River of Two Tongues

Charlie Clemons

To Jim Crute, an excellent Artisan and a good man.

Charlie Clemons

Protea Publishing

This is a work of fiction.

River of Two Tongues
Charlie Clemons

ISBN 1-59344-006-5   Soft cover

ISBN 1-59344-007-3   Hardcover

Library of Congress Control Number: 2003100176

Protea Publishing USA
kaolink@msn.com
www.proteapublishing.com

Dedication

*T*his book is dedicated to my loving wife, Annette, in grateful appreciation for her loyal support of the project and her confidence in my ability.

Her willingness to allow me to read to her, day after day, helped me keep my mind on the target. Her generous contribution of time to edit and proof my manuscript was invaluable.

Most important, though, was the reaffirmation of our love through the required close collaboration.

Charlie Clemons
Saturday, January 4, 2003

Appreciation

I gratefully acknowledge the outstanding work that Johan Du Toit, Publisher of Protea Publishing did on *River Of Two Tongues* and the rapidity with which he concluded his portion of the project.

His artistic ability enabled him to sort through a morass of my photographs until he found just the right pieces to create a cover, which tells as much of a story as the words under the cover.

Charlie Clemons

Acknowledgement

My sincere thanks is extended to Ross Browne of *The Editorial Department* for his clever guidance, excellent editorial direction, patience and friendship.

Charlie Clemons

Chapter One

NEW MEXICO, SPRING – 1900

She struggled to remain conscious and to find the strength to crawl the last few yards to the small stream running alongside the fan of the Sangre de Christo Mountains.

The brief, uncomfortable moments of consciousness were much worse than the blackouts.

The hard, dry buffalo grass on which she'd collapsed felt like needles on her sunburned skin and itched through the rips in what was left of her homespun, cotton jumper that her mother had delicately embroidered. Insects skittered between the fabric of her clothing and the skin of her legs. The sun that she'd so welcomed after the long, cold nights in the wilderness beat down without mercy.

The slightest touch of anything sent rivers of pain to her brain. Even the gentlest of breezes brought intense jerks from otherwise useless muscles that could take her no further.

Memories of the tragedy had been with her for every step of her journey. It was as vivid as though it had happened only a sunrise ago. But she knew different. She had marked every lingering sunset in her memory, along with the chilling calls of the coyote, the rustle of the leaves and the dribble of small stones set loose by some creature of the wild. Every turn and twist of the trail had brought more anxiety. She remembered counting five sunsets, but how many more had there been? She didn't know but everything her family had was gone. She knew that.

Her escape was forcing on her the frantic first steps of womanhood into a world for which she was not prepared.

The unmistakable sensation of being touched was as startling as any she had felt in her short fourteen years of life. It sent shock waves through her body, unearthing an avalanche of hope.

"Daddy?" she said. "Is that you? I'm hot, daddy."

"Hot's not the word for it. You're burning up, Little Miss, but don't worry. You'll be cool soon enough."

It was a rough, dry voice; a stranger's voice. She forced her eyes open, desperate to see something in his face to quell her sudden unease. But the searing, brightness of the sunlight blinded her.

She almost screamed when she felt his arms slip under her despite the slow movement of his hands and his gentle touch. Even so, the pain of the friction on her skin nearly made her faint.

He cradled her in his arms and brought her hot face to his own. His coarse whiskers hurt like the prick of a porcupine quill, but his head provided shade. She again tried opening her eyes, this time just to narrow slits, a little at a time. "Water... Please."

He carried her for a little while before she heard the whisper of a small stream rolling across rocks. The sound she'd been so desperate to hear provided a moment of comfort. When he gently laid her body in the water and began to bathe her with the cool, clear liquid, her body went limp; she knew that she'd be okay.

She opened her eyes all the way and let the blur clear some more.

"Thank you," she said, and tried to look at her rescuer for the first time. From her prone position the man looked like a giant, but his dirty clothing, straggly hair, and dirty fingernails revolted her. Weak as she was, she was suddenly desperate to know more about him.

She started to ask his name but he shushed her with a finger to his lips. Then he took off his hat, filled it with water, and held it just below her chin. Her body's demands made her overlook the sweat-stained dirtiness of the garment. In haste she drank, taking big swallows of the water along with gulps of air.

"More, please," she said when he took the hat away. Intense pain grabbed at her stomach, but she couldn't resist.

A loud belch erupted from inside her. She doubled over and regurgitated most of the water she'd just taken, along with something green and bitter. She turned her face away from the smell, brushed at the dribble on her chest, and then lay back in the water. It was a struggle just to keep her head up.

The man removed his shirt, shook it under the water for a few moments, and then wrung it out so he could squeeze small amounts of water into her mouth. He hadn't said another word.

The sun was beginning to ride the top ridge of the canyon when he first interrupted the routine.

"Did that help a little bit?"

She nodded.

He handed her the shirt. "Hold onto this while I rustle up something for you to eat. Squeeze it like I was doing, so you get just a little at a time. If the cramps start again, stop."

She pulled herself up on the shore a bit and did as he told her. The man was gone only for a moment or two, leaving her no time to make any real sense out of what was happening.

She attempted a smile when he squatted down on his haunches next to her and held out a piece of beef jerky. Her stomach grumbled in anticipation.

"Easy now," he said as she put the smaller piece in her mouth. "Chew it up good and only swallow the juice until the jerky gets tender."

The tough, sinewy meat was so salty she nearly gagged. The man didn't seem to notice. "I've got a campsite at the top of that canyon wall."

Dovey turned her head to the east and looked in the direction he was pointing. All she saw was lifeless, inhospitable boulders and sheer rock faces. Her eyebrows knitted. She looked at him and her lips parted to speak. He answered her unasked question.

"There's no way you'll be able to make it up there tonight, so I'll fetch us what we need. You just rest, and I'll be back a little after sunset."

Sunset? He couldn't leave her all alone. Not here. "Please," she said, surprised by the volume of her voice. "The Indians…"

The man turned and looked at her, with eyes that seemed to pierce her brain. He chuckled aloud, but he wasn't smiling. "You mean like me?"

"You're not an Indian, are you? You sure don't look like an Indian…"

The man paused a moment, and the deep lines in his face melted into a smile. "You're kinder than most folks. Chew that other piece of jerky and try to get some rest."

He smiled again, an awful smile, full of crooked, yellow teeth set off against a straggly black mustache. She tried to smile back, but her stomach had turned sour. She was suddenly eager to be away from him. He turned without another word, grabbed his horse's reins and jerked the creature's head around so he could mount from where he was standing.

He'd looked like a giant when he hovered over her by the water but from a distance she saw that he was really a short man.

She'd never seen big, high top boots like he wore. They weren't the kind the ranchers or the farmers liked to wear. His pants, made from gray, coarse looking material were held up with broad suspenders like her daddy's. But the fringed-style, buckskin jacket told of another place and people. Maybe he was an Indian.

She strained her ears to hear the last of the poor horse's clattering hooves. As the sound diminished into eerie silence her anxiety increased. Every falling pebble from the hillside, every tree branch that rustled in the wind caused her mind to race with questions and uncertainty.

She wanted, so badly, to be gone by the time he returned. Could she? She struggled to rise from her sitting position, winced and tried to pull herself erect by grabbing onto a small sapling. The cramps in her arms and legs told her it would not be possible. She fell back onto the stream's bank and sighed.

As dusk descended on the canyon bottom, the comforting, warm glow from the rock face disappeared. A cool, moist movement of air began to rise from the tall grass along the edge of the stream. Goose bumps crept up her arms and legs, and for the first time she realized that her fever was gone. Her body was no longer blazing hot, and her thirst had been sated even if her hunger had not.

She tried once more to rise. Cramps in her legs allowed only slow, jerky motion and her body felt unstable. After twenty yards of laborious effort, she slumped against a cedar tree to rest. No sense in running. She needed the help of this stranger.

When she awoke, the character of her surroundings had changed. Fireflies sparkled like blinking stars in the heavens, crickets chirped, and in the pale moonlight she could see swallows diving at insects along the surface of the water.

For a precious few minutes she felt very much at peace. Her mind drifted back to the happy evenings, very much like this one, at her home in Kansas.

Her sense of tranquility was shattered by the sound of coyotes calling to each other in their mournful way that always made her think of death. So many mornings, after hearing the coyotes call in the night, she had awakened to find small lambs slaughtered and ewes wailing.

Just as the last of the howls echoed off the canyon wall, a new sound found its way to her ears. It was steady and rhythmic, punctuated from time to time with the clink of metal on metal.

It was he. It had to be.

She hesitated when he called out to her, not really knowing why. He had gone to get food and shelter, and she needed both. She moved, ever so slightly, crushing loose pebbles beneath her shoes.

The man dismounted and walked over to where she sat. "I told you I'd be back, didn't I? Now sit down and let's have us something to eat."

Her nostrils caught the scent of bacon, and her mouth flooded. With trembling hands, she lifted the fry bread with bacon wrapped inside, to her lips. He restrained her hand. "Take small bites and chew it all a long time. I got some beans with me too, so you'll have plenty."

She ate slowly and said nothing. By the time she'd finished, the man had a fire going. "Stir them beans now and again, would you... What's your name, anyway?"

She swallowed the last of the fry bread before answering. "Dovey," she said after a moment. "Dovey MacPherson."

"Well, well. Ain't never heard that name before. Can't say I like it, neither."

"I'm sorry." What a strange thing to say.

He waved a hand at her dismissively. "Don't you worry about that. You probably won't like mine much either. I sure don't."

"I never thought a name was something to like or dislike," she said. "It's just something people call you. It doesn't mean anything."

"Oh yeah? Well, Dovey MacPherson, what if I told you people call me Black Jack Diamond."

She was not accustomed to words soaked in such bitterness, so she sat silently.

"It's Blackjack for short," he said, stretching out his fingers and looking at them. His tone had changed markedly, she thought from anger to despair.

"Anyway, you stir them beans while I make us a shelter. That wind will be blowing pretty hard down this canyon before morning. We'll need all the protection we can get."

She stirred and watched him hack away at a couple of pine saplings, take a long piece of stiff cloth from the pack on the burro's back and use strips of animal hide to tie the cloth to the pieces of pine that he had cut and trimmed. He rammed one end of the wood into the ground and leaned the other end of the structure at an angle against two fir trees. He lapped the ends of the cloth around the trees and tied them securely. Two thick Navaho blankets laid over fir boughs finished the job.

She wouldn't ordinarily have been so interested. But afterward when he approached and smiled at her, it became crystal clear.

"Old Blackjack's gonna look after your needs, Dovey MacPherson," he said, then paused to taste the beans she'd been stirring. "And maybe even some of mine."

A hazy fog hovered just above the stream when Dovey opened her eyes. She yawned, stretched her body and then bolted upright at the sight of the lean-to hanging over her. She pulled back the heavy Navaho blanket and felt the shock of the cold morning. She clutched the blanket; its roughness brought flashes of the prior evening and visions of the strange man who had helped her.

She filled her lungs with air and sniffed at a mixture of scents. There was a foul smell from the blanket next to her that reminded her of bad meat, not rotten, but almost. Blackjack had been there, sleeping next to her. She was sure of it. The idea of it made her cringe.

What should she do? She opened her eyes wide, cocked her head to listen, and felt the beat of her heart accelerate. Her breathing was steady but a bit deeper than normal. Every sense was strung as tight as an Indian's bow.

Though he'd done nothing to threaten her, she would have to be careful and stay alert and patient. She had her mama's nose for trouble, her daddy used to say, and now something told her that getting away from this man would be no easy chore.

The delightful smell of fresh-cut cedar competed with the rancid odor of Blackjack. She turned her head, took a deep breath to cleanse her nostrils and caught the welcome aroma of frying bacon. Her body was stiff and aching, but hunger and thirst demanded she rise.

"Morning, Nana," Blackjack said when she peeked around the corner. "How you feeling?"

Nana? She decided to let it go. "Better, thank you. Whatever you're cooking smells yummy."

"Well, you better come on down and eat then. This ain't gonna stay hot long."

She stood up slowly and held on to one of the lean-to supports until her unsteady legs felt as though blood was flowing through them. Then she dropped the blanket and took a tentative step toward the fire.

"I still feel so weak, though," she said, moving as close to the flames as she dared. It didn't help much; the wind cut through tears in her clothing.

He rose without comment, retrieved a blanket from the lean-to and placed it around her shoulders. He grinned. She turned her face away. "Ah, you look good now, like my squaw. Soon as your hair grows long like hers, anyway."

What did that mean? She didn't even want to think about it.

After breakfast, she tried to scrub the two metal plates and the pan with sand like he had demonstrated, but her fingers cramped and fixed themselves tightly to the metal. He noticed her difficulties, came over to her and gently removed the plates, then began massaging her hands between his own. The warmth felt good and soon her fingers began to relax.

His fingers were long and unusually slender for such a small man. Even more unusual were the tattoos just above each of his lower knuckles, which she hadn't noticed before: nine blue letters, one per finger, and a red diamond on the tenth. As she tried to discern what the letters said, she realized how much darker his skin was than hers.

It wasn't white like hers or brownish-red like an Indian's. It was more like bronze - or even gray - depending on the light.

She ventured a look at his face and saw the same skin color but also deep wrinkles in his forehead and along the side of his mouth. He could easily be as old as her daddy. Maybe older.

For just a moment, she let herself think about her family that she missed so much. But she swallowed hard and choked back the tears. The grief and mourning they deserved would only destroy her right now.

"Can you move your hands now?" Blackjack asked. He flexed his own fingers as he asked the question and for the first time she saw the lettering of the tattoos clearly.

Blackjack Diamond, of course. That the letters and symbol spelled his name made enough sense. But what they were doing there, that was another question.

It was a long circuitous trip from the canyon floor up the mountain to Blackjack's camp on the mesa. He tied her feet in the stirrups, put a rope around the saddle horn and wrapped the other end around her midriff. He jerked the horse's reins and led the way up the sloping trail, which wrapped around a series of increasingly steep hills. By the time they reached the summit, the sun was nearly overhead, and it had become much too hot for the blanket. She was too exhausted to care how much of her body was exposed because of the ragged condition of her clothing, or to give much thought to the lecherous looks Blackjack gave her from time to time.

The camp turned out to be much smaller than Dovey had expected. It was located on a ledge about a hundred feet wide and about half as deep. The western edge of the ledge dropped off sharply, and the rock-strewn canyon below looked ominous. In the side of the abutment there was what looked like a tall shallow cave. Blackjack laid the two Navaho blankets side by side in the enclosure.

Hanging from a tree limb on one side of the camp was a dark skin, oozing water. A cloth covered an opening on the top of the skin and a metal dipper hung by a thong. Two blackened metal rods bent at right angles were rammed into the ground just on the outside of a ring of rocks that contained smoldering ashes. One rod held a metal pot as big as her mother's stew pot and as black as the rod itself. The cross rod sagged at the point where the pot was hanging.

"This'll be your home until you're well enough to travel," he said. "There'll be plenty for you to take care of while I go to the mine, once you're feeling a little better, that is."

"But I can travel now. Really."

"No, you need a while yet. Come on. Let me show you where to relieve yourself. Then you can rest a bit."

He walked about fifty feet and pointed out three smooth logs, without bark, wedged between two groups of rocks about six feet apart. The logs were staggered so that they looked like a bench from the side. Underneath the logs was a sheer rock wall of nearly fifty feet, which sloped off at a sharp angle toward the canyon floor.

"Only use this place. And no messing on the logs, you understand? Here watch me." Blackjack walked across the bottom log until he reached the mid point. Then he sat on the middle log, tucked his feet under the lower one on which he had walked and leaned back against the top log. "See it's easy. Just get your little rear end out far enough and you'll be okay."

She nodded but did not reply. The idea of climbing out there was terrifying.

Yet it was easy to see the sense of such a spot. She tested the security of the logs by pushing on them, gingerly at first and then with a resounding boot. Small pebbles dislodged and thundered down the steep cliff. She jumped back and stared at Blackjack.

It wasn't safe. She knew it wasn't. What would she do?

As if he could read her mind, he kicked the logs hard, walked out on them, then pretended, with great amusement, to slip.

"See, nothing to worry about. The wood is strong, Nana. The rocks are solid. You can either walk out on the lower log and sit on the middle log with your feet tucked under the bottom like I showed you or you can walk out on the middle log and squat."

He looked at her hard as if expecting her to respond. All she could think to do was nod.

"You must be strong, too, and not worry about things little girls worry about."

She quickly turned away and ran to the camp. She wasn't ready to be the woman he seemed to want her to be.

She welcomed the midday rest he insisted she take. She'd slept soundly in spite of her bewildering confusion about this man.

Despite her misgivings, he'd taken as good care of her as she could have asked. Her stomach was no longer churning. Her legs supported her better. The haze through which she had seen things the last few days had begun to clear.

Why should she worry about this man? He hadn't harmed her, only saved her life. She should show him gratitude not distrust.

She stretched her sore body for a moment and turned on her side to slide back into her dream world. The commanding aroma from the campfire would not allow her to have the luxury of more rest. She heard Blackjack's boots scuffling across the rocky campsite floor, and his image paraded across her mind. The memory of the smell of his unclean body displaced the pleasantness of the food. She felt the hair on the back of her neck rise. Every sense was alert.

She squinted at the last rays of the sun and marveled at the rich shades of red, mauve and russet coloring the canyon walls. The sudden brightness prevented her from seeing Blackjack at first, and she jumped when he spoke.

His laugh was more like a cackle, she thought, but even so it was better than the stern look she had witnessed until now.

"You startled me. I couldn't see you because of the sun."

"The name I have picked for you, Nana - Frightened Deer - it fits so well."

Nana? She wasn't going to let him call her that; she'd… No, better not upset him. But she couldn't shake the sense that he was marking his property.

"You look like a new woman. Rest has been good to you. I like the smile and light in your eyes. You'll make a good squaw."

She forced a smile. She shouldn't allow this man to see that she was afraid in any way. She would be kind to him and wait until the right moment to act. Where she would go and how she would survive were questions with less than satisfactory answers. But she would go - and soon.

"What smells so good?" she asked, trying to sound cheerful.

"I trapped a small rabbit and added some of the stuff my number one squaw sent with me. It keeps pretty good back in the mine. I cut off the rotten parts."

He stirred the pot. "It's about ready, too," he said. "If you are."

They ate in silence. She was soaking up the last bit of the

hearty stew with a piece of fry bread when she realized how ungrateful she must seem. "Delicious, Blackjack. Good as my mama used to make."

He ignored her compliment. "Why don't you tell me about your ma. I don't even know where you come from. Or what you were doing in the wilderness when I found you."

The tears she'd been fighting for so many days now again began burning in her eyes. She lowered her head, brought her hands to her temples and rubbed. Knots of tension formed in her stomach and a suffocating feeling of desperation enveloped her. Suddenly she wanted to run fast and far away from everything and everybody, she only wanted to be where she could forget the horror that had befallen her family. The horror from which she had somehow been spared.

But at the same time she wanted to share her grief with someone, anyone, who was warm and real. She wanted to be held in her daddy's secure arms. Or even someone like him. But, not this man. Not now.

She squeezed her eyes tight and swallowed hard. "No," she said loudly, then bolted for the trail leading away from the camp.

He caught up to her in seconds and pulled her close. "Don't cry, Nana. Talk is good. It will make evil spirits leave your body. A shaman told me that."

She held him tightly. Only the warmth of his body was meaningful now. She remained silent. He picked her up in his arms and carried her to her sleeping mat. He lay beside her, caressed her shoulders, moved her long brown hair from the tear-stained cheeks and carefully platted it into two braids at the back of her head. Stifling dry sobs kept her from saying a word.

For the next two days she hardly spoke. She replayed the events of that horrible day over and over in her mind until the scenes ran together and her mind gave up attempting to rationalize the meaning of the tragedy. She cried silently to herself until there were no new thoughts and no more tears. Her face became a placid mask. Blackjack seemed to sense her need for privacy. He let her be, only insisting that she eat enough to keep getting better. On the fourth day, at the early meal, she broke her silence and spontaneously began telling her story. "Indians attacked our home in Kansas near the Cimarron River. They killed my whole family, burned everything we had and left me with nothing."

She stared at him after she said it, her eyes dry, her mind almost blank. Then in a cold, even monotone that sounded foreign to her own ears, she told him every detail she could remember. He didn't interrupt her once. Just let her speak. When she'd finished, he sat quietly for a few moments before placing a hand on her shoulder. "All Indians aren't like that, you know."

She nodded. "I do know that but it's still not easy to be with you," she said. "But I am mighty grateful to you for helping me, Blackjack. I was about to die, wasn't I?"

She saw something in his face change. A flash of anger. A sudden absence of compassion. "Be glad you held up better than your old roan. I found him about a mile up the trail, figured he must have been yours. The buzzards had picked him clean."

There was no reason for him to say that. She'd angered him. Why had she done that? She would never win his confidence that way. She sighed. "That was my daddy's horse. If it hadn't been for him... Well, I don't know what might've happened. It was almost like he sensed the trouble, you know? He ran so fast I could hardly stay on him."

"All the way from Kansas, Nana? That wasn't very smart. I'm surprised you didn't kill him sooner than you did riding him that hard."

Those hurtful words only stiffened her resolve. Don't feel; just think. "Where'd I end up anyway? I thought I was headed for Amarillo."

"Well you made a wrong turn somewhere, then. You ended up closer to Santa Fe. But you don't worry. You're with Blackjack now, and I'm gonna take good care of you." He wrapped his arm around her, put his grubby hand under her chin and lifted her face toward his. He parted his lips slightly. She was startled by the smell of his breath, and her concentration was broken. Before he could do anything further she quickly sprang to her feet and headed for the logs behind the big rocks. He respected her privacy.

Despite her misgivings about the safety of the logs she realized that they served as a convenient refuge where she could think, plan, hope and scheme. She was sure now that his kindness cloaked bitterness.

Why? Did her acceptance of his help and generosity mean that she was obligated to him in some way? Surely he knew she would pay him back when she got to Santa Fe. But why didn't he take her there now, and why did he keep looking at her in such a strange way as though she was a prize animal or something? He's frightening and disgusting; she couldn't stay with him.

She remained behind the rocks for a long time hoping that he'd leave for his mine during her absence. The only solution seemed to be to get away from him, but how? She didn't know where she was, where to go, how far she would need to travel or how she would care for herself.

"Dovey? I got to get going to the mine but I need to talk to you first. Come on back. Now."

She clenched her teeth as she walked toward him. "Yes?"

"I'm taking the burro with me. I've taken the hobble off the horse. You take him down to the water, let him drink and feed. Fill up them water skins and bring'em back. Then cook me some beans for supper. Got that?"

She thought of her mother for a moment and an idea came. "You got any fixings for fry bread?" She continued to smile and watched his eyes brighten.

"Sounds good." He pointed to the edge of the sleeping enclosure. "You'll find everything you need in that box over yonder."

He turned and trotted off toward his mine humming a soft tune. At the entrance of the tunnel he turned, waved and smiled.

She scrounged around in the box looking for the ingredients she'd need. She caught the glint of a metal object. What's this... A package of needles? She might need them when she got away. What else would be useful? She rattled a small tin, opened its cover and found matches. Should she take these now, or wait? She stared at the mine opening and listened. From far inside she heard the sound of a pick on rock. She quickly took two of the needles and a handful of matches. She swallowed hard and let out a deep breath. We'll play the game now, Mr. Blackjack... my way.

✧

Chapter Two

"*W*hoa boy, whoa."

Dovey pulled back on the rein and felt her hands tremble from the effort. She didn't feel strong enough to make the long, twisting walk to the river. Yet, sitting on the back of the horse, looking down at the rocky bottom made her stomach do somersaults.

What if he should slip? No, she would walk and lead him along slowly.

"Whoa."

She stopped when she came to a small flat spot about halfway down the mountain. She flopped onto the ground with a sigh of relief. "Old fellow, this girl needs some rest."

She kicked at a small pebble, and it thundered down the mountain. That would be her if she weren't careful. The horse shook his head, nuzzled her and sniffed the air. His large brown eyes were comforting to her.

"You smell the water don't you? Well, it won't be long if I don't slip on this steep path and break my neck."

From her resting place, she could see the ribbon of green twisting its way through the rocky wasteland extending outward from the small stream that had been her savior. The water birds, rustling along the bank, were the only sign of life. The contrast of brown and green, rocks and soil and the few wildflowers, provided relief from the tension pulling at her. The knots in her stomach began to subside.

How beautiful the land is. But where are the people? She shuddered at the sensation of suddenly feeling very small and very alone.

She stood up, took the horse's leader and continued down the narrowest and steepest part of the trail. She was looking back at the horse behind her, when something gave way under foot. She fell awkwardly to the ground, landing just short of the trail's edge. She winced as every ounce of air exploded from her lungs into the dryness of the rocky hillside. Her lungs were on fire. She couldn't breathe. It seemed as though her head would explode. Darkness was creeping up on her like a shroud being pulled over her head, and she could visualize herself stretched out at the bottom of the canyon.

Blackjack wins the game.

The thought invigorated her fighting instinct. Quickly she took another turn of the rein around both wrists and spoke softly to the horse. She moved as far from the edge as she could with the horse's bridle clenched in her hand taking huge gulps of precious air. As soon as her breathing was near normal she again showered affection on the horse and made a decision.

She swung up into the saddle, leaned back to compensate for the steepness of the trail and tentatively said, "Giddy up."

She shuddered as she looked up at the cliff top camp from the river bottom. The mesa looked even higher from the bottom than it did from the top. Deep gashes in the cliff face, like angry scars, seemed to dance around as the sun and clouds made a game of changing the light patterns. Again she felt small, insignificant and alone in the vastness on every side of her.

She had hardly made it down the path, how could she think of running away? But, yet, how could she think of going back to the camp?

Her only security was the horse's bridle which she gripped tightly, reluctant to release it.

Did he want to be free from Blackjack as much as she did? Would he run away if she let him go? What could she do if he did?

The horse neighed and tossed his head as they neared the water. She looked at the horse's wide eyes, dilated nostrils and the small amount of foam on his lips.

Well, you had to trust somebody sometime. She patted the horse on its neck and dropped the reins.

"Go boy. Drink. Run away if you like."

She kicked off her shoes, followed the horse into the cool water and screamed with delight like the young child she was. It felt good to wade in the cool river water. She scoured the riverbank for edible greens or berries. A small fish darted by her feet and a memory came to her of fish traps her daddy used to make.

She gathered small sticks and struggled to break the tenacious, tall grass growing along the bank.

She needed a knife. That's the next thing she should put in her escape package. And maybe a hatchet.

She patiently stripped the grass into long threads, broke the sticks into similar lengths, and combined the two so that she had a rectangular box with a hole in one end, a larger hole on the other, and a swinging trapdoor.

Her daddy had said, "Make sure the fish thinks he can get out of the trap or he won't go in."

She placed the trap on the bottom with the large hole facing upstream and perched herself on a big rock in the center of the stream where she could watch.

The first small fish swam right through. She adjusted the downstream opening and climbed back on the rock. The sun was nearly overhead now. The exertion, the heat and lack of food were wearing on her. With every failure her determination grew and the words of her mother came to her, "Only people who never do anything avoid mistakes. Try again."

Oh, Mama! A tear came to her eyes. Her parents were gone and so was their love and protection. Except for inspirational memories, they couldn't help her any longer. It was up to her now - forever.

She thrust her shoulders back, cocked her head upward toward the heavens. A sudden strong breeze whipped the tops of the nearby trees stirring the placid, windless day into a semblance of life and action. She listened as the wind whistled through the leaves for a brief moment.

Dovey smiled. Was that you, Mama?

She went back to her trap, made another adjustment to the gate, which blocked the large hole once the fish was inside. She felt sure that it would work now.

She would use the same persistence she had used to make the trap to escape. She would try again and again and would continue until she could escape, as she knew her mother would want her to. Until she could, she would play the game she had started to elicit information from Blackjack. It was just like pretending that she was playing house, as she used to do with her sister and brother, wasn't it?

She bathed herself in the clean, clear river water and washed the buckskin jacket Blackjack had given her to wear over her torn jumper. She slammed the garment on the rocks, over and over, and fussed about not having soap. Hopefully, the odor of Blackjack's body would come out of the garment. She had to have something to properly cover her chest and the small breasts that had emerged during the preceding winter.

She completed her exhausting chores, took a deep breath and stretched her body down onto the cool, green, grass carpet under the cedar trees while she waited for the buckskin to dry. The delicate aroma from the trees dominated all other scents and for a moment took her mind away from her predicament. She decided to rub her clean clothing with the boughs and to take some to her campsite bed.

Already tired and sore from the morning's activity, her leg muscles began to contract into small knots. She massaged them and for the first time was conscious of how weak she really was. She hadn't recovered as much strength as she thought.

The stream trickling along over the rocks made music, or so it seemed, but that was the only sound she heard. Occasionally, the grazing horse would shake his head and emit a sound, but there was nothing else.

To her it seemed strange, to lie in such a beautiful setting without the sound of clucking chickens, squawking geese, dogs barking and all the other sounds she had become accustomed to in her life on the prairie.

How could Blackjack live in this desolation? She wouldn't.

A hawk circled above, coasting lazily, high in the sky. How peaceful he looks. How free.

How free! The thought inspired her. She stretched her memory to recall the maps she had seen in her daddy's atlas. She'd been a little girl then with no reason to care much about the world outside her small corner of Kansas.

On her tenth birthday he had taken her to Dodge City with him. He had carefully shown her the path they would take up the Santa Fe Trail. She pinched her lips, squinted and tried to remember without success. Maybe, if she told Blackjack about her trip, he would supply information without realizing her objective. Maybe.

For the rest of the morning she thought hard about her plan and the things she had squirreled away and other things she needed to get. She smiled at the thought; all part of the game.

A sudden, loud, thrashing sound made her jump to her feet. She scoured the terrain in every direction and waited. It happened again.

It's coming from the stream. "It's a fish!" she shouted, and she splashed into the water to recover it from her trap.

It seemed to her to be the finest fish she'd ever seen. Wouldn't her daddy have been proud of her... and Mama, she told me that the hardest thing about doing something was the will to try and try... Well, Mr. Blackjack, don't be surprised when you wake one morning and find her blanket empty.

The fish plus a few shavings from the jerky provided a bit of flavor for the beans and bread. Blackjack brought one turnip with him from his storehouse in the cave. That was supper.

As meager as it was, she didn't care. She was anxious to get him talking. She smiled as she watched him scoop up the last bit of food, wipe the back of his hand across his mouth and belch.

"Good?" Dovey asked.

"You'll make a fine squaw one day, Nana."

His pronouncement caught her by surprise, there was more to his statement, for sure, but what? What did he expect of her? But the game must go on. She would have to keep him talking. "Me, a squaw? I'm not even an Indian, how can I be a squaw?"

"Squaw means wife. Many Cherokee men have white squaws, black ones, too. My daddy was a half-white and half-black man. He took a full-blood Cherokee woman for squaw."

"So you're..."

His face clouded over. "I'm a mixed up mess is what I am. A rainbow man, that's what a man down in New Orleans called me... just before I shot him."

"You shot a man? Dead?"

"Didn't wait around to find out. They would have strung me up for sure. So I went back to my people on their land in Oklahoma."

"Oklahoma? I see. My Daddy told me that's where President Jackson made the Cherokees go after he bought their land in Georgia."

"Bought? Stole their land! Our chiefs sold us out for five

million dollars. The gold alone, on our Georgia land, was worth twenty million. They stole it!"

"How'd you get here from there, then? Is Oklahoma far away?"

"Four days ride if you don't kill the horse."

"Which direction?"

"Direction? You don't even know where Amarillo is. How can I tell you about Oklahoma?" He chuckled.

She smoothed out the sandy part of the rocky floor with her small, bare foot and made three marks with a stick. "Kansas, where I came from is north. You told me Amarillo is east and Santa Fe is west. She made three x's in the dirt.

"Now, which way is Oklahoma?"

"You ask too many questions, gimmie the stick." He stabbed the stick into the ground so hard until it broke. "There," he shouted. "There. There it is, and all the hateful people that chased me away."

She stayed quiet as he ranted on. Listening to his tirades was apparently the price she'd have to pay to learn what she needed to know. "You've been a lots of places haven't you?"

"More than you know."

"Oh?"

"My daddy was a slave even though he was half white. He belonged to a Cherokee planter that had seven hundred acres near Dahlonega, Georgia."

"Indians had black slaves?"

"Lots. Cherokees ain't dumb you know. Why, long ago they had a written language all their own, a printing press and many educated, wealthy people. They lived in regular houses, not teepees, like the savages out here in the west. They had a government with a constitution very similar to the American one and governed themselves.

"Problem was, they trusted the white man. Although they had fought by the side of General Jackson and helped him become president, he betrayed them."

"So your daddy came to Oklahoma with the other Cherokees?"

"When gold was discovered near Dahlonega, a bunch of miners from North Carolina came to Georgia. Indians were forbidden to mine gold in Georgia for themselves although it was on their land. The miners needed help, though. My daddy was sold to one of them."

"Sold? Like a sheep?"

"Sold!"

She shook her head.

"My daddy was smart, though. After he learned a little bit about what he was doing, he'd sneak into the mine in the middle of the night and mined some for himself. He was patient, not stupid, and only took a little at a time. By the time the march began down 'The Trail of Tears,' my daddy had enough gold to fix him up good. He ran away, disguised himself as an Indian, joined the march, and settled in Oklahoma.

"You must be proud of him."

"Sure enough. He could read and write in both English and Cherokee. Knew his numbers, too."

"Did he teach you?"

"He taught me plenty, mostly about people - things I couldn't understand at the time."

"Such as?"

"What would you do if a drunken slob came into your store and called you a nigger?"

"That would never happen, I'm not..."

"Well it happened to my daddy more than once. I saw it happen one day, pulled my knife and started to jump the counter, but my daddy grabbed my collar."

"What did he do?"

"He sent me to the back, got rid of the man and then came to talk to me. 'Son,' he said, 'Never let a man's words provoke you. Words won't hurt you but you might hurt yourself if you're provoked into foolish action.'"

"Sounds like good advice."

"Never understood it, to tell the truth. It might sound good and all that. But a man's gotta stand up for himself, I say.

"But, anyway that was my daddy, always trying to teach me. Even sent me to school in Massachusetts, so I could come back and run the trading business he started in Oklahoma."

"So, that's why you talk better than most prairie people." She looked down at her feet for a moment in reflection. "I wish I could have gone to a real school. My mama and papa were the only teachers I had."

Blackjack picked something from his teeth with his thumbnail and shook it to the ground. "I hated the school and the entire countryside with its washed-out skies, rain and snow. And the kids there weren't any better. For two years they pushed me, picked fights and called me hateful things."

"That's awful."

"I fixed 'em, though. One of them had a headache for a week when I got through with him. That's when they kicked me out. Wrote to my daddy and told him to come get me."

She did her best to sound sympathetic. "I guess he was pretty disappointed."

"I don't know. I suppose he was, but he'd gotten sick. So rather than coming himself he just sent me money to come by stagecoach. But, instead I got on a boat and headed to New Orleans."

"New Orleans? Where's that?"

He smiled, picked up another stick and drew a map for her. This time he broke off a piece of stick the length of his middle finger. "This will be a day's ride on horseback," he said. "The way I ride, not running like you did."

She laughed at his comment; his joking was a good sign. She had to keep him happy, keep him talking. That was the only way.

"On the ship some men taught me how to play poker. They let me win at first but before we got to New Orleans almost all my money was gone. One of the sailors told me they were cheating, and he showed me how to deal the cards like they did."

"That's stealing," she said.

"I practiced like that sailor showed me, over and over until I learned good. When we got to New Orleans I set out to get my money back. I won big and was getting rich. I was going to go home and make my daddy proud of me." He kicked at the spot representing New Orleans on the crude map drawn in the dirt.

"Go on," she said.

"Indians and whisky don't mix. I started winning big, you see, so some of the big losers got a couple of drinks in me. My hands turned to leather. I couldn't deal. They caught me trying to palm an ace."

She sucked air through her teeth, shook her head and said as sincerely as she could manage, "That's awful. I'm so sorry."

"So you know what they did? They tied me down and tattooed these letters on my fingers. That way everybody would know me on sight."

She kicked at New Orleans, too. He smiled.

"So, when you got home, you told your daddy what had happened? How getting kicked out of school was not your fault?"

She suddenly felt the strange urge to comfort him. But she couldn't bring herself to touch him.

"My daddy died before I reached home, Nana. The Shaman said I broke his heart and he took me to the water to cleanse my spirit."

"I'm sorry you couldn't explain to your daddy."

He seemed to be unaware of her comments. He went on in a sad monotone. "The Shaman's cleansing didn't help. My Cherokee brothers avoided me. Women wouldn't even look me in the eye. I was no longer welcome at council meetings. My own people were rejecting me, so I left."

"Not back to New Orleans?"

"Hardly. I went to Santa Fe, Zuni territory. Down to a new town called Phoenix. People were talking about a great canyon located north in the cool of the mountains. The Navaho people lived there.

"It was a beautiful place, with good weather and nice people. Everyone seemed to accept me, at first. They asked no questions."

"Is that where you got the two blankets we sleep on?"

He nodded. "The Navahos make handsome things. So do the Zunis"

"Why didn't you stay there?"

"Firewater - again. I fell for a woman, but her eyes had no shine when I approached her. When I touched her soft skin I felt it go cold and turn to chicken flesh. She ran to her Hogan and I ran for the whiskey." He talked while he added to the map, which now stretched nearly ten feet across the campsite.

She concentrated on every squiggle trying to remember details. "What's this line next to Santa Fe?" she asked.

"The Rio Grande. It goes for miles north and south and then turns toward the sea. It's kind of like a dividing line between civilization and nothing. I'll take you there sometime when I get enough gold put by. They'll deal with Indians in Santa Fe."

"I'd love to see it. How long would it take us?"

"Four days, if we don't kill the horse, Nana." He cackled again at his joke.

She stared hard at his map and smiled. Santa Fe it would be. Four days to freedom; somewhere over those mountains.

She was startled at his touch.

"Answer me, Nana, are you ready for sleep?"

His voice again sounded angry to her. "Why do you keep calling me that name? My name's Dovey, not Nana."

"Your name is what I say it is. I saved your life. Your life belongs to me now, NANA."

She cringed and pulled away from his grasp. She would not be his Nana, nor his squaw. Never! She meant it. She shuddered at the prospect.

"Tomorrow, we'll go to the water, and I'll repeat the words the Shaman would say if he were here and you'll be my number two squaw."

The moon went behind a dark cloud and his scowling face disappeared from her view. She felt the cords in her neck tighten and her throat go dry. She stood still. Her skin shuddered, like the Navaho girl. She took a deep breath, swallowed and managed to say, "I'll go to the logs." She left before he could reply.

She tentatively crawled out onto the logs, sat, wondering whether she should dash off through the night now or wait until he was asleep. Perhaps tomorrow when he was at the mine would be better.

No solution seemed satisfactory. She shook her head, clenched and unclenched her hands, trying to think. The ugly sound of Blackjack's shout distracted her.

"You gonna take all night? I need to go, too, you know."

With reluctance she left the solitude of the logs. The night was warm but she crawled under her blanket, before he returned. She held the edges of the blanket tightly to her chest and pretended to be asleep.

As he had done on each of the four nights since her arrival, he lay beside her, and began gently massaging her shoulders and back. "To help you get well," he had said. This night he said nothing, but the ritual began.

The sensation of his hands on her sore muscles did feel good, despite her anxiety. Without intent her small body relaxed and her grip on the blanket loosened.

His hands migrated slowly down her back and lingered for a few moments, massaging with a gentleness that made her body tingle. Soon, her breathing deepened and her body started to gyrate ever so slightly. One of his hands brushed across the soft flesh of her stomach and found its way to the small patch of curly hair between her legs.

With his free hand he peeled back the blanket covering her and cautiously lifted her buckskin skirt. The pinpricks of his whiskered face rubbing against her tender thighs interrupted the euphoric feeling. Almost immediately she felt a new sensation. Something warm and moist was exploring the flesh around her private spot. Occasionally, the object teased in and out of the warmth between her legs. The feeling was compelling, and entirely unfamiliar to her. She didn't want it to stop.

She felt him maneuver himself between her legs, gently pull her skirt over her head and lower himself onto her.

The night was shattered by her scream!

Chapter Three

"*P*lease, Blackjack, stop! You're hurting me... Stop, I SAID. STOP!"

Dovey strained to push herself away but Blackjack held her small body pinned. No one heard the cries of rejection or the pleading for help, or Blackjack's laughter as she beat on him with her tiny fists.

"That's right, little tiger, fight. I like it."

His raucous laughter drowned out her screams, and the intensity of his movement increased. Soon, he began moaning, low and throaty. She felt his body tense. His face changed, and his eyes softened. He leaned closer to her, parting his lips slightly. Her body went numb as she looked up at him through her tears.

Time seemed to stop. She couldn't look at his awful face any longer. Her eyelids snapped shut, and a forgotten memory made her gasp. Once, in the middle of the night, when she was a small child, she had heard her mother moaning. Her feet had shivered as she tiptoed across the cold, dirt floor of their one-room sod house and cautiously pulled back the canvas partition that separated the sleeping areas. In the darkness of the room, she could only see a formless mass in the center of the bed, and her heart pumped hard as she tried to understand what she was seeing. As her eyes became accustomed to the flickering light provided by a nearly burned-out bedside candle, her fear changed to curiosity.

She saw her daddy lying on top of her mother, the bedclothes rising and falling in concert with his movements. The moaning sound she'd heard before began again, but this time her mother's lips were smothered by her daddy's. Then she watched as her daddy slowly raised himself so the profile of her mother's bosom could clearly be seen. She watched him kiss her there, then roll to the side, still breathing hard. Her mother pulled the covers over them and spoke soft words to him, which Dovey couldn't hear. The kiss that followed was long and slow, very different from the casual kisses she had witnessed before.

The smell of Blackjack's breath interrupted the memory. Her eyes snapped open. She saw his lips slightly parted and his head moving slowly toward her. She jerked her body and tried to roll him off of her, but he was too heavy. She lay panting, waiting for an opportunity to try again.

He was not going to kiss her again. No matter what else she would have to do she would not let him kiss her... NEVER.

He thrust into her again and brought his mouth even closer, sending a surge of panicked adrenaline through her body. Without thinking, she leaned forward and grabbed his lower lip with her teeth. Then she bit down hard; so hard until her upper and lower teeth made contact with each other through the tough tissue of his lower lip.

Salty blood flooded her mouth. His eyes went wide. He screamed and jerked his body away from her. A milky white fluid spurted onto the blanket in halting bursts.

He brushed blood from his mouth with the back of his hand, looked at it in the dim light, and slapped her hard across the face. Dovey stared in disbelief at a face that seemed hard as stone. She buried her face under her arm and waited for whatever came next. The tension, waiting for the next slap or something worse, was nearly as bad as the slap. She remained silent and listened as he gasped for air. After his breathing slowed a little, he grabbed her shoulder and pulled her upright so that he could look directly into her eyes. "You ever do that again and I'll strangle you."

She rolled away from him and gave in to the retching heaves that had begun rocking the pit of her stomach.

A few moments later, she lay her exhausted body down, closed her eyes, and listened for his heavy breathing. The pain between her legs was subsiding now, but her whole body felt cramped and uncomfortable. Her head pounded with pain.

Was he asleep? She crawled on hands and knees across the rocky campsite surface, paused at the foot of his blanket. When she saw the slow steady heave and fall of his chest, she crept toward the path leading to the logs. A hint of light from somewhere beyond the western hills helped define the path. She raised her tired, sleepless body up onto sore and bruised legs and tip toed the rest of the way to the logs.

She couldn't stomach him touching her again. Better to take her chances in the wilderness.

She reclaimed her small stockpile of items she'd been saving from its hiding place near the logs. She also took the small hatchet from the woodpile. On her silent return trip past the sleeping area, she noted Blackjack's worn boots still protruding from the end of the blanket nearest her and his hat at the other.

She quickened her step down the path toward the river and freedom. Ten steps down the trail, a dark figure stepped from behind a tall, granite boulder.

"I thought so," he said and grabbed her wrist. With her free hand she whacked his shin with the side of the hatchet blade and jerked her hand away. He fell to the ground with an angry groan.

She ran to the other side of the boulder, hid herself behind another boulder and threw some rocks down the trail in hopes of confusing him. She heard him coming down the path shouting, threatening, and then pleading for her to return. She tried to control her heavy breathing as she watched his shadow pass the boulder, but she could not. He stopped, whirled around and grabbed for the hatchet.

He half dragged her back to the sleeping area and kicked at the rolled-up blanket. His hat and boots went sprawling across the enclosure. His cackling voice ricocheted off the canyon walls and even in the still half-light she could see his repulsive, yellow teeth.

"Didn't your mother ever tell you never to trust an Indian?" He laughed loudly, stopped abruptly and began shaking her by the shoulders, hard.

"Now listen to me. I saved your life, which means that I'm responsible for you now. I must clothe you, feed you and see that you have a place to lay your blanket. That's the way our people have always done."

"You don't need to do that. Just take me to my people. They'll pay you for helping me."

"Your people are dead, Nana. Have you forgotten that already?"

"There are others, though. Relatives, friends that live nearby. Someone will pay."

"You lie."

"No!"

"You're mine now, Nana. To do with as I see fit."

"NO!"

"Enough. We have no council house or sacred fire or relatives with gifts for our wedding, but another day will come. For now you must do things my way.

"When the sun warms the waters I'll take you to the river, face east, and say the words the Shaman would say if he were here. We'll drink the corn drink, tie our blankets together and thereby pledge our support to each other. Then, you'll be my squaw. We'll share one blanket instead of two."

Her first impulse was to shout her defiance, but her eyes went to the stinging red marks on her wrist where his grubby fingers had grabbed her. His strength and power were great; she had seen that.

Her only choice was to comply, to play along with his game until she had a chance to run - or to shoot him.

The morning dawned gray with low, ugly clouds engulfing the camp. A sharp wind blew into the sleeping area, making Dovey shudder when she kicked her blanket down. Her body was sore all over and her privates still stung.

"Get up," Blackjack said.

"Why? Where are we going?"

"To the river like I told you."

"Blackjack, I - -"

"Shut up." He grabbed her arm and led her to the burro's side. When she didn't mount, he lifted her, kicking and screaming, onto the back of the burro, ran a rope under his belly and tied each of her feet so tight that the rope cut into her flesh.

"I'm tired of waiting, Nana," he said, "We go NOW." He stood back and approved his work with a smile.

The bitter winds made the trip down to the canyon floor more frightening and miserable than usual. When the procession reached the river, he led her into the chilling water until the current lapped at her midriff. He removed his shirt and threw it onto the bank, raised both arms to the sky, and began a moaning chant.

Her body went stiff. She shuddered. She'd spent most of the night struggling with the question of how she would act if he went through with his ridiculous plan to make her his squaw. She could never be his squaw or his wife no matter what he called it. Why did he even want her?

She thought of the warm, tender words her parents said to each other and the things they did to make each other happy. Her daddy had loved her mother; it was for that reason and no other that he took care of her. But, this vile, stinking man ... this animal, had no love in his heart, if he did he would see that she was returned to Kansas, or maybe Santa Fe.

This "marriage" was like a play. It meant nothing. She wouldn't let it mean anything. She'd fight him again, gouge his eyes, bite him, and shoot him if she got the chance.

The chilling moans changed to a chant, more rhythmic and musical in tone. He carried on for what felt like ages as she stood shivering, waiting for the charade to be over.

Finally he spoke. "You are now my squaw. I will provide for you as I promised. You will do my bidding. There is no other way."

She said nothing. Just sighed and with bowed head took the reins of his horse and followed him up the tortuous path toward the camp and an uncertain future.

Chapter Four

*F*rom her favorite resting place, under the cedar tree, next to the river bank, Dovey's mind went over and over the events of her "wedding" morning. The remembrance of the scene never left her. Many times in the night, particularly after he'd had his pleasure with her, the memory of his terrifying cries and chants screamed at her.

This morning the memories were particularly vivid, but other thoughts were fighting to be heard. Why did she keep trying to run away? He wasn't really a bad man, at least not when he was getting his way. And he did work awful hard for the gold he sent back to his village on those rare occasions when a rider came with supplies.

She had asked him why he did that once and he told her that the villagers would starve without it. She never understood why he didn't take her with him to the river when they came to meet him, or why he slept at the river with them instead of at the camp? Maybe he didn't want them to know of the mine's location. Or perhaps he didn't want them to know about her.

She'd long abandoned hopes of the messenger's assistance in her escape. Their loyalty would of course be to Blackjack. And lately, she'd noticed she'd thought of escaping a lot less. Blackjack talked often of a real life and a real home for them once he'd mined enough gold. She couldn't imagine the children he spoke of, but the idea of living in a village somewhere instead of the camp was certainly appealing.

What she'd come to realize was that in some ways, she really did need him. Without Blackjack, she had nothing. So why couldn't she be a good wife like her mother had been?

The last few months hadn't been too bad. He didn't come to her as frequently as before. And she'd become comfortable with her daily routine of washing, mending, fishing, and checking his traps.

The only thing that gnawed at her acceptance of things was

the realization that a woman always traveled with the messenger who came with their provisions. Was it always the same one? She couldn't be sure but maybe, just maybe, if she could find a way to get to her, the woman might help her.

She sighed at the myriad of familiar, useless thoughts and stared at the glitter of sunlight from the small amount of snow still on the ridge of the western mountains.

It wasn't too long ago that she had nearly reached that ridge before he caught her. He had beaten her badly that night but not nearly as badly as he had last night on her seventh escape attempt. The ice cold water from the river had done little to alleviate the pain in her left arm. And though it had healed to the point where she could use it again, she still felt needles of fire shoot through it often.

The jelly from the leaves of long spiny cactus plants was the only medicine they had. It did little for anything but cuts and rope burns, but she would get more today, apply it and hope for relief.

She recalled seeing the distinctive looking plants in the narrow valley to the left of the trail leading to the camp. She pressed her left arm against her chest and began the slow trek up the winding path. A fresh stab of pain shot through her arm with every jolt of her foot on the rocky path. She breathed deeply, grit her teeth, and continued the slow walk with the delicacy of a ballet dancer, stepping only on her toes.

A big skull shaped boulder on the left of the path marked the turnoff to the valley. Cautiously, she worked her way around the north side of the boulder until she was on the uphill side. She ambled as best she could along the narrow path until finally she came to the crest of the trail, which offered a panorama of the valley below.

Dovey gasped when she saw it.

Long shadows alongside the peaks of red sandstone seemed to quiver as heat rose from the desert floor. Cactus wrens busy with their daily chores dotted the landscape and a single hawk circled lazily overhead. Down below, toward the valley bottom, hundreds of cacti were in full bloom, showing off their beautiful flowers in the most dazzling array of colors. The sight brought tears to Dovey's eyes. How long had it been since she had seen a flower, or color, or beauty of any kind? She couldn't answer her own question.

Time meant nothing to her any longer. She remembered the long endless heat of the summer, the trees turning color, and the short days of winter when the snow was piled high on the campsite floor. The snow was gone now.

Was spring really here?

Despite the loose gravel on the walkway and the danger of slipping, she couldn't resist getting closer to the flowers. For the first time since... how long she couldn't remember... she smiled.

She took a deep breath and tried to drink in the aroma of the setting. She picked an enormous yellow flower, nearly as large as her hand, and held it with the tenderness a mother might hold a baby. With delicacy she inspected each petal, each stamen, each leaf on the small stem. She sat on a rounded rock and stared at her treasure.

Flowers. Spring... she remembered! *"Dovey, honey, come here for a minute. I want to show you something."*

She remembered running to her mother, so happy to be loved and to share with her all the wonderful things the world offered. *"Look, the first flower of spring. That means it's nearly your birthday."*

She remembered the sound of her own laughter then. "The twenty-seventh of April. Right mama?" The memory was so clear, it seemed her mother was standing in front of her.

"The winter I was carrying you, Dovey, was the longest and coldest since we moved to Kansas from the east. There was so much snow I thought I'd never see anything pretty or green again."

Dovey could see herself, sitting on the bench by the duck pond holding her mother's hand. To her at that moment, her mother was the prettiest thing in the world.

"One day the snow melted and you know what popped up? A small yellow flower. The next day you were born and I had beauty in my life again."

"Is that where I came from? Did I pop out of the ground like a flower?"

"No darling. You came from here, inside me. You're a part of me and always will be."

Even now she remembered the warmth of her mother's hand

as she placed Dovey's small hand on her stomach.

Dovey had giggled. "It's not big enough. I don't understand..."

"One day you will. One day I'll tell you all about it."

"When?"

"Someday."

Someday had never arrived.

Chapter Five

"*W*hat's the matter with you girl, if you ain't crying you're puking?"

"I'm sick, what do you expect? I need a doctor, Blackjack. Take me to Santa Fe... please!"

"We'll see. I'll think of what to do while I'm at the mine. Maybe you better rest today."

She stamped her foot. "If you don't do something I'm going to go to Santa Fe without you."

"Good luck finding it." He shrugged his shoulders and chuckled. "You'll be here when I get back. Then we'll see what has to be done."

He was right. She couldn't leave now. Why, she couldn't even walk to the valley with the flowers, but the memories of the first time she had seen it helped her endure her discomfort.

She sat on the stump of an ancient oak at the edge of the camp, staring across the canyon, and let memories flood her mind.

A sudden dash of color moving rapidly across the ground distracted her. She was instantly on guard, thinking it was a snake. But when she saw it again, she realized it was a roadrunner scooting in and out of the cacti, stabbing its beak at insects too small for her to see.

The interruption had stolen the memories. They were gone. An unfamiliar stab of pain shot through her stomach. She changed her position on the stump in hopes that a different position would help, but the pain only got worse.

She couldn't endure it. She had to move. Her legs and back strained as she rose slowly. She grabbed at her stomach, and as though it were yesterday she felt the warmth of her mother's stomach and heard her words: "You came from here, inside me."

The realization triggered an avalanche of fear... Is that why her stomach had stretched? Visions of her mother's words and her stomach, just before her sister was born, raced through her mind.

"I don't want a baby," Dovey shouted.

The wind carried her words to the walls of the canyon and they shouted back at her. Suppose he looked and acted like Blackjack. She couldn't be a mother to a child like that and be reminded of Blackjack for the rest of her life.

She sobbed a long time, aloud at first, and then silently until at last she fell to her knees on the rocky path. She looked to the sky and in a, halting, apologetic voice cried out: "I don't know how to have a baby, Mama."

Chapter Six

"*W*hew, that took a long time to make."

She laid the pot of beans and plate of fry bread on the edge of the coals and rose with difficulty. She tried to stand erect for a moment, to stretch her shoulders backward and her head upward. The orange, yellowish full moon, wending its way from behind the hills in the east, attracted her attention. What a wonderful sight, she thought; it made her feel good. She wished there were something here, in the camp that would do the same thing. She rubbed her protruding stomach, sighed again, and dropped to her knees to spoon the meager rations onto Blackjack's plate.

She thought of the morning meal and of Blackjack's irritable comments about her frequent complaints of pain and her refusal to take the animals to water. She had told him more than once that being so fat made it very hard to walk up and down the steep trail.

"You ain't the first woman to have a baby, you know. Now stop complaining and do your share of work." His words and the sudden confirmation of what she thought was happening to her, were like a slap in the face. The pronouncement seemed to boomerang around the canyon walls, bending her thoughts backward and forward until it seemed her head would explode.

She grabbed her belly with both hands as though to protect it from Blackjack and was startled when he took her hand and gently rubbed her stomach. His voice softened. "A child is coming; maybe the spirits will give me a boy child," he said with a smile. "You did good, Nana. Rest now. I'll look after the animals. Take good care of yourself and make me a strong boy with an eagle's heart."

"I'll try, but I don't know how... my belly and back hurt so much." She watched him shoo the animals down the trail and felt relieved when he followed.

She would try. There was no other way, but there was so much she didn't know. Why couldn't she sleep, and why did she awake with rivers of sweat pouring from her body? How long would the nausea and pain last? Could her stomach stand even more pain from the retching up of the terrible tasting bile that followed the nausea? Perhaps it would all stop when the baby was born.

But, how could she give birth to a baby? What should she do, push hard on her stomach?

The gentlest push told her that was not the right way. She kneeled slowly and rolled over on her blanket, staring at the sky, hoping to see an eagle or something to distract her from the mingled and disturbing thoughts brought on by Blackjack's surprising statement.

No eagle came. No sound jingled the wind chime. No essence from the flowers reached her nostrils. She was alone with her questions. She tried to remember when her sister was born. How did that happen? All she could remember was that one day a neighbor lady came and stayed in her mother's room a long time. She heard terrible screams from inside the room, and her daddy asked her to help him in the fields. When they returned, her mother was holding a small child, a wrinkled, dark-haired girl that looked so much like her daddy... "Oh NO!" she shouted and quickly covered her mouth. Would her baby look like Blackjack? Please, God, let it look like her daddy. How could she stand the pain of having to be reminded of that awful man forever? She couldn't, and the Lord would hear her plea in every prayer she said.

She rolled from one side of the blanket to the other, moaning quietly.

She heard footsteps behind her and watched Blackjack's shadow fall over her blanket. Her muscles tensed as he bent down to look at her, and a new pain stabbed her insides.

His face looked - different, soft, with slight wrinkles around the eyes. She looked directly at his eyes, something she rarely did, and wondered what had caused the change. She never knew which face he would wear.

"No good for you to be like this," he said. "Bad for you and bad for our child."

She nodded, wondering what he could possibly have in mind.

"It's time," he said, nodding his head. "Tomorrow I'll take you to Wesa."

After hours of riding, it became harder and harder to hold onto Blackjack's waist. Her grip began to weaken. She could no longer hold her head upright, and it flopped from side to side in tempo with the horse's gait. She had mastered the technique of short, quick breaths to match the rhythm of the ride, which dulled the pain each hoof beat sent through her body. Now that ability escaped her. She moaned and slumped against his back.

"Whoa!" He shouted at the animal, jerking back on the bit in the horse's mouth. "What now?" He stood in the stirrups and half turned to look at her.

"It hurts so bad. I must rest a few minutes."

"Rest? We ain't stopping until I get you to Wesa. She'll know what to do."

"The cramps... they're awful... your child..." She grabbed her stomach and felt her head nod. She jerked herself erect and gulped the hot, humid air of the valley.

He dismounted and caught her as she slipped to the side. She felt her eyes roll back into her head. She was grateful for the layer of perspiration that began coating her face, driving away the heat of the day. All she wanted was to lie down and let the breeze, as sparse as it was, blow over her tired body.

There were no trees at this lower elevation to provide shade. There was only coarse grass between the trail and the river. On the other side of the trail, acres and acres of rock absorbed the blistering rays of the sun from the cloudless sky, reflecting them onto the weary travelers.

"Drink this water. I'll fill our bags from the river."

She sipped, while he fashioned a crude lean-to, using the same canvas he had used three years ago, the night he had found her.

How wonderful it was to stretch out, to rest, and to let her mind dwell on something else, like the birdcalls in this wilderness. The pain ebbed, and the effect was hypnotic. Her head nodded, and her eyes refused to stay open, but the wind played tricks with her: *"Yes dear, April 27th, that's your birthday."* How could she be so young and yet so old? The time with Blackjack had seemed a lifetime.

It was late in the afternoon when she awoke. A brisker

breeze made the heat more tolerable. Her stomach cramps had subsided.

She began to wonder; should she say something nice to him? Perhaps thank him for his help? He really isn't such a bad man. He had only done to her what every other man does to his wife. That was his right ... wasn't it? Pay back, maybe, for the food and care he provides. Wasn't it the same with her mother? He isn't a bad man.

She wrung her hands. She knew the proper thing to do, the thing her mother would want her to do, was to thank him, but she was afraid to express her feelings. There was no way she could anticipate his reaction to anything. The simplest of comments could stir a rage in him that she had not been able to understand. It was best to keep quiet.

"I'm ready to travel again," Dovey said.

"No you're not!" Blackjack shouted. "You want to kill my son?"

She didn't answer. She knew better.

"You sleep some more. I'll cook. We'll travel tonight, when it's cool."

"I didn't think Indians traveled at night."

"Sometimes it's good to be the rainbow man," he said, and then he laughed long and loud.

The charred skin of the fish he had speared was less objectionable than the worm-laden beans they had eaten for the last two days. The berries he had found tasted sweeter than any pie her mother had ever made. Lord, let there be something different to eat when we reach the village.

Her curiosity about the village was more than she could stand. At the risk of having to suffer through another tirade, she tried to find out more. "Is your village a large one?"

He cocked his head and looked at her as though he'd never thought of the question. "Large enough to hold all the outcasts and misfits, like me, that aren't wanted in the other villages."

"What do you mean, misfits?"

He put his plate down and wiped his mouth with the back of his hand. "Remember when I told you how I was chased away from my home village by those that thought they were better than me? Well, before I left, the Shaman told me of a place where two rivers marry and become one."

"And you went there?"

"He called it 'Fairview.' He told me to take a girl from the village that had disgraced her family. When she was a young girl, her daddy had arranged her marriage to a brave of his choice, a thin, short brave, but a good provider. The girl's skin crawled whenever the brave was near, but she didn't want to defy her daddy. She waited until the council house was prepared for the ceremony before she went to the Shaman to tell him she had taken a drifter to her blanket and was heavy with child.

"It made no difference to me. She was strong, and I knew she could work hard. I took her, and her daddy gave me two goats. The Shaman said he would send other people to Fairview to help grow maize."

"Did he?"

"Before long, every murderer, thief, and drunk from the territory scratched at the flap of my hut. Not only from my former village but from many others."

"You took them in?"

"They became my brothers. I was their leader. I gave them what they needed, and they gave me respect. No person was questioned. No person was turned away."

"Then there must be lots of people in the village. How many? Ten people? Hundred? Thousand?"

He shook his head, "Maybe twenty, maybe thirty braves, depending on how many are in the white man's jail whenever you count, and there's fifty squaws and lots of screaming babies."

"Oh. And your squaw, what's her name?"

"Wesa. That's the only name she wants. She was unhappy with the name her mother gave her, so she asked the Elders to have a name-changing ceremony so that she could choose a name of something she admired. Wesa, the cat, uses its intelligence and cunning to get its way. It's silent, swift and determined, all qualities she admired."

"But… that's an awful…"

"Wesa, Nana, nothing else."

She saw the large zigzag vein on the side of his head begin to pulse, and she nodded quickly. "Does Wesa have children?"

"Only girls."

"So she can teach me?"

"She helps all the squaws in the village."

"When will we get there?"

"Maybe one, maybe two hours before the sun rises. When we hear the first dog bark, we'll stop. Even the rainbow man doesn't enter a village in darkness. We will wait until we see smoke from the cooking fire."

Dogs announced the arrival of the travelers. Heads poked out of the buildings, and a few swarmed around them, welcoming Blackjack and pointing at Dovey, some laughing and others pulling at her clothing. Despite what she felt was a strange reception, all of her senses were directed toward these new surroundings. Is this where she would stay, among the confusion of the buildings placed in what seemed to be a random fashion? The buildings were different than her Kansas house; wooden weren't they? And the people, look at the people, more people than she had seen since her daddy took her to Abilene.

A waft of wind swirled a wisp of smoke from one of the open fires, and with it came an aroma of food. Hunger pangs demanded that she sniff out the source. Alongside the fire was a young girl, not much older than she, attired in a buckskin dress. Her black hair was loose, and it delicately folded over her shoulders. She was kneeling on a woven blanket with a red band at each end, stirring something in a large pan held away from the fire by three poles. Dovey watched the girl take a taste of the ingredients and then pass the large horn spoon to another, older looking girl for her to taste. The older girl returned the empty spoon, nodded, and went back to her task of scraping the inside of a large skin. Dovey's eyes were riveted on the two girls.

Can it be? Would there really be girls she could talk to? Maybe they could help her understand what she must do to have her baby. Maybe. She sighed and felt her body relax from the tension created by coming into this strange and unexpected place.

Blackjack led her around the edge of a hut where she could no longer see the girls. She continued to stretch her neck in an attempt to see everything, even after Blackjack dismounted. He led the horse, with Dovey still on its back, to a building in the rear where a woman was sitting on a stump made into a chair. She had her back turned to the sun.

Two long, shiny braids of coal black hair tied with small pieces of blue cloth extended down her wide back just like the ones he had often tried to make from her hair. She smiled and hoped that the similarity in hairstyles would, in some way, make Wesa like her.

The woman ignored her visitors until Blackjack called her name. Then she turned slowly to stare hard at Dovey.

"We knew you were coming. Our scouts picked up your trail two days ago." But as the woman turned, Dovey felt her smile fade, her lips go taut, and blood race up her neck to her head. She gasped and briefly turned her head away.

The woman's face was pockmarked like the roof of her Kansas home after a hailstorm. Her left eye drooped as though she was trying to see the purple mark on her cheek.

Blackjack walked over to her. "Get up, Woman," he said. "You've got work to do."

He didn't even say hello or hug her, like her daddy often did to her mother when he entered the room.

The woman rose from her sitting position, stood silently before him for a moment, and then turned to stare at Dovey, who stared back, trying to learn everything she could about this woman. She couldn't help noticing her size. She was nearly a head taller than he was and probably twice as heavy. But her fluid movements were similar to a young girl's.

Dovey felt small, and the woman's hard, angry scowl made her feel unwanted. Why had he brought her to this woman? Look how clean her long dress is. She brushed at her makeshift maternity dress and felt the warmth of embarrassment because of its unclean, tattered condition. She hoped Wesa hadn't noticed her clothing.

"Get down off that horse, Nana," Blackjack said.

Wesa looked Dovey up and down, scowled and spoke angrily to Blackjack in a strange tongue. He barked back at her. She stood for a long moment, in rigid silence, with her dark eyes blazing. Then she shrugged her shoulders and began to feel Dovey's stomach, peeled her eyelids back to peer into her eyes, and pinched the flesh of her arms and legs. She stood back, staring at her, as though she were looking at a statue. She ignored Dovey and addressed her comments to Blackjack in English. "No good. Got no meat on her bones. She has no milk to feed baby when he come. Her eyes say she hasn't eaten right food. You go. Leave her with me until your child is born."

'Leave her with me!' Dovey couldn't believe she had heard right. But whatever lay in store for her in this strange village had to be better than what she had experienced lately. 'Please do what she asks Blackjack. Please!'

He hesitated, took a short step toward Dovey, cocked his head, and squinted at her. Then he turned to Wesa, speaking in their language but with frequent looks at Dovey. She saw the older woman nod her head without a change in demeanor.

He's probably telling her about my tries to escape. Don't worry old woman, she wasn't going anywhere until her child was born. Then...?

"Take good care of my son, Woman," he said, in English. He casually patted the woman's shoulder with a scowl that emphasized an unspoken threat.

"I'll take care of the child that this trail woman of yours is going to have, but I won't forget the shame you bring to me in the eyes of the village. Your blanket will cover me and only me in the night." She pointed a crooked finger at Dovey, raised her voice, and in slow, strong words said, "If you try to lie with that one there, or any other, there will be no papoose and these hands will strangle anyone that does not listen to my words."

The size and obvious strength in the woman's hands, the blaze in her black eyes, and the purposeful way she had handled everything convinced Dovey that she was able and willing to carry out her threats.

Dovey's spirits soared. A tingle went up her backbone. Surely, if Wesa is so possessive, that will mean freedom for her.

Dovey smiled and took a shy step forward. The older woman's lips tightened in response and her stinging words of a moment ago echoed in Dovey's ears, 'Or there will be no papoose.'

It was foolish to believe that this woman would help her escape. She'd remain quiet for now or maybe there will be no Dovey either. Wesa's big hands and arms seemed even larger, now that they were standing face to face. Her threat was clear. The woman hated her. How could she ever make her understand she was held against her will? It wasn't her fault, any of it.

Wesa spoke, in her native language, to a young girl lurking around the corner of the squaw's house. The girl bounded away and returned in seconds holding in both hands a gourd filled with chalky-looking liquid.

"Drink," the squaw said.

Dovey looked at the squaw's placid face and hesitated for a moment, but the nearly forgotten aroma of goat milk was too compelling. Her hands trembled as she brought the gourd to her lips, determined to not spill a drop. "Thank you," she said and bowed slightly.

There was no acknowledgment. "Come," she said to Dovey. Then she gave more instructions to the young girl.

The village, as Blackjack had said, was at the joining of two rivers, the one that he had followed and another, larger one that flowed swiftly along as though in a hurry to reach the sea. Many canoes rested on the bank of the larger river. Racks for sun drying fish were on the higher ground. In the distance, further along the confluence, Dovey saw what looked to her like the Kansas cornfields. There were trees and other green things growing in neat rows.

How orderly. How different from the village, where all the houses were scattered, seemingly at random.

She stopped to look and to wonder what else she might find, flowers maybe. She felt a strong arm on her shoulder.

"Come," the squaw said.

Wesa led her down a path until the cool water of the river lapped at her feet.

"Take off your clothes," Wesa said. "Lie down, wash good... everywhere."

The young girl also came into the water, unbraided Dovey's hair, washed her back, and handed her a cake of soap and a piece of cloth.

Dovey smelled the soap as though it were the finest French perfume and lifted her eyes to the heavens in appreciation. A grin came to her face as the first small bubbles of lather appeared on the cloth. She patted her face with the soft foam, rinsed, and looked at the surface of the water to attempt to see if the grime had been carried away.

With precision she scrubbed every inch, every crevice, with great care, not once but twice or more.

As she lay back in the water to rinse, the reflection magnified the size of her stomach so that it looked to her as though it were a giant melon. She arched her neck and inspected it thoroughly. Her small hand traversed the swollen flesh with tenderness.

She had so many questions to ask Wesa. What was happening inside her body? How long was it going to take? How big was she going to get? How wi...?

A strong thump came from within her. What was that? She stared at her stomach, wondering... A second thump; her flesh actually moved. She saw it.

She opened her eyes wide and turned her head to see if the others had seen what happened. The Indian girl was grinning. She waded to Dovey's side.

Wesa nodded. "Good, baby is healthy."

The magic continued. Dovey took the young girl's hand and laid it on her stomach. The baby obliged. Both girls laughed and felt again and again until the spark of life decided it had had enough.

The shared laughs, the mutual discovery of the miracle of life, and the kindness the young girl showed to Dovey sparked an instant friendship that gave Dovey a long forgotten sense of comfort.

"What's your name?" Dovey asked.

There was no sign of recognition from the girl. After the second request, Wesa said, "She speaks your language a little. She will learn. You teach her. Her name is Matushka. Means 'Red Dawn.' First thing I see when she wriggle from between my legs."

"Red Dawn," Dovey repeated. The young girl smiled.

"Your daughter?" Dovey said the words slowly as though thinking of the other part of the equation. "And Blackjack, is he her daddy?"

"Enough talk. You come." Wesa led her to a hut and gave instructions to Red Dawn in Cherokee.

"Lay on blanket. Put knees up. I'll look."

She felt Wesa inspecting the folds of flesh between her legs, then saw her extend her fingers in fan fashion before placing them between her pelvic bones. She grunted in apparent satisfaction.

Wesa took a gourd from Red Dawn, removed the stopper, and poured a small amount of the oily contents into the palm of her hand. "You rub belly and thighs morning and night. Rub good. Don't lay with any man. Red Dawn will sleep on blanket next to your bed. She'll call me when you're ready."

Dovey nodded and rubbed the fragrant oil on her body as instructed. It felt soothing, soft and good. The only thing better was the kindness of these two Indians. Indians, people she had always thought of as savages and killers. A tear came to her eye.

Blackjack would have been just as good if he had only had a chance.

After the second full moon passed, the villagers began the celebration of the Green Corn. Dovey watched from a distance as the dancers paraded around the fire in an incessant movement of swinging arms and stamping feet. One short step, two quick stamps of both feet, a shuffle, and then a step with the other foot, all in time with the tom toms. Shouts and screams pierced the air in random fashion. As the night wore on, perspiration gleamed on the dancers' bodies, the screams became louder, and the drums quickened the pace of the dancers.

A sharp, sudden pain at the pit of her stomach distracted her from the spectacle. She returned to her hut, winced, caught her breath, and attempted to control her breathing. Short breaths were better. She tried to distract herself by listening to the madness of the dancers screaming their thoughts to the sprit world, but the rhythm wouldn't blend with the pace of her breathing.

Red Dawn had not seen her return to the hut, and it was nearly an hour before she found her. "Does it hurt bad? How often are the pains coming?"

"Just now and then. Sometimes twenty minutes, sometimes more or le... I don't know. But the last one, oh Red Dawn, that hurt so bad! When will the baby come?"

"Baby will come when baby ready. Mother says you small, young girl. Might take long time, maybe many hours."

"I can't stand that much pain. Can't we do something to make it happen quicker?"

Red Dawn made a cursory inspection of her genitals, felt her head and began wringing her hands.

"What did you see? Your face, I can see there's a problem isn't there? Tell me!"

Red Dawn shook her head.

"Tell me, what's the problem?"

"I'll get my mother, but first I'll give you some Garden Heliotrope to help chase pain. Don't tell mother I gave you. She wants to wait."

Dovey's renewed screams blended with the shouts of the dancers.

"Not time," Wesa said to the pleading Red Dawn. "You go back. I'll come soon."

Dovey was panting. Her breaths were coming quicker than before. "Oh Red Dawn, oh Red Dawn, please help me. I hurt so bad... what's happening to me? How can I give birth to a baby if I don't know how?" She breathed deeply for a few moments, and the pain began to ebb once more.

Red Dawn bathed her forehead with cool water, pulled up the only chair in the room to her bedside, and took Dovey's hand in hers. "Remember when we talked about babies before the last moon?"

Dovey smiled, "I remember." The scene at the river came back to her.

"Didn't your mother tell you about making babies and birthing them? Haven't you watched other women give birth?"

"She was going to but..." Dovey listened in wide-eyed amazement as Red Dawn tried to find enough words to explain about conception, the growth of the embryo, and the delivery of the baby.

Red Dawn held Dovey's hand as she talked and her face mirrored the tenseness that she was certain Dovey was feeling with the advent of each new spasm.

Dovey thought, 'So, that's why Wesa says that this baby is Blackjack's, because he planted the seed. I won't let him have it! It is my baby!'

Out loud Dovey said, "Thank you, Red Dawn. I think I can

do it now. I want to, I want to see my baby. I want a girl that I can hold and rock and play with like I played with my young sister."

More cramps and pain snatched away the precious memory. Red Dawn paced back and forth, went to the door, and listened. Wesa was nowhere to be seen.

The moon was beginning to fade before Wesa came to the hut. She threw back the cotton cloth covering Dovey, pushed on the moist flesh between her legs, and motioned to Red Dawn. "Give me the Devil's Bit from the basket." To Dovey, "Chew on this and swallow the juice."

Dovey held the short piece of root in front of her and rubbed it on the bedclothes, trying to remove what looked like dirt and fine hairs. It still didn't look clean, but she had to do something to attempt to relieve the pain; so she bit into it at the cleanest spot and held it firmly.

The first cock crowed and Dovey's screams were louder than before. They were coming often now. Wesa paused at the door to say, "See what happens when you take another squaw's man. You're being punished."

"Please, old mother, forgive me. I didn't know what I was doing, ooohhh…"

"Mother, she is truthful, she didn't know." Red Dawn repeated the essence of the girls' earlier conversation. "Please give her some Black Haw for her cramps and ease the baby's journey with Snake Root."

Wesa was stoic, seemingly unmoved by her daughter's story of Dovey's innocence. She looked out into the early glow of the morning and raised her head to the heavens, said something quietly as though for the ears of the Great Spirit only, and turned back to Red Dawn. She nodded, and Red Dawn ran for the basket.

When the ordeal was over, Dovey fell back onto the blanket in exhaustion. She heard the baby's cry and looked through swollen eyes to see a small, black head that seemed to be swallowed in a bright, red blanket. Wesa was examining the child. Dovey reached toward it, but the exertion was too much. She fell back on the blanket, and for a moment darkness overcame her. The first cry of the small infant revived Dovey. She held out her arms, pleading with Wesa to give her the child.

Dovey's heart pounded as the child settled into her arms. She couldn't wait. "It's a boy!" she shouted. "A boy."

Wesa slammed the door as she left.

"Look, Red Dawn, look how pretty he is. Look at his big feet. Do you think they're too big? Of course, my daddy had big feet." She continued to excitedly examine every virtue of the small baby.

"He's perfect," Red Dawn said.

Dovey smiled at her words and kissed the top of the infant's head. "He is, isn't he? I can't thank you enough for your help. I don't think I could have done it if you hadn't explained what was going to happen."

Before Red Dawn could react, the door slammed open and the sun, which was now high over the trees, burst into the room. With it came the stench of Blackjack and the melody of the Yellow Warblers.

Dovey looked up to see the form of a man standing in the doorway, bathed with the glow of the early sun, and even though she could not clearly see his features, she knew who it was.

"Come see my boy," Dovey said.

She felt no anger toward him, only a sense of forgiveness. It was he who had given her the happiness of having a child. The beatings and the pain that he had inflicted were displaced by her feeling of pride.

But, when he stumbled over on unsteady feet and stared through bloodshot eyes, she suddenly didn't want him holding her child. She tightened the blanket around the small bundle and kissed his cheek. The baby rooted for her breast. She guided his small mouth until he clamped his lips around her nipple and began to suckle. She saw his tiny chest move, felt his heart beat, and watched his eyes stare at her for a while and then intermittently close.

Her entire body tingled in response to every slight movement the child made. His body was warm, and so was hers. A feeling she couldn't describe coursed through her heart. She stroked the child's head and her mother's words came to her: 'You came from inside me, Dovey. You're a part of me and always will be.' And you, my darling boy, will always be a part of me, she thought, and I pray that your life will have all the happiness that I feel at this moment.

Blackjack continued to stare without comment.

"Blackjack, I want to thank you for giving me this wonderful child. I've named him Jerry, after my daddy. Isn't that a happy name? Do you like it?"

"Blackjack's son will be called Junaluhska," he said, then turned and left the hut.

She let the comment pass. Nothing was going to ruin the most complete happiness she had ever experienced. But even so, the trauma of the morning was beginning to wear on her.

Her head began to nod. She blinked and held out the small child to Red Dawn and drifted off to the sound of her son's breathing and the memory of the sensation of his warmth against her.

When she awoke, she looked around the cabin but saw only Red Dawn sitting on the floor, staring through the open door.

"Where's my baby?" she asked and felt a chill envelop her body. "Something's wrong with my baby!" she screamed. "Red Dawn, where's my baby? What's the matter with him? Why are you crying?"

Red Dawn ran from the room.

Through the doorway Dovey could see the large frame of Wesa approaching and tried to read the expression on her face. There was none. There never was.

Without comment Wesa changed the bloody compress between Dovey's legs and handed her a cup of liquid.

"Where's my baby? I want to hold it. Please, Wesa, bring my baby."

"You drink. Rest. Talk later."

She drank the tart "tea" straight down in hopes that Wesa would talk to her. Her eyelids became heavy. She blinked a few times until her head fell onto the neck rest.

✧

Chapter Seven

On the morning of the second day, Dovey was awakened by the sharp, incessant cries of a baby.

Something about the tone of its cry tugged at her heart. It was her son. She knew it. She attempted to stand, fighting against dizziness and a spinning feeling in her head. The room was a blur; she started to fall and screamed as she reached out for the wall, or anything that would help her orient herself. Red Dawn ran into the room, restrained her, and shouted for her mother.

"Please," Dovey said, "Tell me what's wrong with my baby. I hear him crying."

"Have some food, rest a little, and then we'll talk," Wesa said.

"No, last time you gave me stuff it made me sleepy, and you left before we could talk." Dovey held her hand in front of her mouth refusing the spoon of gruel that Red Dawn offered. "Please, Wesa, I can't stand to hear those cries without trying to help him. It breaks my heart, PLEASE! Just let me go to him to feed and comfort him."

Wesa cocked her head for a moment, looking intently at Dovey, then nodded.

Dovey sucked in her breath and slipped to the far side of her small bed as Wesa sat her huge body next to her and took her hand. "You hear the cries of another squaw's papoose." She paused and looked away. "Your baby is dead."

Dovey's throat tightened. Her mouth went dry. The woman was lying; she had to be. "No! That's a lie! I heard my baby cry when he was born. I know his voice. That's my baby crying. You lie!" Dovey lashed out with her small fists to strike the old woman.

Wesa smothered the blows, held her arms for a moment, and then quietly laid her on her bed. She held her hand up with the palm forward. "Listen to me. Your baby is dead. We waited until you felt better to tell you." She paused again. "I lost a child, too. I've felt your sadness. My heart was broken also. I'm... I'm

57

sorry."

The old woman walked away.

Dovey swung her legs out of the bed, took one step and fell. She crawled to the door and screamed. "You're lying and you know it! Why are you doing this to me? I didn't take your man; it wasn't my fault. Why do you want to hurt me? Please give me a chance. I'll never let him come near me again; just give me a chance to prove it. And bring my child to me. He needs me. Please."

Her pleas fell on deaf ears. Wesa didn't even look at her. Dovey tried to get up, but her legs were too weak to support her. She fell to the dirt just outside the hut, panting, trying to catch her breath, hoping to determine where the child's cries were coming from.

The cries became louder, and she fixed the direction in her mind. He wasn't far. She would crawl to him if she had to. She began crawling across the hard, dirt surface of the village in the direction of the screams. Every inch she crawled was torture. Her knees became red from the abrasion of the loose sand on the hard road, and a speck of blood dribbled down the side of her leg. But the cries seemed louder. Despite the pain she felt in her knees and left arm, her heart felt light. She was almost there. That was all that mattered to her. She listened for a moment longer, took several large gulps of air, and tried to pick up the pace. 'Mother's coming, Honey.'

Blackjack's dirty boots blocked her way. He picked her up, took her into her hut, and dropped her on the bed. He slammed the door. She heard a scraping sound on the outside of the door and saw it quiver like something was being jammed against it. She hobbled to the door and shook it, but it wouldn't move.

Through the entire night the baby cried, and so did Dovey. At first she beat on the door until her hands bled. No one came. The door would not budge. She fell to her sore knees and cried until, exhausted, she fell asleep. The last sound she remembered hearing was the wail of the baby. Her baby, she was sure.

Before the sun rose, she was awakened by a scraping sound from outside the door. Panic crept into her heart as she envisioned Blackjack returning. Her thighs ached at the thought. She looked for a weapon. Anything would do. She would kill him before she let him touch her again. There was nothing.

The starless night was ink dark. She couldn't see. A rush of fresh air told her the door was open. Soft footsteps were creeping across the floor. There was no other sound. She sniffed the air. It wasn't Blackjack. But, who else would it be? Her ear caught a faint gurgling sound and she smelled the wild lilac scent that Red Dawn loved.

She whispered, "Red Dawn?"

"Baby need food. Mother sick. You feed." Red Dawn's hand found Dovey's shoulder in the blackness of the night, and she transferred the small bundle she was carrying into Dovey's arms.

Her heartbeat accelerated, and it seemed as though blood would burst through her temples as she cuddled the small bundle to her breast. The tiny mouth found its goal, and the bond between mother and son was reinforced.

Twice a day, for three days, Red Dawn made the secretive trip to Dovey's bed. On the fourth day, Dovey heard the familiar scrape on the door, and her body flushed with anticipation. The door didn't open. Dovey heard the angry voice of Wesa and a slapping noise that told the story, 'Red Dawn had been caught.'

In the days and nights that followed, her only contact with her boy was through hearing the lusty wails that pervaded the village. She pushed on the door again, on the walls and the floor; it was hopeless. The exertion caused her to breathe heavily and to perspire. What could she do? The thought ran through her brain over and over, mingled with her confusion about Blackjack's attitude.

Surely he can hear how weak our son's cries are becoming. He must know that he is dying. He wanted a son so badly. Why would he stand back, do nothing, and wait for the child to die? Why had he imprisoned her in this small, stuffy hut when she could be there helping the boy? No answers came to her, but the perpetual question remained: "What could she do?"

In spite of her misery and confusion, she was getting healthier. Her legs held her more steadily now, and the dizziness wasn't as frequent. She didn't let on about her condition when Red Dawn brought her food and water. Still, there seemed to be something in the girl's face and her speech that made Dovey believe that Red Dawn understood.

What could she do? Could she run past Red Dawn when she opened the door? No, she would only be caught before she could attend to the child. Perhaps she could lean the bed on its end and crawl up through the roof thatch. But, what's on the other side? Would she survive the fall?

She put her hands over her eyes, shook her head, and began speaking aloud. The sound of her voice and the answers that were iterated in a tone like her mother's brought comfort. There was no other way she could stay sane. 'Mother, why didn't you tell me about men and babies? If I had known... What else didn't you tell me? What else will happen to make me toss in the night, grow old, and forget the days when I was near you and happy? Help me find a way to get out of this place, mother.'

Dovey felt the pressure of tears in her eyes as she waited for the answer she knew couldn't come, but she didn't cry. She refused to. She clenched her fists, clamped her jaw shut, and refused to cry. She remembered another time when she did the same thing, years before, when her mother was teaching her to spin yarn. She couldn't do it. She wanted to give up, to cry, and to run away where no one would know how thick-fingered she was. She remembered her mother taking her small hands in hers and gently kissing them, saying, *'My darling, many people, especially young people with such small hands, have trouble with the wheel at first. But the ones worth their salt just try harder. Remember three years ago, when the rain refused to fall and the crops were poor. Did your daddy give up? He might have made a fist or two like you did, and his insides may have been quivering with worry and self doubt... But, he didn't quit. He only worked harder. Remember that.'*

The sudden memory of a long forgotten incident was like lifting a yoke from her shoulders. For the first time since she last saw her son, she felt her face relax and the fire in her belly cool. She could do something, and she would!

A glint of sunlight through a crack around the door bathed a portion of the far wall, highlighting details she had not seen on her first frantic search.

She ran her fingers over the wood, inch by inch, pushing as she went, praying for a soft spot or an opening of any kind that could be enlarged. There was nothing. She tried the other three walls. They seemed even more formidable. She sighed. She didn't want to give up, but how many times could she go over these walls? How much could her bleeding knees take of crawling on the hard wooden floor?

She would move the bed and try the roof. But could she do that before Red Dawn returned with her evening meal? Would she be caught and tied up, or would they do something else to her? They didn't need her anymore, did they?

Her baby needed her, even if they didn't.

She removed everything from the wooden bedstead, pulled the frame from the wall, and started to lift. She bent her knees, straightened her back, and lifted. It moved. She panted, groaned and strained, trying to lift the heavy furniture further. If she could only rest a minute, take the load off, and push instead of pull.

She wouldn't give up; she could do it. THINK.

She saw the chair, the only other piece of furniture. She would lift the bed high enough to kick the chair under the end, and then she could push upward. That was it!

It seemed as though her body was now light and flexible. It responded immediately to her intense needs and seemed to be willing to provide a small amount of extra force.

She moved the chair into a strategic position, drank a small amount of water, breathed deeply, reached for the bed, and pushed with controlled force. She knew she could get it on the chair. She eased the chair into position with her foot, carefully, slowly, afraid that the chair would tip.

She let go of the bed slowly, praying that it was stable, and fell to the floor, sweating from every pore. Her injured arm was crying out for her to rest it. Her breathing was rapid, and nausea was slowly creeping up on her. Maybe she had been wrong to drink the water. Why hadn't she eaten more of the porridge that morning?

She rolled onto her right side. Why... a shaft of light no larger than her little finger stabbed the floor behind the bed. Dovey stared, transfixed, afraid to move, afraid that it would disappear. Her hands began to sweat, her heart beat more rapidly, and she slowly inched forward on her belly, still staring at the opening. She extended her hand slowly, then she paused before touching one side of the irregular hole. It was real, not a reflection from the door.

She ran her finger around and around the irregular surface of the hole, pushed, and felt a small movement. She tried to put her finger through but was unable to do so. She looked at the other tree limbs, comprising the wall. They were solid and bound tightly together. Thank God for this small knothole... it's a start.

What could she use to dig with? She scoured the place; there was nothing. Maybe, if she broke off a leg of the chair, she could ram the leg through and make it big enough to get her hands where she could pull on the limbs. But, how would she explain the broken chair to Red Dawn?

Red Dawn. Maybe she's the answer. Maybe she'll help me. She tried before. But if she were to tell her what she was doing and she didn't want to help, then what would happen? Her thought trailed away. She couldn't tell her. Besides, it wouldn't be fair to her. But wait a minute. When Red Dawn brought food that night, suppose she were to keep the spoon to dig with. She nodded. Her wet hands began to dry, and her breathing returned to normal.

She had better rest now, she thought, and prepare for the job she had to do during the evening, but she didn't want to leave the shaft of light. She pulled a blanket down onto the floor and went to sleep with the light shining on her face.

As soon as Red Dawn left, she quickly moved the bed from the wall and began to dig, hour after hour, expanding the hole by minuscule amounts. Her hands quivered with every twist of the spoon. When the spoon slipped, the jarring force tore at her injured arm, but she wouldn't quit.

With every wail the child made, Dovey intensified her efforts. Desperation kept her going, and every square inch felt like a victory and spurred her onward. How much time did she have before Red Dawn came back? Had the cock crowed? She couldn't remember, and then she saw a slight change through her precious hole: the sun was rising. She made one more lunge at the wood, the spoon bent, and its jagged edge rammed into the palm of her hand. She tore a piece of cloth from an old shirt, wrapped it about her hand, and then folded the small pile of wood scrapings into the rest of the shirt. She put the bed back into position and crawled into it, waiting for Red Dawn's scratch on the door.

She tried but could not sleep because of the throbbing pain in her hand, but she kept her eyes tightly closed in hopes that Red Dawn wouldn't know she was awake. She needed to hide her bloody hands, and she didn't want to be asked about the missing spoon.

As soon as her meal was finished, Dovey struggled to move the bed again and immediately began gouging, pulling, pushing, and pleading with the wood to break. She began a new technique. She felt up the limb to find the thinnest section and cut around it on three sides with the jagged spoon. She pulled. A creaking sound began and then exploded into what sounded like thunder to her. The piece splintered into her hands and gave way, and she tumbled backwards. She was breathing hard, perspiring from the exertion. She lay by the hole, as still as she could, listening for outside sounds that might indicate her activity had been discovered. She heard the normal sounds of the squaws going to the fields and the first screeches from the children's ball game, but nothing else.

Cool air, from the north side of the building, facing the forest, oozed through the small opening, providing lifesaving ventilation. Even so, the sweat still flowed from her pores. She swiped at the perspiration on her brow with her forearm. Blood from the wounds on her arm mixed with the perspiration, and a small pink stream ran down her forehead and into her eyes. The diluted mixture stung, half blinding her. She removed her clothing, lay by the opening for a moment, and took a small drink from the tiny gourd that contained her drinking water. Did she dare close her eyes for a moment? The cry of the baby answered her question.

As the sun began to set at the end of the second day, Dovey waited for her evening meal to be brought and prayed that her hole was now big enough.

She winced and held her bloody, raw hands in front of her. The wood was more stubborn now. The spoon was twisted and mangled. Worthless. She threw it in the corner of the room.

How much more could she endure? She looked back at the hole and could not believe what she saw. A greasy iron rod had been poked through. She grabbed the rod quickly and pulled it in. Then she stretched her neck to see if she could see her benefactor. There was no one to be seen, but the cool air drifting in brought a clear fragrance of lilacs. Her heart was now as light as the rod was heavy; she owed Red Dawn so much. But she had better work fast, before someone took it away.

Her pain, thirst, and sleepiness meant nothing now. She rammed at the hole with newfound strength, over and over until large chunks of wood fell to her feet.

She panted, wiped the sweat and blood from her brow, and kicked at the last restraint. Her heartbeat surged. She waited, trying not to breathe while she listened to determine whether anyone had heard the cracking wood. The camp was quiet.

She squeezed through the opening. The jagged wood cut her flesh. She wanted to scream but knew she couldn't. The fall from the hole jarred her left arm. A momentary darkness enveloped her brain as she fought against the fiery hell inside her arm. She rolled to her right, under the house, and waited, to be sure that no one had seen or heard her.

Dovey thanked God for keeping the moon behind clouds. She inched her way in the direction she knew her baby to be, listening as she went for the subdued cries of the infant. She cursed the barking dogs that seemed to be determined to make her task difficult. Which is the right hut? She must not enter the wrong hut, or all of her work would have been in vain. The thought made a shudder run down her spine.

She heard a faint sound behind her. She turned and gasped. Wesa took her by the arm. "Come," she said.

Wesa lit a pine knot in the smoldering coals of a cooking fire and marched through the door of the second hut. Blackjack was sprawled on the floor with a deep wound in his head. The surrogate squaw was cowering in the corner, holding her ripped clothes in front of her. The naked baby was lying on the floor, crying.

Dovey cradled the weakened child in her arms and helped him find her nipple. She walked away. Wesa kicked Blackjack and followed Dovey into the darkness. Dovey saw the slight smile Wesa permitted herself as though she were a proud grandmother escorting her young daughter. Is she going to be my friend?

Chapter Eight

"*W*ound looks bad," Wesa said to the group of braves huddled around her. She held a torch over Blackjack for all to see.

Yellow mucus oozed from the torn, red, inflamed flesh. One brave put his hand on his forehead and the startled look on his face told the others: Blackjack was in trouble.

Red Dawn left the building gagging.

"Will he live?" a brave asked.

"With the prayers of the Shaman, perhaps."

"Can't you do something to help him?" another asked.

"It depends on how fast the rider gets back from Eutec with the Comfry leaves. If it's not too late, they'll heal his wound."

For three days Blackjack raved, shouted and strained at the rawhide straps holding him. He had been given belladonna to calm his madness and a young girl was assigned to bathe his forehead with cool water and to lie next to him when he shivered.

The Shaman had him carried to the water to cleanse the evil spirits that were circling him. A dance was held. Now his survival was in the hands of the Great Spirit.

Once his fever began to subside and the drainage from the wound diminished, attention was directed toward his assailant.

Council members marched into the seven-sided council building, and although only five of the clans were represented, they sat in their assigned seats, passed the pipe and waited for the Elder to speak.

Debate continued on into the early evening.

"Perhaps it was the woman's fault. She has been long without a man. Or maybe it was jealousy because the child she cared for belonged to another," a brave said.

The Elder unfolded his legs and rose. "There is much to consider, and we should let the wisdom which comes with sleep guide us."

The pipe was passed and the debate continued. On the second night it was decided; the woman would be banished. Blackjack would go unpunished.

As long as Blackjack was lashed down with the rawhide strips, Wesa did not attempt to separate Dovey and the baby. She continued to ignore Dovey's insistence that the child was hers.

If she couldn't make Wesa understand, she'd never get her help. What could she say to make her pay attention without risking a refusal to bring the baby to her? Maybe she should relax and find other ways to kindle the friendship she believed was growing.

Each time Jerry was brought to her she kissed and hugged him and examined every inch of the small body. She knew every wrinkle in his skin and every spot to touch to see his wide eyes sparkle with delight.

Her soft voice cooed to him and at times laughed aloud at his gurgle. "Jerry, my little child, mama is happy that your bones no longer push through your skin. You used to be sallow, but my milk has made you pink and soft. Your mother loves you so much. Grow, my boy, grow. What color skin will you have when you are old enough to run on the prairie in the sunshine with other children? No matter, your mother will love you always, but let me rub your soft skin with this sweet oil. Perhaps we can rub away Blackjack's gray."

She rubbed, but dreams of the future caused her to pause. There was no doubting his eyes would be dark, but she hoped they would be the mellow brown of her daddy.

She caught her breath as an image of her daddy, the first in a long time, floated across her mind. Her daddy; oh, how she wished her daddy could see his grandson.

A tear fell onto the cheek of the little one. She kissed the child's cheek and watched his small head turn toward her.

During the five weeks that Blackjack's delirium lasted, Jerry remained with Dovey. Red Dawn came daily to bring fresh water and food. She played with Jerry while Dovey performed her ablutions and took a short walk around the camp, each time with fear in her heart that when she returned to her hut Jerry would be gone.

On a rainy morning during the fifth week she cut her walk short, turned up the path leading to her hut, and saw Wesa's large body entering her hut. She gasped and ran for the hut.

"Two full moons have passed since the baby was born," Wesa said. "You feed him from your breast, morning and night, no more. In the morning you feed him part goat milk, part barley water. Soon we'll put cornmeal in milk."

Wesa's words made her shiver. Was she trying to fix it so Jerry didn't need her any more? She tightened her hold on Jerry. "I don't mind nursing him. It's all right."

"No. It's time for you to work in fields with other squaws. Put baby with other papoose in daytime. Old squaw watch all babies."

"Please, old mother, let me take my baby to the field with me. I'll work harder than any of the others if I can just take him with me."

"No. All mothers must do same."

"You don't like me, do you? You hate me, don't you? Is it because you think Blackjack likes me better? Is that why you try to keep me from my child?"

"I am number one squaw. Blackjack come to my blanket, not to yours. You do as number one says."

"You can have him. I don't want him. Never did. He's an angry man who's full of rage and hate. He forced me, and I fought him over and over. You keep him if you can stand him. How can you care for him anyway? You can see, can't you, that he doesn't deserve your loyalty. He treats you like dirt!"

"How can I not like him? Put your hand on my face and feel the scars and the sores. Look at my fat belly. It was even bigger, full of someone else's child, when my daddy banished me. All of the villagers supported my daddy except Blackjack. He took me, fed me, and warmed my bed." Wesa shook her head and sighed. "I know of his failings, probably better than you, but I know too that he gave me a chance when no one else would. Many times I have wished he would change, but he won't. He's all I have, and I'll never fail him. That is the only way."

Dovey felt her face flush and her eyes flood. How many lives has that man ruined? She clenched her teeth, wanting to say something about the woman's tragic story but afraid of saying the wrong thing. She reached out and took the old woman's hand in hers and felt a slight shudder go through Wesa's body. The glaze seemed to disappear from her eyes, and her down turned lips parted as though there was something she wanted to say but she was not sure.

Blackjack entered the room and stood by Wesa's side as though he were reinforcing her command concerning feeding the baby. The ugly scowl on his face and the bright, red, six-inch scar that ran diagonally across his skull made him look menacing. She handed the small, gurgling child to Wesa and left to join the other squaws in the fields.

For the next five days she fed Jerry in the morning and worked all day in the fields, dreaming of nightfall and the chance to feel his small lips close on her nipple and to watch his tiny eyes search her face. The memory of his giggle when she tickled him and his thrashing arms and legs made the hours of hard work seem like nothing.

Thoughts contrary to these happy ones would not disappear. Wesa's demand that Jerry begin eating only solid food worried her. She would no longer be needed, and although she felt a bit closer to Wesa, the bond was not yet strong enough for the woman to resist Blackjack's demands. Jerry would be taken from her again, she felt certain.

On the night of the sixth day, she bathed her tired body in the river, rubbed her limbs with oil, and lay back for a precious few moments of relaxation. Strange thoughts began to come to her.

Why did Wesa allow her to go to Jerry the night she escaped from her room? She could have stopped her. If she had, Jerry would have died. The shame of having another squaw produce a son for her man would have been erased. Then she could have killed her in revenge for taking her man.

Dovey continued musing on her confusing thoughts until the sharp cry of a crow broke her concentration. She dashed from the river and ran the hundred yards to the room where she expected Jerry to be waiting. As her foot hit the creaking boards of the front step, she began the song she knew Jerry could identify with her, "Mama going to buy you a mocking bi-i-i-rd." With a smile on her face she pushed the door open and... the room was empty! She stood still and listened... nothing. She ran to Wesa's hut and banged on the door. "Where's Jerry? Where's my baby?"

"Real mother get well, come for papoose, take away."

"NO, NO, NO, it's my baby. She stole him. Where is he?" Dovey grabbed Wesa by the shoulders and shook her. "Tell me or I'll kill you!"

Suddenly pain exploded on the side of her head, darkness enveloped her. She slumped to the floor.

She heard Blackjack's voice as she faded away. "Tie her up," he said. "I'll take her with me tomorrow."

It was before sunup when Dovey felt her shoulders being shaken. "Get up. Time to leave for camp."

She'd spent most of the night with her head pounding and her mind swimming in dismay at the prospect of being taken back to the gold mining camp. How foolish to think that he would stay in the village to help raise his son.

"Didn't I tell you to get up?"

She spit at him and tried to strike him but her hands were still restrained.

Blackjack slapped her and called for Wesa. Together they lifted her onto a pony he had bought for her and tied her feet in the stirrups and her hands to the saddle horn.

"She had no food," Wesa said.

"She'll get nothing; no food, no water, until she learns to behave herself and stops her idiotic raving about that damn brat."

"You'll kill her."

"So? That's not your concern." He mounted and kicked the horse. "You take good care of Junaluhska, Woman."

Dovey spit at him again. He laughed and pulled on the pony's rein.

Hate and anger were her saddle mates. Hunger and thirst gnawed at her, but she wasn't going to give in. She gritted her teeth and stared at his sweat-stained, dirty back. With each step the pony made, her resolve to get even with him and to reclaim her child stiffened.

Her strong anger was like a screen that obliterated her ability to think clearly, but suddenly she was able to translate the meaning of his last comment to Wesa, "Take care of my son, Woman." Her heart pounded now with the thought: Jerry's alive. She had to find a way to get rid of this man and return for her son.

Anger turned to hope, and mile after mile her mind raced to think of a solution. Maybe she should be good to him so he'd be distracted, maybe…

No finite answers came, but a glimmer of an idea began to seep through the morass of confusion: Wesa does like me. She wanted him to feed her. She liked the old woman, too. Hadn't she done everything she could for her? It must have been an impossible situation for the old woman. How could she earn her trust and faith? How could she get her to help get her baby? How…?

Blackjack's horse stumbled on the rocky path. He lashed the animal with his whip and pulled back on the reins.

Dovey winced but held her tongue. She felt like shouting, "Anger's not going to keep the horse from stumbling." Anger wasn't going to solve her problem, either. She smiled. Be smart, girl. Think. Think about Wesa. Don't do the same stupid things Blackjack does. Catch him off guard and then run. Or shoot him.

"Blackjack, can we stop a moment? I need to go to the bushes."

"Are you going to spit on me again?"

"I'm sorry for that. Everything happened so fast, I was-"

" Shut up! Just up ahead, by that big boulder. There's a few bushes there," he said.

When she returned, she smiled and held out her hands to be tied. "I really am sorry."

Blackjack looked at her, stood motionless for a moment and coiled the ropes he'd tied her with around one of the saddlebags. "It's almost sundown. We'll stop for the night when we reach the first stream."

She had been right; she had done the right thing. Maybe her chance to get away would come soon.

About two hours after sunup, on the third day, the scenery began to look familiar to Dovey. She knew the camp was near, and the thought of what that meant made her blood run cold. Revulsion at the thought of Blackjack lying next to her and of him forcing himself on her made her stomach curdle.

"There it is," he said. He turned in his saddle and smiled. She cringed when she recognized the leer on his face. She would not sleep with him again, even if he killed her for it; but she must tell him.

She looked beyond him, at the mountainside, and tried to concentrate on the aspens, which had begun to change to a golden shade of yellow. There wasn't much more to see except for the ever-present rocks and boulders and a small group of barrel cactus. Then the river came into view, far down below, slinking along in its silvery path.

Her hands trembled. The knots in her stomach intensified as they neared the campsite. She decided. It couldn't wait; she had to talk to him ... now.

"Blackjack, I enjoyed visiting your village and getting to know your squaw. She's a nice woman, and I'm grateful for her advice. She helped me a lot."

He continued unloading the animals in silence.

"You're lucky to have her, you know. I think she likes me, too, particularly since I was able to give you a son."

"I want more sons."

"You tell Wesa, not me. I've repaid you for saving my life. We're even. Don't come to my blanket ever again. Make me a different place to sleep." She rested her hand on the stock of the rifle and stared at him, waiting for his reply; but none came.

Each time he unwittingly acknowledged the falsehood of Jerry's death she wanted to ask him a thousand questions, but just knowing he was alive was enough for now.

"I'm going to the logs," she said. "When I return, I want my blanket in a new place."

Before he could object, she hurried up the inclined path toward what she remembered as her "Thinking Spot." Every boulder, every bush, and every broken tree limb alongside the path seemed to be just as she had left it. The birds were there. The small lizards scurried about with tongues darting like lightning to catch insects, yet something was different. She paused a moment at the top of the path and surveyed her surroundings, trying to determine what it was that caught her curiosity.

The huge boulders on the south side hadn't moved an iota, but the moss on the north side seemed to have grown and was darker. On the east side, the smaller rocks were intact, but it looked like a river of water had run down from the hillside above, creating small ditches. Now she knew. It had rained while they were away. That explained why she had stumbled on her walk up the path. She looked to the west. The logs seemed the same. She shook her head, and a sense of dread spread over her.

She put one foot onto the lower log, and immediately small pebbles thundered down the hillside. She quickly stepped back and stared. The other end of the top log looked different, dark like it was wet. She shook the log with her foot. A sunbathing lizard quickly crawled from the top of the log and buried itself in the splintered, rotting pieces of the dark end.

She drew in her breath. She couldn't take a chance going out there. Something had to be done to those logs; she knew it. Should she call him? She didn't want him up there, though, when she was there. It was her only place for privacy and solitude. But she had to do something.

She carefully ran down the rutted, uneven path calling as she went, "Blackjack, I almost fell... those logs."

"Damn it, girl, you've been after me about those confounded logs since the first time you saw them."

"They've come loose. I'll fall."

He slammed his hat on the ground and grabbed her by the hand.

"Damn, we've been back thirty minutes, and already you whine like a baby. I should have brought Wesa and left you there. Come on." He grabbed her hand and started up the path.

Dovey pulled her hand away but followed him up the dim path, stumbling on the loose gravel, watching every step she took. This was no time to risk a sprained ankle. She pinched her nose to avoid the oppressive sage smell that made her sneeze.

Without testing them, Blackjack walked out to the center of the lower log. "See? There ain't nothing wrong with these logs. The whole mountainside will tumble down into the canyon before the logs do."

Blackjack gave a vicious kick at the top log. The rotted end of the log split, and the debris and several loosened rocks crashed to the canyon floor. The fall of the rocks caused the anchor points on the lower log to move also. The bottom log dropped slightly, and each end settled in a new position. Small pebbles from the foundation points of the lower log rained down the hillside, joining the other material on the canyon floor.

He looked down, paused for a moment, as still as a statue, and then eased one foot forward toward the nearest end of the log and the safety of the rock ledge. The lower log on which he was walking dropped an inch, and the top one, which he was using to balance himself, shook. He paused, looked down again, and started back in the opposite direction. The log settled further. "Nana, get a rope. Hurry!"

She slipped on the loose pebbles along the path, and blood flowed from her wound. She brushed it aside and continued her rush to the campsite. She grabbed a rope from his saddle and hurried up the hill.

"Tie one end of that rope to a tree or boulder, and throw me the other," Blackjack said. "Quickly, I can hear the log splitting."

She was panting heavily. She gulped air and desperately looked for an anchor. The nearest tree was too far for the length of rope. Could she get the rope around that odd-shaped boulder? Would the rope be long enough?

"Hurry, Nana, I'm getting dizzy."

"I told you not to call me that."

"Okay, Dovey. Please."

"The rope won't reach the trees or the rocks. I'm going to saddle the horse and tie the rope to the saddle horn."

Without waiting for his reply, she raced to the campsite, saddled the horse in less than a minute, mounted him, and dug her heels into his sides to urge him up the path. When she returned, she found that he had lowered himself to a sitting position on the lower log and had grabbed the upper one for stability. The constant peppering of small stones sounded like hail. More rocks crashed to the canyon floor. Blackjack's face had turned ashen, and a look of terror spread across it. His look, which she had never seen before, made cold shivers pass through her body.

With the rope securely tied to the horse, she threw the other end to Blackjack. He lunged for it with his right hand, and with his left hand he pulled on the top log, trying to retain his balance. She watched his fingers dig into the soft wood and claw deep scratches into the log as it began to fall.

He was straddling the lower log now, using the rope tension for balance, slowly sliding along the log's surface. By inches at a time he got nearer to the rock ledge. He wrapped the rope around his left wrist and reached out with his right hand to try to grab a gnarled branch that was anchored into the cliff. He lunged, missed, and grabbed again. The recoil of his body stressed the anchor point of the log beyond its capability, and the second log hit the bottom of the canyon with explosive force. The rope and small branch were his only hope.

"Hold on, Blackjack. Hold on. I'll back the horse."

He held precariously to the tree branch with one hand, found a small toehold in the sidewall, and continued to hold the rope with the other hand. "Give me some slack, I need to tie the rope around my waist. When I do, let the horse back up. Hurry, my hand is slipping." Before he could secure the rope around his waist, the branch began to pull away from its moorings. "Help me, Dovey. Do something! I'll take you to Santa Fe. You can have anything you want!"

She took a quick step forward, reached toward him, and saw his fingers on both hands slipping. She ran back to the horse. If he could just hold on, the horse would pull him to safety. The horse wouldn't move. She grabbed his rein and pulled with all her might, but he stubbornly refused to move. She mounted him and dug her heels into his side as viciously as Blackjack had done. He stood still, tossed his head, and neighed.

Dovey felt a sudden jerk of the horse's body, saw the rope go slack, and heard a bloodcurdling yell. She dismounted and ran to the cliff edge. One of Blackjack's hands had come loose from the rope, and his body swung until it slammed into the cliff wall. The impact loosened the grip of his second hand on the rope, his last hope.

She saw panic on his face and fear in his large, black eyes that looked like the inside of a tunnel. Then a fearful scream, more terrible than any coyote's scream she had ever heard in the still of night, sent waves of chill bumps over her skin.

Dovey clasped her hand over her mouth and watched in horror as his body twisted in freefall to another ledge ten feet below. He was facing upward, staring at Dovey in disbelief. He groaned as he tried to move. She saw a spurt of blood fly into the air and heard the sound of falling rocks as the thin ledge began to crumble. Each creak of the rocks caused his body to inch toward the edge, and then, as though in slow motion, it tumbled down the mountain to the canyon bottom. Then it was over. There were no more screams or rocks tumbling. Only silence.

Dovey gasped, slowly lowered her tired body to her knees, and then, on all fours, peered over the ledge, trying to assess his condition. All she could see was his twisted body, laid out on the ledge, still as a corpse. She had a strange feeling that she should jump down the side of the hill and run to his aid. As the absurd feeling penetrated her mind, she lunged back from the edge. Her body began to shake. She couldn't think what to do. What to do? Her feet were anchored as though they were in concrete. She stared at the sight below her. He was spread-eagled on the canyon floor with his head hard up against a large rock.

Was he dead? Maybe not. Despite the way he had treated her and the misery she had endured, she could not let him die if there was anything she could do. She would have to help him, save him, as he had saved her.

She untied the rope from the saddle, grabbed the horse's reins, and started to mount. Then, her nostrils caught a whiff of Blackjack's scent from clothing in his saddlebag. Hair stood on her neck. Her mind was suddenly flooded with overlapping memories of the misery he had put her through. She could feel the pain of each beating and the awful, chafing dryness that had made her scream with pain when he had violated her. Rage, hate, anger consumed her. She dismounted, grabbed his rifle from its scabbard and dashed to the canyon rim. She eased the safety off, raised the weapon, got his head in the sight, and began to squeeze just like her daddy had taught her years ago.

His body was still. His eyes looked to be closed. A pool of blood had formed under his head.

She could not pull the trigger. She wanted to. She wanted to know, for sure, that he was dead, and out of her life forever. But would killing him purge the terrible memories from her mind, or would his death at her hands bring even more formidable problems? Her trigger finger began to shake, and the strength to hold the rifle began to ebb, as did her resolve to kill. Her mother's teachings from the Bible came to her: Thou shalt not kill.

She lowered the rifle and stared up into the heavens. But that doesn't mean that I have to help him, does it? No! He's probably dead anyway.

She made her way back to the camp and sat looking at the valley below, which seemed to be stretched out forever. She looked back at the campsite and the animals. Everything there was repugnant. She returned her gaze to the valley, strewn with rocks, some bearing scorpions, snakes or cougars. She felt small as though witnessing Blackjack's disaster had compressed her into something different. She thought of the burning of her family home. How many more awful things would she have to endure? She didn't want to think of such a thing and sat silently, as though in a trance.

The sun passed the midpoint in the sky, a bird skimmed the surface of the stream and took a fish, and the reality of the bird's action helped to slowly relieve her shock.

"Dead? Blackjack dead? I'm free!" She shot the rifle into the air, jammed it back into its scabbard, raised the skirt of the new dress Wesa had made for her, and began a dance around the rocks containing the fire pit.

"FREE," she shouted. "FREE!" She danced and chanted the Cherokee chant she had heard so often during the five months she'd spent at the village. With blood pounding in her ears and her lungs screaming from her heavy breathing, she danced until she fell to the campsite floor. She lay still, panting and enjoying the exhilaration and excitement she felt. "Free?"

She crawled to the edge of the canyon rim, hesitated a moment, and peered over. She gasped. He was still there. He hadn't moved. And then she saw buzzards circling high above. He was dead. There was no point in going down there now, even if she'd wanted to.

"Free!" she shouted, and she smiled as the word came back to her from across the canyon.

Then, looking again at the vast, empty landscape, she said in an emotionless, barely audible voice, "Free."

✧

Chapter Nine

She transferred the saddlebags from Blackjack's horse to hers and slapped the animal on the rump. "You might as well be free too, old fellow. You were my only friend for months. God knows you've earned it." She hugged the burro's neck, released him, mounted her pony, and rode calmly down the trail toward the river without a backward glance.

Once she reached the river, she turned the pony in the direction of the Indian camp, retracing as best she could the route she and Blackjack had followed. The events of the recent past blazed through her mind. The hate and anger she had temporarily put aside were rekindled. She set her jaw, squinted, and stared at the trail, ignoring her hunger and fatigue. Only one thing was on her mind: Jerry.

She would find him and be the mother he deserved, no matter what.

With every mile her resolve stiffened. She paid little attention to the silky sheen of the colorful clouds as the sun fell behind the hills. Her ears ignored the sound of the crickets. She continued to ride like a robot until she came to a fork in the trail. She pulled the pony up and tried to read the signs on the ground to determine the correct direction, but the light was too dim. The pony shook his head and whinnied. Blackjack's admonishment came to her: "Don't kill the horse."

The thought made her shudder; this poor creature was the only ally she had at the moment. She led the horse to the small stream running alongside the path, removed his bridle, and let him roam freely to eat and drink. "Well, little pony, you and I are liable to be pretty close for a while. You better have a name. How about if I call you Checkers? Maybe then I can figure out the right moves."

She laughed at her little joke but heard no music. It was hollow and hopeless. The echo emphasized the immensity of her surroundings, her loneliness, and the impossibility of her situation.

She thought back to the long trek into the unknown after her parents had been killed. Look what that had gotten her. How long ago was that? One year, two years? She couldn't remember. She didn't care. What difference did it make? Her childhood, her innocence, her baby had all been stolen.

She swallowed the lump in her throat and tried to push all traces of fear from her mind. She picked up the bridle, took a step toward the horse, stopped, and cocked her head toward the sky.

If she couldn't get away from one Indian, how could she expect to rescue Jerry from a village full of Indians who would immediately want to know where Blackjack was? She paused, smoothed the dirt with her moccasin, and considered the reality of the problem.

Her only chance would be to get Wesa, or maybe Red Dawn, alone and plead for understanding and help. But what if her gut feeling about Wesa was wrong? How could she explain Blackjack's absence? Would Wesa believe she had killed him? Had she escaped from Blackjack only to be confined or killed by Wesa?

Even if she was right about Wesa's affection for her, maybe Jerry had already been sent to another village. Could she take the risk?

No satisfactory answers came, and she could feel her body tensing like a coiled spring.

She clenched her fists tightly and bit her lip. The shock of the bite, the blood on her fingers where she wiped her lips, and the sight of ugly rain clouds on the horizon teamed to release the stifling frustration. She must think with her head instead of her heart, even though the battle to do so was tearing her apart. She couldn't continue like that, not now, she must get help, but she wouldn't abandon him, either.

No tears came, despite the decision she had reached. Instead, she felt her body growing cold and the muscles in her face become rigid. She lay on the bare ground in silence until the moon cast its first splash of color on the water below.

As she sat, a desire to purge herself of her past nearly overwhelmed her. She rose. She felt older. She had to part ways with history and take charge of her destiny. She rose and began walking toward the water. When she was waist high, she threw back her head and spoke to the spirits in the only way she knew how.

"I am the Shaman this night. I cleanse myself of the evil of Blackjack Diamond. I curse his soul; may it rot in hell!

"I curse all men. I resolve that none will ever touch me again.

"I resolve to find my baby no matter how long it takes.

"All the sprits, gods and you, Wesa, hear my resolve!"

Chapter Ten

Snooze Dixon watched through slits in his eyes from beneath his broad-brimmed Stetson, hoping the moon would not disappear behind the clouds.

He'd placed his saddlebags between him and the smoldering embers of his campfire, so that he could see anything that passed between.

There was no breeze to rustle the pine needles or to carry the melody of the night warblers. This night silence was golden and aided his old ears in listening for important sounds.

He cocked his head in one direction and then another. The sound of the first crack of the dead pine branches he'd placed around the perimeter of the camp exploded in his ears. Someone was coming for sure. His heart beat a little faster. His deeper breaths sounded like thunder. He steeled himself. He coiled his fingers around his six-shooter and tested to be sure it was free in its holster. He took the rope in his other hand.

Darkness blinked at him as a silhouette passed between him and the fire. He steadied his nerves as best he could and waited. Timing was crucial. He knew that.

Another crackling sound exploded through the silence. This time it came from over near the saddlebags. He flicked his left wrist and pulled hard on the rope. His right hand went for his gun. He jumped to his feet and rushed at the intruder.

A loud shriek roared through the silence of the night. Snooze froze for a moment and listened as the angry sound continued. It wasn't the sound of a frightened animal, or an Indian brave. It was the shrill, soprano voice of a girl. A young girl.

But Snooze, a veteran of life on the trail, was taking no chances. He kept the tension on the rope that bound the girl's feet and wrapped the other end around her torso. This way she couldn't move.

He kicked at the fire and threw fresh, dry branches and leaves on it. Bright yellow and orange tongues of flame danced upward, illuminating his prisoner's face.

He studied the emotionless face in front of him, and his body turned cold when he thought of how close he'd been to putting a bullet through the head of what could have been his daughter. "What in tarnation are you doing sneaking into a man's camp in the middle of the night? Don't you know that could get you killed?"

She said nothing at first, but her mind was racing. She heard kindness in his voice but knew better than to count on it. "My legs, I think they're bleeding. Please take the rope off. I won't hurt you."

"Hurt me?" the man said, with a forced-sounding chuckle. "How you gonna do that, huh? Slap me and call me a bad name?"

She felt the blood surge to her temple as he laughed at his sarcastic remark. 'If he only knew what she had already been through.' The fire flared up, and she saw the broad smile he had on his gray-whiskered face. She smiled, too.

He unwound the rope and removed it from her legs. There was blood on the end of it. "Guess that was a bit tight. We'll put some joy juice on it in the morning. It'll be good as new."

"Not likely. I'll be long gone."

He stopped what he was doing and studied her for a moment. "I heard you last night, you know. That's why I laid my little trap. Many a rider has tried to steal Snooze's kit before. Ain't none done it. Wouldn't have gone to all the trouble if I'd known what I was up against."

"I wasn't going to steal anything."

"Whooee, you've learned young, ain't you? Ain't never been a thief yet, that admits, after they're caught, that they were going to rob nobody."

"I wasn't, and I don't like to be called a liar." Then she thought better of getting huffy, so she turned back to him and grinned as broadly as she could. "I'm sorry to be angry with you. It's just that my folks taught me to be honest, and I am. I won't shout at you again."

"Where are your folks? Waiting down the trail to do me in after you get me all softened up?"

She lowered her head and stared at her feet. The grin left her face. She clenched her fists and tried to push an avalanche of sad memories out of her mind. "I don't have any folks. I'm just me."

"You're telling me you are just out for a ride on the trail, a hundred or more miles from Santa Fe, and just happen to bump into old Snooze. Don't make me laugh, girl."

"Laugh all you want. I'm leaving." She retraced her steps toward where she'd left her pony, stopped at the edge of the camp, and threw a small sack at him. "This was to pay for the food I was hoping to buy."

She watched as he felt the weight of the pouch, opened it, and spilled a small amount of its contents into his hand. She took another step and shouted back over her head, "And by the way, that wasn't me you heard last night. I was a day's ride from here. I hope whoever it was comes back and shoots you. In fact, if I think about you calling me a liar too long, I might just wish I'd done it myself."

"Go on your way, if you want to," Snooze said. "But remember, whoever's out there might rob you, too. A girl carrying gold would be an easy target."

She silently walked away.

"If you're thinking of making toward Santa Fe to sell that gold, you better head a little more west, unless you want to end up right smack in the middle of the badlands."

She stopped a ways down the trail. She'd never find Santa Fe without some help, and she did have her pistol if he tried anything. They wouldn't hang her twice. "Snooze, it's me, Dovey. Don't shoot."

"I didn't see you carrying a bedroll, so I laid out a blanket for you, over there, on the other side of the fire," Snooze said. "Tie up your horse up yonder, and let's get some rest. We'll settle this thing, between me and you, tomorrow."

Dovey didn't argue.

Waking at sunup had been a way of life with Dovey since her first days with Blackjack, but for a reason she couldn't explain, there seemed to be no pressure to do so on this particular morning. Instead, she stretched, yawned and admired the orange streaks of dawn, which were bending around the fluffy white clouds drifting over the mountain. She raised her head slightly, hoping that he wouldn't notice her movement. She fixed the location of the sun in her mind and looked for the high rise of mountains she'd been riding alongside just before dark. Once she had her bearings, she inspected the camp. It was a simple one, no doubt arranged for a short stay, not like the semi-permanent arrangement Blackjack had. She sighed deeply and lifted her head.

She heard a sound behind her. There he was... Washing himself... In a basin. He was shirtless. His suspenders hung by his side, his small paunch hung over the rim of his trousers, but his arms rippled with muscles.

In the darkness of the previous night, she had seen the grayness of his beard. The hair on his head and chest were even whiter. She stared at him in disbelief. After twenty-seven months with Blackjack, she'd forgotten that men bathed.

It was odd that such a simple thing would make her happy. Why should anything he did affect her? 'Be careful, girl.'

"Ah, good morning. Thought you was gonna sleep all day," Snooze said. He shook the water from his face and hair and ran his fingers through his hair in an attempt to comb it. "Coffee's on."

"Good morning, Mr. Snooze." She smiled and drew in a deep draft of the coffee-scented air. "My, that smells good. Reminds me of the cold winters when my mother used to bring me coffee and milk to help wake me up. The smell was always better than the taste. Haven't had any in a while," she said and passed the cup under her nose again.

"There's more water in that goatskin. I'll take a walk up the trail, look at some outcrops, and see if I can spot some color while the sun is fresh on 'em. Give you a little privacy. I'll bellow out before I come back."

They worked together to clean up the breakfast utensils.

"Them flapjacks, they're my specialty. Don't have 'em too often. Don't want to get spoiled."

"Best I ever had. Even better than my..." She stopped herself.

"Well, the trail's awaiting," said Snooze. "I'll point out the way to you, and you can be on your way."

"Which way are you headed?"

"No particular way, not until my grub gets low. I'll just

mosey around a mite, trying to find some of that yellow stuff like you got."

"And then?"

"Back to Santa Fe."

"You live there?"

"Might say that. Me and my woman, Hatti, got a little business we run together. And I dabble in a few other things when I'm there."

"What kind of business?"

"Listen young'en, if you're gonna be a trail rider there's two things you gotta remember: everybody's business is their own. Keep yours to yourself, and don't pry into anybody else's. Got that?"

"Yep. And what's the second thing?"

"The second thing is to always keep your hog-leg handy where nobody else can get it." Snooze pulled out Dovey's pistol from under his blanket. "Without this, what would you use for protection?"

Dovey gasped, took a step toward the old man and reached for her gun. She could feel the back of her neck tingle. He could have done anything he wanted to. But he didn't. She looked into his twinkling eyes and saw the small creases around them shrink as his smile broadened.

"Guess I got a lot of teaching to do if we're gonna ride the trail together." Snooze handed her the butt of the gun and laughed.

She could trust him. Why else would he return her gun? She looked at him for a moment, wondering how to reply, and the contagious smile on his face released a stream of laughter that had been pent up too long.

The sensation was joyous. For the first time since her imprisonment, she felt a ray of hope. How long had it been since she had laughed? She couldn't recall.

Snooze extended his gnarled hand. "Friends?" he said.

"Friends."

"Just so you know, there ain't no way Snooze was going to let you go off into that wilderness alone. Also, what you threw at me last night was enough to buy a whole cow. You better learn to take care of that stuff, unless you know where it grows on trees."

She reflected on his comment a moment but decided silence

was the best answer.

"Well, I guess my prospecting is over for this trip. I better get you somewhere we can put a bit of meat on them skinny bones and get you into some proper clothes."

"You know what I want most?" she asked.

"I know what I want most when I come off the trail..." He interrupted himself. "Matter of fact there's a couple of things, I guess, but there ain't nothing better than a long hot bath."

"Oh, my. I haven't had a hot bath, since, well, what I want is to wash my hair in soft warm water and to cut these hideous braids out of it. I tried, on the trail, to hack it off with my knife. But look, Snooze, just look at it; it's as ugly as I am."

"Ugly? Shucks girl, you don't know what ugly is, but never mind that. Just know that this old man thinks you're pretty as a spring morning." He put his arm gently around her shoulder. "Besides..."

"Get your hands off me!" Her body went completely rigid. Blood pounded in her temples. "You ever touch me again, and I'll shoot you dead, Snooze. I mean it."

He looked her right in the eye, not mad, just serious. "I understand. You have my word, never again. I promise." He smiled, poured himself a cup of coffee and sat on a log by the cooking fire. "So, why don't you sit down and have some more coffee while we gab a mite."

She took a half step back and looked hard at Snooze's face. *What's he up to?* It was impossible to avoid relating every action, every word, to Blackjack. He had also been kind at first. But instead of the hard glint of Blackjack's eyes, she saw only clear, blue friendliness. The soft wrinkles that popped up around his eyes when he smiled made them seem to twinkle. The hair on the back of her neck lay down. She sipped her coffee. "What's on your mind?" she said.

"Remember me saying a while back that trail riders mind their own business?"

She nodded.

"Well, I'm gonna show you how dumb some old coots can be. Hatti always says that about me anyway. As a matter of fact, lots of people say that. I just let 'em. Makes it easier to get into their pocket."

"Wait a minute, your wife thinks you're dumb? That's awful."

"First off, Hatti ain't my wife. She's my woman. There's a difference. Anyway we got this entertainment business you see. We entertain men, mostly miners and prospectors who blow into town, carrying a bunch of that yellow stuff that makes most folks crazy. I play cards with 'em and get 'em all liquored up. They skonk me, pick up my chips, and laugh. Then Hatti and her girls go to work on 'em. By the time they're through, those fellas are lucky to have their socks left. But for some reason they come back, time and again."

"Why are you telling me this? You don't think I'm that kind of girl, do you?"

He shook his head.

"Well, what's your purpose?"

"Sassy little miss, ain't you? Just hold your horses. I'll get there."

She helped herself to more coffee.

"A few years back I had a fine missus and a young daughter just a mite younger than you, I suppose. The missus ran off one night with a no-good coyote named Gus. Went to the California gold fields, they did. Took the young'en, too.

"Oh, Snooze..."

"Don't much care if I ever set eyes on the woman again, but I sure do miss my baby." He looked away for a moment and sniffed. "Went damn near crazy when it happened. Started throwing gold dust around like it was sand. Hatti worked in the saloon where I went for a snort once in a while. One day I was bad sick. I was feeling like I might as well shoot myself, but I was so messed up I probably couldn't have found the gun. Hatti found me lying in the alley and got two men to carry me up to her place and plop me in her tub. I was too sick to fight back.

"After she had me cleaned up and made presentable, she says, 'Listen to me, you're making a damn fool out of yourself. You know what all the men are calling you now? Do you? They're calling you Snooze, cause you were asleep while Gus Stroh was in bed with your wife, right under your nose.' Of course, I didn't. I didn't know nothing."

Dovey smiled at his high-pitched imitation of Hatti's voice.

86

"So, Snooze isn't your real name?"

"Nope. But it'll do. You can call me that." He nodded and slightly pursed his lips. "Let me finish my piece, now, okay?"

"Who's stopping you?"

"Hatti was sweet on me, you know." A glint came to his eyes as he spoke of her. "When I first started going haywire, Hatti went back to my place with me one night. I was too far-gone to do what she came for, but she rooted around and found my stake. She took most of it. She left me just enough so I wouldn't think that I'd been robbed or just thrown it away like I'd been doing."

"She did give it back, didn't she?"

"Just as soon as I sobered up and we began talking. She wasn't one to go spouting off her mouth to every trail rider that came along. Fact is, I'd known her for nigh onto three years and didn't know a damn thing about her except she was some powerful woman under the blanket. She had a way about her, you know? Made me think I was really something. But it was actually her."

Dovey nodded and avoided his eyes. She'd never heard anyone talk about such things before.

"Anyway, It was nearly sunup before she finally told me why she'd taken up the life she had. After her ma died, her dad decided there wasn't no use in going to town to look for another woman, when he had a pretty little thing right there where he could get at her whenever he wanted."

"You mean...?"

Snooze nodded solemnly. "I'm afraid so. He hurt her real bad, too. She tried to get away, but he caught her and beat the stuffing out of her."

Tears welled up in Dovey's eyes. If Snooze saw, he didn't mention it.

"Finally the old man did come on to another woman. The woman hated Hatti and made her dad chase her away. She arrived in Santa Fe with only the clothes on her back. She had no education or work experience and was starving. She began entertaining men."

"Poor Hatti."

"Yeah, I know." He turned his head away for a moment. "Hatti started to cry about then. She terrified me. I thought she was made with a cast-iron constitution, but all her troubles must've been eating at her guts for a long time. She had no one to share her misery until she fell in love with me, a slobbering old drunk.

"For the first time I saw her without her paint, rouge, and powder, and I wasn't sure I was looking at the same woman. Deep wrinkles in her face seemed to confirm her story. She said to me,'I'm so tired, Snooze. I want to quit this business, but I can't. How else will I live?' I felt like saying but couldn't, 'Damn you, Woman, I've cried enough over one woman, and hear you come getting me all slobbery again.'"

If you're telling the truth, old man, we're going to get along fine. Dovey thought,

Snooze hesitated, coughed, and rolled his eyes upward. "I guess I better put a rope around this yarn and draw it in. Hatti wouldn't agree to hitch up with me, but we did go into business together. We had a bond; we both hated men and didn't mind fleecing 'em. It's our way of paying back. Having the 'Snooze' reputation makes it easy for me to be the stooge. I play it to the hilt. Fact is, my speech has become so affected until I can't even talk civil no more."

He sounded plenty civil to Dovey. She liked the music in the way he spoke, so much livelier than the gloomy monotone of the Indians. "Hatti got a few girls together, mostly girls that had come on hard times. She lets them do the entertaining. She just runs the show."

"There's two things I don't understand. What are you doing out here on the trail? And why are you telling me all this story?"

He smiled. "I'm out here because this is what I like to do. I'm a born rock hound. If I stayed around those no-good scoundrels that come to our place for long, I'd shoot one for sure. Now wouldn't that be a pretty mess?" He kicked dirt on the lingering embers of the fire and nodded his head. Nope, it's best for me to be out here where I can smell the pines and listen to the call of my wild friends. That way, I can get charged up a bit, go back into town with a pocket full of dust and wait for the boys to come take it from me. But the girls gets mine back and most of what they brought with 'em." He winked.

"And?" she said.

"And? Oh yes, I'm telling you all of this because I've seen many girls, some even younger than you, come and go through

Hatti's place in the last seven years. A fellow begins to read 'em. Their facial expressions, the way they move themselves around, the way they react to other people's words tells a lot about 'em. It's more what they don't say than what they do."

"You been trying to read me I guess. Well, there isn't anything to read. So let's just move on down the trail."

"Nothing to read, you say? The way you squirmed and screwed up your face when I was telling you of Hatti's troubles was as meaningful as a roadmap into your soul. But, like I said, on the trail everybody's business is their own. If you want to talk to me... fine. But if you don't, that's fine, too. But talk to someone; Hatti maybe. Don't keep your guts all twisted up. We've buried most of the gals that tried that."

A shiver went down her spine.

What a strange thought; talk to Hatti. Talk to another woman? She remembered her conversations with Wesa and her mixed-up feelings afterward. Would talking to Hatti, a childless woman, be any different? Could Hatti understand how her heart and her head were at war with each other and how her very guts were being squeezed to nothingness by the rope of uncertainty? Which end of the rope would Hatti grab? She'd have to think about his advice, but not now.

She rose, consumed by her thoughts, slowly shuffled to her pony, mounted, and waited for Snooze to lead the way.

Chapter Eleven

*T*wittering birds, anticipating the warmth of the sun's rays, announced the arrival of a new day even before the sun peeked over the horizon.

Dovey was up and ready to ride. Snooze still had a tight hold on his blanket. "What's ailing you girl. Go back to sleep."

"Who can sleep?" she said. "I've never been in a big town before."

"Oh, girl, Santa Fe ain't nothing. If it weren't for the freight lines passing through and the drunken prospectors, anyway. Now you take - -"

"But there are so many people there. What are they going to think of me? Look at me... a skinny little snip with Indian clothes and hair like a rat gnawed on it."

"The ones that's got some sense will see you just like I do, a fine young miss with lots of promise. At least as soon as Hatti works on you a mite."

"Snooze, let's don't go into town this morning. Let's wait until the sun goes down."

"If you don't beat all. First you don't sleep because you're in such a dad blasted hurry to get there. Then, you're up even before me. And now, you don't want ta' go."

"I don't know if I'm ready to let people look at me."

"How about if I tell you what. There's a small dirt farm about a mile, mile and a half south of Santa Fe. The widow Swenson lives there. She's got two girl children about your age. Anywise, we'll stop there, and I'll see if she can sell us a dress for you."

"I can't take her clothes."

"She'll be mighty pleased to help. Besides I'm sure she can use some cash money. They ain't got much."

"Maybe one of the girls could help me with my hair."

"Maybe."

It seemed to her that the whole world had been crowding in around her ever since they had turned north onto the Santa Fe Trail. Dust from the big, mule-drawn wagons seemed to be swallowing her alive. She coughed, spat, and rubbed sleep-laden eyes but she didn't complain.

Before the dust had obliterated her view she noticed a wagon driver grinning and his seat companion waving and shouting at them. "Why are those men laughing? Is it me?"

"They're just friendly souls, girl. Played lotsa' cards with the driver."

With every mile and with every wagon they passed, she felt smaller, like she wanted to hide, to turn, to run towards Kansas and the old sod house she had shared with her family. With every mile, Snooze's smile got broader.

"I can feel that tub of hot water and Hatti's soft hands on my back. Between that and a cold beer... MAN! Gonna go right over and draw a bucket of those suds, don't care what Hatti says."

"You think Hatti's going to like me?"

"I know it. But now, little miss, let old Snooze tell you something. First off, Hatti's gonna be so dang fired het up 'bout seeing me she ain't gonna pay you no never mind. Don't let that bother you none, though, because it won't mean a thing."

A sponge bath, chicken stew with small Swedish dumplings, and an almost new gingham dress with pale blue and white checks seemed to Dovey to be the most precious gifts ever bestowed upon her. She felt warm blood come to her cheeks.

"There's always room for another person or two at our table, Dovey. Come back," Mrs. Swenson said.

"I will, ma'am. Thank you for everything."

"By the way, Dovey, you look stunning in that dress. It fits well."

Dovey grinned, blushed, and looked at Snooze.

"See, didn't I tell you everything was gonna be just fine?" His grin was as big as Dovey's.

She twirled around, and the long dress flew out in an umbrella shape. "But look at my shoes."

"Lordy, lord, lord. Another Hatti for sure."

They rode for only a short while before Snooze broke the silence. "Now, don't go gettin' your drawers in a knot, but take a look over yonder. That's it, just a little west of north. See those two big tall peaks. Soon as we go over that next rise, look right smack dab between 'em and you'll see St. Francis Cathedral. It's the biggest building in these parts."

"Get up, Checkers." She dug her heels into the sides of the startled animal and raced to the top of the rise. Shivering with excitement, she patted the horse's neck and bent over him to hug him tight. She didn't want Snooze to see her face right then. This moment was between Checkers and her.

"Quite a sight, ain't it?"

"Never seen anything like it in my life. I can't wait to see it up close. Does Hatti live close by?"

"Hatti's on this side of town. The good ladies of the Temperance Union kept us from getting a good spot close into town like the La Fonda. Those skunks got established afore we did."

"Are those houses, strung all along the side of that open space?"

"Mostly stalls where folks buy and sell goods that come up and down the Trail. Some are houses."

"Strange-looking things."

"Yeah, well, you sodbusters made 'em different, didn't you? These are made from adobe bricks. The Indians been doing it that way for years. They make 'em with thick walls so they stay cool in the summer and warm in the winter. This here town is pretty high up. But, it still gets mighty hot in the summer. You'll see."

"What's that awful smell?"

"There's a cattle corral down by the train track, oh, about seventeen miles west of town. When the wind blows the wrong way, well... of course it could just be the livery stable. You'll get used to it."

"Silly, I know what a stable smells like. Not that. I'm talking about that sweet smell. It seems like its lying down on the ground, lower than that hideous stable smell."

Snooze sniffed the air with his nose turned up and then with it turned down. "Oh, you must mean the cooking fires. That's Pinion nuts, or maybe mesquite. Nice, ain't it?"

Her head was turning continually, trying to take in everything as they turned off the main trail onto a town side street. "Is that an Indian over there?" Her back straightened.

"Nope, that's a Mexican. Hard to tell apart sometimes until you here 'em talk. There's Indians here, though. Fact is, I heard tell, that Santa Fe's split into thirds between Indians, Mexicans, and what they calls Anglos... that's you and me, you know."

"Quiet now," Snooze said as they approached. I'm going in to surprise Hatti. Tie up the horses in the shade over yonder."

A tall, busty woman with a full head of red hair flew out of the door and raced toward them. "What are you sneaking around here for; you think you're gonna catch me sleeping? Why I had my eye on the trail for the last five weeks!" Hatti said.

Dovey stood back with the horses, waiting and watching them kiss, uncertain what she should do. She felt all mixed-up. A lump came into her throat as she watched the happy reunion.

Hatti released Snooze at last and held him at arm's length. Her gaze then fell on Dovey, who'd been rubbing Checker's nose, pretending to be totally uninterested in what was going on. "My," she said, "what have you brought with you? Another girl for us?"

"This here's Dovey MacPherson. Say hi to Hatti, Dovey."

She greeted Hatti, curtsying as her mother had taught her. As she did, she caught a whiff of Hatti's perfume or powder, a scent she hadn't smelled before. She wrinkled up her nose and turned away.

Hatti smiled, offered her hand. "No need to be so formal, Dovey. I bet you two could use a cool drink and something to eat. Come on in."

"Carlita!" Hatti yelled.

A girl with beautiful olive skin came waddling in, brushing at the perspiration on her lip. "Ma'am?"

"The lord and master has come home at last. Fire up the kettle and pour him a bath. I ain't letting him in my bed the way he is, and I know that's what he's dying for." Hattie laughed and slapped Snooze on his thigh.

"Make it two tubs, Hatti. My friend Dovey, here, has got to experience the joy of civilization, too."

Dovey was barely aware of what was being said. Her

concentration was totally on the room and its furnishings. She casually brushed her hand against the back of one of the two red velvet couches arranged to face each other in front of a huge fireplace. Excitement surged through her body. She wondered at the life-size oil painting of a red headed girl above the fireplace. Could that be Hatti? The buffalo rugs, the paintings, the lamps made with translucent-colored glass. It was all so different from her prairie home. How wonderful it is, she thought, and nearly missed what Hatti was saying to her.

"Dovey, you can stay in my spare room tonight. I know you need a good rest after being on the trail with this old codger. Tomorrow we'll introduce you around and move you over with the girls," Hatti said.

The water was cold before Dovey finally stopped daydreaming and stepped out of the bath. The clean, thick towel felt soft as velvet against her skin. She held it close to her, squeezed and rubbed her body again until the flesh was pink.

She began a search for oil for her skin and gasped when she spotted a mirror on the wall next to the chest of drawers. She blinked, the reflection blinked back. Look how she'd changed. She ran her hand alongside her cheek and up to her forehead. The jagged scar brought memories of Blackjack. Look at my hair; it's lighter. And my face is much darker and... rough. I'm ugly.

She changed the angle of the mirror to view her body. She cupped her breasts in her hands and was startled at their development. She looked at the side view of her backside. It, too, had grown. She thought of the endless days in the saddle, felt for the tender area at the rear and between her legs and was surprised at the leathery feel of this skin.

Was she a woman now? She looked again. Had she ever been a child? She continued to stare at herself, wondering...

The nightdress Carlita had brought was soft and smelled of lilac. The blue ribbon that ran around the edge of the collar was the only thing that was not pure white, the color of peace and hope. Her mind racing with thoughts of her discovery, she carefully sank into the softness of the bed, as though afraid she would damage it.

The crisp, clean sheets, the soft mattress, and the warm, hand-made quilt made her feel as though she were floating.

The sun was well up when Hatti came to her room with a cup of coffee and a smile that looked as fresh as springtime. She placed the cup on the bedside table and ran her soft hand over Dovey's hair. "Dovey, honey, I'm sorry for my comments to you last night. I thought you were another entertainer looking for work. We get so many. Snooze straightened me out, though."

Dovey smiled and rubbed sleep from her eyes. "He also told me you want me to try to do something with this hair."

She again ran her fingers through the ragged strands and shook her head. "Somebody sure did a job on you, didn't they?"

She was so different from what Dovey had expected. She wasn't at all hard or bitter. She acted kind to everyone: Carlita; Taco, the stableman, and of course, Dovey. 'Could she trust her?' Dovey sipped her coffee and sighed.

"I gave your dress to Carlita to wash, Dovey, and I borrowed some things from Rosie, one of our entertainers. I think they'll fit."

"Thank you, ma'am, and please thank Rosie."

"I hope you like blue."

"My favorite."

"Well, why don't you get dressed and come on downstairs. We got a Snooze-size breakfast waiting for you."

At the end of the meal Dovey patted her stomach and belched loudly. A quizzical look crossed Hatti's face, causing blood to rush to Dovey's cheeks. Her eyes darted across the table to Snooze.

"Excuse me. I guess I forgot where I was." She saw the knowing glances between Hatti and Snooze.

"It was good, wasn't it?" Hatti said.

"Carlita outdid herself. Looks like all the gals are glad old Snooze is back," he said.

"There's a nice fresh breeze out back. Let's take our coffee out there. I want you to see my hollyhocks, Dovey."

"You gals go on. I'll catch up." Snooze hurried away.

The two women strolled the yard, stopping here and there to look under leaves for bugs or to discard dead buds. "The soil here is good. Water's the problem. We don't get much rain until July, most years. Carrying water can be hard work."

"Your hollyhocks are beautiful though. We didn't have them in Kansas. My mother…"

Hatti didn't react to Dovey's aborted statement.

"It's a lot of work, but it helps me keep my mind off things I don't want to think about," Hatti said. She paused, bent over, and straightened a leaning stalk. "Sometimes, I get pretty sad with the life I lead out here. But this garden always relaxes me about things." She turned and smiled at Dovey. "Flowers are good listeners, you know."

"I talk to the night wind sometimes," Dovey said, "and other times to the coyotes or Checkers, my pony. In the darkness nothing can see me when I cry."

"There's enough flowers here to listen to two stories, Dovey. If it makes you feel better to cry, go ahead. The flowers have seen the tears of a much older woman, I promise you. They don't mind."

Dovey's eyes were drawn to the pools of dark blue in Hatti's face, eyes that were pleading with her.

They sat in silence on rough, wooden benches. A meadowlark sang. The soft breeze brought the garden's scent with it.

Hatti put her empty cup on the bench beside her. "Can I ask you something?"

Dovey nodded.

"How old are you?"

Dovey cocked her head, stared at Hatti, and swallowed hard. "I don't know! Old enough, I guess, to have a beautiful baby boy, but too young to protect him from the thieves that stole him."

"Oh, Dear, I didn't know."

"It's funny, you know. I never think of my age anymore, but I can tell you to the hour how old Jerry is. My age? The months are running by like a swift stream and I know they'll continue until I have Jerry in my arms again. But I don't care. The hurt I feel and the longing for my son is so strong until everything else seems unimportant."

The tears she had been trying to suppress clouded her eyes and washed down her cheeks. She slumped into Hatti's arms and cried aloud with a sense of hopelessness. She took large volumes of breath in between wails and tried to explain more to Hatti, with sputtering words erupting in varying volumes and pitch. "They stole him. I swear they did. I don't know how to get him back."

Snooze and Carlita heard the commotion and ran to the courtyard.

"Help me get her up to her room," Hatti said.

Snooze supported her on one side, Carlita on the other. They got her to her bedroom where she covered her head with a pillow. Her sobs were quieted, but the spasmodic jerks of her frail body continued.

Carlita brought a pitcher of cool water and a fresh towel and waited for instructions.

Hatti disappeared for a moment. When she returned, she handed Dovey a pill. "Here's something to help you sleep," she said. "When you wake up, I want to hear all about what happened."

"I'd like to talk now, please," Dovey said.

She sat up and placed the pillow behind her.

Hatti motioned Carlita and Snooze out of the room.

"Don't go, Snooze. You should hear this. You should know why I acted like I did when we were on the trail."

Snooze glanced at Hatti, who nodded slightly. He sat down on the bed next to Dovey and patted her shoulder.

Dovey began the story with her sight of smoke pouring through the thatched roof of her Kansas home and told it up to the moment she met Snooze. Nobody stopped or interrupted her. When her monologue was over, there was silence in the room. No one knew what to say.

"Here, Dear," Hatti said after a moment. "Drink a little water."

Dovey sipped the water before continuing. "The thing that drives me crazy is that I really may have been responsible for Blackjack's death." She said the words rapidly and lowered her head.

"Why do you say such a thing?" Snooze said. " He jumped on them logs by himself didn't he? You didn't force him. Why, if he had listened to you, then he'd probably still be alive."

"Maybe he is still alive," Hatti said. "Who knows?"

Dovey shook her head. "I saw him in the rifle sight, lying as still as all the rocks around him. But I didn't go to see. I never made sure. If he was still alive at that moment, my failure to go to him killed him just as though I had pushed him over the side."

She put the glass down and turned her head to the window. "I didn't want him dead, I only wanted to be rid of him."

"Why didn't you pull the trigger when you had him in your sights?" Hatti asked.

"I couldn't. My hand froze as though something was pulling on my fingers. I couldn't."

"Something was pulling on your fingers, all right; it was your heart strings and your sense of right and wrong."

"It eats at my insides though, Hatti. How can Jerry ever love me when I refused to try to save his father?"

"He'll love you. How could he not after all you have done for him and are still prepared to do? He wouldn't be alive if it weren't for you, now would he?"

"But still, his father…"

"Who's going to tell him? Not us, that's for sure," Snooze said.

"I would," Dovey said. "I'd have to. How would we ever be able to develop trust and respect for each other if we weren't honest with each other?"

Hatti kissed her cheek. "Bless you Dovey. You're going to make a fine mother."

Snooze coughed, drew air through his nose, and said in a soft tone, "Hatti's right. Now, what are we gonna do about finding this boy of ours?"

"Ours?" Hatti said.

"The kid's gotta have grandparents, don't he?"

Dovey took Hatti's advice and had a long sleep with the help of the sedative. She woke up feeling more relaxed now that she had told her story, and apparently to the right people. These people would help her; she felt it in her bones.

Hatti beamed broadly at her when she came down the stairs. "Honey, Snooze and me, we been talking all night about what you told us. You're a brave young girl, and Jerry is lucky to have you for a mother."

Snooze nodded.

"So, for your sake and his, we'll do everything we can to help you find him." Hatti kissed Dovey on the cheek.

"Count old Snooze into that party." He held out his hand.

"You can kiss me, too," Dovey said, reaching out for Snooze.

"Now then, how about some breakfast? You must be starving by now."

"Thank you, Hatti, but first could we have a little coffee maybe out in the garden? I'm still a bit foggy from that pill."

Hatti asked Carlita to bring the coffee and to hold off on the breakfast. When she returned she had a large map of the New Mexico Territory. She spread it across the potting table. "Can you show us where Blackjack's village is?"

She looked at the map for a long time and traced every stream with her finger, but nothing looked right. Her scowl deepened. "Snooze, can you show me the spot where you found me?"

He made an X on the meeting place.

"Okay, where's Kansas?"

"Kansas ain't on this map, but it would be up this away if it was." He put a mark on the table to the east and north.

"And Amarillo?"

He made another mark on the table.

Several minutes passed before she slammed the pencil on the table. "I can't do it."

She turned away in shame, but then an idea came to her. "I can't show you on the map, Snooze, but if you will take me to our meeting place I know I can find the camp from there."

Snooze shook his shaggy head, wild from its thorough scrubbing the night before. " Now listen, little miss…"

"Please don't call me that. I'm a woman. A grown woman." She felt the blood rush to her face.

"Pardon me, Dovey. I was about to say that if we were to do what you suggest, every Indian in the territory would hear and feel our first step. Your baby would be a goner, for sure. Most likely sold to another tribe as a slave."

Dovey shuddered at the thought.

"Which, by the way, is exactly what would have happened if you had continued to the village that night. You did the right thing despite how bad you wanted to rescue him."

Hatti nodded. "Snooze is right, honey."

Dovey stared into the distance in stony silence.

"It's happened before. Believe me," Snooze said.

"Dovey, honey, Snooze has been on the trail for many years. He's lived with the Indians, knows their lingo and customs. Please listen to him."

"I can't sit here and do nothing. I have to try."

"Do it Snooze's way first. Please."

"All he's said is don't go looking."

"Not what I meant, litt... 'scuse me, Dovey. We'll look for him all right. Bet your bottom dollar on that. We're gonna do it Indian style though; sneaky like."

Dovey looked him hard in the eye. "How?"

"First we'll go to the Army command and tell them your story. They'll have every trooper in the west alerted and on lookout. Then we'll get every trail rider that comes through Santa Fe ginned up about it. They go into Indian camps all the time like they own 'em."

"I need to go with them. I'm the only one who'll be able to spot him."

Snooze shook his head. "That would mess up the whole thing. These soldiers have to be thought to be looking for something else or just paying a courtesy call to help keep the peace," Snooze said. "But you think on it and give them the best description you can, anything that would make him stand out."

"He has a dark blue, almost purple, mark high up on his left arm, about this long." Dovey spread her thumb and forefinger to demonstrate. "And big, round, beautiful brown eyes."

"Continue to think on it. We need to give the soldiers all we can. We'll get someone to write it all down for us, and you can add to it as you remember things. Think hard on it and then trust the soldiers. They know every non-Indian child in the territory, I promise you. Ain't that many of 'em anyway."

"Suppose one of them finds Jerry. We still have the problem of getting him away from them. How will we do it?"

"Can't rightly say till we find him. Then we'll scheme up something. Don't worry, though; this ain't the first young'en they've looked for. They'll know what to do."

"It's the only way, Dovey," Hatti said, putting her arm around her.

Dovey sighed. "Maybe, but I still hate the idea of sitting

around here waiting."

Hatti poured more coffee and then pulled her chair up closer to the table. "Snooze and I have been talking about that, too. You see, besides the entertainment business, we're in the mercantile and freight business. We want to get that established real well and then get out of the entertainment business. But that end of things ain't going so good."

"What's the problem with the business?" Dovey asked.

"The problem is that Snooze and I don't have enough time to get into it to find out. We keep hoping that our manager, Josh Kendal, will get it turned around for us," Hatti said, "but lately we're beginning to wonder."

"You see, Hatti and me don't know much about that kind of business. We took it in payment for a gambling debt. 'Course, we had to sweeten the pot. We figured if we could run all the other business, we could run that one too. Lordy was we wrong."

"How about Mr.... Kendal, is that his name? What are his thoughts?"

Snooze scratched his beard and squinted. "You tell her Hatti."

"Snooze's belly gets all riled up every time he talks to Josh. There's just something, I don't know..."

"That boy's too much of a Fancy Dan for me. Every time I ask him a question, I end up answering one of his."

"Anyway, he was a clerk there when we took over the business. Since he knew how it operated, we thought he could manage it better'n anyone we knew. At first things changed for the better, and we did good. But, for the last few months, it's been nearly as bad as it was when we started. We questioned him. He said to look in the books. It's all there."

"Is it?" Dovey asked.

"Neither Snooze nor I can read or write real good, so you see..."

"No." Dovey knitted her eyebrows. " I'm sorry and all, but how does all that affect me?"

"Well in the entertainment business, everything's pretty cut and dried. We bank some of the money and divvy up the rest to the girls, Carlita and so on. Don't take much know-how to do that."

Dovey nodded, still wondering how she was expected to fit

in.

"This business with the Mercantile is a lot more complicated. And since Snooze and me ain't got no schooling to speak of, well we were kind'a hoping that you know your numbers and you can learn some more so you can give Josh a hand with his record keeping. Then, maybe together we can figure things out a little better."

"My mama taught me at home. It's not like I went to a regular school or anything. She told me, though, I was clever... I used to read good, but Lord knows I haven't had much practice." Dovey said. Did they really want her to do this?

Snooze looked at Hatti and grinned. Hatti nodded. "Here's what we'll do, Dovey," Hatti said. "We'll get everyone we know out looking for Jerry. We'll tell Josh to take you on as a clerk in his freight office, and we'll get Lily, one of our girls who used to be a schoolmarm, to teach you how to keep books. What do you say?"

"Why don't you have Lily check his numbers?"

Hatti smiled sheepishly. "Well, you might say Lily is choosy about who she entertains."

"Or you might say that she had the good sense to turn Josh away more than once," Snooze said. "And that Josh ain't had much use for Lily since."

They looked at each other and laughed.

"I see." Dovey stared at them trying to read them. Was there anything they weren't telling her?

"I understand what you're suggesting, but, please, let me think about it for a while," Dovey said, caressing the shiny surface of a Snake Plant. "I'll answer you before supper."

These people had done nothing but good for her and probably will continue. Her mama would want her to try to help even if she weren't sure she could. Besides, what else could she do? She had to earn the help she needed. Helping her friends would work. Of course, she would do what they suggested.

The following morning at breakfast, even before Dovey made her intention to help known, Snooze announced that Lily would be joining them that morning for coffee. The words were hardly out of his mouth before a trim, petite girl, who at first glance seemed to be only a few years older than Dovey, entered the room. She paused for a moment and looked at Hatti, who nodded slightly.

Lily smiled as she approached the table. "I couldn't wait to meet my pupil. I'm so excited about teaching her, and apprehensive. It's been so long since I have been in the happy arena of teaching." She took Dovey's hand in her soft, well-manicured fingers. "Dovey, I'm game if you are. Can you stand being around an old woman for a few hours each day?"

Until then Dovey had been tantalized by the way her dark green eyes sparkled when her neatly brushed, long, sandy-red hair swung, changing the light on her face as she walked. Her manner seemed gracious and sincere. She would like this girl - no, this lady. Now that Lily stood next to her, she could see the crow's feet around her eyes and the loose flesh on her neck. But, what is age? It means nothing.

"Thank you for coming over, Miss Lily. I'll try to be a good student."

"Whoa, now. I'm Lilly, no Miss. Makes me feel I'm 'bout ready for the pasture."

Dovey blushed. She couldn't remember doing that before. There was a brief interval of silence. Dovey was beginning to feel a bit awkward at being the center of attention but knew she had to say something.

"Lily, the next thing you can teach me is how to do the attractive needlework like you did on your pretty dress," Dovey said.

"Thank you." Lily rubbed her hand over a few of the stitches. "Do you think I got a bit too much green in it?"

"The green blends nicely with the yellow, Lily," Hatti said. "You know you always look neat and well groomed. I'm not surprised to hear Dovey's comments."

Long hours of intense study, frequent discussions with Lily about many things that were new to Dovey, and the genuine friendship developed by the pair made time important once again. Dovey felt the grip that sorrow had on her heart for so long loosen a bit as Lily's praise of her work slowly pried open her previous self.

"Well, this young lady," she pointed at Dovey, "is the smartest pupil I have ever had. It's a pleasure to teach her and to watch her enthusiasm for learning. And for bookkeeping; why, she not only understands how to create the individual ledgers but understands how they fit together to tell a story; she's wonderful."

Dovey grinned broadly, put her arm around Lily's shoulder, and looked down at the happy face of the diminutive woman. "Thanks to you, Lily."

"I didn't do much. It was your hard work and tenacity that brought you this far in only six months. Clerking in that store ten hours a day and studying afterward had to be tough."

"Is she ready, you think, to take on the bookkeeping?" Snooze asked.

"It would be a waste if she had to keep on clerking there," Lily said.

"How do you feel about it, Dovey?" Hatti asked.

"There's a good side and a bad side."

Snooze cocked his head, grinned and said, "Never know what's coming out of that mouth next. Do you?"

Dovey waited for the laughter to subside. "What I mean is; I won't have as much time to spend with Lily. There's much more she can teach me. Her patience and kindness helped me shake the willies." Dovey put her arms around Lily, and they hugged.

"And the good part..." Hatti said.

"The good part is that I can help two wonderful friends. Working as a clerk has helped me understand the basic business, and the little I've seen of the books makes me awful curious."

The next morning, Snooze escorted Dovey to the Mercantile.

"Josh, this is what I want you to do." He held up his hand. "No, don't say nothing till I say my piece."

Josh placed his elbows on a counter behind him, leaned back, and listened. Dovey watched his face go dark and saw his jaw muscles tighten, relax, and tighten again.

"So, you and your *girl* here are gonna run things, now. Is that what I'm hearing?"

"If that's the way you want to think about it... just put her to work and act civil to her."

"Well, she ain't sharing my office." He pushed a table over by a window. "Get your own chair."

"The light will be good there. It's okay, Snooze. Josh and I will work it out."

Dovey glanced up from the pile of invoices, checks and other business papers that were arranged strategically on her desk and let her eyes wander to the snow piled on the mountainsides. She shivered and clasped her arms around her torso. How had she survived the winters she had spent in the open with Blackjack.

"Is that all you got to do, girl? Stare out of that window?" Josh said.

"I'll finish the posting before I quit, don't worry."

"Well you better. I'm leaving. There's a drover name of Harry supposed to stop by to pick up that load on the end of the south dock. He's late. You stay until he comes; I gotta go."

Dovey stamped her small foot and started to answer but thought better of it.

After he shut the door, she continued matching invoices, bills of lading, payment receipts, and other data with the precision of a born businessperson.

Why did so many of these payment receipts look like the same person signed them? And why couldn't she match the weights on the incoming bills of lading with those on the outgoing? Did they have that much inventory? Something seemed off, but what? She scratched her head and wondered: what was she missing?

Dovey racked her brain, leaned back in her chair, and stared out at the hills that were reflecting the last glimmer of sun as well as the yellow of a full moon.

The unwashed, whiskered face of a man appeared in the window. She jumped back and reached for the pistol in the side drawer.

"What do you want?"

"It's me ma'am, Harry. Don't you remember?"

"Come around front."

"Sorry if I frightened you, ma'am. I knocked on the front door, and I guess you didn't hear me. I came around to where the light was."

"Forgive me, Harry. My mind was far away. You look tuckered out. Come on in and have some coffee."

"No, ma'am, thank you. I'd like to get loaded up so I can be on the trail at first light. Where's my load?"

"I'll show you in a moment. Let's get this paperwork out of the way first, okay with you?"

"What paperwork, ma'am? I don't never fill out nothing for Mr. Josh. He just pays me in cash money, I load up and go."

"That's strange. I'm sure I saw a payment receipt from 'Harry' in the data I was posting. Let me see... here it is."

She showed him the document.

"See, you signed this one not more than a month ago."

"No, ma'am, *this* is my mark." Harry made an x and placed small circles on each corner of the x. "Used that mark all my life."

Dovey studied the mark and the neatly written paper and looked up at Harry's one-sided grin, sturdy, unwavering posture, and the clearness in his light blue eyes.

This man was telling the truth. Either there was another Harry or she had a huge problem on her hands.

"So this isn't your signature? Maybe some one wrote it for you."

"Ma'am, I haven't been here for eleven months. Remember? That's about when you started clerking here."

Dovey pursed her lips and thought hard. "I remember you now. Why haven't you been back to see us? You know we have more freight to move than we're able to get wagons for."

Harry looked around the building before answering. "Because Josh don't want to pay nothing, that's why. A man's got to have a fair wage. Hauling freight through Indian country and trying to outsmart all that white riffraff that's always on the lookout for something easy to steal ain't much fun."

Dovey picked up the receipt and studied it a moment. "Harry, from the numbers on this paper, I'd say that Josh is paying you more than adequately."

"That paper don't mean nothing to me. He ain't doing us right. I only stopped here now because I was passing here anyway and something's better than nothing."

"But..."

"Listen, Ma'am, why don't you ask some of the other drovers about what they get. Maybe I'm the only fool on the trail, but I'd be surprised."

Dovey pinched her lip as she showed him the load. The man

was telling her the truth. She knew it. But what had happened to the difference in the money between what Harry received and what was shown in the ledger as payment to him? Even without answering her question, her stomach turned sour.

Should she review her findings with Josh? Perhaps there was a logical explanation that she didn't see. On the other hand, if ... no she had better not be too quick on the trigger.

Dovey paced the floor, thinking, reasoning and wondering. How could she get more cooperation from Harry to help her unravel her mystery? Then an idea came.

"Harry," Dovey called from the window facing the loading dock, "please come say good-bye before you leave."

"Just got to lash down, and I'll be there."

Dovey paced the floor while she waited, rehearsing what she was going to say. "Harry, I'm sure there's been a bad mistake made. We need good drovers like you. I'm going to talk to Josh tomorrow and try to get him to agree to give you frequent loads at the going rate, plus a little to make up for the past. What do you say?"

"I'm grateful for your thought, but, well, why don't you talk to Snooze first?"

"Oh?" Dovey tried to read the covert message, but Harry looked away.

"Suppose we were to set up a guaranteed load for you every two months. For that arrangement we'd ask you to haul for just a little less than others."

"How much less?"

"Something fair. We'd have to study on it before we get together. Right now I just want to know if you're okay with the thought."

"I'm listening, ain't I?"

"One more thing, in the summer we lose a lot of money because of spoilage on fresh vegetables and fruit."

"Yes'm."

"If you could guarantee us to be here on certain days during the summer, I think we could save as much as fifteen percent on spoilage. We could split the savings with you."

"And pay the regular rate for haulage.?"

"Yes, your established rate."

"Better talk that over with Snooze, too."

"I plan to do more than that, Harry. Vaya con Dios."

Dovey closed the door to the darkened office and leaned against it for a moment, glanced up at the moon, and made a decision.

She needed to be away from the freight office. She needed a place, like the flower garden, where she could think and clear her mind. She had to make sure her suspicions were right before sharing them with Hatti and Snooze.

Then she would have to make a plan to rescue Jerry.

Chapter Twelve

*D*ovey watched in anticipation as Snooze gave the door to Josh's office a fierce kick with his heavy-booted foot. The jam splintered, and the door thudded against the adobe wall. He stepped in quickly, holding his cocked shotgun extended in front of him with both hands.

"What the hell are you doing?" Josh shouted. "Are you crazy?"

Snooze took his right hand off the gun for a moment and motioned forward with his arm.

Dovey walked calmly to the front of the room and slammed a set of account ledgers on Josh's desk, sending a puff of dust exploding into the air. She felt her heartbeat accelerate and her breathing become more intense. Her eyes found his. She watched his fat belly bounce as he shied away. "How dare you people break into my office! What are those books?"

"Why don't you tell us, Josh," Dovey said. Her words were measured, hard, and deliberate.

"I didn't ask for your insolence. Don't forget who you work for. Tell me what all this gibberish is about." Josh began thumbing through the first book, frowned, and slowly laid the book aside, tapping it with his fingers as though in deep thought.

"Well?" Snooze said.

Josh shook his head, sucked air in between his teeth, and grinned. "Snooze, I told you this damn girl didn't know what she was doing. Two years of work, and this stuff ain't worth the paper it's written on." He threw the books to the floor. "Now get outta here, and let me do my work. I got a big shipment coming in today and lots of buyers lined up."

Snooze raised his shotgun to eye level. "Pick up them books. Read the numbers out loud on the last page."

Josh hesitated. His lips began to form a word. Snooze's finger began to move toward the trigger.

With trembling fingers, Josh picked up the ledgers, opened

them, and read the last page of each.

"Read that last one again, you damn maggot."

Josh swallowed. "A net difference of twenty-two thousand six hundred dollars and thirteen cents." The words trailed off as he read. Beads of perspiration covered his forehead. "A mistake. That's all it is, Snooze. You understand that, don't you? Why, this young girl has just made an honest mistake, tha - -"

"This young *woman* made no mistake. Altogether, you owe the company a total of fifty-one thousand one hundred ninety-one dollars and seventeen cents. These books tell fact, not fiction. Every drover on the trail will back me up, and so will the bank manager."

Her heart was beating normally again, but her breathing once again became rapid as she laid out the facts, beginning with the payment discrepancy for Harry and other drovers.

Josh straightened his back, raising himself to full height, and smirked. "That's ridiculous. I didn't - -"

Snooze stuck the shotgun in his ribs. "You got three choices, mister: we march down to the bank and draw from your account whatever's left of the money, or we march over to the pokey and let the marshal look at these ledgers. Or you can make a run for it."

Snooze paused for a moment when a look of confused surprise came over Josh's face. "What'cha thinking? That old man can't see to shoot nothing, is that it? Gonna run for it? Go ahead, try it; but if I catch you, I ain't responsible for what happens to you. Ain't a court in the land that'll punish me for it, neither."

Snooze winked at Dovey. She looked at Josh's quivering lip and nodded back.

"Despite the shortage of eleven thousand dollars and that change," Snooze said when they returned from the bank, "I'm gonna show you our heart's in the right place. We're gonna buy you a ticket on the first stage or put you onto the first drover that might take your mangy hide with him."

"Please, let me go home and get my heavy coat. There's still two foot of snow in the mountains. I might freeze out there."

"Too bad. You ain't going nowhere except outta town."

Dovey stepped up close to Josh, stared at his quivering mouth, clenched her teeth, and slapped him hard. "That's for all the times you patted my ass."

She watched her red palm print fade to pink, turned, and walked away with an enormous feeling of release from the shackles men had used to drag her spirit down.

Snooze gulped in surprise but quickly stepped in front of Josh and said back over his shoulder, "You ladies take this here bag of cash back home. I'll be there directly."

Snooze prodded Josh with the shotgun. "All right, mister, it's the stage depot for you."

"Get all the girls that aren't tangled up with some dude," Dovey said, the moment she threw open the door to Hatti's place. "We're going to celebrate!"

She kicked off her shoes, raised her skirts, and danced around the room. She took the clip out of her hair, shook her head, and loosened the long strands of flowing brown hair that had once been such a mutilated mess. Dovey continued to dance around the room in circles, shouting as she did so.

"I feel happy. Liberated. Free."

Hatti smiled, quietly; she understood.

Dovey's breaths were coming in short, quick gulps. Her eyes were wide. She was trembling. She fell against Snooze as he entered the room. "Is the fat-bellied, bald-headed bastard gone?" Dovey shouted.

"He's gone."

"Whoopee!" Dovey grabbed Lily and swung her across the room, around and around. "I want to celebrate. I want champagne."

Hatti stepped up and interrupted the pirouetting couple. "What's come over you, Dovey? I've never seen you act like this, and I've never heard you use such language,"

"Open the champagne. Let's party," Dovey replied.

"You'll get no champagne until you're eighteen, young lady. Not in my house." Hatti frowned and shook her head. "Now, me and Snooze - -"

Dovey stopped her. "I was waiting to tell you, I finally figured it out. My mother told me once that I was born on April twenty-seventh, the day the first flowers appeared through the snow and in the year the Statue of Liberty came to America. I did some checking and found out she was dedicated in 1886."

"Say what?" Snooze said, splaying out his fingers, one by

one. "That means - -"

"That means that I'm eighteen. I was born April twenty-seventh, 1886. Jerry was born fifteen years later, in the summer, 1901."

"I can't believe it," Hatti said, "but you look it. A pretty eighteen, too. You don't know how many men come through here asking if you're available."

"After two years around your entertainers, I could handle them, too. I know how to make men crawl to me now and how to throw ice water on their fire when I have to. The girls know how much I hate men, and they have been having a grand old time teaching me the finer points of the 'entertainment business,'" Dovey said.

"And the language, they taught you that, too?"

"Not intentionally, but if you don't break out that champagne, I'm going to let you hear some more words you didn't know I knew."

Carlita poured.

Dovey raised her glass and doffed it to Hatti, Snooze, and each of the girls. "To my family. I love you all." She drank quickly and held her glass to Carlita for a refill.

"Whoa there, little filly. Go easy with that stuff. Didn't these confounded girls tell you that once you get an old buzzard's gizzard jumping up and down, you gotta back off and let him make a fool out of himself while you sip with your pinkie in the air?"

"Yep, they did. But they didn't tell me what to do when I get myself in a stew."

The room erupted with laughter.

"I think we all better sit for a spell," Hatti said.

"You know, Dovey, you did a grand job boxing Josh into such a corner. You had him cold. And that left hook you gave him, that was a beaut. Girls you should'a seen her. 'Mess with me,' she said, and wham."

"And it didn't even sting my hand until about three minutes later. I was riding high."

Pandemonium hit the room.

They joked and drank for a bit; then Dovey rose, walked over to Lily, and kissed her cheek. "Lily, I want to thank you. Your patient teaching made it possible for me to help Hatti and Snooze.

It made me so happy to be able to help, and I couldn't have done it without you."

"You're such a natural for the business world until it was easy and a pleasure."

"Well, I couldn't have done it without you."

They hugged tightly.

"Another thing set my head a'spinning too. When I saw Josh cringe, a thrill went down my body, like an electric shock. I breathed so hard until my lungs hurt. I felt that I had partial revenge for the hell that Blackjack had put me through. I, I, I..."

Dovey felt the rush of excitement start all over. She gasped and stepped back.

There wasn't another sound in the room, not even the tinkle of the wind chimes.

Dovey paused, looked at the blank faces, and in pleading tones asked, "Don't you see? Don't you understand? It's like I've taken control. I can do things now; I've proven it to myself."

Hatti took Dovey's hand in hers and raised it to her lips for a gentle kiss. "I understand. We all do. We admire you for caring and for wanting to teach your son. You will make a good mother. Come on now. Carlita is going to be upset if you don't eat some of the food she made especially for your celebration."

The eating, storytelling, and drinks continued until the mantle clock struck two. The last of the entertainers left the party. Carlita had been dismissed long before. Only Dovey, Hatti and Snooze were left, and he was yawning.

"Let's step out on the patio and breathe some of that fresh air," Dovey said. "I need it."

The night air was cold and somehow seemed to Dovey a fitting match for the bright stars in the heavens. She breathed deeply, trying to drink in the aroma of the flowers surrounding the tired revelers and was surprised that the aroma wasn't as distinct as it was in the heat of the day. No matter, she thought.

Dovey's thoughts were interrupted by Snooze. He had been so uncharacteristically quiet that Dovey had forgotten he and Hatti were there, standing in the dark beside her. "Gosh, we're lucky people. Old Josh would've ruined us if you hadn't skunked him. We owe you."

"That's nonsense. You owe me nothing. You rescued me from the wilderness. I rescued you from Josh. You supported me for more than two years. I worked ten hours a day for most of that time. I'd say we are about even. Wouldn't you?"

"Then it's about time for us to sit down and do some serious talking," Snooze said, suddenly seeming more awake. "Hatti, fetch us some candles, will you?"

In less than thirty minutes, a plan was developed which put Dovey's newfound skills to work in exchange for a one-third partnership in all business. She would manage the Mercantile and the freight business, and keep books on everything. Hatti and Snooze would continue with their established work.

"This'll gimme a little more time on the trail," Snooze said in a wistful voice.

The nuance of his speech was not lost on Dovey. There'd be two of them on the trail as soon as she saved enough money, no matter what the soldiers found.

Hatti shook her head. "Snooze, you're something else."

"Well, better head for the corral I guess."

Snooze stood up, stretched, and took his leave. "G'night, partners," he said, tipping his hat.

Partners. Dovey liked the sound of that.

"Honey," Hatti began, "I know this thing with Josh stirred up some hurtful things for you. But you said some pretty bad things about men today."

"You're lucky to have someone like Snooze," she said, "Not too many like him."

"I know you have had some rotten luck, but that don't mean you should go shooting yourself in the foot. Someday, somewhere, a man is going to come along and your heart just won't pay no heed to that stubborn head of yours."

"Never!" Dovey thought for a moment. "I just can't imagine it, Hatti. Even if I wanted that... I just feel, I don't know, like I'm scared or something."

"Dovey?"

"Yes."

"Snooze ever tell you about my pa?"

A lump formed in Dovey's throat. What could she say? She nodded.

"Well you just think of that and of Snooze and me before you use the word 'never,' okay?"

Dovey nodded again. Hatti kissed her on the cheek, blew out the candle, and left her alone with the stars.

She lay down on the bench and gazed at the blinking stars until they blurred. She thought about Blackjack, then Josh, her father, and Snooze. Then, in rapid succession, images of a hundred faces danced across her mind: drovers, prospectors, cowpokes; dancing, cussing, spitting, and drinking, acting like darn fools. Dovey rolled her head back and forth, and the parade accelerated to a rapid pace where they all blended together. A cloud obliterated the view. They were gone. *There's no man for her.* She shuddered and folded her arms around her to protect against the cold of the night - or from captivating despair.

The cloud rolled on by. One more face appeared - the one that made her smile. 'Soon, Honey. Real soon.'

Chapter Thirteen

*T*he sun burst through the slit between the red, brocade drapes covering the window on the east side of Dovey's room. The sharp light, the effects of the unaccustomed champagne, or both, sent sharp needles of pain behind her eyeballs. She thrashed around in the soft bed for a moment, grabbed the pillow and buried her head.

It wasn't enough to dampen the sound of Snooze's heavy boots clumping across the wooden floor. "Is my new partner gonna sleep all day? Sun's been up for two hours. Here, have a look." He pulled the pillow away from her clutches and then threw open the drapes. His grin was as bright as the morning. "Ever see a better day? Maybe old Josh took the gloom with him." Snooze held his side as he laughed. "Laughed so durn much last night until my belly plum hurts."

"I give up. It looks like you aren't going to let your new, hardworking partner sleep. But don't let it bother you; I'll suffer." Dovey said. She tried to keep from laughing at the change of expression on his face. She walked across the cold floor, opened the window wide, breathed deeply of the fresh air that had recently bathed the snow-capped hills on the horizon. "There's a new world out there this morning, partner, all fresh and sparkling and ready for us."

"Yep."

"Well, get on out of here and let me dress, and we'll do some talking on how to benefit from the day and our partnership." Dovey kissed him and held him tightly for several seconds.

"Oh fiddle, Woman. Let me go. Ain't no way to treat a business partner."

"Hatti's your business partner, too. Don't tell me you chase her away."

Dovey came to breakfast dressed in buckskin britches, brown-and-yellow plaid, woolen shirt, and a buckskin jacket thrown over her shoulders. A tinge of rouge gave life to her pale cheeks. Her long hair was twisted into one large braid and secured with a broad apricot-colored ribbon.

"Well aren't you the picture of happiness," Hatti said. "I like your outfit. First time I've seen you in pants."

"I'm so glad you like them. I asked Mrs. Swenson to make them for me. I'm thrilled with them. Can't wear skirts and handle those spitting, cussing, loud-mouthed drovers." She sat and took a small helping of eggs and toast. Her stomach felt a little uneasy. Would this food stay down, or would she be sorry. She hesitated before taking the first bite.

"You know," Snooze said, "I learned a lot about you yesterday. I saw something a lot of folks don't have. It plum thrilled you to make a monkey out of Josh; I just know it did. My insides were churning up and down just like I know yours were." He paused and studied her expressionless face. "I'm right, ain't I?"

Dovey nodded, a little chagrined. She really had enjoyed herself, but she wasn't proud of it. Was she right to be spiteful to men, even bad men? Would her folks have approved? She stared at her food and took another bite.

Snooze saw her nod but waited to see if she were going to say anything. "Those eggs are good, ain't they?"

"Better than yesterday's happening."

"Well, then, I'm gonna give you a chance to have a thrill so big you'll bust your britches."

"Better than yesterday?"

"Better. Last night you said you would put up a third of your dust for a share in our business. If you could multiply all of it ten times, by putting up the rest, would you do it?"

"Nope." Dovey shook her head emphatically.

"Why in blazes not? I thought you were a gambler like me."

Dovey laughed. "Sorry, Snooze."

"You remember last year when the leaves turned color and the snow started flying. I said I was going down south to get my bones warmed up a mite."

"Yes," she said slowly, wondering what he was getting at.

"The trip before that, I didn't tell you about for a reason. I didn't go hunting no gold dust that time. I met up with Scotty down on the edge of town and took him to show him the spot where I found you. I figure someone had to know that place in case... well, just in case. Now Scotty's lived with Indians all over the Southwest. He knows'em and they know he can be trusted. If any body can help you find Jerry, he's the one.

The words sounded hollow to Dovey. Hundreds of people had been looking out for him for two years now. If they couldn't find him, how could one man? "I am grateful for what you're trying to do, Snooze, but I don't know..."

"Let me finish. We got up there all right, but the snow started coming down something fierce. All we could do was make camp, drink coffee, and tell tales.

"Anyway, Scotty told old Snooze a tale about a big gold mine some of the ancient Indian tribes had down near Tyrone. He said when the white men started coming west, them Indians covered the mine and let it sit. They'd rather their sons have the gold than the whites.

"Now you know old Snooze can smell gold, so I decided to hike on down there and have a look-see.

"Ain't no confounded gold there. But there's a bunch of copper and pyrites. Copper ain't worth much, about seven cents a pound these days. But if a man can find a good way of getting that ore out of there, big money can be made. So I staked it and filed on it.

"Next day, while I'm down in town, I spend a bit of my dust, talk to a few fellows about the legend, and do a lot a listening. Soon, a man all duded up in fancy city clothes comes to the place I'm staying and wants to dicker about buying my claim.

"No sir, I tell him. 'Soon as I tie up the water rights, I'm gonna start putting a company together.'"

"I don't get it, Snooze. How does my gold get involved in this? Are you wanting to use it for developmental costs?"

Snooze grinned. "You might say that."

"Snooze, for goodness sake, get this over with," Hatti said. "You can give the details on the trail."

"Trail?" Dovey sprang out of her chair, "I'm not going on any trail, and I don't want to hear anymore about this plan of yours."

Snooze stood in the doorway blocking her exit. "Now don't get all riled up just listen a while fore you tear outta here. Here's what I think we should do, Dovey. First off, I want you to figure the value of the probable reserves. I only got five test holes down, but that'll have to do. Those holes show several feet of ore, and it's grading almost two percent, average. That'll give us a starting point for dickering with old man Russo.

"Then I'm a'gonna dress you up in one of those new-style frocks they're wearing back east these days, and you're gonna use what the gals here learned you to string old Russo along until I can do my part.

"While he's stewing in his juice, I'll go to the claim with my shotgun and your dust. I'll cram the dust in the shells and decorate the insides of a couple of those caves, so she'll shine with glitter. Then I'll cover it up except for a mite. We'll put a few nuggets down in the streambed just below the cave. And whamo, we'll have him."

"Sounds interesting, but suppose he doesn't find the gold; what then?"

"He'll find it. The more we keep telling him there ain't none there, and the more we get all the fellows in town talking about the legend, the more he'll look. He'll try to hornswaggle us. Just you wait and see. Then we got him."

"You're a devil, Snooze Dixon. A real devil."

"That mean you're in?"

She thought for a moment. She wasn't sure how much money she'd need when she took leave to find Jerry, but she knew it was a lot more than she had. If this scheme worked, she could get on the trail a lot sooner. "I'm in," she said. "When do we leave?"

Every day of the next eleven months was torture for Dovey. How could she ever explain her foolishness? Why did she continue to work like a dog and depend on others to find Jerry?

She felt something deep inside her demanding action, her action. The feeling was strong, pulling on her, hard, pleading with her to go. To go and find her son. She had to.

But, now her gold was gone. She had no money to use to search for him. How could she have been so stupid?

She reacted to the hundreds of questions running through her mind by driving herself at the Mercantile. Every penny she was able to bargain away from someone was a minor victory. Even the joy she attained from that was not enough to make up for her major concern about the probable loss of the gold.

"Lily," she said one day, after she had sent the last wagon down the trail. "I can't tell you how glad I am to have you around. Sometimes I think your company is the only thing that keeps me sane."

Of course, having someone to take over the business when she left would be great. Snooze and Hatti would be happy to have Lily run things, and they wouldn't think she had deserted them; so... Just save a little more money and she'd be gone. Wild horses couldn't keep her in Santa Fe.

"Well you just remember, honey. Lily's got a little put aside. I'm so grateful to you for getting me out of Hatti's place, I'll be happy to share. Why don't you go ahead and look up that fellow Snooze told you about and make some plans."

"You mean Scotty?"

Dovey sighed. How much would it cost for her to hire him? And, wonder what she had forgotten... Gosh, one thing after another.

The door to the Mercantile squeaked, and there was Snooze, trying to sneak in. A grin was plastered across his face. Once spotted, he rushed in and spun Dovey off her feet. "The dad burned money's in the bank, Dovey, a whole heap of it."

"You mean..."

Snooze nodded. "I told him there wasn't no gold on that there property, but he was greedy. He wanted to rob us."

Tears flooded her eyes. It seemed too good to be true.

"Whatcha crying for, gal? Ain't this enough for you?" He thrust a bunch of papers in her hand. She glanced at the heading and the official seal on the front, flipped through the accompanying detail, and kissed the long number on the final page, which told one and all that the contract had been probated.

"It's not that. I'm just so pleased to have what I need to begin my search for Jerry. It's hard for me to explain how terrible I felt about being reckless with his money."

"Oh shucks, girl. You know we weren't gonna let you down. I told you I been thinking about you. Scotty'll be here in two days to hit the trail with you. He rode with Captain Wallace, you know.

Wallace had three different Indian wives, each from different tribes. He knew Indians better'n Indians knew themselves. He taught Scotty."

"I'm ready to ride. Lily will look after things for me for a while. Bless her."

Lily nodded. "Hatti says it's all right, Snooze."

"Sure it's all right. For the last few months, Hatti and me been talking about closing down the entertainment business, anyway. It might not be a bad idea for us all to be outta town for a while, in case old Russo gets his drawers in a knot."

"Why don't we close up the Mercantile, too? You can come with me, Hatti, and the rest of the girls to San Francisco and on to the Sandwich Islands. The gals are already buying up all the feathers and fancy things in Santa Fe. You oughta smell 'em too, mm, mm ... pretty. I don't rightly know if we'll ever come back."

"We'll keep the business going, Snooze. One day, though, Jerry, Lily, and I might come calling on you, so don't spend all your money at once."

Dovey, Hatti, Lily, Snooze and most of the girls partied the rest of the day, but not as wildly as they had when Josh was sent packing. Even so, Dovey was up before dawn, huddled near a kerosene lamp, writing note after note, trying to think of everything that she needed to do before leaving.

She read the list over for the third time and nodded. It would do, at least until she had an opportunity to meet with Scotty to make a plan, but maybe she should talk to the bank manager about transferring money if she needed some on the trail.

She smiled and crawled back into bed. Now she could sleep without the feeling of helplessness that had plagued her - forever, it seemed. She knew whom she would dream of now.

Chapter Fourteen

"*H*atti, you and Snooze didn't have to get up to see us off, you know that," Dovey said.

"Course we didn't," Snooze said, "but who could sleep with all these here women chattering their heads off?"

"Besides, honey, we weren't going to let you get away with a half filled stomach," Hatti said. "Ain't seen a trail rider yet that can cook worth a hoot."

"God, I'm going to miss you two." She stepped toward Hatti and hugged her. "Thanks Hatti and you too, Snooze. You have been great." She kissed his cheek.

"It wasn't a one-way street, Little Miss," Snooze said. He quickly stepped back with hands raised to ward off the expected reaction from Dovey.

"I wouldn't love you as much as I do if you didn't kid me once in a while, Snooze. I hate to lose you to those 'Little Misses' in the Sandwich Islands." She kissed his cheek and quickly turned away.

She nodded to Scotty who was patiently holding the horse's reins. "We'd better leave, Scotty, if you're ready."

She looked to the side and dabbed at her eye. She saw Carlita and Paco standing in the background. "Hold on for a moment, Scotty. Thank you both for everything. I'm glad that I had an opportunity to say good-bye." She hugged Carlita for several seconds and then gave Paco a peck on the cheek. "Vaya con Dios, amigos."

Scotty mounted.

Dovey bit her lip and took one last glance back at her friends, with hand poised to slap the horse.

"Wait, wait, don't go yet."

Dovey heard the clomp of sturdy shoes running along the tile floor. "Lily, is that you? I told you not to get up this morning, but I'm glad you did."

"I was afraid I had missed you. I want you to have this book of poems, but I had a hard time locating it. Otherwise I would have been here for my share of the hugging that I know went on."

Dovey dismounted, threw her arms around Lily, and squeezed. "Bless you, Lily. I'll treasure this book forever." Dovey held the small book over her heart and smiled at Lily.

"I can see that Scotty is about to bust to get you on the trail, honey, and I'll let you go in a minute. First, though, I must tell you that my insides are so riled up over your departure until it's tough to keep from bawling..." Lily held her hand up to stop Dovey from answering. "I don't know what you're feeling - anxiety, impatience, hope, fear, probably all of them - but at night read those poems. You'll find a lot of things to think about and to comfort you."

As Lily talked, Dovey thumbed through the book, stopping here and there. "There are words in here I don't understand, Lily."

"It doesn't matter. You'll understand the message of the poems and you'll learn the meaning and the beauty of the way the words are strung together. Go now, before I hug you so tight until you can't go."

The steady clop of the horse's feet sounded to Dovey like drums echoing from within a cave; go... stay... Jerry needs you... later...

"We'll pause on the knoll up yonder for a mite, and you can give 'em a last wave; then we better move out smartly if we're gonna make the river camp by nightfall," Scotty said.

At the top, she turned for a final look at the group of friends still watching her progress. Her thin body shook. She rubbed her arms, hunched her shoulders, and quickly turned away before the emotion of the moment strangled her reasoning.

"Cold up here at this time of day, ain't it?" Scotty said, rubbing his own body.

She nodded and looked at him quizzically. She wasn't cold. Why had he said that?

On the east side of the knoll, the warming rays of the early morning sun began to beat on the chests of the travelers. Despite the welcome warmth from the sun, the air remained fresh, crisp and stimulating, providing something different for her to think about. The excitement and anticipation of the coming adventure slowly replaced her despair, and memories of Lily, Hatti, and the others ebbed.

The pair rode in silence for a mile or so. Dovey couldn't contain herself, there was so much to see and experience that she had to share her feelings. She knew she was chattering away. It wasn't like her, but something was compelling her. Why doesn't he say something? He seems nice enough but was she going to have to talk to herself for the whole trip?

Scotty rode on silently until about midday.

"Whoa!"

"What are you stopping for?" Dovey asked after dismounting. "I thought you were anxious to make our river camp before dusk?"

He pointed to the sun. "Not anxious to kill the horses," he said. "They need . . ."

Dovey didn't hear the rest. She swallowed hard, squeezed her eyes shut, and struggled to prevent the laughing face of Blackjack Diamond from exploding out of her memory. "How long, Scotty?"

"I reckon an hour will do."

"No, I mean how long before we get to the first village?"

"Want to talk about that later, maybe while we get the grub together tonight. As a matter of fact, there's lots on my mind that we need to talk over."

"I been talking to you all morning, but you don't say much. Don't you like me?"

His eyes snapped to her, punctuating an expression she couldn't quite read.

"I'm your guide. Paid to take you where you want to go and to look after your welfare. That's my job."

"What's that got to do with not talking to me?"

"Lots. What would you do if something happened to me? Say I got snakebite, or took an Indian arrow, or perhaps a cougar attacked me."

Dovey stared out at the grazing horses, watching the swishing tails combating the flies.

"Well, you wanted to talk. I just asked you a question."

"Sorry," she said. "Snooze gave me the impression that this wasn't something I'd have to worry about. He said you did this all the time and that you were good at it."

His face softened a notch, but he kept his gaze on her. His gaze was met with a stare focused on his cold, gray eyes.

"Well are you?" she asked.

"Ma'am, it seems to me that you just answered a question with a question. Now please, tell me what you'd do."

She sighed loudly to express her disapproval. "Well, I can't imagine anything like that happening, but if it did, I suppose I'd turn around and retrace my steps."

He half-smiled at that. "Oh, you would? Well, just this morning we crossed quite a few trails that'd take a body all sorts of places. You remember how many?"

Dovey shook her head.

"So the way I figure it, you wouldn't have the first clue how to get yourself back to Santa Fe, would you?"

Dovey stood up and looked away. "This is morbid, Scotty. I don't want to talk about sad things. I've had too much sadness."

She felt a firm grip on her shoulder spinning her around. "If I'm gonna be your guide, ma'am, you gotta listen to me and do like I tell you. Otherwise we might as well turn back now."

She looked back in the direction they had come and shook her head. "I don't have an answer for your question; that's why I hired a guide."

"I thought so," he said with a self-satisfied grin. "You were paying attention to all the wrong things. When you're going where we're going, ma'am, you need to look as much backward as forward, you hear? I didn't see you check your back once."

Dovey nodded. She recalled Snooze frequently looking over his shoulder as they traveled the long miles into Santa Fe, many years before.

"Okay," he continued, "So this afternoon as we ride, I want you to stay quiet unless you got a problem. Concentrate on the trail. Looking back will give you a sense of direction and a better feel for the things around you. Watch for water, not just the water you see flowing in the streams, but note where green spots sprout up among all this brown. Listen to everything, and pause if something sounds strange. Keep conscious of the wind direction. Smell the air. Concentrate!"

"I'll try." She turned to stare at the odd shape of a butte on her left and thought about what he was telling her. One day, hopefully very soon, she'd be the one with the responsibility for protecting Jerry in similar circumstances. It was good advice.

"Okay, Scotty, you're right. I'll start paying attention. No more chattering." For the first time since she'd met him, he smiled at her, and then nodded with a slight wink of his eye.

To Dovey the afternoon ride seemed endless. She attempted to stay focused by looking to the rear frequently, smelling the air, and watching the waft of the grass, but her mind kept snapping back to Jerry. Scotty had said he wanted to talk about him. Why? Did he know something he hadn't told her? The question lay on her brain as heavy as an Indian ceremonial hat. He knows something. She knew he did. No, that's ridiculous. Surely he would have told her. Be patient; she couldn't get flustered or make Scotty mad again. She needed him. That much was clear.

The sun was nearly horizontal in the western sky when Scotty's big roan stallion sniffed the air, snorted, and shook his head violently. Dovey's mare picked up the pace so that she was nearly abreast of the stallion.

Dovey dared a spoken word. "What's the matter with them?"

"Water. They smell the river on the other side of that there rise. That'll be our camping spot."

Dovey shifted her sore backside in the saddle and sighed. *Finally.*

After Scotty had tended the horses, built a fire and, laid out his bedroll, he spoke for the first time. "This meat Hatti sent with us is still cold; you think you can do something with it?"

"What else you got?"

"Look for yourself, but remember there ain't no stores out here. So go easy."

"How long you think we should plan for?"

"That's one of the things I want to talk to you about."

"Good." Dovey lowered her weary body onto a sandstone boulder, stretched her legs out straight and removed her floppy hat. "Talk. I'm listening."

"Ma'am, are you wholly sure that this Blackjack fella died when he fell off the cliff?"

Dovey thought for a moment. "Why do you ask?"

"Because it makes a whale of a difference how we proceed."

"We've talked this all through several times, Scotty. I want to follow the plan we decided on. I must go back to the mine, or his dirty face will dance through my mind forever. I can still see his open mouth and wide eyes staring at me, pleading for help. I have to try to reassure myself that his death was an accident for which I wasn't responsible. I can't live with the uncertainty. I've got to go there."

"Okay, then. Let me put something else to you, something I hadn't thought about until this morning. Suppose - and now remember, we're talking possibilities - suppose he didn't die? Ain't it possible we could walk right into him at the mine? He'd have the high ground to hear you tell it. Might put a bullet through us before we ever saw him."

"Dead men don't shoot people."

"I know he looked dead, but you didn't make sure, did you?"

"I was his prisoner for three years, Scotty. I panicked. I couldn't..." She turned from him, squeezing her fists, trying to control her breathing. She couldn't lose control; he wasn't really accusing her of anything. "He's dead, I tell you! I saw him lying on the canyon floor staring open eyed at the sky."

"Regardless of whether he died or not, suppose someone else found him and decided to rummage his camp. Don't you think they would find the mine, and wouldn't they be working it now?"

"And you believe they would harm us?"

"Think of another thing: suppose someone in his village decided to check on him after he hadn't returned for the festival he promised to attend, or for any other purpose. What would that person do?"

"Are you saying we shouldn't go to the mine?"

"Maybe not, at least until we know what we'll find there."

She remained quiet for several minutes, staring into the fire, and then took a deep breath. "So, I suppose we shouldn't go to the village either." She held her breath waiting for his answer. She wanted to visit Wesa if she was still alive. Surely he could see the sense in that.

"Not just march right in, if that's what you mean. Until we know what the situation is, secrecy is the best friend we got."

"But Jerry's in the village. I know it, I feel it."

"This ain't no time to let your heart do your head's thinking. Remember, it's your son's life we're dealing with. If Blackjack's as crazy as you tell it, he'd rather kill him than let you take him away."

"But I told you Blackjack's dead, damn it..." Even as she said it, she realized she couldn't be sure.

Scotty seemed to understand that she needed time to think. He kept quiet and waited for her to finish preparing their small meal using the ham and pickled beets Hatti had sent along.

They ate in near silence, each waiting for the other to speak; but for an occasional reference to the night sounds, nothing more was said. Dovey cleaned and put away the cooking utensils and reached for her bedroll.

"Sleep well, Scotty."

"You, too."

She turned on her side and felt the poetry book in her jacket pocket. Pleasant memories of her friends chased away her feeling of despair. They were all so happy to try to help her, and so was Scotty, really. Why had she been so belligerent with him? His logic was sound; she knew that. Tomorrow, first thing, she'd tell him so... wouldn't she?

She felt her eyes blink and her head nod, but she opened the small book to the preface and strained to read: "Love is not without travail..." The book fell from her hands.

Three miles down the trail, Scotty pulled up the roan and let Dovey come alongside. "We got about two miles to travel, and then there's a fork in the trail. We can take the right fork, ride east for two more days, and we'll be almost to the mine; or we can take the left fork, ride nine days, and be at the army command headquarters at Fort Dodge"

"Left." Dovey said.

The heat in the anteroom outside Captain Campbell's office was stifling. The eastern shutters were closed to lessen the impact of the morning sun, and no air stirred. Dovey fanned herself with a dog-eared army pamphlet, slapped flies, and silently pleaded for someone, anyone, to come through that door to prove their trip had not been in vain.

She should have eaten more last night and this morning. She knew that now, too late. The pangs of nausea swirled in conjunction with the thoughts of uncertainty, and she tried hard to fight back with positive thoughts. It's silly, she decided, to worry about how the captain would react before she even met him.

Stomps from heavy, spur-laden boots behind the closed door became louder. He's coming. She knew it. What should she say?

The door opened, and a tall gray-haired man with a thick, walrus-style mustache stood in the doorway and called, "Scotty?"

Scotty turned to face the captain.

"Scotty, Scotty MacLean?" the captain shouted. "Naw, it can't be."

"Howdy, Captain. I look different, I guess, in these here civvies."

"You look fine, man. Lost some weight and a little hair, but the wild life will do that to a man, won't it?"

"It's been a while, Captain."

"A long time... I believe it was at your mustering out ceremony right after Jinni, er, ah..."

"It's okay, Captain, I can accept it now; she's dead you know."

Dovey looked quizzically at Scotty, wondering about Jinni and whether she should say anything. It didn't seem that Scotty had any intention of introducing her.

"So, Scotty, what brings you here? Can I help you some way?"

"I hope so. I agreed to help Miss Dovey MacPherson here with a problem she has. You better hear the story firsthand, and then you can advise us."

"Howdy, Miss, and welcome to Fort Dodge."

Dovey extended her hand. "Thank you, sir."

"I'll be glad to try to help, but come on into my office. It's a bit more comfortable in there."

Once seated, Dovey began to relate her story as fast as she could speak.

The captain quickly interrupted. "May I ask a question now and then, Miss?"

She nodded, caught her breath, and then resumed telling the

story at a more relaxed pace. The captain kept his eyes on her and seemed to be paying close attention.

When she finished, Captain Campbell walked around his paper-strewn desk and cleared a small place to sit, close enough to Dovey for their knees to nearly touch.

"Miss MacPherson, you're a brave young lady. I admire your tenacity and your dedication, and I would very much like to help."

"Thank you, Captain," Dovey sighed, settling back in her chair and brushing at her eyes. Maybe they had done the right thing coming here.

"Let's start with some of the cold, hard facts facing us. If we all understand the full problem, our planning should be better."

"Makes sense," Scotty said.

"Miss MacPherson..."

"Please sir, call me Dovey."

"Dovey, some of the things I will tell you may shock you, but you need to know the facts so that you can be prepared to face the danger and to protect your son, understand?"

For a moment Dovey shifted her gaze from the highly polished buttons on the captain's coat to the mounted elk head behind his desk, rubbed her turbulent stomach, and turned to see Scotty nodding his head slightly. "The truth never hurts anyone. That's one of the things I remember my daddy saying."

"Last year, 1907, we had seventeen reports of missing children in my command alone. We recovered six, one of which was so terrified until she'll likely never recover. She was kept naked, in solitary confinement in a space so small she could hardly turn around. Her body was covered with bruises from beatings and repeated rapes. Her mind went into another world; probably the only defense she had.

"We found four bodies, badly mutilated, and the rest are unaccounted for."

His words were like knives to Dovey's stomach, but she had to hear the rest. She nodded for him to continue.

"President Roosevelt has sent a message through the command structure demanding that we make the rescue of such children a top priority. We're doing that."

"So, there's hope then?"

"There's always hope. Please understand, though, it's not an easy task we're faced with. I'm sure you know there's so much land out there until it's hard for us to be everywhere, even though the Indians seem to be. Their intelligence network is an amazing thing."

Dovey sighed. Is that all anyone can say, 'It's hard, miss'. Well, it had been darn hard for her too, but she wasn't going to let that stop her. She knew it was hard or otherwise the people Snooze had sent out wouldn't have come back empty-handed.

"Captain," she said, "These children you're talking about, they're white children? Belonging to non-Indian families?"

He nodded. "That's right. Usually kidnapped or found somehow or other. Sometimes we're not sure."

"Then, isn't our situation different from that? Remember, Jerry is the son of a village elder. He's part Indian, too. Doesn't that mean that he's just living among the others, just as though he had an Indian mother?"

"That's one reason we need to find out if this Blackjack's still alive. Times have gotten real hard out in some of these villages. With a white mother and a dead father, there's no telling what they might do with the boy."

Dovey swallowed hard. Wesa was her only hope, just as she knew it was all along. "But, if Blackjack's alive…"

"Ma'am, let me suggest that we take this one step at a time. The first thing we need to do is find out if that's the case."

"That should be easy," she said. "He's either in the village or at the mine."

"After the fall he had, I doubt if he's up to any more mining," Scotty said.

"No use speculating," the captain said. "We'll send out a team or two to check his village, the mine, and a few neighboring villages. They'll find out about Blackjack even if they don't find the boy."

"Count on me, Captain."

"Me, too," Dovey said.

"It wouldn't be wise to let you ride with the men, ma'am. It would send a confused signal to the Indians, but you can be a big help," the captain said.

"How?"

"Scotty, I'll ask you to be in charge of this expedition. I'll assign four troopers to do your bidding. You can make up a story about getting permission to bring a wagon trail through their territory or whatever you like. You know how to do it."

"And me?" Dovey said.

"I want you to sit with the troopers every day while they're making preparations. Tell them every last thing you can think of about your boy. Everything. Don't leave out even the smallest fact. Also tell them about Wesa, Red Dawn, the village, the mine, and even the trails."

"I'll do my best, Captain, but I lie in agony many nights trying to get a picture of him in my mind. I know he's now large enough to run and play with the other children, but all I can see are his big brown eyes twinkling in front of me and... Captain, he must look much different now after all this time."

Dovey walked alongside Scotty's horse right to the stockade gate and stood there waving, until even the rider's dust cloud had dissipated. The many possibilities raised by the troopers raced through her mind: 'I'll bet he took his gold, grabbed the boy, and hightailed it east,' one had said. And another, 'Naw, man, you don't get up from a fall like that and go dancing the next day. He's holed up somewhere.' Then a third, 'We'll get his ass, though. 'He's dead, man, didn't you hear what the little lady said?'

Dovey shook her head. She would go crazy if she had to keep thinking about the things those men had said. She had to do something to take her mind off all these possibilities. She had to get Captain Campbell to give her some work to do.

One day of anxious waiting followed another. Assisting Captain Campbell with his record keeping was challenging, and the other small chores he found for her helped to control the torment of not knowing where the team was or what they had found.

At the end of a long day, she closed the account book she had been working on, laid it aside. In a tentative voice, without preamble, said to the captain, "How long before the men will return?"

"I can't answer that, maybe three months. They have to proceed so cautiously. But if these were any significant news, I'm sure Scotty would send us word."

"I'll go crazy hanging around this fort with so little to do. I can't help but fret," Dovey said.

The captain smiled. "This is my third year here, and although the whole fort isn't more than a hundred yards in each direction, and the view from the parapet gives the same rocky, treeless, dusty view in all directions, I haven't gone mad yet."

"How in the world do you stand it?"

"See that shelf over there? That's my salvation: books."

"Books?"

"Don't have many, twenty-two if the soldiers have returned them all, but you can see by the smudged pages that they are well-used friends."

"Every night I read a poetry book a friend gave me, but I can just about memorize the words now. I'd like to try something different."

"Have a look and take what you like. I tried to bring a wide cross section with me. Like you said, the same old thing gets tiring, doesn't it?"

One night she had fallen asleep reading a tattered edition of the King James Bible. The reading candle was still burning when a challenge from a sentry jarred her from her sleep. The responding voice was Scotty's. She was sure of it. She threw the bedcovers to the side and ran to the quadrangle clad only in her flannel nightdress. Breathing heavily, she shouted, "Scotty, is that you? Is Jerry with you?"

"This snow is ten inches deep. You'll get pneumonia in that outfit. Git back inside and I'll be there in a minute when I see to the horse."

Dovey rubbed her arms and body to try to control the shivering in her body, but it didn't help. She made coffee and began to sweep the floor as she said to herself, *be calm, be calm. you'll know in a moment.*

A burst of cold wind accompanied Scotty into the room. He slapped his hat against his chaps, sniffed the air, and headed for the coffee. "It's been one tough ride," he said. "I'm frozen to the bone."

"Scotty, please, where is he?"

Scotty shook his head, looked over at the open Bible, and

said, "Only God knows for sure." His words were softly spoken and his manner said more than his words.

He hasn't found him. Is there any hope? All that time and money... and nothing. What could she do?

"I'm sick of Indian camps and villages, nineteen of them, so you see we were riding hard all the time."

"But, what did you find out? Is Blackjack alive? Did anyone know Jerry?"

Dawn was beckoning by the time Scotty finished telling the story of their trip.

"One thing I'm sure of is that the people at the camp at the river with two tongues were lying. I speak Cherokee pretty good, and I could detect tension in their voices. The scroungy devils knew something, and they wouldn't talk. Either Jerry was there, or he has been recently. I'd bet my life on it."

"Then let's go there now, today, and flush him out. Wesa or Red Dawn might help us," Dovey said.

"We couldn't find Red Dawn. You're lucky though that Wesa is still alive."

Dovey smiled for the first time since Scotty had walked in.

"That's the worst Indian camp I've ever been in. Dirty people lying around doing nothing, and the crops look like they're dying. It looks like no one cares whether they grow or not."

"It's changed then. When Blackjack was in charge, he at least had people working."

"That's the other thing, Dovey. Blackjack is alive. You didn't kill him."

Dovey gasped, felt the blood drain from her face, and felt every muscle tense to its breaking point. She covered her mouth with both hands. *Had she heard correctly... alive?* "Alive? Are you sure? How do you know?"

"When I first reached the camp I asked for the headman. There was lots of talking in low tones among the braves before someone said, 'Blackjack gone away.' I told them I was a friend of his from another place and asked them when he would be back. That's when a heavyset squaw with a scarred face walked up to me."

"Wesa," Dovey said.

"What do you want with Blackjack?' she asked me. I told

her that a friend of mine had something that belongs to him and wants to make trade. I also told her to send a messenger to Occana when he agrees to trade. Well, she asked me for my friend's name. I thought on it and decided to take a chance. So, I told her it was you. I also said that you wanted to thank her for her help a few years back."

"What did she say? When can I go there?"

"You can't. Wesa stared at me for what seemed like minutes and told me that Blackjack is not dead and that everyone in the camp knows you pushed him off the cliff. He'll kill you, Dovey. If you go there the other braves will skin you. I told her that you didn't try to kill Blackjack- that he fell. Wesa looked at me a long time in silence and then walked over to her house. Just before crossing the threshold, she turned to face me. Her face was hard, and her black eyes seemed to penetrate my brain when she said, 'I want Dovey to tell me what happened. When she speaks I know my ears will hear truth.'

"Here's a map. See where this river leaves the lake and rambles south. She will meet you at a spot off the main trail, here, where I have made an X. Her next trip will be when the moon is full during the month of the big bear. I reckon that's four months."

"I can't wait that long. There's no telling what might happen to Jerry in that time."

"After waiting nearly six years, four months can't make much difference."

"But it does, and you know it. I'm wondering if you even care?"

"What? Now look, Dovey, I'm too tired and hungry to argue. I rode nearly thirty hours to get here with what I thought was good news, and you don't see it the same way. I think I better sleep a bit before I say any more."

What was the matter with her? She shouldn't have said that. "I'm so sorry. I'm just so frustrated, I..." She quickly closed the short space between them and hugged him with all her strength. The touch of a man felt strange to her but was not as bad as she had thought it might be. He placed his hands lightly on her shoulder, and the two remained in silent reflection for a few moments. "Please forget what I just said. I know you've worked hard to help me."

Scotty tousled her head with his cold, leathery hand. "You got every right to be worked up. We'll talk more about it after I've had some shut-eye."

He picked up his bedroll and left, letting a cold draft of air drift across the room.

Dovey rose to clear the breakfast plates.

"Let that wait a moment, Dovey."

Dovey knit her eyebrows, put down the breakfast plates she'd just cleared from the table, and looked at him as he sipped coffee. She sat down and rubbed her hands together, waiting.

"Well?"

"I'm sure you remember that our agreement was to include a full year's pay, whether or not we found Jerry, and provided for an optional extension." Scotty said.

"Of course I remember. I put the money in your bank, didn't I? Are you asking for more?"

"Your pay is fair. You're a fine young lady, and I'm sure you'll be a great mother. But this just ain't my kind'a work. I'm going stale and soft. I need to be back on the trail with other trail riders, people I can talk to about other things. I can't take any more talk about Jerry; it's all I hear from you, night and day and ... well, you see."

"You mean..." She stood up and leaned across the table. "You're telling me you want to leave me out here in the wilderness. Is that what you're proposing?"

"No ma'am. I wouldn't desert you. I'll take you where you can get home safely."

"Where I want to go is to Blackjack's camp. Dead or alive I'm not afraid of him."

"I'm sure you ain't, but think of how many people you'll have to confront to get the boy. The only sensible thing you can do is to go to the meeting place that Wesa suggested and pray she shows up. In the meantime, go home, rest, put some meat on your bones."

Scotty emphasized his point by patting Dovey's thigh. Dovey caught her breath. They both looked at each other but said nothing.

She shook her head, picked up the dishes, and walked away

to clean them in the washtub on the verandah. She swished the water around in the big tub, scrubbed the plates automatically, and stared at the greasy film that rose to the surface of the water. In a near trance, she watched the blue, yellow, and gray streaks until it seemed to her that an image had formed. *Bess, it's Bess.* An idea came to her. With her back turned toward him, she brushed back her hair with her fingers and unbuttoned the top button on her blouse. She looked down at the floor for a minute, traced her foot back and forth, and made a decision. She couldn't be left alone now. She had to do whatever was necessary to keep him from leaving, anything. She stood tall, smiled and let a song come to her lips to help chase the butterflies that had come to her stomach.

The unexpected song attracted Scotty. "Are you that glad to get rid of me?" he asked

"I just had a surprise. A friend's face seemed to form in the grease and soapsuds. It surprised me."

"Never heard you mention any friends."

"It was one of the girls that works for Hatti and Snooze. She was good to me and gave me good advice."

"Ooooh ... I see. Well, Miss, better think on advice given by those that work in such places."

"What did you say you were going to be doing, Scotty?"

"Didn't say, but if the job is still open when I get to St. Louis, I'm gonna take a wagon train out west, all the way to Oregon, if we make it."

"Sounds exciting," she said with an enthusiasm she didn't feel.

"Better get yourself ready to ride. We've put the captain out too much already. I'd say our work here's done."

"Ride where?"

"Didn't tell you, did I? First I'm going to take you to the place where Wesa plans to meet you and then show you how to get there from Santa Fe. Then, we're gonna intersect the Santa Fe Trail and go north a bit to a stage stop. I'll hop one for St. Louis, and you'll head south for Santa Fe."

Maybe not. Dovey smiled at her thought. Not if she could help it anyway.

The riders were saddled up, the horses snorted, and a fog of their hot breath sprayed the cold air.

"Well your mounts are ready whether you two are or not. Travel well, and Dovey, cook that venison I gave you a long time. Old men like Scotty have wiggly teeth some time," Captain Campbell said.

"Right, Captain. I'll remember that crack," Scotty said.

Dovey pulled up on her horse's reins so she could lean over to shake the captain's hand. "Thank you, Captain, for everything. I'll bring Jerry to see you one day."

He nodded, paused, and said, "I hope so, ma'am. I surely hope so."

"Before you ask I'll tell you; two days and a mite," Scotty said.

"For what?"

"To reach the stage line."

The wind shifted so that it blew from the northwest, and a light powder of snow began to fall. The riders bent their heads into the wind and protected their faces with scarves as best they could. Normal conversation was out of the question, but it was all right with Dovey, for it gave her time to think of what Bess had taught her and how she would go about it. Then he would have no choice except to continue with the search.

Scotty waved for her to come alongside. "I wanted to make a few more miles today, but this snow is coming down faster than fuzz off'n a thistle in a high wind. I think we better cut over to those hills and see if we can find ourselves a rock ledge or a cave to camp in."

She swallowed hard and nodded. "Good idea."

"Well, this is about the best place I've seen along this trail," Scotty said, once they got settled. "As long as I don't stand up quickly, anyway."

"A girl could do a lot worse. Cozy place like this in the company of a handsome man." Dovey said, smiling and laying her hand across his.

"Handsome, is it? You've been on the trail too long."
She tried to read his face. It told nothing except that he wasn't unhappy about her compliment.

"It's not that," she said, trying to keep her voice steady.

"Oh?"

"Well, till now we've had a business relationship."

"And ..." He was smiling at her, not just with his lips. His eyes twinkled a message also.

There was no doubt in her mind, now, that he had a pretty good idea of what she had on her mind. "You told me our business was done, so it's not necessary to hide my feelings anymore."

"Your feelings?"

"The way you do your job, your courtesy to me, your knowledge... That's the way a real man should be. I admire you so much, and I'd like to say it in nicer, more romantic words; but I haven't had much practice expressing my personal feelings."

She stepped to the far edge of the enclosure out of Scotty's view, removed her blouse and shift, then quickly put the blouse back on with the top two buttons undone. She smoothed her hair and sighed; she had to do it. She had to. Maybe it wouldn't hurt so bad this time. She stirred the stew again, smelled it, and then tasted. "I think it's ready; here, you taste."

Dovey took a spoon of the liquid to Scotty and bent over to serve him. "More salt?"

"No, they're perfect. I mean the stew is perfect."

"Well come on, let's eat."

Besides some small talk of incidental trail remembrances, not much was said as the hungry travelers finished the stew.

"Well?" Dovey said.

"Best I can remember. You'll make someone a fine wife one day."

She crossed to his side of the fire, knelt in front of him so that he was sure to see her cleavage, and placed her hand on his thigh. She had to send him an unmistakable message; she knew that. "Scotty, I'm so appreciative of everything you have done for me. I wanted to do something really nice for you in return, something you wouldn't forget, ever."

She kissed him and was surprised to find his lips firm and attentive, as though they had been waiting for her. He took her hand, stared at her lips in silence for several seconds, and rose, assisting her to rise also. He picked her up in his strong arms and carried her to her sleeping place.

His lips went to her neck, and tingles went down her spine.

He rolled her on her back, caressed her skin, and kissed her deeply. With each touch, her anxiety lessened, and a feeling she had never known made her desperate to share with him something her body had forgotten and her spirit had never known.

An eagle's cry announced the dawn and caused Dovey to open her eyes first. She was momentarily startled to find herself in Scotty's arms. What had she done? The thought of trying to trap him felt wrong. She hung her head for a moment, chastised herself, but couldn't rid herself of the pleasure she had enjoyed. Is that wrong?

She tried to lift his arm, and slits in his eyes peered at her. He pulled her back to him and kissed her.

"That was one hell of a thank you, Dovey MacPherson."

"Come closer," she said, "There's more from where that came from."

He backed away from her and sat up. "Not if we're gonna be on our way. Judging from the light out there, I'd say the day's gotten a jump on us already."

Why had he backed away from her? She washed herself hastily and wondered, what had she done wrong?' Why wouldn't he lie with her? Maybe he's too shy to look upon a woman in the daylight... That must be it. She would have to put him at ease.

"I guess it's hard tack and beans; maybe there's a little jerky left. But never mind, day after tomorrow we'll make up for it at the hotel," he said.

"That sounds wonderful. How long has it been since we've even seen a hotel? I can't remember. But after we leave, I'll see that your belly stays full of good things as long as we're together," she said.

"Whoa up there, Little Filly. Ain't nothing changed; I'm going north and you're going south."

"Then last night meant nothing to you. You used me like you would any old whore."

"Used you?" he shouted, standing up directly in front of her. She winced and threw up her hand to ward off the expected blow. He stood for a moment, staring, shaking his head and pursing his lips as though he were resisting saying more. But his words exploded across the campsite. "If you were thinking what it sounds like you were thinking, I'd say you were the one doing the using."

He took a step away and quickly spun back around *"Wanted to thank you,* my hide. It's all about that damn kid of yours, ain't it? Well, I'm sick of it. Sick of it, you hear me?"

"Isn't there a place in your heart where Jerry and I could nestle?" Her voice sounded small, almost helpless, and her eyes darted away from him.

"Jerry and you, huh? Why don't you face facts and get it through your head that you know nothing about this son of yours. You're obsessed, that's what you are. Part of me hopes that you don't find him, 'cause sure as shooting you'll not be able to let go of him, ever."

"Stop it!" Dovey clenched her fists and closed her eyes. "Please..."

"You never thought about it did you? You're always 'Jerry this' or 'Jerry that,' but let me tell you something. His name ain't Jerry, I promise you. And he might not be pining for his mama like you make him out to be."

He paused a moment and then spoke in a quieter voice. "I'm sorry, Dovey, but what I'm saying is, how do you know he's not happy with the life he has?"

"How could he be?"

"Well, if he's with his father... Many boys love their daddies; for all you know, he and Blackjack might be hitting it off just great."

"Blackjack is a hateful, evil man. He'd be the worst thing for Jerry. I won't let him get anywhere near him."

"You ain't the one calling the tune, are you?"

She slammed her hat on the ground, and the embers from the fire glowed brightly. "I'm done listening to this crazy talk of yours. You want nothing to do with me. Fine. But don't you dare question my devotion to my son."

"I wasn't," he said, "not like you meant it, anyway. What I am questioning is, if it's right to be so sure that he's unhappy? Suppose he loves his father and likes living the Indian life? Would you just step in there and whisk it all away from him? Or do you love him enough to let him go?"

Chapter Fifteen

*T*he glimmer of dawn, streaking through the hastily built lean-to, slowly forced Dovey's eyes open. She yawned, stretched, took a deep breath, and sniffed. There was a different scent, one she remembered. It was near, but she couldn't place it. Was it animal or human?

She wasn't sure, but she would take no chances. She felt for her pistol with one hand, grabbed the blanket and threw it one way, rolled the opposite way, and bounded to her feet, gun leveled for action.

"Would you try to kill me, too?" The somber words came from the darkest shadows of the enclosure.

A chill went down Dovey's backbone. In the partial light, the form, although as still as the dead, was beginning to take shape. *Wesa!*

"Old Mother," Dovey shrieked, "I knew you'd come. If my hands weren't shaking so, I would think it was a dream."

Wesa remained still and silent.

"I was so anxious to see you. I came three days early. I thought I saw you yesterday, just after midday, in the distance, walking alongside a horse pulling a sleigh."

"I saw you on the hill, searching the trail," Wesa said. "The reflection of your silver pendant was as bright as a signal fire."

Dovey fingered the pendant, blushed at the thought of her mistake, put down the gun, and walked nearer to Wesa. Light from the opening was shining on the woman's face. Dovey stopped when she saw the stiffness of the wrinkled face and the piercing, black eyes, so different from the memory she carried of her from the day Blackjack made her return to the mine.

"You don't trust me, do you? That's the reason you were searching the trail from the top of the hill. You were looking to see who I had brought to take rèvenge for what you did to Blackjack, weren't you?"

"No! I did nothing to him. Believe me."

142

Wesa rose, exposing the rifle she had concealed under her blanket, and thrust it, stock first, at Dovey.

"This weapon will be a better one if you decide to kill me; it's just like the one you fired at him."

Dovey laid the rifle on her bedroll.

"You speak of trust; I would cut out my heart and exchange it for yours if that would recover the trust that I know we once had. Because then..."

Neither woman blinked or moved as they stared into the eyes of the other. The mournful howl of a wolf up in the hills broke the intense concentration.

"We have a lot to talk about," Dovey said. "Let me put the coffee on the fire and offer you something to eat."

"No, we talk first, and then I decide if I share your food."

"Well, I need coffee. It'll only take a minute."

While Dovey prepared the coffee, Wesa spread a blanket on the ground and sat cross-legged with her back to the sun. "Sit," Wesa said. "Give me your hands and answer my questions."

She was glad her hands were no longer perspiring and that her breathing was normal. She had to stay calm.

The old woman's hands were warm and rough. Memories of her hard work at the village of the river with two tongues softened Dovey's concern.

Dovey watched as Wesa closed her eyes, tilted her head upward, and silently moved her lips. Her grip continually tightened until she opened her eyes, took a breath, and had a long look at Dovey. "Tell me what happened at the mine."

Dovey's smile was ignored. The woman's grip remained strong. "Old Mother, I swear on the life of my son that what I will tell you is the truth."

She paused for a reaction, but there was none. "It's no secret that Blackjack brought me more misery than a person should have to bear. He found me five days after my whole family was killed. He made me his prisoner and had his way with me freely, despite my tears and pleas. I was barely fourteen and totally ignorant about men.

"I wanted him gone, Old Mother, more than anything else in the world. But I didn't want him dead. It's not in me to kill anything. I didn't want him to die. I could have easily shot him, but when I brought the rifle to my shoulder, my heart grabbed my hands. My mind said, 'Leave, get away, you're free of the torment this man has put you through'; even then, my feet were as though they were paralyzed. I waited... if he had moved, I'm sure I would have gone to his aid on the canyon floor. He's dead, dead - get away. That's all that my brain would permit me to tell myself."

Wesa closed her eyes, tightened her hold on Dovey's hands, and listened to the rest of the story.

Dovey paused for a moment when the story was finished, waiting for the woman to speak, open her eyes, or release her hands. She did none of these, and Dovey watched her lips move again in silence.

Finally, she opened her eyes, stared at Dovey for several moments, gradually released her grip, stretched her legs, and winced as she eased her rotund body to a standing position.

Did she believe her?

"Let us have coffee and food now," Wesa said.

Dovey watched the down-turned mouth slowly reach a neutral position. The pit of her stomach tightened as though a thousand ropes were pulling in different directions. She wanted to speak, but no suitable words came. She cautiously closed the gap between them, hesitated for a moment, and then hugged Wesa, tightly. She rested her chin on the woman's shoulder and commanded herself not to cry. Wesa's strong arms folded around her, and the ropes squeezing her insides flew away.

"Thank you . . ."

Wesa nodded.

"I have something to share. White man's bread, jam, and oranges from Arizona," Dovey said.

They shared the repast and spoke of life in the village of The River with Two Tongues and Dovey's experiences since leaving Blackjack. It seemed to Dovey that the sun was galloping across the sky, and she knew that before the next dawn the old woman would be gone. Had she not been courteous long enough? Had she not listened to all the tales of Blackjack, Red Dawn, and the other villagers?

"Thank you for sharing the news of the village and the people. Please express my feelings to them for health and happiness. There is a matter we have not yet spoken of," Dovey said, finally. "Jerry, my son. What news of him? Is he healthy and happy? Is he well cared for? Is there someone to love him and teach him like I wish I could do?" Her words gushed out like a stream that had burst its bank.

Wesa didn't answer. She stared into her cup and swished the coffee grounds around and around. Dovey offered more, but the old woman shook her head. "Sometimes, my daughter, the Great Spirit places two people together with a bond as strong as the sap on the pine tree. Nothing can separate the two. What the one wants, the other is bound to provide. I'm not strong enough to pull away from the bond given me."

"You're talking about Blackjack, aren't you? You're not going to tell me about my son because that unwashed, cheating, bastard of a man won't let you!"

Dovey tried to stand, but Wesa gently took her arm. "The Great Spirit gave us a code similar to the one Moses brought from the mountain in your religion. The path I must walk is clear to me. It may not be the path my heart would choose, but it is the path that will honor his trust in me." She looked hard into Dovey's eyes. "I cannot speak of Junaluhska."

Junaluhska? Dovey caught her breath. The name tore at her insides, but she said nothing for a moment. It seemed impossible for this meeting to have happened without her finding out something. She had to convince her to help. "The Great Spirit is wise and gives good council, but doesn't he also speak of respect for all, and doesn't he command that all work together for the benefit of mankind?"

Wesa slowly nodded her head.

"Then is it wrong to help me find Jerry? You are clever, Old Mother; you'll find a way, if you wish, to follow all the Spirit's teachings."

Wesa turned her coffee cup upside down and pressed it into the earth. "The words spoken here today must stay within us like the air in that cup. I wish to walk alone now. We'll speak again when the sun reaches the mountaintop."

"Before you go, please hear these few words: my God says, 'Forgiveness is Godliness.'"

A few hours later, Dovey saw Wesa slowly walking up the trail, carrying something in her hand. With each step the old woman took, Dovey's breathing became more rapid.

"For you," Wesa said as she approached with hand extended, holding a bunch of wildflowers.

"How beautiful."

"I remember you often picking flowers when you lived with us. They don't have the sap of the pine tree, but I hope they bind us as close and as long as the spirit lives."

"Thank you, Old Mother. They will."

"Junaluhska talks to the Shaman often. He enjoys matters of the mind more than going with the other boys to kill food for the table."

"Is he well? Is he happy?"

"Well? Yes, he's never sick. He loves sport, and his friends beg him to play on their side always."

"Happy?"

"Most of the time, yes, but sometimes I wonder. He likes to be by himself often, mostly after long talks with the Shaman. I asked him once what he thinks about. He shakes his head and says, 'People.' I asked him what people, and he walked away."

"Old Mother, please, where is he?"

"With Red Dawn in another place. She loves him very much."

"At the village?"

Wesa shook her head. "I will not betray Blackjack's trust further. His location will stay within me."

"Does Blackjack love him?"

"More than I ever thought he would." She smiled. "He's teaching him how to lead our small village. Whenever he visits and his father is home, which is seldom, Junaluhska is with him always."

So… he wasn't living in Blackjack's village. That meant he would be harder to find.

Dovey watched the sun come from behind a large gray cloud and begin to paint the sides of the mountains in the west. In contrast to what she was hearing, it was soothing. She let her mind wander to what she had learned over the last sixteen months. Two images dominated all others: first, Captain Campbell's words, 'We recovered six -'

The second image chased away the foreboding feeling, and she clenched her fists and teeth. Damn that Scotty! He knows I love my boy. He knows his happiness and health is foremost in my mind. How dare he ask me not to pursue him further!

Dovey saw Wesa nod and nearly fall from the tree stump on which she was sitting. She couldn't let her sleep now. There was much more she needed to know.

"Old Mother, I would like to visit Red Dawn while I'm up this way. Where can I find her?"

The woman smiled. "When the rabbit sleeps, the fox pounces," she said.

Dovey blushed. "I didn't hear your answer."

"I'll tell Red Dawn you asked for her, and perhaps she can come to this spot the next time I come, if you want to visit again."

"Please, Mother, please. Name the day, I'll be here and I'll bring with me whatever you feel the village could use. I've heard that your crops were not good this year."

"When six moons pass, during the time of the changing leaves, I will be here. You can bring corn if that pleases you. The village will be grateful."

"Before you rest, tell me why Red Dawn left. Did she marry?"

"You have said many bad things about Blackjack. I close my ears to those words, and many times I close my eyes when I see him falling in the path from the white man's poison. My eyes opened, though, when he tried to take Red Dawn to his blanket. My ears heard her cry out, and the pinesap melted for a while. I took a hatchet from the woodpile and rescued her. Before morning, I had sent her to another place."

"How can you stand it? Don't you want her close to you like I want JERRY?" Dovey emphasized the name.

"I see her sometimes. She is happier now and has eyes for a strong brave in her new place."

"Suppose you never saw her. Don't you love her?"

Wesa took her hand. "That *is* love. Love as I understand it. It was hard to accept until I asked myself, whose happiness is more important, hers or mine?"

✧

Chapter Sixteen

The door to what was now Lily's office at the Mercantile burst open. It was Hatti, disheveled and out of breath. "I couldn't wait another minute. Wait till you hear what I saw, or what I think I saw, anyway."

Lily looked up from her desk, head cocked.

"Last night I was coming out of the millenary shop across the street from the stagecoach stop, and I saw her."

"Saw who?"

"Dovey."

"Dovey?"

Hatti nodded. "Sure as I'm standing here. I didn't realize who it was right away. Her hair was a lot darker, with streaks of gray, and she had this hard look on her face. It can't be, I thought at first. She was so pretty when she left and all. But then I got to thinking that if this woman wasn't dressed all in black and wearing men's boots like she was... well, she'd look a lot more like Dovey, least if she smiled, maybe."

"I'm smiling now."

Hatti spun around, eyes wide. "Dovey?"

Dovey swung her legs off the couch where she had been resting and listening and stood up. Without a word, she walked toward Hatti, arms spread wide. They hugged for a good thirty seconds before Hatti backed away, took her by the hand, and looked her up and down.

"Used to be so pretty?" Dovey said. "Nice to see you too."

Hatti pointed a scolding finger at a laughing Lily. "And thank you, dear, for letting me run my mouth like that in front of her." She turned back to Dovey.

"You girls ought to be ashamed of yourselves. Ain't I just the horse's behind?"

The three of them laughed.

Hatti went on, "Honey, we been worried about you so much... God, it's been a long time... not a day gone by when Lily and me haven't looked out these windows hoping you'd come riding in with a little boy on your saddle. Been so long, we were beginning to worry something had happened. But it's all behind us now, ain't it?"

Dovey felt her torso stiffen. She turned and stared out the window for a moment, wanting to tell them things, but was afraid that she'd break down if she tried. Not yet, she decided, let their friendship chase away some of the hurt first. She rubbed her stomach and winced.

"I'm telling you, Hatti," said Lily, "I've had about all the surprises I can take. First it was Dovey, last night, and then you this morning. Who knows, the next time that door swings open it may be a handsome man that'll carry me away screaming."

"Screaming with joy, no doubt," Hatti said.

Lily and Hatti's laughter was contagious. Dovey shook her head at first and then laughed along with them, slowly at first, and then it was as though a dam had broken, carrying much of her frustration along with the flowing water. A hot ember of failure burned in her stomach, but the laughter quenched the fire. It was so good to be back. And being sad wasn't going to change anything.

"Dovey, that couch is going to break your back if you sleep on it another night. Why don't you check into the hotel where Hatti is staying?"

The thought of a hot bath and a fresh change of clothes reminded her of her first trip with Snooze and the luxurious bath at Hatti's.

"Right now I can't think of anything better," Dovey said.

"Shall we meet for lunch at noon?" Lily asked. "I'll make arrangements for a room where we won't be disturbed."

The gray in Dovey's hair did not wash out. It wasn't dust. Nor did the deep wrinkles in her face disappear. What had disappeared was the meager amount of meat she had on her bones when she left Santa Fe. She looked at herself in the mirror, as she had done after coming off the trail the first time. This time she could easily see her bones underneath her skin. There was no surprise or distaste. Like most other things, nowadays, it was just the way it was.

She ignored the makeup and perfume, but she politely donned the flowery dress from the Sandwich Islands that Hatti had brought to her. It hung loosely. Dovey cinched it up with a cord from the window drapes, put on her boots, instead of the sandals provided by Hatti, and clomped down the hall toward Hatti's room.

A porter showed them to the private dinning room that Lily had arranged. The room was spacious but a bit musty smelling. There was only one window, and the drapes were closed. Dovey wrinkled her nose and stood at the entrance, reluctant to be surrounded by the foul smelling air. She hadn't been inside much lately.

The table, set for three, had a gingham cloth, white cotton napkins, and a small bouquet of fresh garden flowers. Dovey smiled, walked to the table, and ran her fingers over the long petals of the zinnias.

Hatti returned from opening the window with a quizzical look on her face.

"Hatti, you're looking at me like it's the first time you've seen me. Have I changed that much?"

"No, honey. It's just that the dress I brought you hangs like it would on a scarecrow. You been sick or something?"

Dovey did her best to smile. "Sick in my heart, I guess. Not the way you mean. But these flowers here..."

Hatti put her arms around Dovey and held her tight. "Been a while, hasn't it?"

Dovey nodded.

They sat down, and two waiters began bringing food to the table. Dovey didn't talk much, just let Lily tell her about things in Santa Fe and Hatti talk of her time in the Sandwich Islands.

"Honestly," Dovey said, once the meal was over, "I'd forgotten just how good food could taste. Best I've had since Carlita prepared my farewell dinner. How's she doing, by the way?"

"Fine, fine," Hatti said. "Stayed behind in the islands. Found herself a man, you know."

"Lucky fellow," Dovey said.

"Maria and Bess also got hitched over there."

"Maybe I should have gone with them," Lily said to no one in particular.

"So what about Snooze, then?" Dovey said, smiling at the thought of him. "Away on one of his jaunts? Salting another mine, maybe?"

Hatti coughed and looked away.

When nobody responded, she said, "He's still the only man besides my daddy who's ever been really good to me. I'd love to see him."

"What about Scotty?" Lily asked.

Dovey looked into her lap for a moment, pushed her plate away from her, and sipped her iced tea. "That's something I've been asking myself every day since he left."

"Left?" Hatti said.

Dovey supposed it was now or never. She refilled her glass of tea and told her friends the story.

There were no suggestions for her when she finished. A search of their faces met only sadness and compassion. She had counted on receiving good quality advice, which they both had given so readily in the past.

"I just can't believe Wesa wouldn't help you," Hatti said after a moment of silence.

Lily nodded and added, "Well, what I find hard to understand is Scotty's decision to leave."

"At first I couldn't either, at least not after what I did for him. But then I realized that he had no idea how hard it was for me to welcome him into my bed. He couldn't have known what that meant to me or how badly I'd been hurt by Blackjack. To him, it was just what I told him it was. He owed me nothing, and I had no right to expect anything. It was sheer desperation on my part, I guess."

"So..." Lily leaned in close, a mischievous smile on her face.

"So?"

"So you told us what happened, but you didn't say if you liked it or not. It had to be a whole different experience from what you had with Blackjack."

"Oh, Lily," Dovey said, her face suddenly feeling a little hot. "He was just so gentle and loving about it. I never thought I'd say this, but it was really just... well, amazing."

Hatti smiled and nodded her head in satisfaction. "I told you, girl."

Lily smiled, too.

Dovey paused for a moment, then stared down at her folded hands. "When he left, he accused me of being obsessed with finding my boy. Said he couldn't stand being around me every day jabbing on about Jerry."

"What did he think you were going to talk about, his good looks?" Hatti said. "Men are stupid. Don't give that a second thought."

"Well, it's not that simple. He also asked me how I knew that Jerry wasn't happy where he was. And if taking him from the only home he's ever known into a life of uncertainty would be the best thing for him.

"I been thinking about it lately. I hated him for saying it at first, but now I'm wondering if maybe he's right. Maybe it's selfish to try and get him back at this point. You think that's possible?"

She stared into two expressionless faces. Neither woman said anything, yet they both looked slightly uncomfortable.

"It has me so confused that sometimes I think I'm going insane. I've done everything I can think of to find Jerry, and I still can't. Sometimes I think I'm being punished. Sometimes I think it's fate. But most of the time, I feel like I am doing the right thing but I've overlooked something, left something undone."

"Oh, honey..." Hatti started to speak, but a noise at the entrance interrupted her. A tall man, with a slate-gray face partially hidden by a high-collared starched shirt and a cravat, strode toward them. The hotel owner was doing his best to keep him from interrupting the private luncheon, but the man paid no heed.

When he was a few feet away, he removed his beaver skin fedora, bowed slightly, and spoke in a high-pitched, excited voice. "Henry Stillwell, President of El Grande Mining Company. Sorry to barge in on you ladies, but it's imperative I speak immediately to Miss Lily Perkins."

"That's me," Lily said, annoyance in her voice. "Can't this wait?"

Stillwell offered his card. "I'm afraid not. My entire operation is held up waiting for supplies that I'm told are locked in your store yard."

"May I introduce my friends, Mr. Stillwell? This is Hatti, and Dovey MacPherson, on your left, is the owner of the freight line."

Stillwell bowed and offered his hand. Dovey ignored it, challenging his right to interrupt their meal with a penetrating stare into his eyes. She was surprised by the softness she found there, quite a contrast to his biting voice and clipped demeanor.

Lily kissed Dovey on the cheek and excused herself. Dovey watched the two of them leave and shook her head.

"Handsome fellow," Hatti said.

Dovey just nodded. "So," she said after a moment, "what about Snooze?"

Hatti's eyes moistened. "There's no easy way to tell you this..."

"Oh, God!" Dovey said, throat suddenly tight. *It couldn't be. Not Snooze!*

Hatti nodded. "The easy life in the islands must have been too much for him. He went to bed one night and just never woke up."

Dovey's chest felt heavy. Breathing was difficult. But she managed to stand and take Hatti in her arms. "I'm so sorry," she said. But the words were soaked in tears.

They stood there for a moment holding each other tight. Dovey kissed Hatti on the cheek and stood back in reflection for a moment.

"You just can't count on men for nothing, can you?" Dovey said, her tears giving way to a choked, sad laugh.

"Don't go talking like that, now," Hatti said. "Snooze would be rolling in his grave if he thought his leaving us would make you think that way."

"Well," Dovey said, "I know it sounds selfish but he's the only man I know who never let me down. And now-"

"I know, honey, I know. But it's just like with you and Jerry. Sometimes all we can do is be thankful for the time we had."

Had? It was odd hearing his name in that context.

"A boy does need a father," Dovey said.

A few moments of silence passed between them before Dovey spoke. "Hatti?"

"Yes."

"If Snooze were here, what do you think he'd say?"

"You mean in regards to your dilemma?"

Dovey nodded.

"Well, he'd probably ramble on a bit and tell you not to make a hasty decision. As you said, it's a complicated matter. But in the end, he'd probably say something like do what needs doing. He always was a big believer in following instinct. Drove me crazy sometimes, but that's the way he was."

Dovey took Hatti's hands in her own. "Right now, my instinct's telling me that as long as he's happy and well cared for..."

"It might be best, honey. For the both of you."

She couldn't reply. She felt like her heart was breaking.

Chapter Seventeen

*T*he recently installed, electric carriage lights blazed a twisting trail up the hillside road leading to the El Posada Country Club. The club, perched on the edge of a cliff on the western side of the Catalina Mountains, sparkled like a jeweled beacon.

The "room" Henry had talked about turned out to be a three-room suite, complete with a marble bathroom and a balcony boasting a panoramic view of the Tucson Valley.

A silk negligee with matching robe and slippers lay perfectly arranged on the bed, an assortment of exotic perfumes on the bedside table beside it. On the pillow was a purple velvet box.

"Happy Anniversary, my dear. Why don't you open your present and then join me on the balcony. We'll have a glass of port in the moonlight."

Dovey Stillwell opened the box and gasped. "Henry... you shouldn't have." She held the beautifully carved cameo broach in front of her. "It's exquisite."

She looked at the back and read the inscription: "Forever." She smiled. *Straightforward and direct; how else?*

"You like it? It's was made by the same man who did your wedding ring." Henry was beaming.

She looked down at her hand and smiled.

"I love it. And there still isn't a day that goes by when I don't think back to that night when you slipped this beautiful gold band on my finger. My life was so crazy until then."

Henry smiled and led her out to the balcony. "That was the happiest day of my life. I'll never know how to thank you for saying yes."

Dovey held up the brooch. "This is a wonderful start."

She moved to the balcony railing taking a moment to admire the panoramic view. "Henry, there must be hundreds of small, twinkling lights running down the hillside and onto the valley floor. It's a happy feeling." She sat, took his hand from across the table, and said after a few pensive moments, "Can I ask you something?"

Henry nodded. "Anything."

"What took you so long?"

He stood up, walked around the table and took her into his arms. As they kissed, a warmth touched her and a tingling came over her flesh. But she wasn't ready to make love yet. There were, indeed, things that needed to be resolved. She gently pushed away from Henry's embrace. "That didn't answer my question."

That made him laugh. She loved to see him laugh. But then his face became serious. "You weren't ready, Dovey. It was so obvious your heart was shattered. I hurt for you, so much, during those years. I felt impotent, absolutely worthless, when I couldn't help. I'm just grateful I had the patience to let time do its job."

"You did help, Henry. The dining and the dancing, they were like tonics for me. You taught me how to have fun again, reminded me that life was to be enjoyed. You helped me extract myself from a mire of hate and self-pity. If I had continued to drift along with that ugliness I can't imagine what kind of person I would have turned into. If I hadn't met you…"

"Never mind, my love." He took her hand in his and slowly raised it to his lips. "I love you, Dovey Stillwell. You're the best thing that ever happened to me. We're a pair."

"And you to me, Henry. Happy Anniversary."

After another kiss, they parted and sat side by side. Henry began pouring two glasses of port.

"I wonder sometimes…" He stopped pouring, smiled broadly, and in a rich, sonorous tone said, "How one heart can have so much kindness in it."

"I don't know how you put up with me sometimes," she said. "Me and these black moods I get into." Dovey looked away for a moment. "I know there are times when I am distant, preoccupied, and don't immediately respond to your caress."

Henry straightened his glasses and waited for her to look at him. "You forget, my dear, that I was married once before. I have a comparison. Inez was happy at the beginning and always ready to join me in bed. But she loathed the idea of pregnancy. That's why we adopted Isabella."

Dovey sipped her port, wondering where this was going. She hated hearing about his first wife, and he knew it. There was a lot she didn't know about the woman and didn't want to know.

"Then Juanita was conceived in spite of our efforts to the contrary. And suddenly, my happy, loving wife was as angry and mean as anyone I'd ever met.

"At first I thought her attitude would change for the better once she had a baby nestled in her arms. It didn't. As the child grew and began developing a personality that brought pride to my heart, I waited for Inez to at least show kindness to the child. After a while, I began to realize that she wasn't the same woman I'd married. It was just after Juanita was born that she took her own bedroom. She became more of a housemate than wife, and a damned ornery one at that."

Dovey considered the sad story for a moment or two and patted Henry on the thigh. "You deserved better, Henry."

Henry walked to the rail, sniffed, dabbed at his eye, and put his arm around Dovey, who had walked up to stand beside him. "Dovey, the way I look at it, you've had a lot of pain in your life and in some ways still do. Of course that's going to get you down sometimes. But I want you to work through those things, and I don't expect you to be cheery about it. Just so long as you let me back into your heart. And you always do."

Six years and this man still continued to amaze her with his kindness and understanding. She hoped her gaze at him conveyed her appreciation. She couldn't find words to express it.

After a moment, he took his hand from hers and fidgeted with the stem of his glass. "What's really sad about it was how terrible she treated Isabella and Juanita. That's probably a big reason that you and the children are having what I pray are adjustment problems."

Dovey raised her eyebrows and studied the sincere look on Henry's face. "My love, I'm afraid your daughters and I are well beyond an adjustment period. Juanita and I seem to be doing well, now that she sees that I'm not trying to replace her mother, but Isabella is another story. Her wild mood swings, negative attitude and questionable truthfulness confuses me.

"My failure to get Isabella's respect makes me sad. I love my son so much and for years wanted to have him near so that I could talk to him, love him and care for him. When you proposed I suddenly realized that I would have children, even though I hadn't given them birth and that I could administer to them as I would have my own child. It hasn't worked that way. I'm still trying but Isabella..."

"Yes, I know. I love my daughters, both of them, but I'll have to admit that something is just plain wrong with Isabella. As a matter of fact that was one of the few things Inez and I agreed on. We took her to a psychologist once but she put up such a ruckus until we didn't follow through."

"Henry, let's leave this discussion for another time. Tonight I only want to talk about you and me, happiness and togetherness."

Henry kissed her, long and hard. "I agree, darling, but there's one more thing I want to tell you. I had hoped to have a very special gift for you tonight. My heart's broken because I can't give it to you."

"Henry, I love the brooch, and especially the inscription, which echoes my feelings. What could possibly be more special than that?"

Something about the way he was looking at her told her exactly what he meant.

"Junaluhska...?" It was still odd to say the name. That, however, was what she'd resolved to call him when she'd made her decision, so many years back, to let him live where he was happy.

He nodded solemnly. She grabbed his hand and clung to it. "I didn't want you to know about it, but about six months ago, I hired a man named Dennis Pinkerton, a partner in a well known agency back east, to try and find him."

Dovey gasped. She felt the blood drain out of her face. She paused, afraid to ask the question, but her eyes asked for her.

He shook his head. "Pinkerton went to the territory you told me about and tried everything. Rewards, threats, bribes... nothing worked. He did find Wesa, but she wouldn't even listen to his questions, much less answer them."

That was no surprise. Dovey had met with Wesa quite a few times and had encountered the same refusal. It strained their friendship, but Dovey never gave up. They continued to meet like clockwork.

"When Pinkerton told me this, I suggested he hire a local Indian to keep a quiet eye on Wesa. If she were still in touch with

Junaluhska, I figured there was a chance she might go to him."

Dovey nodded.

"Now I'm not sure of the details, but someone, a girl, I think, found Pinkerton before he left the village and told him something. She said that Junaluhska was attending a school in Massachusetts. She didn't know the name of the school, but she did know that he went by the name of William Stewart."

It must have been Red Dawn.

Dovey let go of his hand and stood up to walk to the railing, her legs a little unsteady.

He stood up and followed. "Knowing that, I was sure that Pinkerton would be able to find him. It didn't take long, actually, but by the time he did, it was too late."

"What?" A cold chill crept up her spine.

Is he dead . . . could it be?

"What do you mean, too late?" Dovey asked the question slowly, as though she were afraid to hear the answer.

"I'm sorry, Dovey. That's why I didn't tell you about this; it was never a sure thing, and I didn't want to get your hopes up. But Pinkerton's colleague on the East Coast did find a prep school in Massachusetts with a William Stewart registered, but not until eleven days after he graduated."

Eleven days! Dovey thought for a long moment before she looked at him.

"I think I'd like to go there, Henry. I know it won't help me find him, but at least I can find out something about him. My God, William Stewart. A prep school? The East Coast? It's all so different than I had imagined. I need to know more about it."

Henry took her face in his hands. "I thought you might say that. And if it's really what you want, by all means, go. But give it some time and think about it carefully. A great deal is at stake."

"Was this Pinkerton able to pick up his trail after he left? Was he headed back this way, maybe?"

"I'm afraid we don't know. Everything we've been able to find out suggests that he caught on to the fact that we were looking for him. My guess is that he changed his name again."

"So he could be anywhere."

"Well, we do have one hopeful possibility. The Headmaster told us that he was an excellent student, rated in the top five percent of his class, actually. A good athlete, too."

A surge of motherly pride went through her. She smiled. It was the first reliable news she'd heard about him that gave her any faith that he was healthy and well adjusted.

"There's more, Dovey. During a counseling session, he revealed considerable interest in both business management and in mining. He asked the school to explore opportunities for his entry into a western college. He showed particular interest in the University of New Mexico at Albuquerque."

"Let's check it out then, Henry. Then I'll decide what to do about approaching him. If I can just see him once, I'll know what to do... I know I will."

"Pinkerton already has. No William Stewart registered at any college west of the Mississippi. That's why we think he changed his name."

"So close, yet..." She threw her arms around Henry, rested her head on his shoulder, and let the tears flow.

"Don't worry, my dear. We won't give up."

"I know, Henry. I know."

After a few moments of silence, she placed her arm around his shoulder and stroked him lightly. "Finish your port," she said, "and come with me."

Henry ignored the port and followed her into the bedroom.

"I'll never forget this night, Henry... nor will you."

Chapter Eighteen

"*T*hat was a long, hard ride for a twelve-year-old, but it had to be done. It's important. You'll see why when you hear what I got to tell you," Blackjack said.

"I'm not tired, father. I'm strong like you, see?" Junaluhska stretched his lean, angular body to illustrate his point. He smiled broadly in hopes of demonstrating the pleasure he felt to be on the trail with his father. "But I wish you hadn't punished yourself so. We could have taken three days to make the trip instead of two."

Blackjack sputtered. No one was allowed to question him, but he gave his son more leeway than he gave others. He shook his head, then swept his arm toward the panorama surrounding the high plateau to which they had ridden. "My son, look at this place and never forget it. Let every rock, bush, tree, and the small stream be so deep in your memory until you can see it in the darkest night."

Junaluhska stood tall in his saddle for several moments and let his eyes drink in the beauty of the snowy mountain peaks on the western skyline. He turned to his father. "I remember you telling me, my father, that my eyes were not just for looking but for seeing. I will remember each thing as you have taught me."

Junaluhska's words were met with scowling silence. He waited for his father to speak but saw only a stare, like a trance, that made him feel a little uneasy. "Father, Is this the place where the evil woman called Dovey MacPherson tried to kill you?"

"Why else would I have brought you here?"

"This place is peaceful, father. How strange that someone would want to kill in such a beautiful spot. There must be something wrong with her."

Blackjack snorted, frowned, eased his saddle-weary body to the ground and winced. His leg throbbed with pain and the gritty feeling at the base of his spine burned with every move he made.

"Come," he said. "Make us a fire, and we'll eat while I tell you a story." He eased his pain with a swig from the bottle he was carrying. A smile crossed his lips as the firewater did its work. Pain was replaced with anger.

He threw his hat to the ground, glared at his son, and demanded, "Look at this scar on my head between the folds of hair. Put your fingers on it, feel the deep, ragged lines and think how ugly it must have been when it was newly made. Rub your fingers back and forth over it until the sickening thought of it burns in your brain. Close your eyes and let the feel of this symbol of failure be repeated in your heart so that at night, before you close your eyes, it will be the last thing you think of, until one day, you get revenge for me."

"Revenge?"

"I have waited to this day, your twelfth birthday, to tell you what you must know. You are a man, now. It's time you knew the whole story. "That scar is where the thief, Dovey MacPherson, hit me with a rock. As I lay helpless and unconscious, she rolled me off this cliff, onto the ground below, where she thought I would die. But I fooled her. I lived!" His voice rose in intensity as he spoke the final words and ended in loud, cackling laughter. Sun bounced off the few yellow-stained, rotting teeth left in his mouth.

Junaluhska shivered at the thought of his dad lying on the canyon floor. Why would she have done that? What an evil woman she must be to try to kill a man like his father. How could anyone kill anything?

"When I returned from the dreamworld, my body felt like there were a thousand porcupine quills in it. I was afraid to move. I opened one eye so that only a slit of light penetrated. I was looking up at the sky. I remembered my father's story of Chief Howling Fox who played dead for three days until his attackers broke camp. He then crawled to the safety of the trees and made his way back to his village."

"I know the story, my father. It is repeated at our campfires as the legends of our people are taught. Chief Howling Fox is a symbol of bravery that helps keep our people strong and united. And now, you are an equal symbol. The courage of your escape will also be repeated for all to hear, for all time. I will see to it."

Blackjack continued his story, as though he had rehearsed what he would say to his son, and ignored Junaluhska's response. "I was surprised how much I could see through slits in both eyes.

The first clear sight was of vultures circling overhead. I knew then that I had been lying on the canyon floor for sometime. But I wasn't sure that Dovey had left. Maybe she was watching me. I moved my head a fraction of an inch clockwise, and as I did, I saw the glint from her rifle barrel. It was pointing directly at me. I remained calm and motionless.

"I felt a thud by my side where the bullet hit the ground, and then I saw a puff of smoke and heard the sound of the gun ricocheting off the canyon wall. I steeled myself for the next bullet. It only grazed my pants leg, but I flinched to give her the impression she had hit me and then I lay still.

"She didn't fire again. Dusk came, and I heard the horse's hooves on the rocky trail going south. So I stayed still until dark came, and I figured I was safe."

"You're brave, like Chief Howling Fox." He smiled and patted his father on the back. "How did you get back to the village?"

"My leg was broken, and my spine was damaged; but I managed to crawl to where the burro was feeding. It took every bit of my strength to pull myself onto his back. Once I did, I passed out. When I came to again, the burro was walking slowly down the trail toward the village. I patted his neck; he brayed and kept going. He went home on his own."

"Why did the MacPherson woman hit you, father?"

"Son, gold makes people crazy. They'll do just about anything for gold. Remember that, your very life may depend on it.

"Do you understand why I want revenge?"

"Revenge shall be yours, my father."

"I worked seven years for that gold. I was saving it so that I could buy a small farm near Tulsa, where you could have a good education, like I wanted. That hateful woman destroyed every hope, for me and for you. Find her. Kill her."

"I'll avenge you, father. Where is she? I need to make a plan. Will you help me?"

"Yes, we must plan. NOW!" Blackjack shouted the word.

"I'll describe her to you on our return trip, but remember this; her left arm is crooked, and there is a three-inch scar under her chin. She fell. She also has a purple birthmark on her right thigh that looks like a scorpion."

Junaluhska rubbed the mark on his arm, looked at Blackjack, but chose to remain silent.

"I don't know where she is. Her home was in Kansas, but I don't think she went back there. She asked me many times about Santa Fe and about Amarillo. I heard the horse go south, so perhaps she tried to get to Santa Fe."

"Show me the way, my father."

"As much as I'd like to see her dead now, this very minute, I know it isn't practical. Her spies would spot a twelve-year-old Indian boy, in a moment. No, we must be patient.

"If you're going into the world of the white man we must get you ready. You must be wise in the ways of the white man. After you learn, we will sit at the campfire and make a final plan. While you are studying, I'll have our brothers in the north, south, east and west look behind every tree, under every bush, until we find her and know every move she makes. Then we'll decide how slow her death can be."

Junaluhska's eyes clouded over and his flesh tingled as his ears absorbed his father's chilling words. He said nothing, but his mind was alive with thoughts.

How could he kill? He deliberately missed with his arrow so that he didn't have to feel the blood of the deer running across his hands. He shivered when he thought of the wild turkey, fluttering in agony with its neck twisted by the hands of his comrades. How could he kill? But how could he not do the will of his father? He must make his father proud, and he must prepare himself to lead the village after his father returned to the Great Spirit.

His skin felt cold, his throat cried for moisture and his head pounded from the dilemma that twisted his head and heart into knots.

"My father sent me to a school in the east years ago when I was sixteen. At that time, Grant Preparatory was one of the few schools that would accept Indian children. They had special programs to help Indians catch up to the level of the other students. Although I would have preferred for you to be nearer to me I haven't been able to arrange it but I have been able to get you admitted to Grant.

"You will be known as William Stewart so there will be no connection with your Indian heritage. You won't be laughed at, like I was, when I went to school. But despite the name change, never forget that you are descended from the greatest people on earth, the Cherokee Indians.

"When you are educated and know the customs of the whites, you can find Dovey, reclaim my gold and then kill her, slowly, so that she'll suffer the same pain I've suffered. REVENGE!"

"REVENGE!" Junaluhska said, and he began to dance around the dying embers of the fire. Blackjack drank the remaining whiskey and danced also, until he fell, face down, on the rocky surface.

Junaluhska covered him with a blanket, stood over him a moment and said, "We'll dance again, father, when you have your revenge."

Junaluhska turned slowly, went to the cliff's edge, and studied the stars for endless moments looking for a message. When none came, he felt compelled to speak. With timber in his voice that sounded richer than his years, he cried out, "Great Spirit, I know my duty... I will obey my father and bring honor to his legend and to the tribe, but please, I need your help. Replace my heart, the heart of a sheep, with that of a mountain lion, for I will need strength. Also add wisdom to my brain, for I do not understand the meaning of revenge. Do not allow my skin to crawl along my body, like the flesh of a chicken, when I feel blood on my hands. Let me find a way to honor my father and earn his respect without taking a life."

Soft tears rolled down his cheeks. "Thank you, oh Spirit, for the darkness that hides my shame."

Chapter Nineteen

*L*oneliness and apprehension were Junaluhska's companions as the train rattled across country, taking him to a situation so foreign that it wasn't possible for him to even speculate.

Even so, he tried, but almost every effort to conjure up a vision of his new surroundings brought only disturbed, troubled questions.

Why hadn't his father come to the station to see him off? Had he angered his father by conferring with the Shaman about the justness of revenge? Was his father sick?

For three days, no one except the conductor and the dining car steward had spoken to him, but others in the car were talking, making friends with each other and occasionally laughing.

Why didn't someone talk to him?

The train left the flat land of the Midwest and began to wind through the green hills of the Shenandoah Valley. It stopped to add an engine for the climb out of the valley, through the tall mountains, and onto its final destination: New York City.

"Thirty minutes, folks. You can get off, stretch your legs and breathe some of this fresh Virginia air. Three short blasts on the whistle will let you know when we're ready."

Even before the door was open, he sprang to his feet. Whoa, what was the matter with him? His legs; they were stiffer than if he had ridden a horse all the way from New Mexico.

He walked up and down the platform rapidly, with his wide shoulders held back, backbone erect, and head looking straight ahead. He breathed deeply as he walked, and the fog of depression slowly ebbed.

"Board... All aboard!"

He was at the far end of the platform. He picked up his pace and felt perspiration gather on his lip. He brushed it away and smoothed his hair. The short stubble surprised and angered him. *Why did they insist on doing this to him? He must look stupid.*

He pushed hard on the heavy door from the vestibule, and it

slammed against the wall. Heads turned to stare at the noise.

He ignored quizzical faces and moved down the aisle toward his seat in his normal, fluid way. Near his seat he paused, checked the seat number, and watched a tall, skinny, dark-haired woman of about Wesa's age fuss with her luggage. Sitting across from her was a young girl with hair the color of honey.

"Is there something you want, young man?" the dark-haired one said.

"I believe you've taken my seat."

"Nonsense. Here, look at my ticket."

He reached for the ticket, but his fingers seemed to be as stiff and unresponsive as his legs were before the stop. He dropped it.

Without hesitation he reached for the ticket, which had fallen on the lady's shoe. The younger girl reached also. Their heads collided with a resounding thud.

"I'm sorry. Please forgive my clumsiness, I..."

"Please, don't worry. It was only a glancing blow; besides my head is probably harder than yours, or so my father would say."

The young girl extended her petite hand. "I'm Sarah Forester, and this is Hanna Floyd, my chaperone."

The pit of his stomach seemed to shrink as he touched her soft skin with his callused hand. He didn't know what to say; instead, he stared into the deep brown orbits that seemed especially crafted to match her smile.

She pulled her hand from his and said, "And, you are?"

"William. William Stewart. I'm on my way to school."

"Really, which school?"

"Grant Preparatory, in Massachusetts."

"I don't believe it. Hanna, did you here that?" She turned back to face him. "That's less than a mile from my school."

For a moment, all Junaluhska's anxieties and concerns deserted him. If a nice girl like her was headed for a school near Grant Preparatory, it certainly couldn't be a bad area.

"Then it's especially nice to meet you, Sarah."

He flashed a big smile. The first in a long time. "None of this solves our seat problem," her chaperone said. "Where is that conductor?"

"I'll get him, Mrs. Floyd."

"Sorry, ma'am," the conductor said. "You're in the right seat but the wrong car. May I show you the way?"

"Wait, if you are comfortable, you can stay here," Junaluhska said. "I'll go."

Hanna looked at the conductor. "It's fine with me. I would hate to move all this luggage again."

The conductor winked at Junaluhska and pulled a pad from his pocket. "The other seat isn't reserved, so you can all sit here if you like. Then nobody has to move anything."

Neither the green forest climbing the rugged hills nor the changing leaves of gold and brown could maintain Junaluhska's attention. He was captivated by Sarah's femininity. They sat in silence as the train lurched onward, and each time he turned from the window, she seemed to be looking at him with a half formed smile.

He felt his hands go clammy. He started to say something but his tongue felt thick. No words came. He turned back to watch the scenery roll by for a while but the scenes were a blur. His mind was on Sarah. Finally, he gulped and started a conversation. "Excuse me, Miss Sarah, have you been to New York City before?"

"Yes, it's a wonderful place. I hope you have time too look around a little before heading north. I'd be happy to show you except that Hanna and I have plans that we can't change."

"No, I have to be at school on the fifth to register, There's no time."

"If you are registering so early, you must be a freshman."

"It's my first year."

"I'm surprised. I thought you were about eighteen, my age."

"Did you really? Well, I'm fifteen." *Well almost, he thought to himself, smiling.* "I guess I grew too fast." *Why had he lied? He was only fourteen, and besides, what's it to her?*

"What do you plan to study?"

"I'll decide at the end of the second year. At first I have to work on stuff I should know but don't. How about you?"

"Ultimately, I want to study Philosophy but it's hard for a girl to get into a university for such studies. I talked it over with the principal at my school. Through him and with the support of my parents it has been arranged for me to go to a Quaker school for young ladies. It means that I will have to spend nearly five years in high school instead of four."

Philosophy, what is that?

Junaluhska climbed into the taxi for the ride to the train station to catch the train going north and waved at Sarah until the cab turned the corner. He tightly clutched the scrap of paper she had given him with her contact information on it, carefully folded it and placed it securely in his new billfold, which he still found difficult to use. Her memory and the anticipation of seeing her again would fill the miles left on his journey.

As soon as he was settled, Junaluhska wrote to his father to describe his trip and to outline for him his course of studies. As an afterthought he added a postscript: 'I have met a friend who intends to study Philosophy.' He pronounced the word several times, but each spelling was different. He reached for the small dictionary he had recently purchased at the insistence of his English teacher, carefully copied the word, pronounced it several times, and then read its meaning. He closed the book, and then, as though struck by lightening, he grabbed for the dictionary and impatiently hurried back to the strange word. He knew he would need to know more about this word. Sarah will know. Where is she, how could he find her among all these buildings and people?

He walked the mile to Sarah's school which was nestled among hills with large boulders dotting the hillsides blending with graceful cedar, maple and oak trees. Although it was a small campus it seemed to be deliberately designed to provide privacy for each building. He strolled along the tree-lined streets trying to look nonchalant as though he knew exactly where he was going, hoping that she would miraculously appear. He tried to ignore the glances of what seemed to be hundreds of young women, laughing, talking and gesturing. Should he stop one of them and ask for the Philosophy department or for the school's headman?

He couldn't. He thought of the horrible experience his father had with these eastern people. The very thought frightened him. His despair deepened.

"William, William . . .WILLIAM."

He heard the shouts, but the strange name didn't register. He continued to walk, conscious though of rushing footsteps gaining on him. He glanced over his shoulder, gasped, and the feeling of excitement expressed his heart's message.

"Sarah, there you are. Nice to see you. I've looked everywhere for you."

"You have? It didn't seem so; you wouldn't stop when I called."

"I'm sorry. My mind was far away. I didn't even hear you."

"I thought so, otherwise I wouldn't have chased after you. A girl doesn't want to believe she's being ignored you know." She was looking him right in the eye, a playful smile on her face. "Or at least this one doesn't. But how have things been going? You getting settled okay?"

"Pretty well, yes, but I'm struggling with one thing. I could sure use a bit of help." He blushed slightly, "I'll explain later."

"Well, not today. I'm on my way to lab. Sorry. How about tomorrow, Saturday? You don't have any classes on Saturday, do you?"

He shook his head. "No classes, but I do have to help out at the library to repay one of the teachers for tutoring. I need it. There's so much taught here that I haven't had. Catching up is hard work."

"Okay, Sunday then. Suppose you join me for church, and we'll go to the church picnic afterward."

He'd never been inside a church before. What would the Shaman say if he found out?

She sensed his hesitance. "Come on, it'll be fun. We can go swimming, or take a canoe and paddle up the river. That way we can find a secluded spot where we can talk as long as we like."

Junaluhska thought of the imposing building on the hill across from the student union building, and he shuddered for a moment before Sarah's warm smile chased away his apprehension.

"Good. We'll do it."

On Saturday it seemed to Junaluhska that the pile of books to be filed was enormous. Would he ever finish? He needed to be alone to think and consider whether he should go through with something so radical as a church visit.

An attempt at sleep brought nothing but questions.

All right, calm yourself.

He picked up the pillow from the floor, rammed his fist into it, and tried to sleep again; but the daze of half sleep compounded the endless questions he had of himself.

What do they do in that big building? Would he be asked to pray to their God? Should He tell the Shaman? Would he be separated from Sarah? He wouldn't know how to dance to their songs... What would he do when the dance starts... just follow along? Is there no other way to gain her confidence and develop a friendship?

As soon as dawn broke, Junaluhska dashed to the window, staring, praying for rain, hoping for postponement of the picnic. His feet seemed to drag on the way to the church, his armpits felt warm and moist, and a voice somewhere in his conscience was demanding that he turn and flee. But then he saw Sarah waiting anxiously at the bottom of the long concrete stairs leading to a huge arch, the entrance to he knew not what. He watched her, nodding at the other parishioners and darting glances down the tree-lined street and then at her watch.

As he watched, the sun came over the eastern hills and added sparkle to her hair. Her face looked soft and touchable. He no longer heard the voice in his mind. His heart was in charge now, and the previous discomfort was replaced by a tingling in his insides. "Good morning, Sarah. How nice you look; yellow suits you well."

"Hi." She brushed at a small piece of lint on the skirt. "It is pretty, isn't it? Hanna picked it out."

He blushed slightly. All this girl stuff was so new to him.

"We better go in. The service will start any minute."

Junaluhska took a deep breath. "Uh, I think I should have told you before, I, er... I've never been in a church."

"Never? Then what creed do you live by?"

"I'm sorry. I don't understand the word *creed*."

"Never mind, we can talk about that later; we should go in now. You just do as I do, and everything will be fine."

"Will we be together?"

Sarah wrinkled her brow and paused for a moment, apparently contemplating the question. "Of course, did you think this was a Moslem church?" She giggled and offered her hand. He felt softness and warmth, even through her delicate white glove and that strange feeling in the pit of his stomach returned.

He decided, at that moment, there was much about this young lady he needed to know.

The large, circular stained glass window at the rear of the church was ablaze with hues of blue, red and gold; the candles spotted around the building flickered as though trying to keep count with the soft notes the organist was playing. Most people sat quietly, as though contemplating their inner thoughts.

It was a friendly, peaceful environment that Junaluhska found soothing. Even so, he was grateful for the reassuring touch of Sarah's hand.

Doctor Liston's sermon was on the perils of war and the effects that The Great War was having on the moral fiber of many young people. "It is time for us to go back to basics and remind ourselves of the fundamental facts that form the basis of our religion," the minister said, looking out over the crowd with his dark, sharp eyes, giving the parishioners time to contemplate the significance of his pronouncement.

"Each Sunday for the next several weeks, I would like to devote a part of the service to these fundamentals."

Junaluhska shifted uneasily in his seat. The minister's words bothered him for some reason. What are the fundamentals? Should he listen to these strange ideas? Perhaps he would listen once and then explain to Sarah that he couldn't return. But on what basis could he do that without explaining his background.

Dr. Liston continued, "It is arguable, I suppose, as to which of the fundamental beliefs is the most important." He cocked his head and focused on several young people sitting in a pew to his left. "But rightly or wrongly, I have chosen to begin with *The Ten Commandments,* for I believe that these supreme laws offer the clearest guidance to our young people concerning what it means to be a Christian."

Dr. Liston raised his voice two octaves, at least, and thundered out: *"THOU SHALL HAVE NO GODS BEFORE ME."*

A chill went up Junaluhska's spine. He parted his lips as though to shout out, and then he heard: *"THOU SHALL NOT KILL."*

Why? Not even for revenge?

The rest of the sermon was a blur, completely overshadowed

by the two concepts iterated by Dr. Liston. They were indelibly impressed on his mind, not as facts, which he believed, but as further conflict with the beliefs and duties ingrained in him.

Dr. Liston finished, the music began, and Junaluhska bowed his head and closed his eyes as he saw some of those around him do.

"What? I'm sorry; I was thinking of something. What did you say?" he said.

"Are you thinking of the sermon, I saw your body tense up and your jaw drop when Dr. Liston began reciting the Commandments. I thought for a moment you might challenge him."

"Very perceptive. I'm confused."

"Let's get changed and come back for the picnic. We can talk it all through. My specialty is philosophy, remember."

Junaluhska selected a canoe after careful consideration, asked for advice about currents and stopping places, and began a smooth, short stroke to ease the small craft through the water.

"Are you comfortable?"

"Yes, but I don't see how you could be, the way you're kneeling like that."

"It's the only way I know. I can't tell you how good it feels to have a bit of exercise."

At Sander's Island, he pulled the boat ashore and quickly made a crude lean-to to ward off the chill of the wind.

Sarah spread out the lunch she'd purchased at the church picnic grounds and offered him a sandwich. "So," she said in between bites, "are you going to tell me what happened in there?"

"In where?"

"The church, silly, during the sermon. Your body tensed up like a spring when Dr. Liston began talking about the Ten Commandments." She paused as if awaiting a response, but he remained silent. "I thought for a moment you were going to challenge him, or something. But then you just nodded, and we seemed to lose you after that."

"Is that what you think you saw?"

"Do you deny it?"

He didn't answer.

"Then I'm right. What was your problem?"

"I wouldn't call it a problem... it's just, well, call it confusion. Your minister's words were compelling, and most of them seemed to make good sense. Just take the time when he raised his voice and thundered out 'Thou shall not kill'; not everyone believes that, or there would be no wars. I'm confused."

She looked at him for a moment. He got the sense that she was sizing up his desire, or perhaps willingness, to talk about it further. "Well?" she said, then paused for a bite of her sandwich. "You sure have me in suspense, you know."

Junaluhska frowned, looked at his feet moving back and forward at the end of the blanket like a fan and wondered: How did he ever get himself into this conversation? How could he ask meaningful questions without giving away what he shouldn't?

He sat silently.

"Well?"

"The water's beautiful, isn't it?"

"Are you teasing me?"

"No, but..."

"Relax, would you. Something's bothering you, and I'm dying to know what it is."

Junaluhska traced the path of an ant with his finger, and urged him away from the food. *We all have problems, don't we little fellow?* He rose, walked to the water's edge, and tossed a crust of bread to the ducks.

Sarah followed, took his hand in hers, and squeezed. "So?" she said.

"I'm troubled by something a friend told me, a friend out west. He has been told by his father that he must do something that he feels may be wrong. To do it could ruin his life. To not do it would dishonor his father and bring him much shame."

She nodded. "A rock and a hard place, huh?"

Junalhuska smiled slightly at the phrase he had not heard before but recognized how well it fit.

"That's it. He doesn't know what to do, and he's asked me for my advice. Until this morning, although I had great concern over the action needed, I still thought the path he should take was clear. But... now..." He threw another crust to the ducks, turned, and looked into Sarah's eyes. "Tell me something. How could your minister proclaim in such a loud, confident voice that HIS God was the only one?"

A look of surprise crossed her face. "Wow, William, that's taking off in a different direction. I take it you don't agree."

"How many religions are there in the world, fifty, a hundred, five hundred? Does each think their God to be the only one? Aren't there more ways to live than by the narrow utterances of one almighty?"

Why did he let his voice rise like that? It sounded ugly.

"I'm not sure I know the answer to that, William, but what does that have to do with your friend?"

"The point which affects my friend is the second thing he said, 'Thou Shall Not Kill'; he put no rope around that. He didn't explain. Surely there must be some justification for killing."

"Well, there are wars where people are forced to kill each other, but even then, many believe that is wrong."

She curled her fingers over her lips and turned her head away from his steady gaze. "Why don't you tell me more about your friend?"

"A woman tried to kill his father, and she stole the savings he had earned by years of back-breaking work. His father has sworn vengeance on this woman and has made the boy responsible to see that vengeance is done."

"You mean his father wants him to kill this woman?"

"How else would he get revenge? Where he comes from, a son obeys his father always." Junaluhska kicked the dirt. "Of course he has to kill her or face committing a crime against his own flesh and blood." He paused and breathed deeply, knowing he had said more than he intended. But he knew, too, that to understand the things that had him so mixed-up he would have to trust someone. Intuition told him Sarah was the right one.

"What about a crime against God? Whatever one believes about God, killing, for any reason, is wrong," Sarah said.

"According to your minister, that's right. In some places, dishonoring your own father is a worse crime. That's what makes this problem so difficult."

"But that's stupid."

"What!"

"You heard me. I don't care where your friend comes from or what his father's teachings have been. You just don't kill people. Period."

"But..."

Honking geese broke the intensity of the moment. Sarah jumped and started laughing. Junaluhska imitated the distinct sound with precision, and his effort was rewarded by more honks.

Sarah glanced at her watch and began folding the blanket with a slow, automatic movement as though the blanket was the furthest thing from her mind. She stopped before the folding was completed and stared at Junaluhska packing the food hamper. "The next time you see your friend, William, you might tell him this; absolute right or wrong is not the same all over the world. People differ for many reasons, most of the time because of their cultural background."

"But when you're confronted with two views that seem so right..."

"Even if your friend does come from a place where they believe killing for revenge is justified, it's still up to him to decide for himself what *he* considers to be right. Then his actions should demonstrate his beliefs without fear of the opinions of others."

Junaluhska brushed another ant off the hamper, waiting a moment or two before answering. "Did you ever question whether your God was real? Is he more powerful than any other? Did you ever lie in your bed in the comfort of night and dare to say that you didn't really believe what you had been taught since birth? Did you?"

"I think everyone has."

"Yet, here you are, going to church on your own accord."

"William, you have to understand that there are two parts to the church; theology is the mainspring, but take your mind away from the God part. Do you remember the commandments Dr. Liston spoke about: lying, stealing, and coveting another's wife. These philosophical points are what interest me. I like to debate such issues and compare them with other thoughts that have been developing since the beginning of time."

"I saw a book in the library where I work with a picture of a near naked man, a small man, with a tiny bow and arrow in his hand. I skip-read a bit of it, but one thing I remember is the religion of these people, Bushmen, I believe. Did you know that they believe that an almighty delegates his power to things like fire, bushes, trees, and other things?"

"The tip of the iceberg, William. You should read more about them, and you'll find that they also have strong philosophical principles, many of which differ from Christian principles."

"Suppose my friend had been taught that revenge is an honorable thing. That's a philosophical belief, isn't it? Why should he be punished for something others feel is right?"

"I have read of the views of some of the ancient cultures, Indian tribes, and also of the views of some of the Arabic cultures. It's a complicated subject, William. But one thing is clear; your friend must establish his own set of values and make his own decision based on reasoning. Once again, I ask you to tell him, PLEASE, not to follow the will of others blindly, without understanding the consequence of his actions."

Many venues saw the progress of their relationship. No conclusions were reached concerning Junaluhska's basic concern about revenge and religion, but new and different things solidified their interest in each other.

On a Sunday in late September of the third year Junaluhska had been at Grant Prep, he slowly propelled the boat close to the shore toward Sander's Island.

"How beautiful the trees are, William. Each time I think I've seen the best one, we come around a bend and there is another."

"I like the soft yellow ones best."

"I'm surprised, I would have thought you would prefer the dark red ones... sort of like your mood. Positive and bold."

"Remember the dress you had on the first time we went to church? It was the prettiest dress on the prettiest girl I had ever seen."

"It was yellow, like the trees you admire... I want to kiss you."

"You'll have that opportunity as soon as we are around the next bend."

Perspiration from their naked bodies mingled under a light blanket until the intensity of their expression of love gave way to fatigue and blended into kisses, caresses, and soft words. He turned to her again.

"No," she said.

"Darling?"

"Not until we have a serious talk."

"We have had serious talks for nearly three years."

"But not about the subject I wish to discuss."

Sarah reached for her clothing, dressed, and poured two glasses of lemonade. "Come sit beside me."

"I love you, William and I believe my actions prove it, but I'm unsure about your feelings."

"How can you doubt how I feel? Aren't I always with you?"

"I can't explain it. You confuse me. You seem to be obsessed about revenge and killing. Yet, when that thug tried to rob us last year, you ministered to his wounds after you knocked him out. You had his gun and could have killed him, but you didn't. Surely, if you had, that would have been considered self-defense. And when we found the dog, which had been hit by a car. You cared for that animal with tenderness as though it were your son. Which person are you?"

"I am the person who finds you the most desirable creature ever created, and I want you, now." He moved nearer to her and reached for a hand that was withheld.

"Your words comfort me, but instinctively, I feel there're problems which we haven't discussed."

"Such as?"

"Where do you come from, William? Even after three years, I know almost nothing about your life before Grant. What are your parents like? Why don't you ever talk about them? Why had you never been to church, and what is your true religion? And most of all, why do you have such an obsession with the concept of revenge?"

"It's late. Perhaps we should go," he said.

"If you wish to go, we shall, but I won't come here with you again."

"Please don't ask me about those things, I CAN'T!"

"In two weeks I'm meeting my parents in Boston for a Christmas party. I had hoped to invite you and present you as my fiancée. What can I say to them to give assurance that the man I love is not a madman, or worse?"

"William the 'Mad Man,' how perfect. Or should it be William the Savage?" Junaluhska jumped to his feet and danced around the blanket, singing, laughing and chanting until his breath came in waves and his lungs hurt from the exertion. He fell to the blanket, turned away from Sarah, and fought against the need to cry, scream or shout.

Madman... would he ever be anything else?

"Madmen don't give away their secretes," he said.

Sarah did not return to Grant after the Christmas Break. Loneliness enveloped Junaluhska like a fog off the river. He found comfort in her church and silently prayed for enlightenment.

He had to find the right way, whether she was there to help or not. He must. Some day he'd return and explain everything to her. She would understand, regardless of what he decided to do; he was sure of it.

Perhaps he would find the answers in the new book Sarah had given him at Christmas, *Plato*... 'What is a JUST man?' Socrates had asked.

Chapter Twenty

Junaluhska could hardly remember the trip he made four years ago across the same bleak plains he was now traveling. He did remember the tugs he felt on his heartstrings as he had waved good-bye to Wesa and Red Dawn. He remembered twisting in the saddle, time and again as he headed to the train station, looking back for a glimpse of his father, who hadn't even showed up to see him off. He hadn't really expected any show of affection. But a good-bye... would that have been too much?

All during the years that Junaluhska was away The Great War had raged in Europe. He had often wondered about his father. Was he getting enough to eat? Things were scarce during the war. The government wouldn't make his father participate in the war, would they? Surely not. Of course, men of courage are needed and the Cherokees are strong fighters. Every one knows that. But, yet, somehow things are different with Indians. The government has strange ideas about his people. In the history books he studied at Grant College Indians are portrayed differently from the true stories he had learned at the campfires.

But many things are different in the outside world. He knew that now. And The Great War had done nothing but add to his confusion. He had heard President Wilson say on the radio that things will never be the same for we are now living in a different world. How true that is. Had it been good for him to get an eastern education? He had learned much but many questions, some personal, were still unanswered. Why does his father act so strangely sometimes? Was it because he was ashamed of having dishonored his own father by being expelled from Grant or perhaps because he was not full blooded Cherokee like he wanted to be. Neither answer explained his attitude toward the MacPherson woman. That's a separate issue he imagined. But even though he did not completely understand, he loved his father and would show him respect.

Such thoughts rolled around Junaluhska's brain as he stared

at the endless, cornfields dominating the countryside. Great tribes of warriors used to ride through this land. Even the white man's history books told of that. And now...there wasn't a village to be seen. Why?

He shook his head. Four years of schooling seemed to raise more questions than answers.

He needed to be back among his people to think about all the differing views he had been exposed to so he could decide on many things.

Blackjack Diamond sat in the shadow of a large, oak tree watching puffs of smoke and steam dot the cloudless, July day as the train lurched it's way around the last bend before reaching the Occana station.

The train's whistle announced it's pending arrival at the station and Blackjack felt an unusual feeling in his heart. His boy, Junalhuska would sit with him by the fire tonight. How long had it been?

His question stimulated a rush of other thoughts: Dovey deliberately loosened those logs. He was sure that she had but why? He wouldn't have hurt her. She's evil; that's why. She wanted him dead. She wanted his gold.

He winced as he tried to move. Look at him, all crippled up, barely able to walk. What use was he now? Even some of the elders turn their heads when he approaches. He hated the woman that caused all of his problems.

The screeching wheels of the iron horse brought the three-car train to a stop and the wheezing steam from its cylinder's pronounced arrival. Only then did Blackjack raise his bent, aching body to peer through the dust for a glimpse of Junaluhska.

The only passenger to disembark was a tall young man with dark, black hair that was cut after the fashion of eastern people. He was wearing a dark suit and carrying a valise.

Blackjack stretched his neck to attempt to look beyond this broad shouldered man and a sound floated by his ears. It was a voice, a vaguely familiar voice to be sure but it was deeper, stronger, more musical and mature.

"You look well, my father." He resisted the temptation to

hug the old man, who now looked so old and frail until he thought he might break in his arms. That was not the Cherokee way. He stood as straight as the tall pines, waiting for his father to speak.

Blackjack cocked his head upward, questioning, wondering... "Junaluhska? Is it you?"

"Yes, father. I'm happy to see you. Are you well?"

Blackjack ignored his comment and question. Instead he said, "I have waited long. Come, we'll ride now, away from this dirty, noisy place with all its hateful people. We'll stop by the stream, talk, share some food and begin our final plan for our revenge."

"Yes, my father."

Plan? It seemed that nothing had changed except that his father's speech sounded odd, not like the eastern speech. And his clothing... his father was truly different than the white man. No wonder he has different beliefs. Well, no matter, he had decided now how he would handle the 'Revenge' question. But, he hadn't decided how to let his father know. Junaluhska shook his head. He looks so ill. Could his father stand to hear what he had to say?

"This willow tree, here at he bend of the stream is as old as the legends of our tribe," Blackjack said when they'd stopped and dismounted. "It has heard many secrets and like you respects what it has learned. If it could talk it would carry the stories and the pride of our people forward forever as you and your children must."

"It's quiet here. Only the birds and the soft music of the water bathing the rocks in the stream will disturb us. Please lie down on the soft grass, let the cool wind refresh you and let me brush and braid your hair and place the special eagle feather I brought for you. I will tell you of my life in the east and of the thoughts that have paraded through my mind since we last sat together," Junaluhska said.

"There is no time."

"But it's been..."

"No matter. My days are long like the evening shadows. The Great Spirit is tugging at my hand. We need to talk of important things. We need to talk of the MacPherson woman and the things you must do." His voice increased in intensity and his face changed from the dark red of the sun to a bluish cast. He choked and struggled to get the last words beyond his lips. Junaluhska looked up and noticed that dark clouds had formed on the horizon.

He dipped his father's head between his knees, gently patted his back and rubbed his shoulders. Blackjack recovered but grimaced when he saw the ugly cloud forming in the east. "A sign, Junaluhska. A sign that says we must finish our business soon."

"Rest father. We'll talk later."

"NO!" the old man shouted. "No!" He pulled the eagle feather from his head and stabbed it into the ground. "This is what you must do. Stab her. Kill her. I have waited long for this. I'll wait no longer!"

Junaluhska gasped when he saw the trace of blood in his father's spit and he turned to face the black cloud. "Not yet, great spirit," he whispered, "Please."

"What?"

"Nothing, Father."

Blackjack took several deep breaths, crossed his hands over his heart and began his story. "Since you left, Junaluhska, our brothers have served us well. One of our brothers in the west has found the woman we seek. I have rewarded him and he awaits you in Santa Fe. You'll know him by the scar he carries from his right eye to his left lip, placed there by the sword of a white soldier."

"Is he sure it's her? How can he be positive?"

"By the crooked arm and the scar I told you about. He saw both. There is no doubt."

"I must be sure, Father."

Blackjack struggled to his feet, reached for a limb on the ground and tried to lift it above Junaluhska's head. "Do you doubt my word?"

He easily restrained his father from striking the intended blow but suffered from the angry stare of the older one's eyes. "Please father let me speak of my feelings."

"You will speak to me only of a plan to kill that woman; to kill the woman that disgraced me before the tribe. The woman that stole my gold is your enemy and the enemy of the tribe. Speak to me only of REVENGE."

He bent his head away from the demented stare of his father and waited.

"The MacPherson woman gave our gold to a man named

Stillman. They bought many businesses including two large ranches in the Arizona territory. The woman lives on the ranch near Tucson."

"Are there many people on the ranch? Would it be easy for me to get to her?"

"For an Indian, easy. Too easy. Shooting her from the seclusion of the dark or even stabbing her when she goes for her long rides would not be a fitting death. She must die slowly like she thought I did."

"But Father..."

Blackjack held up his hand. "Speak when your Father is finished." Blackjack moaned, grabbed his leg and fell to the ground. A second dark cloud appeared.

Junaluhska went to the stream, removed his shirt, soaked it through with cool water and returned to squeeze the life giving liquid into Blackjack's mouth. He bathed his father's brow with the damp cloth, silently said a prayer to the Shaman and softly chanted "The Song of the Elders".

Blackjack's horse neighed, shook his head and reared as though disturbed by a snake or some other unknown creature. The sound startled Blackjack and his eyes popped open instinctively responding to the warning of the trail. He looked around as though in a trance and continued his story from where he had left off. "Twice each year the Stillman's tour their properties. They end their tour in Santa Fe. The man returns to Arizona by himself and Dovey rides the trail. I asked one of our brothers to follow her."

Junaluhska watched the scowl on his father's face harden and saw the wrinkles around his eyes tighten. The jaw muscles looked as though they would split and he shouted out, "Wesa... that's where she went; to see Wesa."

"But why? Doesn't my second mother feel as you do?"

"They greet each other like sister's. What they talk of not even the keenest ears can hear."

"I don't understand, Father."

"Who understands? Who knows? I was going to kill Wesa with my bare hands at first and then I decided to wait and let her bait a trap for us." Blackjack cackled until the fluid in his throat strangled him into sputtering silence.

A small tear appeared in the corner of Junaluhska's eye as he propped his father up. "Rest, Father, please."

"Rest? Never, until..." he gasped for breath and glanced where the clouds now obliterated the sun and then with effort said, "You see it don't you, son? You see the plan?"

"I'm not sure, Father."

Blackjack's breathing was now shallow and frequent. "Go to Santa Fe, get a job any where you can watch for the woman to arrive. Try to get hired by the woman called Lily Perkins at the Mercantile which the Stillmans own.

"When the deer's coat turns and the leaves change color she will visit Santa Fe. Follow when she rides the trail toward her meeting with Wesa. When she makes her first camp, ride in swiftly, grab her, take her to the camp I showed you on your twelfth birthday and fling her over the cliff. Let her lie on the canyon floor where she can see the buzzards circling in the sky. She'll know... Blackjack has been AVENGED!"

"Avenged?" shouted Junaluhska. "The word is poison, father. It's like an endless chain that drives people crazy beyond reason. They become so inflamed until the wisdom of the Shaman and the Christian God is no longer heard."

"Are the ways of the Christian God what I sent you to school to learn? Have you listened to this GOD and now refuse to honor your father?" Blackjack's body was shaking. His words were indistinct. His eyes rolled back in his head.

Junaluhska knelt by his side. "I love you father." His sonorous words were emphasized by a touch on Blackjack's shoulder.

He waited a few moments and continued. "You sent me to school to learn, father which I did. My teachers taught me well from the many books, which carry words of wisdom from many lands and times. But I also learned from others as I tried to understand what life is all about. My time was used completely and beneficially. I'll always be grateful to you for giving me the opportunity that I know you wish you could have completed. At the end of my schooling I sat in a quiet park with only the birds to keep me company. I tried hard to condense all that I had learned into something which would help me decide how I would live my life. It became clear to me that I must use all that I had learned as background for making my own decisions for which I alone would be responsible. A person must think for himself and act accordingly. I will find a way to bring honor to your name but it must be done my way."

"You must do as I say. The woman must die." His voice was lower now, his eyes were glazed, large veins stood out on his temples but his stare was intense.

Junaluhska bowed his head and spoke softly. "Only the being that provided life has the right to take it."

"What are you saying -?"

"I'm saying that I will not kill for revenge or anything else. I will not!"

Blackjack tried to rise. He coughed and bloody spit dribbled from his lips. "If you do not respect your father and will not listen to his words, I must tell you a story that I intended to never let pass my lips."

"Rest Father."

"No. You must hear this; Dovey MacPherson killed your mother."

"No, father, no. Red Dawn is my…"

"Red Dawn and Wesa raised you but your mother, a full blood Cherokee, Alonah was killed by Dovey when you were only six months old. Your real mother caught her trying to steal my gold while I was in the mine. I heard a gunshot and quickly ran out but it was too late. Your mother was lying there in a pool of blood. That's when the woman hit me over the head with a stone and threw me over the cliff."

Junalhuska felt the blood drain from his face at first. He closed his eyes and the significance of the horrible story his father told him began to work on him. He saw his hands tremble and felt the beat of his heart accelerate. He clenched his hands tightly and began a silent prayer for direction.

It had all seemed so clear to him. He was so sure that to kill was wrong. But could he allow an evil woman like this Dovey woman to live. She had robbed him of his mother's love. He would never again know her caress, or the warmth of her lips on his cheek. The woman had cheated him. She had stolen gold from his father but she had stolen something, even more important, from him.

The thought caused Junalhuska to clench his teeth. He

pounded his fist into the ground trying to chase from his mind the ugly thoughts that were rapidly replacing his conclusions of the last few months.

"Tell me of my mother. Was she pretty? Where is she buried?"

Blackjack remained silent.

Junalhuska could not be still. There was too much turmoil in his mind. He rose and walked by the river, keeping a close eye on his dad as he did. He replayed his father's words carefully in his mind and wondered. He returned, sat alongside his father, looked into his father's eyes to see if any of his questions could be answered. He was treated to an icy stare. He would save most of his questions until his father felt better but there was one question that had to be answered now.

He sat by his father again, cradled his small body and massaged his shoulders for several minutes. Then in a clear anxious voice that seemed to break at the conclusion asked, "Father, how could anyone kill my mother? She was a good woman wasn't she?"

"My boy, look at the cattle in the fields or the goats or the sheep and at the other children in our village. It has been arranged by the Great Spirit for the females to produce the young that carry our existence onward. Women feel honored to perform this task. When, for whatever reason, they can't fulfill this strong need, they frequently become jealous of other squaws that can. The jealousy can grow to strong feelings of hate and bitterness."

"You believe that's why my mother was killed?"

"Why else? Dovey could have taken the gold without harming your mother but she didn't. She killed her. She deprived us both of your mother's love and affection. Now do you see why I want revenge?"

"You should have told me, father. I would have understood. Now what do I say to Red Dawn? Do I pretend I don't know and continue to live a lie and force her to do so also?"

"I'm so sorry, my son. We did what we thought best. It seemed too horrible for you to grow up without a mother. At first, we just left you with Red Dawn so that there would be someone to care for you. As you grew so did the affection for each other blossom. It just happened. Can you see that?"

"It was my happiness you were concerned about."

Junaluhska's eyes moistened slightly. He looked away. It was quiet except for the tinkle of the small stream and the Meadow Lark's song. His mind raced.

Should he let the tragedy of his mother's death change his well thought out feelings on revenge? Should he tell his father of his need to think through the latest turn of events?

There have been enough lies. He should let his father know his feelings. "Father, I'm confused now on the proper way to honor your memory."

"There is only one way. Kill that woman."

"I can not promise that. But you will be revenged."

"Go then. You're no longer my son. Go walk with the women for that is where you belong."

Junaluhska jumped to his feet and shook his fist at the swirling, black clouds that had invaded the river valley. Streaks of lighting responded and the first drops of rain dented the water's surface. He raced for the wagon and returned with a blanket to cover the old man's tired shoulders. An expressionless face, wide eyes and an open mouth greeted the boy - turned man.

Chapter Twenty-One

Dovey lifted the brim of her large straw hat, mopped her brow, and surveyed the results of the mulching operation that she and Juanita had undertaken.

"Don't you think it's about time to call it a morning, Dovey? That sun is getting pretty angry."

"I know. Yes, we must. Nine AM on a July morning in Tucson is not the time to garden, no matter how much one enjoys it. But hand me the trowel, and let me just finish this last little bit."

"If you must."

"While I'm at it, why don't you hop inside and ask Angela to bring some iced tea and a cold cloth?" Dovey finished her chore, took a last glance, and breathed deeply, inhaling the lingering fragrance of the roses.

She closed her eyes while she waited on the west patio for Juanita and let her mind run free. Sometimes, she thought, maybe God asks one to give up something they want very badly to test them. And then he replaces that desire with something else of similar value. If Junaluhska had been with her, would she have been the same type of mother to Juanita? Would she have tried as hard to understand Isabella and her idiosyncrasies?

Before she could process her thoughts, Juanita came striding through the folding glass doors connecting the library with the west patio. "Oh, sorry that took so long." She handed a cold, damp cloth to Dovey and placed hers around her neck.

"Angela will be out in a moment with the tea. Isabella made a ruckus about getting her breakfast before Angela served the peasants. That's you and me, you know."

Dovey chuckled. "Yes, I know, but let's not be too concerned about Isabella's attitude. It may be a disguise for something, you know. Love perhaps."

"Could be. Love causes strange behavior sometimes. You know, I remember reading a story once about a young girl that shot the man she loved because he was married and she knew that she could never have him."

"Oh, my! Let's talk about something else."

"Good. There's something I do want to talk about, but I don't know how to put it."

"Just say it, dear. I would like to think we could share anything."

"First, I want to say that I'm very sorry for not being kinder to you when you first moved in. I wasn't old enough to understand what happiness you would be bringing my daddy. But I treasure every laugh and every joke he has made since then. You made us a family." Juanita walked around the table, kissed Dovey on the cheek, and grasped her hand. Dovey kissed her hand and squeezed it hard to try to stem the flow of tears that seemed to want to flow.

A child of her own. Dovey smiled at the thought, and her body relaxed. How hard she had tried. "My dear - -"

"Please let me say one more thing while my heart is open. I thought six months ago, or so, that you were insane when you asked me if I wanted to join you in these early morning sessions in the garden. I don't think I had ever seen the sunrise before."

Dovey started to reply, but a thought from one of Captain Campbell's books ran through her mind, 'When someone wants to talk, the greatest thing you can do is listen.'

"Daddy was there when you first asked me. Do you remember?"

Dovey nodded.

"He smiled broadly at your suggestion. It seemed to please him. That's why I did it. I wanted you to know that."

"You must enjoy it, for you work pretty hard out there."

"Dovey, enjoy is not a strong enough word. I adore working in the garden. Of course, I curse when I break a nail or get scratched by the rose thorns, but all that is carried away with the wind when I look out on the beauty we have created.

"But, you know what the best part is? It's being with you, doing something together, like a real mother and daughter would."

"Dovey, It's wonderful to work alongside you. I can let my mind drift and my thoughts go wild, and I know you won't interrupt. Yet, when I settle on something that needs to be aired, you're always there to listen, question, and make me think things through. God bless you."

"It's the magic of the flowers. I don't want to bore you by rehashing what I've probably told you a million times; but believe me, if it hadn't been for Hatti and her flower patch... but, never mind.

"I'm glad we could build a loving relationship. It wasn't easy, was it? It's been good for your father, too. I only wish that I could find some way to reach your sister."

"My sister... Well, would you look at that?" Juanita jumped to her feet to fold back the glass door so that Isabella could walk onto the patio with the tea tray.

"That's nice of you, Isabella. Thank you," Dovey said.

"It's only because Angela burned her fingers. Don't get any wrong ideas. Besides, I want to talk to both of you. What's all this nonsense about a surprise birthday party for me? Whose bright idea was that?"

"I don't know what you're talking about, sister."

"The hell you don't. Do you think it's going to placate me now that father has refused to buy me a motorcar? That wasn't his idea I'm sure. 'Sugar,' he said to me, 'It's just that you aren't yet old enough to drive. I would be worried about you out on these lonely roads by yourself. You need to have instruction and learn about safety.' Now, those aren't his words. He speaks more directly. Which one of you destroyed my dream? I know you both hate me, but why would you want to destroy the one thing I want so badly? It would have given me freedom to get off this darn ranch."

"Your father made his own decision, Isabella, as he always does. I did, though, plant some seeds in his head, but for your own good. I was concerned for you. I suggested to him that we get driving instructions for you and - -"

"Driving instructions? And who says I can't drive? What do you think Al and I do, lie around in bed all day?"

"Isabella, how can you talk about your fiancée like that?" Juanita said.

Isabella glared at Juanita but said nothing; then she whirled and ran to Dovey's flower garden. She kicked at the marigold patch and started pulling on the rosemary, all the time screaming at the top of her lungs.

"See, old woman, see? How does it feel to lose something

191

you care about?"

She whirled around, grabbed the first thing she saw, and screamed at the pain from the rose thorns.

"Stop it! Stop it, Isabella stop it, NOW! Do you hear me?"

"Look what you've done to me. Look at my hands. Won't I look pretty for the party tonight? Damn you, Dovey MacPherson!"

Dovey reached for her hand. "Here, dear, let me see what I can do for you."

Isabella slapped her hand away. "Get away from me. Leave me alone. Haven't you done enough already? And as for that party, forget it. I'd rather be out with Al anyway."

"Isabella, Mr. Brougham has been especially invited to the party tonight by your father."

"For what? So you three can spy on us and you'll have more information to use in trying to kill our romance? Remember this: I'm twenty-one today, and tomorrow I can marry anyone I want. Don't be surprised if I come home tomorrow night as Mrs. Aloysius G. Brougham."

Henry stepped from the library just as she shouted the last few sentences. "You won't be coming home to this house unless you discuss the matter with Dovey and me first, and that statement does carry all the implications that you think it does. Now what's been going on out here? I could hear shouting as soon as I got out of the car."

"Nothing, Henry, just a misunderstanding," Dovey said.

"It was no misunderstanding. I hate her. She made me lose something, and I returned the favor; and that is probably not the last of it."

"Isabella, did you pull up all those flowers?"

"Yes, father dear, I did." She grabbed a hunk of rosemary. "Here, you want some?" She slammed them at his feet.

Henry looked at the plant for several moments in silence, took a big sigh, and addressed himself to Dovey. "Please ask Angela to see if she can stop the bleeding in Isabella's hands, and then I would appreciate talking with you and Isabella in my study in, say, thirty minutes. And you *will* be there, miss.

"Juanita, most of what I intend to say to Isabella is personal, but I'll call you toward the conclusion because you will also be included in what I have decided."

Isabella sauntered into the study five minutes late. Henry ignored her and continued his discussion with Dovey about repairs that were needed for the house. When five minutes had passed, he abruptly turned to Isabella. "You were a toddler when you were brought into this house. From that day, you have received as much love, benefits, and concern as any child in America has. Yet no love is returned. Why?"

"Oh, is that what's wrong with 'Daddy Po'? You want your little baby to cuddle up on your lap, is that it? Well, if you had said so when I was a child, maybe I would; but no, where were you then? Off at some damn mine or something. And that damn wife of yours. What did she care, as long as some nice fellow invited her to the club?"

"So."

"Yes. So."

"I had a call from Doctor Levitz yesterday, asking to meet with me over breakfast this morning. I did, and that's why I came home early. I've reached a decision about you and your status in this family. The doctor tells me that it's been six months since you have seen him, and he felt it wasn't right to hold my retainer so long."

"How would you like to go there and be bombarded with all kinds of ridiculous questions?" She turned her head to the side, pursed her lips to look as though she was going to kiss something, and spoke in baby talk. "'Do you love your mommy?' That's the kind of drivel you get from him. Who needs it?"

"He needs to know your feelings before he can help you, dear," Dovey said.

"Who needs help? Maybe you do! But don't worry; he knows how I feel now. 'Which mommy?' I asked him. 'The opportunist that sleeps with my dad now, the first Mrs. Stillman that didn't know I existed, or maybe the whore that conceived me, whoever that might have been?"

Isabella pulled a cigarette from her bag and leaned back in her chair with a self-satisfied grin on her face. "Oh, excuse me; I forgot, young ladies aren't supposed to smoke." She laughed loudly and squashed the cigarette on the carpet.

"I had hoped to have a sensible conversation with you,

Isabella, but since that isn't possible, let me tell you what's going to happen. At dawn tomorrow, you will be out of your bed, and you will replant those flowers you tore out of the flower garden."

"Never."

"You'll do it exactly as Dovey tells you to."

"When pigs fly."

"Then you will come to my office and start reading about company business. In the fall, we'll take you and your sister out to one of the operations, maybe Santa Fe, to get your hands dirty. You'll see then what people have to do to earn a car, not just demand one."

"And if I don't?"

Henry smiled for the first time. "I think you know the answer to that. By the way, I'm going to the office now. I'll inform Mr. Brougham that the party for the evening is called off and so should the engagement be until you learn to be an adult."

"Damn you, and you too, Dovey. This was all your idea. I know it was. I'll pay you back one day. You'll see."

Chapter Twenty-Two

Junaluhska's shoulders glistened with perspiration as he performed his morning exercises. He breathed deeply at the conclusion and extended his muscular arms toward the sky. "I dedicate this day to you, my father. Rest with the comfort that I, Junalhuska, will avenge you. The day draws near. The story you told me about my mother's death hangs heavy in my heart and has made me question my beliefs. My soul is in torment. It shouts at me, 'It is wrong to kill'. But another voice shouts nearly as loud, ' It is wrong to dishonor your father.'

"To have to walk the paths of life without my mother's footprints to follow in is devastating to me. I will have no warm bosom to remember on the nights when I am cold and the dark threatens, no scent to tell me she's near and no one to laugh with. The woman stole my life as well as your gold. Something must be done with her but what? Is killing the only way.

"I go over your story every night before I sleep. Where did the woman come from, father? Not many women ride alone in that desolate country. How did she know you were mining gold and why would she kill my mother without cause? I wonder...

"I listened to your wisdom and changed my name to Jason Martin. Although I had to belittle myself in the beginning, I managed to get a job with the Lily woman. In a few moons, the trees will begin to turn, and I will pray to the Shaman every night. I ask for the patience to wait, the knowledge to know the right type of revenge for you and my mother, and the courage to undertake our mission. Smile, my father, and rest well."

At the conclusion, he stroked the molting hairs of Blackjack's sweat-stained hat, ran his fingers over the eagle feather he had brought from the east, and moved to the side so the sun could shine on the memorial he had so carefully placed.

But it seemed that every leaf that Junalhuska plucked from the tall, spiraling aspen tree was greener than the last. The deer's hair remained short and tan. Would the cold wind never come?

White powder had dusted the tops of the Monetary Mountains by the time the Stillmans arrived for their inspection of their Santa Fe business.

From his small desk at the rear of the large, general-purpose room, off to the left of Lily's office, Junaluhska had a limited view of the entrance that afforded him a glimpse of anyone entering the building.

The door swung inward, and a stream of light swept across the office floor. A masculine voice called Lily's name, and the tall frame of a man wearing a fedora and a black greatcoat entered, only to stop as though waiting for an answer.

Lily screamed. The heels of her stout shoes echoed her excitement as she ran toward the man. "Henry, Henry Stillman? Heavens, I'm so happy to see you. Where's Dovey?"

"Right here, my dear. Beside my man, where I'll always be. You remember Isabella and Juanita, I'm sure."

"Of course. Welcome girls."

Juanita curtsied and offered her hand.

Junaluhska heard Dovey, DOVEY, D O V E Y, like it was echoing across the canyon floor. His instinct was to dash out, to kill, to snap her neck, right there, with his bare hands, to kill them all. The bitterness in his throat galled him; every muscle became tense. He shook his head. It was difficult to think. He had waited so long to encounter this woman. He had planned so many ways to deal with her, to fulfill his obligation, and now he stood paralyzed. What to do? There were too many things involving this woman; more time was needed.

He saw a vision of his father's frowning face and heard his words... 'Kill her slowly, if you intend to show me respect'.

But as he listened to the woman's soft, kind tones his blood went cold. Hair stood on the back of his neck, as he gasped in surprise at her genteel manner. Is that really her? She didn't look like the woman he had imagined. Junaluhska stretched as far as possible in an attempt to see without being seen. A swish of a long gray skirt, a pair of riding boots, a glimpse of a hand, and she was gone.

He struggled to hear the words that were mixed with the

frequent laughter coming from Lily's office. A word here, a word there, but nothing that would assure him that this strange woman was really the woman he sought.

On the second day, Henry Stillman brought his valise to the office, said good-bye to Lily, and turned to Dovey. "It's not necessary for you to come to the train, darling. I know you're anxious to finish your review and be on your way. I hope Wesa has good news for you this time."

"Kiss me, Henry, and remember that I will count the days until we are together again. I love you. Vaya con Dios."

Junaluhska watched Dovey turn away and dab at the corner of her eye.

"Jason," Lily called.

A knot formed in his stomach. Was she calling him to come in there, in there with the Stillman woman? It couldn't be.

"JASON!" The call was louder and more imperative.

The gray-haired woman had her back to him as he entered. Jason stood so that she couldn't see him unless she turned. He waited.

"For goodness sake, Jason, what's the matter? I've never known you to be so shy."

"Can I do something for you, Miss Lily?"

At the sound of his voice, Dovey turned partially toward him. Her wrinkled face disguised the slight smile Junaluhska thought he saw at the corner of her lips. She was not like the pictures in his nightmares. Where was the fire in this devil's eyes?

He stared in disbelief. He barely heard the introduction that Lily made and recoiled in surprise when Dovey offered her hand.

"Jason! Didn't you hear me? This is Mrs. Dovey Stillman."

"Sorry. Glad... glad to meet you." He took Dovey's hand in the tips of his fingers and shuddered. His skin tingled, and small bumps thundered up his arms.

Lily shook her head. "She'd like to see the General Account ledgers for fiscal year 1919 and the first accounting period of this year. Please place them on my desk and stay available to answer her questions. Thank you."

"Right away, ma'am." Jason hesitated a moment. "Ma'am, may I have a word?"

"Certainly."

"I've received bad news from my home back east. When Mrs. Stillman has finished her review, I would appreciate some time off. I can't say exactly when I'll return."

"Of course, Jason, take what time you need. You've certainly earned some time off. I'm sorry about your news. Anything we can help with?"

He shook his head. "I'm afraid not, but thank you."

Each time Dovey called for Jason, he scrutinized her face, looking for the telltale scar without finding it. Have the wrinkles of age hidden it? Or was this not the right woman? If only she wouldn't wear those long-sleeved blouses.

Junaluhska arose at first light the next morning. "My father," he said, "Today's the day you and I have waited for. The Dovey woman, if it is she, will begin her journey for her meeting with Wesa. I'll be on the trail. Revenge will be ours before the next full moon."

His words trailed off at the end and were barely audible by the time he finished. Thoughts of his intended victim entered his head, but his heart also spoke to him about her kindness.

Why was she hiding her real self?

He mounted and rode to the knob of a secluded hill, where he could be alone with his thoughts while he watched for the dust of Dovey's wagon. Soft cirrus clouds floated by, filtering the sun that provided much-welcomed warmth on this October morning. The yellow aspens, washed by the morning's soft breeze, were populated with hundreds of chirping birds. Despite the beauty and the pleasurable scene, he could not shake the unease in his mind and the dread in his heart.

The memory of the softness of her voice, the touch of her callused and work-worn hand, and her near smile haunted him.

On the horizon, dust meandered upward, reaching for the heavens and announcing that Dovey had started her trek. His sharp ears detected the sound of the creaking wagon before he could clearly ascertain that it was THE wagon, transporting the she-devil.

He lifted his arms to the sky, crying, "Oh Great Spirit, guide me. Do not let me stain my hands with the blood of an innocent one."

He let the wagon's dust be his guide as he followed waiting for her to make camp.

The embers of her fire were smoldering, as the moon seemed to struggle to surpass the tall peaks to the west. Junaluhska stood in the shadows, waiting, hardly daring to breathe, straining to get a glimpse of the woman's left arm, and praying for a signal from the Great Sprit.

Nothing occurred.

Should he wait? Should he grab her now and ride like the wind to his father's former camp, or would morning be better, when the horse was more rested and darkness would not hinder their travel? Maybe if he took her to the mine she would break down and cleanse her soul with a confession of the story his father had told him… or would she?

The night was long. Junaluhska jumped at every howl of the coyote. Was she leaving? Was that her? Sleep was intermittent, punctuated by hideous visions of blood dripping from his hands or of him swimming in a thick, sticky bath of red liquid with gray hair floating o the surface. Slowly his eyelids succumbed to the weight of worry.

The sounds of squeaking wagon wheels thundered through Junaluhska's mind. He bounced to his feet. The wagon was gone. He ran to the bend in the trail and caught a glimpse of the wagon lumbering along. It was too late. "I must talk fast, my father. I failed you last night, but as sure as the eagle flies, I will not fail again."

Dovey took the right fork in the road just after midday and began a climb into the hills. A waterfall thundered down the mountainside in the distance, punctuating the stillness of the open land with its music. Junaluhska reined in his horse and admired the beauty of the scene. No wonder our people like to roam the land and be part of the union of all things. And - -

A sudden, bright flash pierced the darkness of the hillside. The pinprick sharpness of the flash made him blink. Even so he watched closely and read the signal; a single flash, a pause, and then again and again. He recognized the identification sign. It was

Wesa. It had to be. Just as his father had said, the two women greeted each other as sisters. But why?

He remained in the shadows, watching the animated conversation. He could not hear their words, but he noted the soft touch of Wesa on the shoulder of the Stillman woman and the responding smile. Their talk was often interrupted by long periods of silence, but each new thought appeared to be spoken with respect and dignity.

As the shadows lengthened and the crows called out the coming of the night, Junaluhska checked that his knife was securely fastened to his belt and began creeping closer, on his belly, a few feet at a time, like the cougar at the edge of the sheep herd. He was close enough now to hear Wesa's heavy breathing as she stoked the campfire and turned the corn cakes causing the aroma to fill his nostrils with memories. Then he caught her first words.

"Little daughter, I'm ashamed to offer you this meager food tonight. The harvest was poor this year."

"To talk with you is all the richness I need, old mother. It's been a long time."

"I'm sorry the words I say to you are not the ones you wish to hear, but I can tell you nothing I haven't told you before."

"Perhaps one day, before the Spirit calls you, your memory will find some small bit of information for me. Something hidden, perhaps, in that special place in your mind reserved only for the things nearest to your heart."

"Perhaps."

"We share many things. Shouldn't we share all?"

The pair ate in silence. Junaluhska waited, occasionally fingering his knife but wondering what it was the Stillman woman wanted to know from his second mother.

Perhaps he should wait until he knew what they spoke of. There was no reason to hurry.

"The deep wheeze in your chest and the tremble in your hands worry me. Did you use the money I gave you last year to go to the doctor?"

"We have had great famine in our land, daughter. Now that Blackjack is with the spirits, we have no leader in our village. We have only starvation, sickness, and misery. Many have tried and make much noise, but they do nothing to make the cows give milk or the corn grow." She coughed and grimaced with pain.

"We had hoped that Junaluhska, son of Blackjack Diamond, would return to lead us, but that has not happened... I used the money to buy maize for some of the children. They need more than an old woman whose days grow few."

"No," Dovey said. "You must take care of yourself. I won't have that! Before I leave tomorrow, I'll give you a letter to the doctor who treated me the time when your Spirit came to help me recover. He will see that you get the treatment you need, hospitalization if necessary. You will go. If you do, I will see that the children in your village are fed. If you don't, I wash my hands!" Dovey snapped the last words out so that it rang across the forest like the echo of the jackal calling to its mate. "Goodnight." She patted Wesa on the shoulder and left the campfire.

Dovey's sharp words made Junaluhska jump to his feet. He was ready to run to the aid of Wesa if the Stillman woman tried to harm her. "KILL!" flashed across his mind. He tugged at his knife, but the sheath was twisted on his belt. He stopped... the sign. The Spirit had given him a sign.

Wesa turned in his direction and bent her head, testing her keen ears. She peered into the darkness for seconds. Junaluhska dropped to his knees, held his breath and waited. Like Chief Howling Fox, he played dead, waiting until his second mother turned away.

He lay still on the forest floor, thinking. The sign, what does it mean? Was he to spare the life of the evil one, or delay killing her until she feeds the children? What should he do? Did the sign mean that there are more important things to be done? Perhaps it meant that he should return and be the village leader, as his father had taught him. But what can he do for them without money? Dovey has money. But how could he get it from her if she were dead?

The sun laid its first orange rays on the gray cloud, which was covering the mountaintop like a tablecloth. Junaluhska stared at the beauty and breathed in the morning freshness. A flock of geese flying in their tight V-shaped formation, honking their way south, broke his concentration.

Sander's Island; that was where he had last seen geese. Oh Sarah, how he missed her. He was still confused, even more so now that he knew the story of his mother's death. Could it have been her God that gave him the sign not to kill last night? Would her God stay with him and guide him, or must he turn once more to the Shaman?

'Come to peace with yourself,' Sarah had said. 'Only act when your heart does not weep because of your actions. Think.' Her words were clear to him.

He would think with his mind, not his heart. He would do the right thing. Until he could look in the still water of a pond and say to himself, 'This or that is the right way and is the way I will act forever,' he must have an alternate plan.

The children of his father's village needed him now. They needed food, money, and medicine. How could he ignore that?

"You have a reprieve, Dovey MacPherson," he shouted to the sky, "but maybe not for long."

Chapter Twenty-Three

Sleep for Junaluhska was beyond thought. He stared wide-eyed at the heavens, trying to find something, anything that would stimulate answers to the riddles in his mind. He found none. He brushed at his eyes trying to clear the mist or haze that was dulling the twinkle of the stars, hiding the depth of the great sky from him. Or maybe it was mist from tears of desperation. Thank God for the darkness, where a man can be a child if he needs to be.

He thrashed around on his blanket, trying to force himself into a trance like the Shaman. He breathed deeply as he listened for the night calls of the animals and the birds. He did everything he had been taught, but the ways of his ancestors were not helping.

He turned his weary body so as to rest on his elbows and watched the faint luminescence of the river lazily wandering down from the mountains. A sudden, sharp hiss from the reeds on the opposite bank made him flinch. He pushed himself into a crouching position, and his right hand instinctively went to the knife at his side. He wiped at his eyes with his other hand and peered in the direction of the sound. He watched the slight movement of the high grass as the creature worked its way along the bank, slowly and stealthily as if on a hunt. This type of killing he understood. He would not interfere, but caution was the watchword of the Indian; so he waited. He needed to be sure that the action of the small one was the total action, not a diversion to get him in the open for a larger cat to take him down.

With patience, schooled in him from boyhood, he waited as still as the mountainside. A faint, purple glow with a hint of orange ran across his shoulders over the water and down to the town miles below. The railroad tracks that had brought him from the relative happiness of the east to the troubled situation of his homeland glinted, drawing attention and memories. Thoughts of the east, of the Stillmans in the town below, which was now bathed in sunlight, and of the message from the campsite the night before, all these ran together in a hodgepodge of confusion. He threw back his head and laughed loudly, almost hysterically. Tears rolled down his face. A small wildcat came plainly in view and so did his thoughts.

"There's more ways than one to skin a cat, you know!" he shouted. How stupid that saying had seemed when he first heard one of his eastern classmates say it. Now its meaning was clear. Sarah's advice and the discussion between Wesa and Dovey clearly made him lean toward an alternate method of revenge, but his father's demands were powerful. There are indeed two ways to skin this cat but when the time comes, will he able to maintain control?

For many months, he had repeated to himself all that his father had said on his dying day. Something bothered him, something he couldn't put his finger on. Suddenly he thought of the wildcat and how cleverly he was hidden. Even fifty feet away, he couldn't see the cat's ears that marked the type of cat he was.

How had his father known about Dovey's scar and crooked arm if she just suddenly appeared and he hadn't seen her before? That's what he claimed, wasn't it? Why were Dovey and Wesa friends if Dovey had tried to kill his father? Had the whiskey destroyed his father's memory, or... had he been untruthful to him? Sarah was right.

The pressure that had been bearing on his heart was gone. His legs no longer felt wooden. He knew he could run, jump, ride, and smell the glories of the prairies. The stars would twinkle tonight; he was sure. He knew, too, that somewhere the Shaman and the Stillman's' God had had a powwow and a solution had been found.

A clear head would be needed to understand the path he must now take. He readjusted his blanket and slept soundly.

The call of a crow jerked him awake, and he was chagrined to see the sun halfway to the top of the sky. He kicked off his moccasins and his buckskins, stood proudly in the morning sun for a second to enjoy the warmth on his bronze body, and then dashed for the water. His leap carried him nearly to the other bank. His head breached the water's surface, and he saw the wildcat jump backward, hissing as it did.

"Don't worry, little friend, Junaluhska will never kill."

Long, fluid strokes carried him far upstream until he came to a dam on which beavers were working. He paused and watched these busy animals continue their creative effort. What a wondrous thing! He never tired of watching the beaver. The beaver, like no other animal of the forest, seemed to plan. He must plan, too.

"Your gold will be back with the tribe soon, my father, and you shall have revenge, not quite like you wished, but…" He laughed aloud again. "I'll kill two birds with one stone."

His eastern education, he thought, and he began a slow stroke downstream toward his entry spot.

"Did you hear that, Isabella?" Jaunita asked.

"Hear what?"

"Someone laughing."

"All I can hear is these damn horse hooves pounding the ground. And pray tell, who in their right mind would be on this desolate road at this time of the morning, and what would they have to laugh about?"

"Come on, sister, you didn't have to take Lily's suggestion."

"Nevertheless, I'm going back. I need a hot bath after riding this absurd animal for two hours."

"Okay. But let the poor animals have a drink, and we can share the hot chocolate we brought."

As the animals approached the water, one neighed and shook his head wildly.

The sound exploded in Junaluhska's ears, and he immediately dived below the surface of the water and swam to the reeds rooted in the slippery mud of the riverbank. He surfaced only sufficiently for his eyes to be above water, and when he saw nothing, he raised his head and heard the tinkle of female voices.

He cocked his head. *That sounds like the Stillman girls.*

He watched the girls sipping their drink and then saw Juanita slip off her shoes and stick her feet in the water. It was the Stillman girls. He waded a little closer to try to hear what they were saying.

"Ooh, that's chilly. For a silly moment, I had the idea of slipping out of my clothes for a morning swim."

"That's stupid, Juanita."

"Well, Dovey does it, and so does daddy, occasionally."

"If you take up doing what Dovey does, you'll end up just as hateful as she is."

"Why *DO* you say that?"

"Juanita, you know as well as I do that the only reason Dovey married our father was to get his money and ours too. Why do you think we have to go through this ridiculous training period at the Mercantile? At least it's Jason that's teaching us, instead of 'Miss Prissy Lily?'"

Juanita did not answer.

"I'll tell you why; it's because she wants us to fail. She wants to show us up in front of our father. Then she'll tell him, 'See, they're stupid. They can't manage money. Henry, give me the money, and I'll look after them after you're gone...' Don't you see?"

"No, I don't see. First of all, after the war, daddy was almost broke. If it hadn't been for the money Dovey put in the business, we would have all lost everything. Have you forgotten that?"

"Well, where did she get that money? She surely didn't earn it."

Junaluhska caught his breath when he heard Isabella's words. Was that what happened to his father's gold?

Isabella rose, grabbed her horse's reins, and prepared to mount. "Are you coming, Juanita?"

"Not until I say something that I should have said to you long ago. You're wrong about father, and you're wrong about Dovey. You're wrong to the point of paranoia. How could you possibly believe that Dovey would steal? She's been nothing but good to both of us. I can't stand to hear you talk like that."

"So, Miss High and Mighty knows more than her older sister. Is that why the old man hugs you, and that old witch sometimes, like he used to hug me? Because you know everything?"

"No, it's because we're kind to him."

"You're so stupid, Juanita. You think you know it all, and you're just waiting to be taken, just like father was. You're right. I despise her. I could kill her!"

"ISABELLA! Please don't say that. You can't mean it."

"Just let her try me, sister, and you'll see how wrong you are."

Jason shivered at the venom in this girl's words, but his heart pounded with excitement.

"Why are you so angry? There are many times when I don't understand you, Isabella, but this time you frighten me with your talk. You should see the way your face is contorted... it's like you're someone else when you get like this. Please stop. I can't stand it."

"Well, here's something you'll understand. My adopted mother and father liked me until they brought you home. After that, I was just someone to boss around."

"So you blame me?"

"I blame the whole damn family. All of you are always telling me what to do, especially Dovey, damn her."

"That's what mothers are supposed to do."

"Mothers are supposed to love their children. When is the last time Dovey hugged me? Do you wonder that I am angry? Do you wonder why they sent me to Doctor Levitz, the shrink? 'Just for talks,' they told me. Ha!"

Jason's foot slipped on the slippery mud. The sound of the splash couldn't have been missed.

He dived below the water.

"I saw a man in the water, Juanita! Grab your horse and ride."

Isabella dashed down the trail without looking back.

Juanita had one boot on when Junaluhska's head parted the water among the reeds. In a panic, she threw her second boot at the formless face covered by strands of long black hair and dashed for her horse. She managed to get her booted foot in the stirrup but dropped the reins. Her horse panicked, throwing her onto the rough trail. Juanita's head hit a root of the willow tree hard, and she lapsed into unconsciousness.

Stopping only long enough to pull on his buckskin trousers, Junaluhska rushed to her side and felt for a pulse. It was strong and rhythmic. He breathed deeply but winced when he felt the bump on the back of her head and saw warm blood from the wound oozing over his hands.

He whistled for his horse, took the sleeping blanket from

behind the saddle, and laid it gently over the delicate frame of the freckle-faced girl. She looked so small and helpless lying at his feet. The need to protect her was strong. He tore a piece of cloth from the bottom of her skirt, wet it thoroughly in the river, and cleansed the wound as best he could. He held the cold compress lightly to the wound, and gradually the flow of blood stopped. He bathed her head with cool water and wiped the dribble from her face. The touch of her soft skin was electrifying.

Juanita's eyes opened for a moment. She blinked. A flicker of recognition crossed her face before she lapsed into unconsciousness once more.

He reapplied the cold rag to her head and prayed for her eyes to open again. They were blue, weren't they? No, gray, or maybe hazel. He wiped at the dribble again and let his hand linger on her cheek for longer than necessary to clean it. He ran his fingers through her hair to straighten it, and her eyes opened again.

He quickly removed his hand and leaned back away from her. "Please, I won't harm you. I'm trying to help."

Her eyes are hazel.

Juanita only groaned, "What happened?" Her voice was barely audible.

"You fell from your horse."

"Where's Isabella?"

"She... she left."

"Left?"

He nodded.

Juanita sat silently, as though trying to determine what was happening.

"How do you feel? Do you think you could sit up for a moment?"

"My head is throbbing, but I don't think I broke anything." She slowly moved each arm and then her legs. "I'll try to stand." She took the arm he offered and tried to pull herself up. "Oh, that kills my head." She started to slump. He grabbed her around the waist and gently placed her with her back against the tree.

He looked at her pale face. "You've lost quite a bit of blood. We better get some fluids in you. Sit there a moment, and let me get you some water. Drink this. As soon as you feel strong enough, we'll try to get you home. It's nearly midday. People will be worried, and you may need to see a doctor."

"I'll try now. Will you help me?"

The two-mile ride to the Mercantile was slow and uncomfortable for both. Despite that, Jason's main concern was the knowledge that at the end of the trail he could no longer hold this soft, appealing woman in his arms. Would holding her ever be possible again? Wrinkles stretched across his face. For a fleeting moment, he thought of jerking the horse's head around and dashing off into the hills. Discretion said, no. Why did life have to have so many impossible situations?

Her legs were too weak to support her when she dismounted. She slumped, and Jason caught her, cradled her in his arms, and walked with her to the door of the Mercantile.

Lily was the first to rush to the door shouting, "Here she is... DOVEY... Here she is!"

"Finally!" Dovey marked the spot in one ledger on which she was working, made a quick note, and rushed to the door. She popped her head around the doorframe, her eyes wide at the sight of a man in buckskin... an Indian... carrying a small girl in his strong arms.

Her world went black as she fell to the floor in a faint.

Chapter Twenty-Four

It was late on Saturday, the end of the second week of Jason's instructions, when Isabella yawned and leaned back in the high-backed cane chair which she had drawn up so near to him until their knees touched. She actually smiled.

"Well, Professor, what rating are you going to give this poor little girl when Her Highness, Queen Dovey, asks?" Isabella let the hand she had placed on Jason's lower thigh meander upward a fraction, just enough for it to be recognized as intentional.

He felt awkward. The light touch of her hand was not unpleasant, but he felt uncomfortable. This was a different Isabella from the one he knew.

He rose to his full six feet two inches and calmly said, "You mean Mrs. Stillman, I guess. Why would she question me?"

"Oh, but she will. Don't you understand how much this woman dislikes me? She'll do anything to try to discredit me with my father. Won't you please help me?" She tilted her head slightly to one side, reached for his hand, and squeezed. "You won't be sorry."

"All I can say is that if I'm asked, I'll tell the truth. My heritage demands that."

"Your heritage? Ha! What's that got to do with anything? Haven't you ever heard of being your own man?"

He shook his head. "Sometimes that's simply not an option."

"Why not? Nobody, not even Dovey, can make you do what you don't want to do. Stand up to them like I do. Decide for yourself what you want to do. You'd be surprised to know what I'm thinking of doing."

He studied her pinched face. The strong set of her jaw had squeezed wrinkles out along her lips and around her narrowed eyes. He wondered if she suspected he'd overheard her pronouncement at the river.

"I'm not good at riddles, Isabella, but I am interested in hearing your thoughts. These walls are too thin; perhaps we should talk elsewhere."

"Why don't you come to my room at the hotel? My sister is spending the night at Lily's place."

"Another time, perhaps. I'm going to Juanita's get well party tonight."

"Oh, please. Don't you think Juanita has milked this injury for all it's worth?"

"I believe it's Miss Dovey's way of thanking me for helping. I feel a little embarrassed to go, to tell you the truth."

"Then, don't go... I refused."

"Tomorrow's Sunday. Why don't we take a ride together? We can stop up at the river, have breakfast, and talk all we want," Jason said.

"Me on a horse, twice in one year? You're insane. Besides, I don't intend to get up before lunchtime, not on the only day I can rest."

"How about I get the hotel to make us a lunch, hitch up a team, and we'll go to a spot I know by a small lake? There will be no one there to hear our conversation."

"Fair enough. I'll be ready by noon."

She was only fifteen minutes late for the hour-long buggy ride. She sat stiffly, silently staring straight ahead, seemingly oblivious to the warm, pine-scented breeze that helped temper the cool air drifting down from the hillsides. Jason whistled along with the call of the birds, and they cried back as though he were one of them. He glanced at the stoic Isabella from time to time, told her the names of the birds he was mimicking, and followed with other conversation. Nothing seemed to engage her, but he was not concerned; his mission was not romantically inspired. All he wanted to know was whether he and Isabella could work together on what was possibly a mutual goal: getting the Stillman money.

It was difficult for Junaluhska to concentrate on the fine meal the hotel had prepared. Even the fried chicken and the still-warm potato salad took a secondary place to the thoughts running through his mind.

How could he get her to open up to him? How much should he dare tell her about himself or his intentions?

He realized she had asked him something, apologized, and asked her to repeat the question.

"I asked you why you wanted to come way up here to this desolate spot and then sit there like a dummy without saying anything. I thought we were going to have a serious talk."

"I'm sorry. I guess I'm not very accustomed to female companionship."

"You mean you don't have any girlfriends? Handsome man like you... What are you, a 'Dandy Boy?'"

"A what?"

"Oh never mind. I thought maybe you were bringing me here to try to seduce me, but... Well..."

"Look, Miss Isabe..."

"For Christ sakes, man, cut out that damn Miss business, and tell me what you want. It's obvious you have something on your mind, and it isn't what I thought. Spit it out."

Silence prevailed for several moments.

Junaluhska began clearing the picnic supplies. A grin slowly surfaced on Isabella's face until a full-faced smile appeared. "It's all about Dovey, isn't it?"

His body went taut. Every sense became alert. "Why do you say that?"

"Because I see how you stare at her every time she walks past. You watch every move she makes, not with lustful eyes like you have for my sister but mean, scowling eyes. There's almost hate on your face. Why?"

"That's a strange thought. I'm not conscious of..."

"Don't try to kid me. I know what I see. At first I was overjoyed. I thought you'd try to take her away from my father but no, not a 'Dandy Boy.' That's not going to happen."

"To see your father split from Dovey, that would make you happy?"

"Anything that gets rid of that woman would make me happy."

"Anything? Surely you don't include death as a solution?"

"The more permanent, the better."

"She looks pretty healthy to me. You may have to wait a while to get your wish."

"Even the healthiest can't dodge a bullet, Jason."

He feigned surprise. "You couldn't hate her that much, could you? Not enough to kill her?"

"Don't I!" Isabella's lips snapped shut, and she glared at him. "And you? Are you man enough to do it?"

"I don't think I could kill for hate... revenge perhaps."

"Revenge? That's a stupid reason."

Junaluhska bristled at her caustic remark, his backbone stiffened, and old arguments surfaced. "Not in some cultures it isn't. It's seen as a matter of pride and respect for those whom you honor by providing revenge. Only those with sheep's blood in their veins would fail to honor a dying man's wish to be avenged - especially if that man were his father."

"Well, well, listen to us. You sound downright primitive. What are you trying to do, convince me that there's some manhood in that body of yours? Words won't do it, Buster." She mockingly pursed her lips and offered a mock kiss while rubbing her chest against him.

Junaluhska countered the ridicule by pressing his lips forcibly against hers for seconds. There was no magic, no compulsion to do more. He released her and gently pushed her away. She drew in her breath and stared in disbelief.

"You can't buy a man, Isabella, and I don't appreciate your continual insults. Still, if there were a compelling reason to work together, say against a common enemy, well, I might put my feelings aside."

"There's no way I would work with you, no matter what the reason, you heathen. Ha, revenge, indeed! Wait until you see my understanding of revenge. You'll come crawling to me on your knees then." She strode toward the wagon with her head high and eyes looking straight ahead.

Junaluhska stood still, thinking of her last words. Chills went down his spine; the word "STUPID" echoed through his mind over and over. Was he stupid? Was he so compelled by one-way vision that he couldn't see the obvious? This woman was helping him, but not in the way he had thought. She was changing his perspective. He had been so sure that Sarah's way was best - then, his father's story about the death of his mother made him even question Sarah. The complexity of providing for the people in his home village drove him again toward Sarah's way, but now there was Isabella and her strange ideas. He needed to think more, perhaps talk to others before acting. He walked to the wagon.

Both remained silent as the wagon rumbled down the rutted road toward Santa Fe, until finally he asked a question that was troubling him. "Is there another way for you to, how do I put it, to settle your score?"

"Such as?" Isabella asked.

"Doesn't your religion say that it's wrong to take another's life, no matter what the reason?"

"What do you know about my culture or *my* religion? You... You heathen. That's the only word I can think of. Do you think those fancy schools in the East know anything about *my* religion, what I believe is right, the way I live?"

Junaluhska thought for a moment before answering, his mind drifted back to another lake scene like this, but one in the summer, with green willow trees bending their graceful limbs toward the water. The memory of the light scent of Sarah's perfume displaced the scent of the pines and cedar trees around the lake. Nor was that all he remembered. Sarah's lips were soft, sweet, and eager. All they had done in the soft grass by the lake had seemed so right, so perfect, so certain to go on forever. Why couldn't she have understood that he wasn't ready to marry before he had avenged his father?

Damn revenge!

Damn Sarah for getting him so confused. He had known what was right at one time.

"Without saying I do or don't understand your thoughts, what I'm asking is whether you're not wanting revenge in your own way as well? Do you want her dead or just gone?" When she didn't say anything, he continued. "What about finding a way to take her money from her? According to you money is all she lives for. Isn't that why she married your father? Isn't it all about money? Wouldn't it be better to take the thing she values most?"

"Well, Mister Moralist, isn't stealing just as heinous in the eyes of the law as killing?"

"Perhaps in the eyes of the law, yes; but in one's heart, if the money is used in the right way, helping feed starving children, for instance, wouldn't that be just compensation?"

"You're an idiot, Jason, you know that? Why I came on this ridiculous outing with you I'll never know.

"My father's getting old. There isn't much time, and I intend to do anything I have to do to protect what's mine. You do whatever you want to. But know this; if you ever speak of my intentions to anyone, you'll regret it more than you could imagine."

"Isn't there another way?" he asked.

"Maybe." Her teeth sparkled from the glint of the sun. She laughed a coarse, husky laugh for a moment, and her face changed to a mask of hatred.

"I'll help her find that stupid kid she's always crying about and kill him, right before her eyes."

Chapter Twenty-Five

*J*uanita leaned her head back, reached out to place her hands on Jason's shoulders, and gasped for breath. "Please, Jason," she said between gulps of air, "please, let's rest a minute. You're too much for me."

He pressed her small hands in his, drew her close to him, and fought an irresistible urge to kiss her. If the band had not ended its stirring tune at that moment, to a crescendo of happy applause, he would have.

The walk across the dance floor helped him rein in his emotions, and the broad smiles of those at the table seemed to punctuate the thought of romance in bloom.

Henry Stillman, who had returned to Santa Fe to escort his family home, rose to his feet, kissed his daughter on the cheek, and clasped Jason's shoulder. "You two looked wonderful out there. Not many people dance the Charleston anymore."

Juanita giggled, saying, "That's probably because it's so tiring."

Jason reveled in her happiness.

"It looks as though the girls from your neck of the woods taught you as much as the professors," Dovey said.

'Girls from your neck of the woods.' Those words rattled through Jason's mind, and memories of the lovely Sarah, of her soft kisses and warm body, made his skin tingle with excitement. He looked at Juanita's compelling hazel eyes and knew that as pleasant as the memories of the past were, they were just that: memories. He had new memories to create and a willing companion to help, it seemed.

"*Excuse me.*" Isabella raised her wineglass in mock tribute to Jason and smirked as she rocked her head from side to side.

"Now don't get jealous, Isabella," Henry said. "Jason's going to give you a turn around the floor. Perhaps when the music is a bit slower."

"Oh, no, I'm not going out there and work myself into a

sweat like some people."

"That's enough," Dovey said. "Come, Henry; this is more our style, don't you think?"

As Dovey walked past Juanita, she leaned forward, whispered in her ear and smiled. Juanita smiled also, and both sets of eyes looked at Jason. He felt a glow on his face. Was it the heat of the room or the excitement stemming from Dovey's actions? They were talking about him, weren't they?

He watched the couple glide along with the music, snuggled in each other's arms as though the present moment were the only thing that mattered.

The woman looked and acted like an angel at times, but he'd seen her crooked arm. He was sure of her identity now, but it was still hard for him to believe that she was the woman who killed his mother and tried to kill his father. What he didn't know was what to do about it. Why is she so damn nice sometimes? He wished he had never been around her, never met her; then it would be easy to do what he was commanded to do. How could he plan, now, with the confusing thoughts she caused him to think?

"Excuse me, ladies. I was lost for a moment, watching the dancers. They're good, aren't they?"

"Isabella has decided to retire, Jason," Juanita said. "I thought you might wish to escort her to her transportation."

"Certainly."

"I don't need a Dandy Boy to escort me." Isabella threw her fox fur cape around her shoulders and marched out with her head held high.

Jason watched Isabella stride across the floor with her hips swiveling. He saw other young men turn to watch her movements, and he wondered if her walk was deliberately provocative. Her long blond hair swayed in frequency with her hips, and the upward tilt of her head gave definition to her full bust line. From every perspective, she looked like a man's dream, but Jason felt no desire for her. He turned his gaze back to Juanita, so different from her sister, in every way. Someday, some way, she would be his. How, when, under what circumstances, only the Great Spirit knew - or maybe God. First, Dovey MacPherson had to be dealt with.

He took Juanita's hand and led her to the dance floor. "This

217

slow music is not only for old people, you know," he said.

"I do know... it's for lovers, too."

His heart felt as though it skipped a beat. He began to lean his head downward so that his lips were nearly upon the full, enticing redness of Juanita's upturned lips. Before contact was made, a voice sounded behind him.

"Sorry to interrupt," Dovey said. "Henry Stillman has worn me out. We'll leave you young folks now. We have an early train in the morning and need our sleep. Might not be a bad idea for you either, Juanita. Save some fun for our next visit. Somehow I get the feeling you won't object to joining me on my next trip to Santa Fe."

Juanita's cheeks turned red. She looked at Jason, smiled for a moment, kissed Dovey on the cheek, and hugged her father tightly. "We'll walk you to the motorcar," Juanita said, reaching for Jason's hand.

When the car turned the corner, the waving couple joined hands, and he led Juanita into the now deserted lounge. "Are you game for more dancing?"

"I'd love to, Jason, but my poor feet are crying for mercy. But if you would like to sit somewhere and maybe talk for a little while."

"I got an idea. Let's hitch up a buggy and go for a ride in the moonlight."

"That sounds wonderful."

The warm, happy look in her eyes told him the time was right. He leaned forward and kissed her tenderly.

"Take me to the lake, Jason. Take me where you took my sister."

"I don't think we had better go up to the lake, Juanita."

"Why? You like me, don't you?"

"That's the problem. I like you too much. Ever since that day at the river."

He paused for a moment, hesitant to say more, but the brightness of her eyes encouraged him.

"The truth is, when I carried you up the walk to the Mercantile that day, I wanted to just turn around and keep walking forever. I wanted to find a faraway cave and keep you all to myself, never to let you go."

"Jason, I love…"

"Please don't say those words. Five weeks is not long enough to get to know one another or to say such meaningful words." He quickly covered her lips with his and let the lingering embrace speak the volumes of words that his heart wanted to say.

"Whether you want to hear it or not, I'll say what I want to; I LOVE YOU, and just so you'll know, I've never said that to anyone else," Juanita said.

A prickly perspiration burst over his skin. He gasped. He watched tears form in her eyes but stood motionless and silent. Her breath was coming in quick, shallow drafts. She started to speak again but instead turned and ran for the elevator.

Desire melted the glue holding his feet to the flowery carpet. He caught up to her as the elevator door clanged open. He tugged on her arm. "Let's go on that buggy ride after all. Not to the lake, though. We have our own special place. The river."

Her eyes were still wet, but her smile denied that she was unhappy. She nodded her head and allowed him to lead her.

Giggles sprang from the throats of the shoeless couple as they dangled their feet in the cold river water and shivered, with arms entwined. The warmth of their bodies, pressed against each other, fought off the cold of the water and added to the thrill of being alone, with nothing but each other to command their attention.

A fish jumped in the water near them. Juanita screamed. She rolled backward, away from the water's edge and onto the grassy bank. Jason followed, laughing and teasing, with a fullness in his heart that he had never known.

They rolled together in the darkness, hugging, probing, kissing, and feeling the wonder of each other's bodies. There was no other world, only theirs, by the river, in cozy darkness.

A coyote called. His mate answered. The two lovers listened.

Jason rolled onto his side and stared not into but through her eyes trying to see into her soul. She looked back, eyes wide, and offered her slightly parted lips. The night was suddenly shattered by another forceful call from the coyote on the other bank, directly across the river. Jason leaped to his feet, reaching for a non-existent knife with one hand and for Juanita's hand with the other.

He shouted at the top of his voice; there was a rustling in the riverbank reeds followed by a complete silence that could only come from such a release from danger.

"We'll build a fire. That will keep him away."

Juanita excused herself and stepped behind a large tree while Jason prepared the fire with an efficiency born from practice. The near automatic work allowed him to think of the evening's activities.

What was the matter with him? How could he think of love? Love requires honesty, devotion, and common goals. Could he ask a wife to help him kill or steal? Of course not. How could he be true to a wife when he couldn't even be true to himself? He was a coward. He didn't even have the courage to honor a commitment to his dead father. He couldn't make another commitment until he did. That had to come before any thought of a life for himself.

He lifted his head toward the heavens, and his long black hair spread across his broad shoulders. The confusion eating at his very being transfixed him into a near trance so strong that he was close to crying out to the Shaman in the ancient dialect of the Cherokees.

His ears picked up Juanita's delicate footsteps on the dry, brittle debris under the large willow tree. His trance was broken, but his face remained blank, refusing to reveal his confused state of mind.

Juanita returned from where she had been, straightening her hair and adjusting her clothing. She stood silently, admiring Jason's regal bearing. His shirtless upper body glistened from the light of the fire. The intermittent bursts of flame made his muscles seem alive and powerful.

"Jason, I wish you could see yourself. The silhouette the fire provides makes you look like the wooden Indian down at the cigar store." She laughed at the thought.

"Shadows play with a person's mind, don't they? Let me tell you about a game my father and I used to play. 'Look,' he would say. 'See the Gray Wolf... there.' He would point and illustrate with his hands, and when my young eyes were convinced I could see the Gray Wolf, my father would start a story. Usually a story to make a point, like 'one must not lie' or 'one must honor their father.' And because the Gray Wolf told me to, I would listen and obey. I learned from those stories and many nights I would lie silently and think of what the Gray Wolf had told me to do."

"That makes my flesh crawl. For a moment I thought I could see the Gray Wolf myself, reflected off the glaze of your eyes. What memories."

He stared into the fire for several minutes before speaking again, and when he did, his voice was harsh and nearly without expression, as though he was reading a prepared text under duress. "I remember when he once told me a long, involved story about a woman who had tried to kill someone that had saved her life. She repaid his kindness by pushing him from a tall cliff when he came to the rescue of his wife."

"She murdered him?"

"He didn't die, although his spine was badly injured."

"No! What a terrible story." She moved closer to him. "I'm not sure I want to hear anymore."

Ignoring her comment, he continued. "The pain from his injuries was so bad sometimes until he wondered if he should continue to live. He couldn't work his mine anymore and was almost useless in the village where he lived. He pleaded with the Shaman to help him find physical or spiritual relief. None came. His mind gradually deteriorated so that he was consumed with grief and a desire for revenge."

"The poor man. The Shaman's medicine didn't help?"

"Nothing helped except for the White Man's poison, which made him senseless at times." Jason waited a moment before continuing the story. "Revenge was an impossibility. He was too weak to travel to find her. But he had a son. A son whose mother this woman had killed. He made his son an instrument of this revenge. He taught him to hate this woman, whom he had never known, and convinced him that she had taken everything from him: his mother's life, his father's happiness, wealth, and livelihood..."

"Please don't tell me that the boy killed the woman."

"The boy was a coward. He didn't do his father's bidding, but the thought of his broken promise consumed his every thought. One night, it is said, he went to sleep as normal, and in the chill of the dawn, with the sun walking up the far side of the world, he began to dream of getting the courage to do what his father had asked. He found himself standing over the woman, with a long knife in his hand, ready to plunge it into her heart."

"Jason, please, don't say any more. I don't want to hear this story... please, take me home."

"No, please... let me finish. It is told that the boy's hand paused at the pinnacle of the thrust and he felt a strong hand grab his arm. He turned to look into the glowing eyes of a second young woman, with long, blond hair falling across her face so that he could see no features except for her burning eyes. 'NO,' she said in a deep voice that belied her femininity. 'NO, thou shalt not kill. There are other ways to honor your father; come with me.' The boy walked beside her as she floated through the air into a large building, where soft organ music calmed his angered spirit. She stopped before the statue of a tall, kindly looking man with a beard and a smile. 'Listen, son, listen to the message, and learn.'"

Juanita mouthed Jesus' name but said nothing aloud. Something was obviously troubling Jason very deeply. She reached forward and patted his hand. "It's okay, really; tell me the rest."

For the first time, he seemed to be aware that she was there and that he was, in his own way, revealing the torment he needed to purge from himself.

Softly and more slowly he said, "The dream continued for years, always the same, but each time the message in the big building was different. As the boy began to understand the messages, the intensity of the woman's red eyes dimmed, and at last she began to take on a benevolent look. The great conflict in the boy's mind had become a skirmish. The boy began to believe the conflict could never be resolved but perhaps something could replace it, something satisfying, so that he would not be seen as the coward that he is."

"Coward? That boy was no coward. He is the strongest man I have ever heard of. How many people would stand up for what they believe is right despite such tremendous outside pressure? Not many.

"I wish I could help him...whoever he might be."

✧

Chapter Twenty-Six

Juanita craned her neck to get one last glance at Jason's wildly waving arm. Puffs of smoke from the train's stack interrupted her view and made it seem as though Jason and Lily, who stood at his side, were bouncing up and down. The train rounded a curve, and the small, receding figures were no more.

"Good-bye, Mr. Gray Wolf," she said softly, oblivious to those around her. A pang of sadness weighed heavy on her. She shook her head to chase it away and spoke openly to Jason, hoping that the wind would carry her message across the miles.

"We'll work on those demons again when I'm back in Santa Fe, Jason."

She stood for several moments at the rear of the private Stillman car, peering through the engine smoke looking to see if she could get a glimpse of Jason's Gray Wolf. There were a few things she wanted to say to that Gray Wolf, and yes, there were an awful lot of questions he needed to answer.

The shrill blast of the train whistle and the rocking motion of the car made any hope of seeing the face impossible. She sheepishly looked at her family to see whether anyone had noticed her actions or heard her words. Only one pair of eyes was focused on her; Dovey's. The focus was benevolent and understanding, not the hard, faraway stare she normally had. There may have even been a slight smile trying to make itself seen.

Juanita gave Dovey a slight nod and sat silently in the seat across the aisle from her father and diagonally facing Dovey. She was intrigued by Dovey's obvious interest in her. It seemed that Dovey's attitude toward her had changed since the night Jason brought her home from the river. Why? What was different? Did it have something to do with Jason? Of course, they were a lot alike, so mysterious, and both given to introspective silence. And there was something else, something she couldn't put her finger on. It was a mystery that she would have to think about. And thinking of mysteries, where did Dovey come from? She'd never heard it mentioned.

She stole a quick glance at Dovey, who was now concentrating on her knitting, and turned back, wondering what would be the best way to initiate a conversation about her past and, perhaps, about Jason.

Dovey stretched her back, flexed her fingers, and broke the silence. "Henry, the best thing you ever did was to buy this private car. I don't think I'd be up to this trip anymore, otherwise."

Her father placed his newspaper on the seat beside him and parted his lips as though to speak but fell into a coughing spell instead. Henry grabbed his heart and bent forward.

Dovey gently held his head between his knees for a moment, patted his back, and shook her head. "Henry, please…"

After a moment, he drew himself up to his normal, dignified position, and Juanita breathed a sigh of relief. "It was a good idea," he said, winking at Juanita, "but hardly the best thing I ever did." He looked at Dovey and smiled. "Because that, Mrs. Stillman, was marrying you. You have made me very happy."

Juanita watched a tinge of red come to Dovey's cheeks and smiled at the affirmation. *She does make him happy. Why can't Isabella understand that?*

After a moment, her father turned to the area behind where they sat. "Isabella, come up here and join us, please. We have things to discuss." Henry reached across the aisle and patted Juanita's hand. "And you, young lady, did you dance the night away?"

Isabella plopped in the seat across from her. "You don't get grass stains on your party dress from dancing. I'm surprised at Dandy Boy."

"Isabella, that's rude and unladylike. Apologize to your sister," Henry said.

"I'll apologize when the moon turns blue."

"Isabella!" Henry's face turned scarlet. Dovey quickly put her knitting to one side and moved to Henry's side.

"That's all right, Henry. It's just a joke between the girls. Juanita doesn't mind, do you, dear?"

"Of course not. I have nothing to be ashamed of. Can I get you some water, daddy?"

He didn't answer, but Dovey nodded. "Please ring for the

porter, too. I think it's time for morning coffee."

It took only a few minutes for the coffee to be served. Dovey took a sip, replaced her cup, and took Henry's hand. "Now, dear, why don't you begin?"

He took a long, thoughtful sip of coffee and turned to face the girls. "I'd like to know what you girls thought of our Santa Fe operations. It's time we stated talking about you two taking a more definitive role in one of our businesses."

Juanita bit her lip. To think of the rationale behind such a suggestion was awful. Her eyes moistened.

Nobody said anything for a moment.

"I'm sorry father. I know you were hoping that one of us would take an interest in the business but it just isn't right for me. I do want to contribute something to help the family but give me a little more time. Okay?" Juanita said.

"It's all right, my little one. You tried hard. Dovey told me of all the extra hours you put in working with Jason." He smiled and Juanita blushed. "What about you Isabella, what have you to say? You know this plan was devised to help you. What would you like to try next?"

"Nothing to do with this damn business and certainly not with Dandy Boy Jason."

"I thought not. Incidentally, I know of your clandestine marriage to Brougham before we left on this trip. Both you and Al defied my wish and humiliated me in my own office."

He looked at Dovey, who nodded, a little uncomfortably then turned and patted Juanita's hand. "It's all right, my little one. Don't blame yourself, and for whatever it may mean to you, I think Jason is a fine young man."

"Fine young man, indeed!" Isabella shouted over the sound of the incessant clicking of the rails and stood facing her father and Dovey. What would you say if I told you that the 'fine young man' tried to get me to join him in a scheme to kill somebody and to steal every blessed thing they had?"

Juanita gasped and watched as the blood left her father's face. He squeezed the seat armrest with his right hand until his knuckles turned white. He reached for Dovey with his left. Before he could reply, Dovey drew her body erect and, with a voice that sounded as hard and cold as a judge at hanging time, said, "I'd say you are a liar or insane!"

Isabella whirled to face Dovey. "Funny, you saying that, the person who has the most to lose from not believing me." She turned on her heel and stalked away to sit at the opposite end of the car.

The story of the Gray Wolf raced through Juanita's mind. What did it all mean? Why would Isabella say such a thing? She turned her gaze from her family toward the high, red sandstone cliffs through which the train was twisting around contours where thousands of Indian ponies had trod in the centuries past. But even the beauty of the cliffs, the cacti, the Joshua trees, and the accent of shadow and brightness could not quell the questions raging through her mind.

"Juanita... Juanita, dear, come sit by me for a moment." Juanita delayed for a moment, dabbed at her eyes, and nearly fell in Dovey's lap as the train lurched around a sharp bend.

"Sorry," Juanita said as she grabbed the hand extended by her father. She then added quickly, as though it were weighing on her mind, "I'm sorry about the dress, too. It wasn't Jason's fault, though."

"That dress is the last thing on my mind, my girl. It's your welfare that concerns me more," Henry said.

Dovey laid her hands on Juanita's. "Your father and I both think highly of Jason. He's a hardworking, intelligent, loyal employee, and the courtesy and respect he shows Lily is commendable. But, we wonder, do you think you have known him long enough to get, well... involved with him?"

Juanita raised her eyebrows, looking first at Dovey, then at her father. "That's just what Jason said. He thought it wasn't right to make commitments when we would be away from each other so long. But I..." She stopped for a moment, then blurted out, "Something's bothering him. Something bad. We have to help him."

"What do you suggest we do, daughter?" Henry asked.

"Do you know where he comes from daddy? He never talks about his parents. Perhaps he's... maybe, he might have been married?"

Henry and Dovey exchanged glances. Juanita raced on. "Maybe someone he knows needs help, and maybe he doesn't have enough money to help them, or maybe - -"

Henry interrupted, saying, "Sometimes, my girl, it is prudent to let sleeping dogs lie."

"Not when you want to hold that dog in your arms and caress him. Not when you know in your heart that the poor thing needs you "

"Not when you love someone," Dovey said. There was kindness in her eyes. "I know the feeling, Juanita."

"You do understand, don't you, Dovey?"

"My darling, Dovey understands love like no one else in this world. If she didn't, would she stay with a tired old man like me or dedicate her life to the child that was taken from her?"

Dovey kissed him on the cheek, wiped a tear from her eye, and said, "Love is always a two-way street, Jua... my daughter."

Juanita's pulse quickened, and a smile came to her face. She knit her eyebrows and let her mind freewheel until Henry's renewed coughing demanded her attention.

Dovey patted Henry on the back again. "Sit still, Henry, and don't let all this weigh on your mind. It's clear that we think alike on this issue. I'll explain our thoughts to Juanita. You rest."

"Yes, father, please."

"Last evening, Henry and I discussed you and Jason a bit. We saw the stars in the eyes of you both as you danced. That's when it occurred to us that we knew virtually nothing about Jason. We had no reason to wonder. He did his job well, was polite to Lily, and everything has always been fine.

"This morning, we spoke to Lily about it. She couldn't add a thing. They've talked plenty, of course, but he always steered the conversation away when it veered toward his past."

Juanita nodded. She'd had the same experience with him many times.

"It seemed strange to us that he had not confided in someone. Now that your actions have confirmed that the sparkle in your eyes is more intense than one night of dancing would demand, we think it's about time we discover what this young man is all about."

Juanita felt the back of her neck heat up and felt a tingle in the pit of her stomach. "I agree. We should, but yet I feel strange about it. It's like, well, spying."

Dovey's eyes brightened. "I think I understand your concern. Sometimes moonlight loosens a young man's tongue. Did he tell you anything that you would like to share?"

Juanita thought for a moment. "Not much. He speaks often about the East but not about specific places. Which is strange because he has such unusually broad knowledge of the plants and animals you find around here. He knows every bird, for example, and can mimic them as well as anyone I've ever heard. Imagine."

"That's not so strange. Maybe nature is a hobby."

"Maybe. He's a confusing person in many ways."

Dovey leaned forward and asked, "How so?"

"It's hard to explain. For example, he told me a strange story about a dream of a Gray Wolf. I wish I had paid more attention in my psychology courses, but what I got out of his story was a feeling that he was tormented by the difference between right and wrong under varying circumstances.

"He alluded to beliefs he was taught in early life that are being challenged by a recent discovery of Christianity. It's like he's tormented by something. Not something simple like, is it right or wrong to lie? It's more like..." Juanita drew in her breath as Isabella's earlier words screamed at her: *"to kill someone."* Juanita was silent.

"I believe I understand you, child," Dovey said. "We'll rout out the real Mr. Jason, don't you worry."

Dovey sat back and looked at Henry, who until then had only listened and nodded in agreement from time to time. "You'll find the young man as clean as driven snow, don't worry. But do your investigation promptly. I want some grandchildren." Henry raised his voice. "And it doesn't look like anyone else around here is going to produce one."

Isabella stalked back to confront Henry. "If Mrs. Stillman," Isabella paused to let the full effects of her sarcasm penetrate, "would produce that fictitious son of hers, you'd have a grandson, wouldn't you, old man? Then 'Lady Dovey' would have her claws deeper in you, and you could justify giving me even less of what I deserve."

Isabella's high-pitched, loud laugh sent shivers down Juanita's spine. She thought of her sister's hateful words on that day by the river. Isabella was capable of anything. My lord, she would have to watch her very carefully.

"For your information, Isabella, Jerry is a real person. Our agents are close to finding him, we believe. They'll do the same with Jason. So if you want to protect 'your money,' you and that husband of yours, Mr. Aloysius G. Brougham, better get busy, or is he a 'Dandy Boy' himself?" Henry said. His hands twitched, and his breathing accelerated.

"Damn you all! Go ahead, find 'Glory Boy' if you can, but don't be surprised if you find him one morning at his mother's feet with his throat cut or a bullet through his head; crazy women do strange things, don't they - *mother?*"

Chapter Twenty-Seven

*T*ime was the enemy now.

Despite the pledges made on the train, frequent visits to Santa Fe by Juanita, and Henry's continuing interest in a grandchild, the year following the trip produced nothing but weariness and grief. Henry's health deteriorated, and as it did, concern and despair took a toll on Dovey and Juanita. The only constant was Isabella's insolence and erratic behavior, which was causing everyone increasing concern. There was no way for anyone to know what was lurking in Isabella's mind.

A second autumn gave way to the harshness of winter, and the desert seemed as bleak as Henry's mood. The frustration of the unhappy household wore on Dovey's nerves, and as the mountain snow melted with the warmth of a new spring, the desert bloomed with the suddenness of thunder across the Kansas plains of her yesteryear. Riding out among the acres of cacti topped by flaming red and yellow flowers was her only relief. The rides made her forget, at least temporarily, the torment of the months following the upsetting train ride back from Santa Fe.

On a cool, cloudless morning following a difficult night with Isabella, it was two and a half hours before Dovey reined in Checkers Number Two, tossed the reins to the stable-boy, beat the dust from her denim riding pants, and patted the horse's nose. "Thank you, old girl. It was good, wasn't it?"

A grin appeared on the groom's face.

"Have to talk to someone, Jose. El Patron doesn't ride with me anymore."

"Si, Senora."

She never knew, for sure, whether Jose understood her. Trying to wrap her tongue around Spanish words was too tiresome sometimes.

She stopped in the scullery, removed her shirt, and washed the dust from her neck, arms, and face. She was no longer embarrassed to show her crooked left arm, as she once had been. It was Angela's turn to smile.

Dovey chuckled. "Don't say it. I know it by heart. 'Senora, this place is for pots and pans. Wash your pretty face in your beautiful bathroom with all the mirrors and pretty pictures.' Right?"

Angela pretended to pout, but her dancing eyes gave her away.

Dovey squeezed up against her large, soft bosom and held her tightly. "Don't worry; I love you, Angela. I didn't mess up your scullery too badly, did I? Oh, has El Patron had breakfast?"

Angela frowned. "Si, his kind of breakfast."

Dovey grimaced. Angela's words stabbed at her heart. Oh, God, how could she keep him from killing himself? The thought thundered through Dovey's mind. She was barely aware that Angela was saying something else.

"What? Pardon me. I was, er… thinking of something I need to do. You said?"

"Can I fix you some breakfast, Senora?"

"Huevos Rancheros con salsa y tortilla, por dos personas. Donde es El Patron?"

"En el patio del sud."

Angela normally laughed at Dovey's broad pronunciation, but not this time; she seemed to understand the seriousness of Dovey's order for two. "Maybe some of the small, veal sausages, too, Senora?"

"Good idea. You know what the old man likes, don't you?"

Before walking onto the patio, she stepped in front of the mirror on the wall across from the powder room and admired the hammered silver frame. She brushed her hand across Henry's gift. She had to help him.

She loosened the yellow ribbon holding her hair in place, shook her head so that her hair was fluffy as Henry preferred, and loosely retied the ribbon. She rechecked her clothing for dust, practiced her best smile, and stepped forward. "Good morning, darling." She kissed him on the forehead. The strong smell of brandy confirmed Angela's implication.

"Your cheeks look flushed. It must have been warm for your ride this morning."

"Not bad. I went early but took the long way back, through the citrus groves. How beautiful the trees are... maybe tomorrow morning we could ride out there together."

"Maybe."

"Come sit in the swing with me, Henry. I feel happy and young today. I need you beside me." Dovey took both his hands and tugged slightly.

"Easy, dear. That ride back from Santa Fe yesterday has me sore all over."

"Then don't do it anymore. Quit. Lord knows, between us, we've got plenty of money. Why, this ranch alone is worth millions. Don't you think it's about time to retire?"

He frowned and shook his head. "There are some things we haven't talked about for a while, Dovey. You seem so content running the ranch I haven't wanted to bother you with other business details."

"Oh?" She could hear the apprehension in his voice.

"Since when did we start holding things back from each other?"

"Hand me my glass, please."

"You know how I feel about brandy before breakfast."

"Don't..."

"I know... I'm not going to growl at you. Your liver will do that. But, I *am* going to insist that you have breakfast with me. I'm as tired of eating alone as you are of traveling. Deal?"

She forced a smile, kissed his forehead and helped him from his chair. "I asked Angela to serve on the east patio. The sun's up high enough not to be a nuisance, and if there's anything that will loosen your tongue, it's the view across the valley toward the Catalinas. Come."

She watched him pick at his meal in silence. The veal sausages were the only things he finished.

Bless Angela.

"Did Lily like the doilies I crocheted for her?"

"First thing I did was to give them to her. You should have seen her face light up. If her smile was an indication, she loved them. I brought a small parcel from her and a letter. I'll get it."

"Not just yet, darling."

"I'll not go near the brandy bottle. I'll get it." No one was going to tell Henry Stillman what to do, that was clear, not even if it meant saving his life.

She cringed at the thought. The shadow of loneliness crept across her soul and the old feeling of bitterness that followed Scotty's desertion and Snooze's death wrenched at her guts.

She did not open the package he placed on the table. No one was going to tell Dovey MacPherson what to do, either.

"You said Lily was well?"

"Yes, but like me, she's worn out. She's worked hard to build the Mercantile into a big business. Of all our businesses, it's probably the biggest revenue producer. Its return on equity is over thirty percent. Can you imagine that?"

"She has always been a doer. I know she's clever, too. She taught me so well. You have never seen anyone get more pleasure out of anything than when I caught old Josh cheating."

"The war years are what damn near killed her," Henry said.

"Why doesn't she get some help?"

"She's tried. No one seems to meet her standards. She chases them away almost as soon as they start and puts in fifteen and sixteen hours herself."

"We can't allow that, Henry."

"If you can figure a way to stop her, you're better than I am. But there is some hope. Jason continues to learn rapidly and does more and more for her. In fact, he's so good with accounting Lily intends to let him do it all, including the banking."

"That will take a big load off her shoulders."

Jason. The name always seemed to pique curiosity in Dovey's mind. A year of background checks had still not produced a thing. She thought about his comment to Lily, 'I don't want to talk about my childhood; it's too sad.' Oh, well...

But, on the few occasions when they worked together, Dovey had always felt strange, as if he were watching her carefully and not liking what he saw. He never smiled at her, never spoke unless spoken to. The truth was that he really made her uncomfortable. No wonder she worried about not knowing more about him.

She shook her head, as though trying to chase away those thoughts, and looked up at Henry. There seemed to be sadness in his eyes.

"Look, Dovey, before we go on with the rest, I need to tell you a bit of bad news." Henry coughed, patted Dovey's hand, and said, "Hatti died about a month ago."

"Hatti is dead? Why didn't someone tell me?"

"She was away on a trip to San Francisco. Nobody knew until three days ago. Lily told me that her letter to you explains what happened." Another wonderful person... gone. Not you too, Henry.

Dovey put her forehead in her hands. Ice water seemed to replace the blood in her veins. She would never be able to change things. It's the way God meant it to be, she guessed. She stared out across the ranch entrance road with its Ocotillo hedge and admired the orange flowers sprinkled along the graceful limbs of the bushes.

"Look, Henry. Watch that cactus wren fly right into its nest in the Saguaro. Isn't that marvelous? Hatti would have been thrilled to see that." Why hadn't she brought Hatti here to see the ranch?

Hatti's life meant something to her. She would not let her death destroy the memories. Perhaps she could reproduce Hatti's flower patch and perpetuate the significance that small patch of beauty had on her life. She thought of Hatti's kindness and her clever way of distracting her from her troubles. She'd do it, and she would place a statue of an angel at the entrance.

Dovey looked across the table at Henry's watering eyes, bent shoulders, and quivering right hand.

Old man, who knows how much time you have left? We'll learn from Hatti's passing and not wait until it's too late. We're going to build on our memories, now.

"Angela, Angela! Pack a picnic lunch for two, por favor. Send to the stable and tell them to harness Ross and Rover and to hitch them to the old Brougham."

"Come on, Henry. We've got some living to do."

Chapter Twenty-Eight

*T*he water on the lake was still. The shadow of a small bass swiveled along just below the surface. The pungent aroma from the dried grass on the hills dominated. Not even a small bird disturbed the silence.

"When I was a child, Henry, our family had a pond, smaller than this. I used to love to take my shoes off and wade along the shore and skip rocks across the surface." She slipped out of her shoes, untied Henry's laces and pulled.

"So, the stodgy, old Henry Stillwell can laugh. I didn't think it was possible."

"That slime on the lake bottom would make anybody laugh. It tickled my feet. But, what about the bitter Miss Dovey? You aren't exactly the epitome of the laughing woman now, are you?"

She studied his face. Harsh lines were already replacing the laughter lines. "Something else is on your mind, Henry. No one else died, I hope."

Every sinew in his body tensed up. His eyes clouded over as though near tears. His silence worried her.

"Roll over, Henry, on these buggy cushions. I'll massage your back. Sleep if you want to. We'll talk later."

She began the gentle work of kneading his knotted muscles with her fingers and sang softly to him.

Suddenly, a torrent of words erupted from his mouth. Lying on his stomach seemed, in some way, to accentuate the high pitch of his speech.

"Did I hear you right?" Dovey said when he had finished. "We're broke? How can that be?"

"I didn't say 'broke.' Only that we're in deep financial difficulty. We will be broke, though if things don't break just right for us. We're over leveraged."

"Whoa, there. Back up and go over that again."

"Remember the war years; we kept buying every mining

property that came on the market. Greed had us in its fist. Sure the copper price exploded for a while. We did well. But now demand is lagging, and the increasing cost of hauling ore to concentrators has put us in a squeeze."

"Go on," Dovey said.

"Our margin right now is essentially zero. When we service the debt, we're running at a loss. Our capital reserves are being eaten away. And the damn unions won't give us a break. Operating costs are going up steadily, and productivity is going down."

"So why not sell some of the less efficient properties, pay off some of the debt, and wait for a sunnier climate?"

"Nobody wants a copper mine just now. There's too much production from Africa, Peru, and Chile, where the labor costs are unbelievably low. Even the bank doesn't want to take a defunct mine. They would rather restructure the debt."

He rolled over and looked at her in the eye for the first time since the conversation started. She smiled at him, took his hands in hers, and squeezed. "Henry, I'm glad it's only money you're worried about. Hell, we can fix that some way. We'll stew on it for a while. Remember, old Snooze taught me a few tricks; maybe we'll have to use one of them."

"Things are a bit more sophisticated these days, Dovey."

"Maybe, but we'll come up with something. Don't worry. Come on. Help me load this stuff in the buggy. We'll cogitate on the way home, or do you want to go wading again?"

Henry grinned. "Another time, love."

The buggy reached the crest of the hill forming the western side of the lake, and Henry pulled up the horses.

"You're a devil, Dovey Stillman. You knew if you got me up here, where I could see our spread, I would get a different perspective. But it is beautiful, isn't it? God, I'm glad it's in your name."

He put his arm around her, pulled her to him. "What more could a man want; a beautiful woman by his side, acres and acres of pasture and farmland, and a castle to come home to?"

"A little more water wouldn't hurt. That new grapefruit grove I had planted over theeeerrr..." Dovey let the word extend for emphasis as she gestured to the south, "is having a tough time."

"Henry, I've got an idea I'd like to run past you after I have a tub. I'll meet you and the brandy bottle on the western patio in an hour. We'll watch the sun go down, together, like we used to."

The sun put on an awesome display for them. The reds and oranges seemed to be doing battle to see which could be the more expressive.

"Ah, see that?" Henry said. "A cloud. The mistress asks, and the gods provide."

Dovey thought about her thirsty grapefruit and sighed, "If I had a dollar for every Arizona cloud without water, our worries would be over."

"Back to that, is it?"

"Yes, back to that. I see you took me at my word." Dovey motioned to the brandy bottle. "Pour one for me, too; a big one."

"That's a surprise," Henry said.

"Might as well travel the road together. Who knows, maybe the reaper will come for us both at the same time. I'd like that. I don't want to be left alone again."

"So, tell me," Henry asked, once she had her glass, "What's this idea of yours?"

"Well..." She took a long sip of the amber liquid before answering. "You said we were nearly broke. The way I read it, we're just cash poor, right?"

"That's only semantics, Dovey. Call it what you like, but the fact is we don't have enough money to service debt, and soon we might not be able to meet payroll."

"Put like that the situation sounds serious." Dovey squinted, tapped her forefinger across her lips for a moment, took another sip and then nodded. "Hmmm. Out of all our businesses which has the most potential for future profits?"

"I've never made such a comparison. Time has to be put into that equation. Are you talking ten, twenty, a hundred years, maybe?"

"Let's just say within the likely time span of our family."

He drained his glass, stared at her for a moment. "The copper business probably, but not without lots of headaches along the way."

"I would have thought you would have said the ranches. With the firm hold we have on the water rights and the towns growing like weeds all around both of them. That land is going to be worth hundreds of dollars, maybe thousands, an acre, one day, and think how little we paid for it."

"Your point illustrates the difference between you and me, Dovey."

"Isn't it great there is a difference?" Dovey said, running her hand down Henry's thigh.

Henry shuddered. "No, Dovey, I'm serious. You've demonstrated patience and determination, over and over, as you've searched for your son all these years. You would be happy and content to sit on that land, farm it, nurture it, and accept the small return you could earn while waiting for the big payday. Wouldn't you?"

"And you?"

"I have to have action. The infighting and competitive attitudes of the business world challenge every part of me. But lately the crookedness that sometimes occurs in the business world, the unions, it's all tearing me apart. How much more my heart, stomach, and brain can stand I don't know. Yet, I feed on it. It's better than a shot of brandy. I must stay with the copper business."

"Wouldn't running the ranch be enough challenge for you?"

"It's a different world, Dovey."

"Well I don't want you to quit and wind up like Snooze." She brushed back his silver hair and smiled despite her thoughts. She could see him slipping, aging right before her eyes it seemed sometimes. Better for him to go happy. "I guess it's settled then. We'll do whatever we must to keep the copper business alive and hopefully profitable."

"Then there's something you should probably know." He looked away and sighed. "I haven't told anyone about this yet, except the investigators I have working on the situation, because it's personal. If the information the internal auditors have turned up is true, we're being robbed by our own family."

"You know who it is?"

The color in Henry's face lightened, his pupils dilated, he hesitated. "I want to be absolutely sure. That's why I have private investigators working on the problem. When and if we make an accusation, I want it backed up with facts, and I want to know we have the entire problem under control. I don't want a Titanic situation."

"You suspect the son-in-law, Al, don't you?"

"Yes, but I don't believe Isabella is cooperating with her husband. But, who knows?" He bowed his head and stared out into the fading light.

She left him with his private thoughts for a moment. It wasn't hard for her to imagine the pain and anguish he must be feeling. Some people just weren't meant to have families or that type of happiness. Thank God she and Henry had been able to create their own brand of peace and tranquility even if it hadn't been the classic emotional romance the new "Flicks" were showing.

She cleared her throat, brushed at her nose, and cried inwardly for her man... *He wouldn't.*

"What should we do, Dovey?" His voice was barely audible.

"We should raise every nickel we can, pay off as much debt as we can, and restructure the rest."

"I agree. But, raising cash isn't that easy."

"It will be if we sell the businesses that are good cash cows, such as the Mercantile and the freight business. We have bargaining leverage there."

"Those are your businesses, Dovey. I can't touch those."

"I can, and by guppy I will. And another thing, I'll mortgage the ranch I bought in Mesa. People will jump in line to loan us money on that."

"It's too big a risk, Dovey. I can't let you."

"Try and stop me." She looked at him with an expression that left no doubt about how serious she was.

"Fine," he said finally. "But, under no circumstances will I borrow one cent on this place. I'd turn in my grave if I knew this place was exposed and that you, Angela, Jose, and the others didn't have a roof over your heads."

"How about the Mercantile and the freight business?"

"Sell them. Hell, they're the only significant cash producers, but I can't argue with you... Sell," Henry said, "On one condition."

"Which is?"

"We must provide complete security for Lily and insist that the new owners retain the existing employees... except for Jason."

"Why? Mysterious he might be, but he's done nothing

except good for us."

He threw back another glass of brandy, stroked his chin for a moment, and then broke into the first smile since he waded in the water.

"You're a devil, Henry. I see those eyes twinkling like polished diamonds. What's in that devious mind of yours?"

"That's just it. He's a real comer and as much a number hound as you are. I'd bet anything he'd jump at the chance to help us with our problems."

"You mean by exposing the traitor?"

Henry nodded.

"Sounds good. But, isn't the minerals business specialized enough so that Jason might have difficulty discovering what we need? We could be completely ruined while he's still learning."

"Look what you did. You could hardly read and had no mathematical experience. You did what you needed to do."

"I had to. My friends were depending on me."

"Well, we'll give him a power-packed indoctrination and support him with some good and trustworthy people. He can do it."

"We do have an easy way to ease him in. Call it a reward for being a loyal employee at the Mercantile. We'll bring Lily down here and introduce them both at the same time so that he isn't singled out. I'll stage a dinner party and invite all the family," Dovey said. "Maybe I'll wear my flowered dress Hatti brought me from the islands."

"You love to tease me about the dress that I first saw you in, don't you?"

Dovey grinned.

"Well, don't forget your boots. That'll distract attention away from Jason."

"Come with me, Henry Stillman. I'll teach you about distraction."

✧

Chapter Twenty-Nine

*D*ovey pulled back the white, cotton paneling between the velvet drapes framing the windows in the great room and gasped. "Henry, you've got to see this; it's beautiful."

He turned in his chair and looked briefly at the light dusting of snow covering the landscape. "Probably be gone in the morning," he said and turned back to stare at the fire.

His indifference, which seemed to Dovey to be commonplace these days, didn't diffuse the excitement she felt at the surprise snowfall. "Oh, I could look at this forever!" She put her arm around Henry and squeezed. "Sometimes I miss the clean, soft snow we had in Santa Fe. I always thought of it as a cozy blanket for Hatti's little flower garden. Every winter I stand, searching the Arizona sky for just a glimpse of the same freshness, but all I ever see is the cap on the mountains."

Henry continued to silently stare into the crackling flames of the giant fireplace, which fit the mammoth room. The shadows from the flickering fire emphasized every crease in his face. The dark lines under his eyes looked more dramatic than normal. The bony hand lifting the brandy glass to his dark lips shook. Small drips of brandy fell to a spotted shirt. How uncharacteristic of her darling.

A knock on the door brought the sad moment to an end. They looked up to see Jason, a solemn look on his face, being ushered in by the night man.

Dovey watched his face as she greeted him warmly. As usual, Jason seemed guarded and tense, refusing to make eye contact with her.

Henry remained sitting. "Good evening, Jason. Would you join me in a brandy?"

"No, thank you, sir."

"You have the report?"

"Yes, sir."

"Read it aloud, please."

"The report is in two parts, sir. There is an executive summary followed by a detailed report with an appendix containing an exhaustive amount of backup material. What would you like to hear first?"

"Is there any doubt whatsoever that your backup material gives a fair and unbiased justification for your conclusions?" Henry asked.

"No, sir."

"Then read the summary."

Jason read, "In conclusion, the facts clearly demonstrate that Aloysius G. Brougham, Executive Vice President and Chief Executive Officer, and Zack Karras, Sr., Vice President and Chief Operating Officer, did, with intent, defraud the El Grande Mining Company of the amounts stated."

Dovey could read nothing from Henry's face. From the moment Jason had begun reading, his face had been like a death mask. His eyes stared at the fire, but she felt sure that he was looking beyond the fire, beyond tonight, into the future, contemplating the action he must take. She had hoped that Al wouldn't be proven to be a part of the deception, not his own daughter's husband. GOD!

Jason and Dovey glanced at each other, both waiting for Henry to react. Henry's hands were folded together in his lap. He looked as though he were in a trance. Dovey patted his hands.

"I'm sorry, darling," she said.

Henry jerked his head up, gave a quizzical look at Dovey and sighed. "Jason, I must ask you again. Are you absolutely positive of your numbers and of your findings?"

"Sir, I knew that Mr. Brougham was a family member. I took every precaution. I had competent people helping me throughout the eighteen months' work. I stand by my numbers."

"But, Jason, how could they possibly steal as much as they did without getting caught?" Dovey asked.

"To put it simply, they set up a dummy company to invoice for nonexistent material. One of the men cleared the invoices and authorized checks to be paid to the bogus company. The second one signed the checks." Jason shrugged his shoulders.

"Thank you, Jason. That will be all," Henry said.

At the entrance door, Dovey offered her hand.

"Thank you, Jason. I know that preparing and reading that report was a difficult thing for you to do. You did well, and I'm grateful."

"Goodnight, madam."

Would she ever get through to this young man?

"We must talk, Dovey," Henry said.

"Put your boots on. We'll talk as we walk. The fresh air and the beauty of the night might help us chase away the demons that are hounding us."

"Not tonight."

"Put those boots on... if you want to talk to me."

The nip of the late winter air made Dovey's face tingle. She inhaled the glory of the fresh desert air. Even the snow couldn't take away the acrid aroma she had come to love.

"I believe the moon is going to cooperate, Henry. Let's walk around the abutment and see if the snow has made snowmen out of the saguaros."

A coyote howled. The sound seemed to carry forever in the stillness of the night. Dovey stopped, took Henry's hand in hers, and thrilled at the sound. An answer came, and another. The birds seemed to be excited by the calls, and for a few minutes the desert was alive with the symphony that can only be played in such a natural place.

The beauty of the scene cracked Henry's hardened facade.

"Dovey, do you remember that spalled-out alcove on the other side of the abutment?"

"You mean the place we camped near while the house was being built?"

He nodded, A hint of a smile showing on his moonlit face.

"Well, I remember lying in your arms, next to the fire, listening to the sounds of the night, feeling like the luckiest girl in the world," Dovey said.

His hand slipped from hers, and his arm went around her shoulders. "You were so light in my arms, I felt like Samson. Your body was soft, tender... the golden moonlight and the reflection of the fire made your skin glow like soft satin. Sometimes I think that was the most perfect night ever. I didn't want it to end."

"We've had many wonderful nights like that. We'll have

more."

"I hope you're right." Henry paused. "First, there's this... this thing we have to deal with. Let's go sit in the alcove."

"Got any matches?"

Henry got a small fire going, stumbled backward, and sat down hard.

"Darling, are you all right?" She kissed him.

"Now I am." He kissed her back.

Dovey poked at the fire.

"You know, Henry, I could see your wheels turning all night. You knew what Jason was going to report even before he arrived. What decision have you made?"

"I haven't. This damn depression the country is facing is the worst ever. It has me terribly worried. And if that weren't bad enough... can I afford to fire the only people in the organization that have the experience and knowledge to keep the operation running? Can we carry on with a rudderless ship? Or is it smarter to let them keep running it and allow them to skim off what they can? That way, at least, the company can keep going. We'll make some money, and those that depend on us will keep their jobs."

"Henry, you know the answer to that question."

"All right, damn it, I'll fire them. To hell with the company and the family! I'll be destroying what little cohesion there is in the family, but at least we'll have Juanita's support."

"The other way you'll be destroying yourself. I prefer to destroy them rather than you. Besides there isn't a person in the world that can run the organization better than you."

"Not anymore, Dovey. I'm over the hill. Tired, worn out, done for. I can't take it on. I remain president in name only. If I could have made up my mind which of those bastards could have run the company, I would have resigned long ago."

"There's another way, Henry."

"Go ahead."

"We'll fire those two, have the board name you chairman. You can still have a passive role; but the outside world will see you as the leader, and the stock price won't suffer. In my nine years on the board, I have picked up the fundamentals of the operation. Lily and I once ran a pretty good show on our own, you may remember."

"I see. You would be president. Lily would be your executive, and you would call on me for consultation."

"That's the general idea. I would want to go outside, though, and hire the best mining engineer and/or metallurgist I could find to take care of technical and operational problems. Depending on who we found, we may make him Chief Operating Officer," Dovey said.

"I think you're overlooking one important player who has the potential for making a great contribution."

"You're thinking of Jason, aren't you?" When she said his name, she felt her face flush. Why did she have these foolish reactions to Jason? She must stop that, this minute.

"Yes, Jason, but I think we need to get him out in the field. We'll work out a plan so that he can get familiar with all the operations, get his hands dirty, and learn the reality of life on a mine."

"That's necessary, I guess, but I hate for it to happen. It'll break Juanita's heart for Jason to leave."

"Can't be helped. Besides, if there is any substance to their relationship, they'll work it out."

"Well, it isn't every day an old woman gets to play Cupid. I'm going to talk Juanita into taking a job also," Dovey said.

"Doing what?"

"I don't know yet, but it's going to mean that she has to travel to the same mines on which Jason will be working."

He actually laughed. "Dovey, that poor boy doesn't stand a chance. With two of you plotting against him, he's done for." He paused for several seconds and stared into the fire, which was beginning to gray out along the edges.

"You know, I believe the arrangement you suggest is a good one, but I think we need to intensify our background search. Before we do anything more to support their romance, we should be sure of whom we are supporting. It would kill Juanita if Jason turned out like that damn Al Brougham, a crook, or worse."

She nodded. 'Or worse.' Those two words froze the blood in her veins. Isabella's menacing threats delivered on the train stabbed at her heart. Could there be a conspiracy? Was the problem more involved than they believed? Did Jason bias the report to remove suspicion from himself? Oh God, no, please! She had. .

almost convinced herself that Jason was, well. . . Dovey felt dizzy, gasped, and steadied herself against the rock face of the alcove, breathing deeply. Get a hold of yourself woman! Hysterics won't solve the problem.

She regained control. He was still lost with his thoughts. "How about the board? How will they react to such a plan?" she asked.

"Not likely to be a problem. Besides us, we only need one more vote because those two thieves will be fired by executive order before the board meeting. I'll get an injunction to tie up their stock until they are criminally prosecuted.

Two days later, Dovey was sitting at the boardroom table, listening once again to Jason's report. This time he read the long version. Every detail of the scam was discussed thoroughly, each one a blow to Henry's esteem and confidence, she knew. But, he sat tall and almost looked relaxed as he fielded the barrage of questions.

"How could this have happened? Surely someone should have picked up on this. What the hell were the auditors doing, sleeping?" When the hubbub died down, the oldest board member stood and cleared his throat.

"Henry, are you sure the facts in this report are correct? The last thing this company needs is a libel suit."

"Would I have called this meeting if I had not investigated thoroughly? Is that the kind of leadership you've come to expect of me?" The tone of his words was bitter, and the last several words were more a shout.

Dovey took one look at the anger in Henry's face and interceded. "Henry has spoken to both men individually. They've admitted their guilt. They've been relieved from duty, and their stock has been placed in escrow until the board decides whether we should pursue criminal charges. Any other questions?" Dovey asked.

"Only the obvious," another director said. "How in hell are we going to run the company with the two principal operating officers no longer available?"

"That, gentlemen, is the primary reason for this meeting," Henry said with a much calmer voice. "Jason will distribute to you another folder containing a suggested reorganization plan. Please review the plan, interview any of the suggested participants you wish, make recommendations for filling the technical position we discuss and suggest any alternative plans that appeal to you. We'll meet again one week from today at seven-thirty A.M., here in the boardroom. In the interim, we will operate in accordance with the plan."

Dovey watched him scan the room, eyes hard as though daring a confrontational comment. None came.

"Meeting is adjourned." He snapped his portfolio closed and strode from the room.

Dovey found Henry standing with his back to the door in front of the large plate glass window overlooking a downtown street. So many people had recently jumped to their deaths in some of the larger cities, as the Great Depression raged onward. That thought grabbed at Dovey. She froze and stared for a moment to try to interpret Henry's intent. She knew that whatever his intent, he was hurting inside. The question of how to help him alleviate the pain transcended her fear. She forced a smile. "There you are. I was afraid you had already gone to visit one of the plants."

"No, not today. Today is for thinking."

"Well, you've earned a day of peace. The tact and dignity with which you handled a horrible situation made me very proud of you."

"It was the hardest thing I've ever done. When I walked into that boardroom, my knees were shaking. I looked down the table, saw you and your Mona Lisa smile and I knew - -" Henry swallowed hard and Dovey thought she saw a glaze of mist in his eyes.

"Let's move on. It's over. Forget it," she said.

"It's not over yet. Any minute I expect Isabella to come crashing through that door. I would like to deal with her alone, if you don't mind. Then I'll come to the ranch. I know the water's too cold to go wading, but the lake wouldn't be a bad place to do a bit of soul-searching."

Henry's premonition was correct. Isabella nearly knocked Dovey over as she turned toward the glass double doors leading from the elevator lobby to the entrance of the Stillman Company offices.

"You bitch! You did it, didn't you?" Isabella's tone was soft but icy, her face rigid, as hard as the marble floor under her feet. "You found a way to discredit Al and me. That's a slick way to steal my inheritance. Damn you!"

Dovey only stared into her hate-filled face, longing to express feelings she had kept to herself too long, but Henry had said he wanted to deal with her. She stepped to the side. Isabella blocked her way and slowly lifted her brass-knobbed parasol above her head. The elevator bell caused Isabella to jerk her head to the left before she could bring the crushing blow down on Dovey. As the doors slid open, Juanita shouted an alarm and ran to place her arms around Dovey.

"Isabella, are you crazy? What's the matter with you?"

"Crazy! Crazy? You little slut, you're the one that's crazy. All you can think of is fucking that big stud of yours. Well, when he steals the rest of the money, you'll wish I had bashed some sense into the old woman's head."

Henry responded to the commotion. "Isabella! Get in here. I have things to say to you. I know there's no use to demand an apology."

"You're full of jokes aren't you, old man. I'll come. I have a few things to say to you, also. First I have one more thing to say to *Mother dear.* Look behind every tree, old woman. At night, when you stand at the window brushing that straggly hair of yours, wonder: Is that shadow out behind the saguaro your son, who probably hates you for deserting him, or Jason, or your dear, darling daughter Isabella? I hope, as the sound of the rifle shot ricochets off the mountains, your last thought will be: Which one was lucky enough to have the honor of ridding the world of your venom."

Dovey watched Juanita's catlike movement and saw her handprint turn Isabella's cheek red.

Isabella ran her fingers over the spot and glared first at Dovey and then at Juanita. "Maybe there'll be two shots," Isabella said and spun on her heel.

Dovey watched Henry's face twist into a mask of terror. She quickly reached out to him. He gasped, grabbed his chest, and slowly slumped against the wall and onto the hard marble floor.

Chapter Thirty

A simple granite cross, on the hillside overlooking the ranch, marked the site where Henry rested. Soft, billowing, cumulus clouds dotted the far western horizon; appropriate on this day, as an accent to the panorama that Henry loved best.

The rest of the funeral entourage had left for the ranch house at Dovey's request, except for Jason. To her surprise, he stayed and stood respectfully to the side while she said her farewell words to Henry. When, at last, she laid a chrysanthemum across the loose earth, Jason approached, placed his coat around her trembling body, and held it in place with his strong arm.

It was the first time she could remember that he had ever touched her, other than a casual handshake.

"Amazing, isn't it?" she said. "Henry was such a knowledgeable man, yet he never learned the names of flowers. They were all chrysanthemums to him." She smiled and looked up at Jason. "Isn't it odd how relevant small things seem sometimes? Our years together were full of little things that meant so much to us."

Jason nodded.

"You understand, don't you, Jason?"

"I understand that you loved your husband with a deep love that put him first in your mind and action."

"The girls would have expected me to place an extravagant bouquet of roses, I guess."

"They have different ideas, I'm sure."

"You bet they do. Of course, Juanita is different, but today even she seems distant.

"Did you see their reaction to my flowery dress and cowboy boots? They expected me to be swathed in black, like them."

"That's customary. I'm sure you had a good reason for your, er... costume."

"There's no disrespect intended, Jason, if that's what you

mean. Henry would have approved. We both knew the significance this outfit had for both of us."

Tears flowed down Dovey's cheek, even as she laughed. "Jason, if it weren't for this *costume*, my name would probably still be MacPherson."

Jason had turned and taken a few steps toward the car when he heard the word. "MacPherson," he repeated; the tone of his voice was hard.

He looked over the hillside, and the shadows of the clouds dancing over the rocky surface painted a vision of his father's twisted body as clear as a portrait. He gulped. At least he had an image, awful as it was. For his mother, he had none. This woman had stolen that from him. The vision erased his memory of the logical promises he had made to himself. He reacted. Good sense deserted him. She was in a perfect place to be thrown, where she would bounce off the rocks, to lie, until the buzzards picked her eyes. He stepped quickly toward her with hands partially raised. Loose gravel betrayed his otherwise silent step.

Her body went rigid. She gasped.

"Jason, what's the matter? Your face…"

He stopped and looked at her. The sadness was gone from her face, replaced by wide eyes and skin stretched by fear. A wave of guilt washed over him. She was a kind woman, regardless of her past. And now she was alone.

"I didn't mean to frighten you. For a moment, I thought I heard something in the bush. I ran back to check and tripped on the loose gravel. My clumsiness made me angry. I guess it showed. Gee, I'm sorry I startled you."

She explored Jason's countenance; his hands were trembling, and his eyes were blazing. Her instinct told her, that there was more to this than he was letting on. What is it?

She recalled Isabella's accusations and continued threats. Are those two working together? Should she confront Jason now, have it over once and for all? Should she? No. Today is Henry's day. Her day would come.

"Let's go, then. We shouldn't keep people waiting. I know Isabella is dying to get a look at Henry's will."

The ride down the hill passed in silence.

Dovey ignored the staring eyes when her boots clomped across the hardwood floor. The sumptuous spread on the buffet table was of no interest. She marched to her chair in the lounge.

"Mr. McCracken, please take Henry's chair." She motioned to the chair on her left. "You may begin reading the will as soon as Jason arrives. He's seeing to the motorcar." Dovey brushed away the glass of brandy offered to her by Angela.

"Take seats, please," McCracken said. "I realize this is a time of sorrow for all; please accept my profound condolences. I apologize for intruding on your grief so soon after the burial, but it's the way Henry wanted it. 'Get it over with, man,' he told me. 'I don't want people mooning about. As soon as the last shovel of dirt is placed on me, read the damn will.'

"I'll try to get through this as rapidly as I can. In the interest of expediency, I ask that you hold any questions until after I finish. Thank you."

Murmurs went around the table. Isabella looked straight at McCracken, almost as in a trance. The intensity of her gaze made Dovey shudder.

"As always, Henry Stillman was definitive in what he wanted. As you'll see in a moment, he had a specific way he wished to make his points. I assure you of the legality of the method chosen. There is confirming backup for filing with the Probate Court."

"Please, Mr. McCracken, just proceed," Dovey said.

"Henry had a phonograph record made, Mrs. Stillman. I would like permission to play it."

"If it is germane to the will, do so."

McCracken lowered the arm of the phonograph he had set up in the corner of the room. A few seconds of static introduced Henry's unmistakable, nervous cough:

"Now don't expect a serenade by Rudy Valle." Henry's scratchy voice rattled with laughter.

"You'll permit the dead one little joke, won't you? I didn't have occasion to laugh much when I was alive, except when Dovey and I were alone sometimes.

"Here's the way it's going to be:

"Title to everything I own becomes the sole and unequivocal property of my darling wife, Dovey (MacPherson) Stillman.

"At her sole discretion, she is requested to provide an annual stipend of up to one hundred thousand dollars to each of my daughters. The stipend is to be paid if, and only if, my daughters show the respect to my wife to which she is entitled. Mrs. Stillman will adjudicate assessment of their compliance..."

Isabella's chair scraped across the floor as she lurched out of it, pointed at Dovey, and screamed, "YOU!"

Dovey turned and watched as Jason calmly escorted Isabella from the room, ignoring her hysterics.

McCracken cleared his throat. "Sorry for the interruption, Mrs. Stillman. Shall I continue?"

"Please do."

"...An annual fee of twenty-five thousand dollars is to be paid to Jason Martin, for him to manage the execution of the aforementioned stipends.

"Annual bonuses to all ranch employees and other personal employees are to be continued as Mrs. Stillman and I have previously discussed.

"This is my total and only will.

"The balance of this recording is for the ears of my devoted wife and my two daughters, who I love with every fiber of my being. I would like that to be known by everyone.

"Good-bye, all. God bless."

Chapter Thirty-One

Part of the collar of Dovey's flowery dress peeped from behind the cozy dressing gown Angela had insisted she put on. Crocheted, woolen booties, Angela's Christmas present to her, replaced her cowboy boots, which had been wiped clean of dust and placed by Henry's chair. The last few embers of the fire still made points of light dance from the prisms of the crystal glass on the side table, containing the partially consumed glass of milk

"Can I help you to bed, Senora?"

"No, dear. But, please, you turn in. I'll be all right now. Thanks for sitting up with me."

"Is there anything else I can get you?"

"Not tonight. Just get yourself some rest and don't bother with breakfast in the morning. Sleep late. It's been a hard day for all of us."

The kitchen door closed behind Angela. She had turned off the electric light, but Dovey saw the glimmer of a candle flicker through the crack under the door; she heard the soft melodic tones and rhythmic sounds of Spanish as Angela quietly read her bible.

The dignity, respect, and genuine love of Angela's actions provided the tranquilizing effect she needed. She felt her body grow warm and her facial muscles relax. She looked up at the spot above the mantle where she planned to place Henry's portrait and saluted him with the balance of the tepid milk: "Vaya con Dios, mi querido."

Not even the drama of the previous day or the lateness of the night would allow her to sleep beyond the birth of the new day. She cracked open one eye and saw the glimmer of half-light from the open window. She turned toward Henry's side of the bed and tested to be sure. The cold, clammy, unwrinkled sheets seemed to emphasize what she knew in her heart. He was gone. *Some nightmares are real, I guess.* There she went talking to herself again. "What the hell do I care? I'll do it if I want to. No matter whether I say it aloud or under my breath, my darling is gone."

She placed her thick feather pillow over her face and let the tears roll. She hadn't allowed herself the luxury of crying since it had happened, except briefly at the gravesite.

When the uncontrollable wail turned to intermittent sobs, a vision of Blackjack Diamond lying on the canyon floor began to form. She jerked the pillow away and scoured the room. There was no one there. Dovey's body shook, not from fear, but from the frustration of having Blackjack's memory intrude on her grief.

She would not allow such impertinence. She'd fight it. She would show him, the miserable excuse for a man. Do you dare show yourself again?

She crammed the pillow back over her face. Blackjack's grinning, toothless image began to surface, but almost immediately it faded away. In its place she saw herself lying on the canyon floor. On the rim of the canyon was a young man. His features were not readily identifiable, but there was no mistaking the sneer on his lips.

She leaped from the bed and stood like a statue in the middle of the room with nothing on her mind except Jason. Shivers engulfed her body when she recalled how much Jason's tortured face of yesterday looked like the one in the vision. If Jason were her son, why would he want to kill her? That was his intent; she was sure of it.

She had been so sure of his identity, but he wouldn't, would he? He knows nothing about me. He can't know that I gave him up once for his happiness. But is he happy? His actions, except when he's with Juanita, certainly don't make it seem so.

Over the months she had watched him stare into space for minutes on end, nod his head, then wag it as though he were debating a serious problem.

Should she go to him, comfort him, and attempt to establish a new life together? If she only knew what was troubling him and if she had proof of his identity, then she could make the right choice. Perhaps her counsel would help him with whatever was bothering him. She felt sure he was Jerry. She felt it, but how could she go to a young man that she had worked with for several years and say to him, "Hug me, son; I'm your mother." That's absurd, but the whole mess is absurd. She couldn't imagine the reaction or understand the shock that he might feel. It could tear his world apart, and depending upon the seriousness of the problem she was sure he was facing, it might push him over the edge. He might even lose control.

No, this was not the time. She must wait to express her love to him. He needs to come to grips with his problem without additional complications; she owed him that. It had been twenty-two years since she'd decided that his happiness was the paramount thing in her life, more important than her desire to hold, comfort, and teach him. A short while longer... maybe she could even figure out some way to . . . Oh, damn it!

Despite Dovey's entreaty, Angela was awake at dawn also. Breakfast was waiting. "Where shall I serve, Senora?"

"Here in the kitchen, and please join me."

Dovey picked at her breakfast and listened as Angela talked of her family and particularly of the pride she felt in her son's accomplishments at school.

"I had a son once." Dovey was surprised at her admission. She had told no one in Arizona

"Senora?" Angela seemed not sure she had heard correctly.

"It's a long story. I'll tell you about it sometime. I don't want to delay your trip to church just now. But it's strange, isn't it, that as you get to know someone, one of the first things they talk about is their family?"

"It's something people know about, Senora. It's something people feel. Most of us are proud of our families."

"I've never heard Jason mention anything at all about his family. Have you?"

"Mr. Martin is quite friendly to me. Sometimes when he waits for you or El Pa..."

"That's okay, Angela. We must talk about him. Go ahead... El Patron...?"

"Mr. Martin would sit with me in the kitchen and share coffee. He loves my apple fritters. He asked about my family but never told me a thing about his."

"Nothing?"

"Nothing; but he often asks things about you and your

family."

Dovey nodded her head in contemplative silence. We'll find out, Jason. She sipped her coffee while Angela began cleaning the table, and memories began to flood her mind. How was she going to find out more about Jason?

Visions of Wesa interrupted that thought, and events regarding her floated through her mind. She remembered the scowl on Wesa's face when she had first arrived at the village of the river with two tongues. Dovey shivered. She thought of how jealous Wesa had seemed. Would she have killed her if it hadn't been for the child? She understood the anger. What she couldn't understand was Wesa's change toward her. She felt sure that Wesa intentionally looked the other way when Red Dawn helped her administer to Jerry. But why? Had her fight to save the child meant more to Wesa's motherly instincts than did her desire to have Blackjack exclusively?

But, Old Mother, there are things you are hiding from me. She felt it in her bones. When we next meet, you *will* come up with some answers, or you may join Blackjack in his resting place. Her patience had reached its limit.

"ENOUGH!" she shouted.

Chapter Thirty-Two

"*J*ason, slow down, please. My lungs are burning." Juanita stopped, brushed the perspiration from her brow, and gulped for air.

"Am I too fast for the old lady?" Junaluhska laughed and threw up his arm to ward off the blow he expected.

"Just wait until we get to the top of the hill. I'll show you who's old."

They stood at the crest of the hill, arms locked around each other, breathing heavily, but laughing.

"During my indoctrination period into the company, your father brought me up here. I've loved the view and the solitude of the place ever since. It's always been a place where my mind could roam freely. I've made some important, personal decisions here."

"I hope some of those personal decisions include a marriage proposal." She hadn't meant to say that, certainly not in such a tart tone. There was no use starting another argument. God knows they had discussed marriage often enough. It always seemed to end in an argument or in passionate lovemaking.

He took her by the hand and walked her over to a large boulder near Henry's grave. He sat, pensively, for a few moments. "Juanita... My darling. I do want to marry you and have for a long time. Not only because I love you like I have never loved anyone else. But also because I need the calm, peaceful relationship we have. How empty my life would be without your loyal and trusting support. I do want for us to marry... but..." Junaluhska leaned forward to kiss her lips.

She turned away. "I've tried hard to understand your reasoning, Jason. I can't."

She started to rise. His mind flashed back to a similar scene with Sarah. Does a man ever learn? Losing Juanita as he had lost Sarah would destroy him. He stood alongside her, placed his hands on her shoulders, and lightly pressed.

"Please, honey, sit."

"What's the use?"

It hurt him to see the pallid bleakness on her face. Her emotionless words sounded like an automatic response that he'd heard before.

Junaluhska stumbled over a few syllables, but it felt as though he were choking on his tongue. Nothing he said expressed what he felt. He wasn't making sense. He knew he was getting nowhere. He kicked a small rock. He picked up another and threw it and then whirled back to face Juanita with his eyes blazing.

Juanita smiled slightly. "Well, does that make you feel better?"

He kicked another rock. "Yes, damn it, it does."

"All right, we've both expressed our frustrations." She tried to catch his elusive eye.

"Now, what do you say? Shall we have another go at dealing with what we must?"

He looked at her freckled face and small pug nose, a face he loved to touch. He took her hand and felt his anger and feeling of desperation slowly ebb. "Sorry," he said softly, without looking directly at her.

"It's okay."

They sat silently for several moments, gazing out across the acres of grapefruit trees. Mixed thoughts were racing through Junaluhska's mind. The thoughts Sarah had shared with him would not leave him. He shuddered. He had to do or say something that would provide assurance for his love. He had to. But could he dare tell her what was troubling him so? No, not yet. Or could he? He could feel his neck getting warm and his palms beginning to sweat. The possibility of confiding in her, or anyone else, was terrifying. His limbs, his vocal chords, all of him seemed to seize up. It's an impossible situation… Whether he confided in her or not, she would probably abandon him. Who wants to live with a person who has kept such a terrible secret to himself all this time?

"Jason… Jason, didn't you hear me? I asked you a question."

"Sorry."

"There were two things you said earlier that got my attention. You referred to me as an old lady, actually."

"But, I di - -"

Juanita held her hand up. "Wait, wait. "Let's not get all riled up. I know you meant nothing by it. You were kidding and I accepted it as such. Nevertheless, age is a serious matter, especially for women of childbearing age."

His body stiffened. Why hadn't he thought about that?

Juanita stood and walked over to Henry's cross and softly rubbed her hand across the lettering. "You know, he was counting on us to provide a grandchild."

"Soon, Juanita, soon. I believe that I'm close to having a solution to my problems. I..."

She shook her head and looked at him with a placid face. "Soon is not good enough, Jason. There's another thing," she said. "You spoke of my loyal and trusting support. Isn't trust a two-way street?"

"You mean - -"

"I mean that as long as you keep your thoughts and your problems all bottled up inside, we'll never be ready to marry. I mean that you must trust me enough to know that I'll support you no matter what ghosts are chasing you."

He looked away from her. The sun eased behind a small cloud, and the cross turned dark. So did his spirits. He felt depressed, but then he remembered joking with the old man about a grandchild. He smiled at the thought.

Almost in a daze, he began to speak. "Your concern about trust causes me to think of Dovey and the love and trust that she and Henry had for each other. It's always seemed to me that she has as many ghosts in her closet as I do. And although they are such different people, they apparently overcame the complexities of their lives and dealt with some very serious matters that may have wrecked some marriages."

He paused and looked back at the cross. "Would their marriage have survived without trust?"

"I don't see how it could have, Jason. Trust is a matter of respect and shows faith in a person. Would you like to live in an emotional vacuum, where we never shared our thoughts or worries? If so, we have nowhere to go. Perhaps today should be our last time together... maybe the old lady can find someone else that will trust her."

Small dark clouds began to gather over the valley.

Juanita took a drink from her canteen, kissed him on the cheek, and started down the trail.

He stood erect, as though frozen in place, until she was nearly out of sight. "Wait!" he shouted. "Wait, I... I want you to know something before you leave me."

He caught up with her and directed her to a fallen tree trunk. The armpits of his shirt were soaked, his neck itched from the hot blood coursing through his veins, and his head pounded at the thought of what he was about to say.

The sky continued to darken.

"I love you, Juanita. I want to marry you now, this day, but I know I must earn your trust."

"I'm not asking for much, Jason."

"I know. It's just that it's so complicated. It's taken me years to even understand it myself and to decide what I believe is right or wrong. I have made a decision about what I must do. I'll do it soon, and then we'll see whether you still have faith and trust in me."

"I'm not sure I understand."

"I'll try to explain, but it's hard to know where to begin."

"Why don't you start with the story about the Gray Wolf?"

"The Gray Wolf? Why?"

"It seemed to me that you used that story as symbolism to make it impersonal. But there was no doubt in my mind that something was troubling you badly, something that you wanted to talk about, but you were afraid to do so. Am I wrong?"

A few raindrops fell. Junaluhska looked at the sky. "Perhaps we should go," he said.

"Not until we finish our conversation, or is it finished? Have we started down a path of understanding only to find the trust issue blocking our way?"

He began speaking, slowly, without inflections, as though he were being forced to confess to some wrongdoing. "My deceased father did not believe in the Christian religion or any other, as far as I know. He did believe in the ancient code of Hammurabi, 'An eye for an eye.' He believed in vengeance so strongly until the last words before his final breath were: 'You must swear to me that you will avenge me' ...I swore that I would."

"My God, Jason... the woman... the woman on the cliff in

260

the story... that's the person you have sworn to take revenge against? Isn't it?"

He hesitated and wiped the perspiration from his lips. "Yes."

"Who is she? What kind of revenge are you contemplating?"

He opened his palms and let the raindrops beat on them, looked at the horizon and saw the wind blowing the brittle tumbleweeds rapidly across the desert. "Can't we let this go to another time?" he said. "You can't imagine how it hurts to talk about a burden that has plagued me for years, a burden which often denies me sleep. Contentment for me doesn't exist."

Tears welled up in his eyes.

Juanita put her arm around his shoulder and patted it softly. "I only want to help, my darling. Now that you have begun, I know you'll feel better if we talk it through."

"I haven't cried in so long..." His sobs were soft. "Telling you those few things seems like someone pulling a cork out of a bottle of hot liquid. There's a sudden fizz, then relief; the pressure's gone. That's the way I feel now. Bless you."

He took both of her hands in his again. "I wanted to resolve my problem long ago, but my feelings were so mixed until I couldn't deal with it. At fourteen I knew what was expected of me, and although I cringed at the thought of it, I was willing to obey my father. Revenge would be his."

"You told me once that your father died around about 1919 or so. It's a long time to carry your burden. Why haven't you acted?"

"He wanted me to kill."

"To kill? Who?"

Junaluhska ignored her question and looked at his hands. "These hands were not made for killing, not even the most insignificant thing. I could not."

"But the oath you swore to your father was compelling, wasn't it?"

"It was the fuel that drove me over a twisting, rocky road for years while I tried to reason for myself. A young woman whom I went to school with back east, named Sarah, once told me that I needed to think for myself and to take action that I believed in. She also introduced me to the Christian religion. That only exacerbated my confusion."

"Good for Sarah, but I hope she stays back east." She chuckled.

Her humor helped him get his emotions under control. He blew air from puffed up lips. "Whew."

"Jason, if you want to talk more after we get home, it's all right. I no longer question your trust, although I realize there's much more to know."

The brief rain shower had ended. The clouds had dispersed, and the bright sun had begun drying their clothing.

"There's one more thing I want to say," Jason said. "I have spent years reading everything I could get my hands on about various religions with the intent to satisfy myself that there *was* a religion that was right for me.

"I read countless philosophy books trying to understand why people thought like they do and how these thoughts were applied in the religious sense."

"All because you didn't want to kill?"

"I couldn't kill, but still, I had to honor my father's wish. Trying to find a suitable alternative is what was driving me crazy. But somewhere along the way I realized that I had two important facets of living mixed up: Religion and Philosophy."

"It still gets down to what you believe, to whom you should be responsible, and which tools you should use to live your life in accordance with your beliefs," Juanita said.

"That sounds so straightforward now... can you imagine what I went through trying to reach that decision on my own? I argued with myself over and over. I came to one conclusion and then another. Then something would happen to make me start all over."

Juanita shook her head, looked at the ground for a moment, and tested the air with the palm of her hand. "It looks as though the shower is over."

"So is my quest."

"You mean..."

"I've gone back to the first philosophy book I ever read, Plato."

"What is a Just Man?" she said.

"Good for good's sake. That's the way I intend to live my life. Although killing was never a realistic option for me, I did think extensively about stealing from the person involved in a sort of Robin Hood fashion."

"And now?"

"My plan is to approach the person and talk with them openly, without malice. I'll give the person an opportunity to repent for their crime against my family. If the person does... Well, it'll be over. If the person doesn't repent, I'm not sure I'll be able to retain my composure."

Approach the *person* Juanita said the words softly to herself, nodded her head slightly, knitted her eyebrows, and looked at him. His eyes were dry now. Color had returned to his face. She eagerly received his firm kiss. "Thank you, Jason. I can't express how wonderful it feels to have your trust."

On the trek down the hill, Juanita turned and looked up at the small cross. It won't be long now, Daddy.

Chapter Thirty-Three

*D*ovey fingered the jeweled replica of the old, rusty branding iron that Henry had used when he first started his Tucson ranch. She slowly shook her head, as though in disbelief, and smiled at Jason. "This must be the most thoughtful gift any retiring president ever received."

"You deserve it, Dovey. You did wonders with the company after Henry's passing."

"Thank you. There is only one thing that would have made the evening better."

"I know, if Juanita had been there to share your happiness."

"Tell me again, Jason. Where did she say she had to go?"

"I'm not clear on it. The connection was so bad, and she was so excited, it was difficult to understand. Back east for something of major importance is all I got out of it."

The driver turned the car into the ocotillo-lined driveway leading to the house. Dovey sighed. "I'm so happy, Jason. I don't want the night to end. Why don't we have a brandy together before you go down to your quarters?"

Dovey heard a soft gasp from Jason as they stepped out onto the patio off the library. The night was crystal clear without even a hint of moonlight, making the starlit panorama even more dramatic than normal.

"Amazing, isn't it?" She pulled a chair out for herself at a small table and gestured for him to do the same. He was standing motionless, staring up at the sky, his face full of awe.

"You're truly blessed," he said quietly, before taking his seat.

"I have Henry to thank for it," she said. "Sitting out here at night was one of the simplest of joys for him. He always said that the stars helped him to relax and the moon helped him see things clearly. He probably made his most important business decisions right here on this patio."

She reached for the brandy decanter and half filled the two

snifters she'd brought out with her.

She offered him a glass. "Reminiscing is a strange activity, isn't it, Jason? Lord knows Henry and I had our share of problems to deal with, but when I think about him, it's only the good times that seem worth remembering."

He took a small sip before answering. "I suppose it's natural to filter any unpleasantness from thoughts about someone we care about."

He sounded much less guarded than usual, which pleased her. She really needed someone to talk to tonight, and as strained as things sometimes seemed with Jason, his company was of comfort to her for reasons she could never quite understand. They sipped in silence for a while, but it was surprisingly comfortable.

"Can I ask you something, Jason?" she said after a few moments had passed.

"Of course."

"You remember the strike at the copper mine a few years back?"

"Remember?" he said. "I often wish I could forget it."

"Me too." She took a deep breath before continuing.

"Did you ever have any thoughts about who loosened the lug nuts on the general manager's car?" She took a sip of brandy and looked at his face closely. His face showed no surprise or anxiousness over the question, which she took to be a good sign.

"That was such a tragedy," Jason said. "But, there's no denying it worked to our advantage."

"That's true," Dovey said.

"Wasn't it sort of fitting in a way?" he said. "The way he used to race up and down that snake of a road! It was just a matter of time until someone got hurt. Better him than someone else."

"But that was sabotage, Jason. Not something that needed to happen. The poor man could have died, for heaven's sake."

He put his brandy glass down and looked at her, his brow wrinkled with concern. "This wouldn't be what your question's about, would it?"

"Actually, yes." She paused for a long sip of brandy. "We never did figure out how the newspapers got word of his accident so quickly. And since the negative publicity pretty well ruined any chance the union had of winning the strike, Henry always assumed that, maybe..."

"Maybe what?" Anger suddenly flared on his face.

"That maybe it wasn't a union member at all? That maybe someone on our staff thought it was worth killing one of his colleagues to sway public opinion? This isn't an accusation, Jason," she said, "but Henry did wonder if it could have been one of our own. Someone trying to cause an accident, not the man's death."

"And you thought that someone might be me," he said.

"Henry considered the possibility," Dovey said. "I told him he was being ridiculous and never gave the matter a second thought."

"Until now?" he said, voice flat.

Dovey just looked at him.

"I hope you don't mind my saying how much I resent his suspicion."

"Of course not. Lord knows Henry wasn't perfect. But, think about it.

"What happened that night could have been murder. There's no way the perpetrator could have intended anything else."

"You think so?"

With some of the tension having dissipated, she refilled both their snifters.

"And the sad thing was, it wasn't even worth it," Jason said.

"Worth it?" Dovey said. "Are you suggesting that under other circumstances it would have been?"

"Does it sound like that to you?"

"It sounds like you're suggesting that it's okay to kill somebody if you have a good enough reason. That surprises me."

A look of consternation crossed his face, molding his features into an expression unlike any she'd ever seen. "Why do you ask?"

"No reason really," she said. "I found your comment provocative, that's all."

He stared at her for a moment, shiny eyes appraising her. Then his face softened, and he began twirling the stem of the brandy snifter with the fingers of his left hand. "I have often wondered if sometimes the ends justify the means," he said slowly. "The reason I find Mr. Stillwell's accusation so upsetting is that I think it's unconscionable to take a life, for any reason. It's a crime against man and a crime against God."

"I find that comforting, Jason."

"But at the same time, I can't entirely dismiss the uncontrollable impulses or circumstances that can force a person's hand. Perhaps sometimes killing is justified, if not even right. It's a question of having the wisdom to know when that's the case and, if so, having the courage to follow though with it."

She noted his voice had taken on a peculiar character, thinner and less resonant, almost as if it were somebody else talking. His hand shook slightly on the glass. Suddenly she didn't want to talk about this anymore. "I can't say I agree with you, Jason, but this kind of talk makes my skin crawl."

"It's a sad subject, indeed, but I believe it's something we need to discuss... but, perhaps another time," he said.

"So tell me then, how long have we worked together now?"

"Twenty-two years," he said, "or thereabouts."

"Good heavens," she said, letting out a long breath. "It's amazing how quickly time passes. But Jason, I want you to know that they've been good years for me, all the better because of your presence."

He looked away for a moment.

"The strange thing is, enigmatic as you are, and you are enigmatic, Jason, I've always felt close to you in a manner that I find impossible to describe. You'll probably laugh, but at one point I even wondered if it were a romantic attraction."

She interrupted her monologue, waiting for a response. He remained silent.

"Your silence tells me you believe that to be as ridiculous as I do. Let's go inside, Jason. We've counted enough stars for one night. Besides, this brandy is causing my brain to say things only my heart should hear."

"Maybe it is time."

He waited for her to get up, and then followed her inside, somewhat hesitantly.

She stopped by the doorway and turned to face him. "I've embarrassed you, haven't I? I'm sorry."

"Not at all. You surprised me, but only because I've had confused thoughts about you as well. I don't think it's possible to work together in such intimate ways without establishing some extraordinary feelings about the other person. Until you mentioned it, I had never tried to define them, but hearing you say that..."

"Perhaps we should forget this conversation before we regret it," Dovey said.

"Perhaps. But it strikes me as comical that you call me enigmatic. I've often pondered how much I know about you in some ways and how little I know about you in others."

"I know the feeling," Dovey said. "When I first had the thought of nominating you as president of the company to replace me, I realized that I knew virtually nothing about you except what I had gleaned from day-to-day work experiences. I couldn't justify making such an important recommendation without being sure that there wasn't something sinister in your background I ought to know about. You know what I found?"

"Nothing bad, I'm sure, or you wouldn't have carried through with the nomination."

"Nothing, period. Nothing! How can that be?" His tense posture and hard face told her she'd struck a nerve. She watched him carefully as she continued.

"A man without a past? I fired the investigators and hired new ones. And all to no avail. They still weren't able to find out a thing about you. It's as if Jason Martin didn't exist before we met you."

"Is that a problem for you, Dovey?"

He sort of spit her name at her. She'd angered him, she was sure of it. "It was more a curiosity at first, for the company's sake, and, in truth, for Juanita's. No one has a totally empty past unless there's a reason. It drove me crazy for a while. But at last I decided that your conduct, dedication, and obvious ability superseded any problems of your dark past, if in fact there are any. I suppose I'll just have to be content with that."

"Thank you for understanding."

"Relenting is a better word, Jason. I don't understand, nor can I relax my curiosity. There have been instances that have really made me wonder."

"Things I've done?"

"Yes."

"Such as?"

"Your behavior at Henry's grave site, for one thing. I wasn't satisfied with your explanation that day nor am I now. Just what were your intentions?"

Jason walked stiffly to the tall window overlooking the garden and stared at the darkness without speaking. His fingers ran slowly down the drapery cord, and she could tell that every muscle in his body was flexed.

Suddenly, he spun around to face her with the cord wrapped around his fingers. "My intentions? You want to know my intentions?" His voice increased in intensity as he spoke. "You want to know who I am, about my background, my youth? Is that what you want?" He took a step toward her. She stood, stunned, overwhelmed not by fear, but by what she saw in his eyes and face.

Her breathing quickened, and her pulse started pounding. He stood in front of her, dark skin now almost beet red, his hands separating from one another, stretching a length of drapery cord between them.

All she could think about was a nightmare from her past; the cold, angry eyes of Blackjack Diamond, the eyes that were glaring at her now.

"I was glad when you invited me here tonight. I recently told Juanita I intended to approach you about some serious issues that have driven me half-crazy. But I see now that it would be a waste of time."

He took a step closer. She tried to move but couldn't. "Jason, I - -"

A door opened behind them. She spun around to see Angela standing there, looking at Jason quizzically. "Did I frighten you, Senora? Is everything okay?"

Dovey nodded as she told Angela that everything was fine, though she wasn't at all sure it was.

"I'm sorry to interrupt, but I have message for Senor Martin."

Jason's eyes were wide, his pupils dilated. He looked down and shook his head, as though surprised to find the drapery cord in his hands. "Yes?" he said.

"A woman call for you. At first she seemed no want to leave message. She was hard to understand, but I wrote what I think she say."

He took the piece of paper and glanced at it for a moment. "Excuse me, please," he said. He turned and headed quickly for the door in an uncharacteristically hasty exit.

"Are you okay, Senora?" Angela said, once he'd gone.

The truth was that Dovey was far from okay. What would have happened if Angela hadn't walked in? Dovey shook her head and felt chill bumps run up her spine. "Where did he go, Angela?"

"I remember message," Angela said. "'Crystal needs you at Phoenix General Hospital. Hurry.'"

Chapter Thirty-Four

*J*ason breathed a sigh of relief when he read the bright, red neon sign at Picacho Peak filling station saying, 'OPEN'. He quickly pulled in, gassed up and grabbed a bag of peanuts and coffee to go. Leaving Tucson at such a late hour, without filling up, hadn't been very smart. He realized it now, but the unexpected excitement of seeing Wesa's code name had caused him to forget everything.

Something had to be terribly wrong with her, he knew. She would never have sent such an abrupt message otherwise. What could it be? She looked fine the last time he had seen her. Jason begin thinking... man, it's been a long time, not since his father's funeral. Maybe if he had visited and kept her appraised of what he was doing... well, it's too late now.

The uneven road surface bounced the car's headlights up and down, casting intermittent flashes of light on the saguaros on the side of the road. The hot, dry, desert air pulled at the perspiration on his body. The whine of the tires and the noise from the wind rushing through the open windows nearly drowned out the cowboy music on the radio. His nerves tightened with each mile as his concern about Wesa intensified. She had been like a mother to him, the only mother he had ever known. But her kindness never quite chased away his questions as to what his real mother had been like? Was she pretty? What would his life have been like if Dovey hadn't killed his mother... if she really had? Why did he continually question the story his father told him before his death? If only his father had lasted longer, surely he would have explained the inconsistencies in the story about the murder.

It seemed to Jason that his tires were mired in molasses. Time dragged. Thoughts sneaked up on him of his tumultuous life and the gut-wrenching trauma that assailed him and followed him like a shadow. Why had his father put him into such a predicament? It was a situation he knew he would never understand. He had spent so many years preparing to deal with the problem of Dovey MacPherson. And, for what?

He reflected on his thoughts for a moment and then grinned. It's ironic as hell isn't it? He had spent all those years driving himself, working, scheming, trying to position himself where he could recover his father's wealth and what happens? He laughed. He became rich himself. He was now the President of the company, the God Damn President, and along with the deal had come Juanita, the loveliest woman a man could have. And he would have Juanita, because, ironically, he had taken the advise of another woman. He was his own man now. He would not kill, but even so, he knew he still had to confront Dovey, as he had told Juanita he would, before he would feel as though the blood running through his veins was like that of a Mountain Lion. The thought snapped him out of his dream world.

"Enough of this," he said aloud. He turned up the radio volume higher to drown out such absurd thoughts.

Despite the lateness of the night, the glow of the city's lights allowed Jason to see South Mountain in the far distance. In thirty minutes he would know Wesa's problem.

He tried to remember the prayers the Shaman taught him so many years ago. The words were buried somewhere deep inside his subconscious, he was sure. But they hadn't helped when his father was sick, what good would they do now?

He took a deep breath and as he expelled the inhaled air other words flowed from his mouth; "God is our refuge and strength…"

His back arched into a rigid bow. His hands gripped the steering wheel until his knuckles turned white.

Those words were Dovey's, not his. How dare she intrude on this personal moment?

The lights in the hospital corridors had been dimmed for the night, but the clean white walls still glistened. A moan from one room and the smell of antiseptic brought the hair on Jason's neck to a state of alert. He tiptoed down the hall along with the white clad nurse wondering what he would find. Wondering what action he needed to take.

Wesa was asleep. Her dark hair was plaited in its familiar shape, her hands rested comfortably at her side, and her breathing was steady. In the partial light Jason was sure she was smiling.

He stood reverently at her bedside for a few moments. There was no change. He motioned to a chair at the side of the room. The nurse nodded.

The length and excitement of the day overcame his determination to stay awake. He succumbed.

It seemed to him that a far away voice was calling him, like in a dream... "Junaluhska, awake my little man. Junaluhska..."

He opened his eyes, saw the white of the ceiling, and the small shaft of light coming from behind the edge of the window curtain. His eyes were drawn to the voice from the bed in the partially, darkened room.

"Mother," Jason shouted and went to her side. A tear formed in his eye as he pressed his cheek against the soft wrinkled face.

"I knew you would come."

"What's the matter? Why are you in the hospital? Are you being well cared for?"

"My heart has seen too many summers. My brain has been down too many trails."

"You're young yet."

"The great spirit knows my age better than anyone. Still he gave me time to be with you once more." She grabbed her chest and began coughing a dry, terrible sounding cough.

"Please, mother, don't talk."

"I must. You must know that which lays heavy on my heart... If it isn't too late."

"No, mother. Rest."

"The great spirit will decide when I should take my long rest."

She was breathing only through her mouth. He saw her chest rise higher than before. He ran his hand across her brow and caressed her coarse hair. "Speak if you must, but don't exert your self. I'll patiently listen."

"Something troubles you, Junaluhska. What is it?" Wesa's eyes opened wide. Her lips twitched and the wrinkles at the edges deepened. Her face darkened. "Have you avenged your father?"

He felt as though his body was shrinking. He wanted to run, to hide, to do anything but admit his failure. He fingered the white sheets, looked down and then into glazed eyes sunken in her bronze face that seemed to be turning purple as she awaited his answer.

"I have failed, Second Mother."

Strangely, she smiled at this. Just for a moment.

He cocked his head and watched as color returned to her face and a mist spread over her eyes. "I cannot justify my weakness. I have dishonored my father and shamed myself."

His shirt was wet with perspiration. His head was bowed. "I've been too ashamed to tell you about the path my heart has convinced me to follow. That is why I haven't been back to the village since my father's death and why I haven't shared with you the details of my life.

She reached for his hand and tried to squeeze.

"For a long time I struggled with the rights and wrongs of life and allowed my indecision to tear me apart."

"You would have honored your vow to your father if you could. The spirit knows that and so do I. But, sometimes blind trust and devotion are not the right things. The spirit knows that, too.

"You should feel no shame, Junaluhska. Your father... He had his ways and you have yours. There is no shame in that." Her sympathetic words warmed his heart, but at the same time fueled his anger with himself.

"I have told myself the very same thing, but it doesn't erase the guilt I feel. I did listen to his words with respect, though as he laid out a plan for revenge. But, then I told him of my own feelings about revenge and killing. Even before I finished, he was on his feet cursing me, flailing at me with a tree limb, stumbling and coughing. Then, finally he fell to the ground." He looked at her for a moment, his vision blurred by tears. "He went to the spirit world without hearing all that I wished to say. I don't think I could have changed his mind, but at least I could have made him understand."

"Understand what?"

"That the need of our people was greater than the need for revenge. And that..."

She nodded at him encouragingly, but said nothing.

"That it just isn't in me to do harm to another. And all the rationalization and pleas to the spirit or to God, will not make it different. I am what I am." He waited for a reaction. Somewhere far away church bells sounded the hour. A nurse's heels clicked on the corridor floor.

Wesa's wheezing lungs seemed to be desperately trying to fill themselves. Jason placed his damp hands on hers and his lips silently mouthed, " God is our refuge and strength."

Amazingly, her struggle to breath diminished. Again, she smiled. Her eyes brightened. "Junaluhska, you must listen well to my words. It is important that you hear and that you believe what I say. Only then will I be able to rest in peace."

He nodded.

"I loved your father for reasons perhaps you and you alone could understand. Many people feared his temper. They didn't know the calm, peaceful man I knew and I think that you did also. They never listened to the soft loving words he spoke. Some people said he was crazy and at times he was. But he was a good man in his heart."

"I know that, mother."

"But, good men do bad things sometimes, especially when provoked. People didn't understand the hurt he felt when his father died or the guilt he felt because he had cursed his father for putting black and white blood in his veins instead of pure Cherokee blood.

"When he was home the sun would shine, the rains would bless us and the crops would be bountiful. He gave those things to our village. He sent us gold from his mine. I gave him my love and devotion." She paused for a moment, a hesitant look on her face. "I also gave him my word that his secret would go to the grave with me."

"What secret?"

Wesa's pupils chased the white from her eyes and Junalhuska stared at what looked like black, glistening, river pebbles. She raised her head with some difficulty, but quickly let it fall back onto the pillow. She gasped, took several quick breaths, rolled her eyes back into her head and shouted. "It is I that dishonor his name, not you!"

"I don't understand," Junalhuska said.

"Your father didn't warm my blanket for more than two years. I sent him food from time to time but he remained in his camp, scratching for the gold. One morning when the corn was only knee high he rode in. Dovey, heavy with child, was with him. She was only a child herself. She was weak, hungry, and her head was hot with fever. He demanded that I take care of her. I looked at her stomach and felt betrayed. I was so hurt by what he'd done that my first thought was to kill her and their baby once it was born. But my anger melted when she had a boy. Your father always wanted a son, which I was never able to give him. So I have a brother then. Is that what you're trying to tell me?" Wesa held her hand up.

"We gave the baby to another squaw who had recently given birth and told her to feed and care for Dovey's child. But the baby wouldn't feed from the breast of a stranger and nearly died. One night Red Dawn took the baby and brought him to Dovey. The crying stopped and the child ate until his little belly poked out from beneath the skin and bones he had become.

"Red Dawn didn't tell me what she had done, but I found out. At first I was furious, but, then, for the sake of the survival of the child and for Blackjack's happiness I choose to look the other way."

"You loved my father a lot didn't you?"

"So much so until I nearly ruined two lives. I hated Dovey because she could give your father what I could not. But, when I saw the way she loved you, my mother's heart went out to her. How could I kill her? I asked the Great Spirit to tear the thought of harming her from my mind so my heart could be at peace."

'Loved You?' Junaluhska's body had jerked taught at the words. Had his ears tricked him? Was he misinterpreting? The look on her face suggested that he hadn't. It was a look full of sorrow and regret. A look of penitence.

"You're saying that Dovey... That Dovey MacPhearsen Stillwell is my... Mother?" He uttered the words slowly and deliberately, his fists clinched so hard his knuckles were white.

Wesa nodded solemnly.

His father's words echoed in his mind over and over: Dovey killed your mother. That had to be true. It *had* to be.

Why was Wesa lying to him, then?

His head swam with rage and his first instinct was to walk away. This woman had betrayed him and didn't deserve another moment of his time. Without a second thought, he turned abruptly toward the door.

"PLEASE, Junalhuska, don't leave yet. There's more you

need to know."

Her shout got the attention of the floor nurse, who poked her head inside the door. "Is there a problem here?" she asked.

"No problem," Wesa said.

"Please sir, wait outside for a moment while I attend to your mother. You'll find coffee in the cafeteria if you wish. I'll be about twenty minutes."

He was glad for the interruption. Glad that he had not done what his instincts told him to do.

He poured himself a cup of black coffee and sat down by a nearby table. Someone had lied to him and he wasn't sure who.

He loved his father and he loved Wesa, and he trusted them both. But one of them had not told him the truth.

It was far easier to believe his father. For if Wesa spoke the truth that meant his father had intentionally schemed to have him kill his own mother. How could anyone even conceive of such an evil deed? It couldn't be true; that's a preposterous story.

But, why would Wesa lie? She'd always been nothing but good to him. Would she act differently now, on her deathbed? No, she wouldn't. He stared at the steam from the coffee urn wafting up toward the ceiling. That's it. She is trying to prepare herself for meeting the Great Spirit.

He stretched his legs out under the table, closed his eyes and tried to clear his mind. It didn't help. He had to know more.

When he got back to Wesa's room, her eyes were closed. He wondered for one terrible moment if she were dead.

He touched her lightly on her shoulder and the weary eyes opened. A faint smile welcomed him.

"Bring your chair closer to the bed. Please."

He did as she requested.

"Junaluhska, every word I say is the truth. I swear by it on your father's grave." She held out a piece of paper.

"Take this. The nurse wrote the address of Red Dawn for me. Red Dawn will be pleased to confirm everything I will tell you. She wanted to for many years but would not betray my trust."

For almost an hour she talked in brief spurts while he listened, afraid at first to ask the questions he knew had to be asked. But the more she spoke, the more he trusted her words. Finally a torrent of questions exploded from within.

"She didn't know that my father lived after he fell?"

"Not for many years."

"She doesn't know that I swore to avenge my father?"

"She feels that you carry a huge burden on your shoulders and is curious but doesn't know who you are, Junaluhska. In truth, I might have told her if I really believed you would do as your father demanded. But I know you well, and I thought you would never do it."

She paused for a moment before continuing. "Out of strength, not weakness."

"So Dov... my mother has been trying to find me for thirty three years?"

Wesa nodded. "Yes. Your mother seemed to sense that I knew more than I was willing to tell her and that I was the only link to your whereabouts. That's why she took care of me and arranged for me to live in the old age care facility in Pima. There I was able to chase the loneliness of old age by making things with my hands and by learning to speak English properly. The money she put aside for me allowed me to come here for medical treatment."

"And she still asks about me when she comes to see you?"

"She never gave up, Junaluhska. She accepted that she had no power to change things, but she could never let you go completely. She'd come to me to feel closer to you?"

"She never realized who I really was? Never even suspected?"

Wesa thought for a moment before answering. "I think she did suspect. She talked to me many times of the handsome man she knows as Jason who works with her. But she dismissed such thoughts as fantasy."

He smiled and nodded his head.

"Since I've been sick I've thought about your mother, your father and you. My loyalty was misplaced. It would have been better to... Oh, so many years."

She closed her eyes, reached out for Junaluhska's hand. "Your mother helped me because she is a kind woman. She knew, years ago, that I would never tell her what she wanted to know. Perhaps she could see that Blackjack had caused me as much pain as he had her."

"My mother," Jason paused after saying the word as though it were the wrong choice of words, "is a wonderful woman. I have witnessed her kindness with many less fortunate people. That's one of the reasons that I couldn't bring myself to - -"

He grit his teeth to repress the taste of bile slowly creeping from his stomach. He shuddered and looked away.

"She loves you, Junaluhska. Never have I seen a mother's love demonstrated more strongly, for so long. To give up her search for you broke her heart, but she did it out of love and the thought that you were probably happy wherever you were. Never forget that."

He turned to the window and stared out into the brightness of the day but saw little until his eye caught a flicker of a Cactus Wren darting into her nest to feed little ones. Back and forth she flew on her mission of mercy.

How dedicated she was. He wondered if she knew that one day her babies would just fly away.

He whirled back to face Wesa and deliberately walked to her bedside to stare into her eyes. "I get it. I understand your purpose now. 'Forgive me, son, I was wrong.' Is that what you're telling me? Well is it?"

"Junalhuska - -"

"Don't call me that name. I'm Jason, the son of Dovey. I would slit my wrist and drain the blood of my father from me if I could."

"Please, Jason - -"

"No, I won't listen. Besides, if what you say is true, you let my father poison my life with his lies. You withheld the key to happiness from a woman you call a friend. You took her money and stood silently by, knowing her son might kill her at any moment."

Wesa nodded sadly, but said nothing.

"Forgive you? Never. I give you my pity, my sorrow and my concern but not forgiveness."

"I don't expect your forgiveness, Junaluhska." Her words trailed off into silence. "But I am so very sorry." She said it with disarming humbleness and sincerity. She reached for his hand, which he withdrew.

"I understand your anger, Jason, but I don't think you yet

understand all the reasons I felt I had to tell you the truth."

"I understand all I need to understand."

"Do you see how you have transferred your hate from Dovey to Black Jack and me? Hate will destroy you. You'll never have peace in your soul with that attitude."

"That makes me laugh. Who taught me to hate? Who schooled me so well until my very life was ruined - -"

"Stop it, Jason." Wesa's soft, conciliatory voice hardened for a moment. She placed her hands on the bed and struggled to rise, panting and wheezing as she did. Once she was sitting she paused and held out her arms as she used to do when he was a young boy. Tears were running down her cheeks.

"You're a man now. You have proven that and I am proud of you. But I can not go to the spirit world without trying to help you see the fork in the road that will lead you down the path of happiness."

She waited for a reaction that did not come. "As I said, you're a man now. You'll make your own decisions. But if you must hate let it be me that you hate, not your father." She coughed and reached, for a towel on the bedside table and nearly toppled from the bed. Instinctively Jason caught her, returned her to the bed and handed her the towel. Her time worn face touched his. He felt her hardened, callused hands and heard her gentle thank you. The ice that had been chilling his bones began to melt. He thought of other days when he was a boy, and the hugs and warmth that this old woman had given him. His heart opened a little.

"You were saying?"

"Hate me Jason if you must hate someone. That's what I said."

Jason looked away from her pleading eyes.

"We both know that your father's mind sometimes didn't function as we all would have liked. Can he be held responsible for something, which he couldn't control? I say, no! Because when he was his normal self he was as kind as any man that has lived. Who else would have taken to his bed a fat, pocked-marked woman who's own father had disowned her? He couldn't help himself. But I could. I could have stopped this quest for vengeance before it got to be a disease. I could have shown Dovey where you were and helped her… but, I didn't."

"No, you didn't and there's no way you can change it or make amends."

"I know, but even my support of your father's twisted ways and the heart aches I caused Dovey did not cause you as much harm as my failure to teach you how to love and how to accept love.

"Now you have no basis for transferring your emotions from hate to love. You're lucky you haven't yet married Dovey's daughter. How could you have possibly fulfilled the needs of a wife and how could you have accepted her love without stumbling over your crutch of hate? The bile and bitterness that seeps from your heart wouldn't have let you."

Jason shifted his feet and looked away. "You're wrong."

"If I had taught you how to truly love you would be like your mother. She loved you enough to give you up for the sake of your own happiness. Think of that the next time you want to take your anger out against someone." She held out her arms to him again.

Jason stood inches away from her out stretched arms, glaring at her as though hypnotized. He watched the tears cascade down her pleading face. He took a step, paused and buried his head in her bosom. Their tears mingled. He kissed her cheek and then held her tightly for moments.

Jason sat back on the bed, silently reflected for a moment then took her hand in his. "My thoughts are too confused for me to do or say more. Yet, life must go on. I'll think about you. I'll pray to Dovey's God to show me the way of forgiveness and to teach me to love and be loved. Maybe someday I can say, 'I forgive'. The great spirit would not believe me if I said it now."

Chapter Thirty-Five

Despite a sense of urgency to get back to Tucson to do what he knew he must, he was not ready. He stopped frequently, wondering what he should say, trying to plan at least his opening remarks. Should they be confrontational: "Why did you desert me, mother?" Or perhaps he should apologize for her near death at his hands. He felt his flesh crawl. How could he expect her to forgive him and to receive him as the son he wished to be; a loving one?

He kicked at a rock on the roadside as he made his way back to his car turning his head away from a dust devil swirling off to his left. He brushed at the sand, which was now covering his clothing. Damn this desert with its dust, rocks, cactus, and scorpions! He kicked another rock.

Maybe that's the answer. He would just go in, pack his bag, and leave. He didn't have to ever see her again, did he? She left him, didn't she? No, an immature approach like that wouldn't work, besides he'd lose Juanita.

His touch of the scorching steering wheel jerked him back to the real world. He would have to do more thinking and perhaps talk things over with Juanita when she returned from her trip. That's it!

For the first time in two days, Junaluhska smiled and drove in contemplative silence as he negotiated the long, twisting ocotillo-lined driveway leading to the Stillwell ranch. Even though the sun was already slipping down behind the western hills, he parked under the spreading limbs of the solitary pepper tree, which Dovey considerately had planted for shade.

A slit of light was seeping from around the edges of the heavy, brocaded drapes covering Dovey's window. She was probably dressing for dinner.

"Dovey," he said aloud, the word seeming awkward to his lips. He breathed a sigh of relief over his decision not to confront her yet with what he'd learned. But, that time would come, and soon. With Juanita's help, perhaps they could find an answer to the riddle.

The house was uncharacteristically quiet for this hour, making the prospect of getting to his room unnoticed easier than he had anticipated. He bent his tall body at the waist and leaned forward, passing the kitchen door in silence as he made his way toward the back of the house.

He threw himself on the bed and stared at the whiteness of the ceiling, which was only faintly illuminated by the rising moon. It took nearly ten minutes of deep, steady breathing before his nerves began to calm and his mind began to relax. As the tension released, he felt himself fall into a comfortable limbo, somewhere between wakefulness and sleep.

His eyes were still open slightly when the image of the Gray Wolf perched himself on the windowsill and Junaluhska watched his lips whisper to him, as he had done for so many years. "You are your own man now. Make your own decisions, but be willing to take responsibility for your actions. Do what you must, but consider the effect your actions will have on others."

After a few moments, the apparition disappeared. Junaluhska leapt from the bed, raced to the window, and peered into the night. The full moon now bathed the landscape with warm, golden light, and the only sound he could hear was soft guitar music coming from the hired hand's quarters. He filled his lungs with the cool night air, rubbed his body vigorously, and smiled.

"Junaluhska," he said quietly. He was proud of the name, and it would be good to have it back. Dovey ... his mother ... would probably want to call him Jerry. Surely she'd understand, though. Any mother would.

He reached to a shelf in the closet and found his buckskin trousers. Their smell was distinctive, yet he'd almost forgotten it. He dug through an old suitcase and found the moccasins Wesa had given him when he'd seen her at his father's funeral. They, too, bore the smell of tanned leather, the smell of his own past, which would no longer have to remain a dark secret.

As he closed the suitcase, he saw the bone-handled knife his father had given him for his tenth birthday. He was so proud on that day, and he'd listened with such pleasure to the story of how his grandfather had given it to his father many years before.

"Was that a lie too, father?" Junaluhska said aloud. He thrust it back into the suitcase and was about to replace it on the shelf when the memory of the Gray Wolf's words stopped him.

Bare-chested, he strode from his room, through the kitchen, and into the night. The bone-handled knife dangled proudly from his side.

The sound of screeching tires pierced the calm and quiet of the evening. The crunching of gravel followed, under unmistakably frantic footsteps.

The door burst open.

"Where is he?"

"Senora!" Angela said, tuning around quickly. "I'm sorry, I - -"

"Enough!" Isabella said, voice shaking slightly. "Just tell me where he is."

"Who?"

"Jerry, Junaluhska, William..." Isabella said. "It's hard to keep track of the many identities of the elusive Jason Martin, isn't it?"

Angela's hands went to her face in a gesture of stunned surprise. She crossed herself and shook her head slowly.

"I no understand. Senor Martin, he - -"

"He what? I checked his room, and he wasn't there. But his car's here. Now where is he?"

"He leave maybe a half hour ago for a walk, I think."

Isabella stomped out of the kitchen, scowling. She returned a few moments later with her hair jammed carelessly under a dark felt hat and attired in long black pants stuffed into a ratty pair of old boots. Her turtleneck sweater was pulled up to partly cover her face. All the black emphasized the white knuckles on the hand squeezing a rifle.

"Senora," Angela said, voice hushed. "Where you going?"

Isabella stopped at the door and turned. "Never you mind. Just tell 'Mother, dear' that she has me to thank."

She laughed a hideous, cold, joyless laugh before slamming the door behind her.

Juanita dashed into the house, grinning from ear to ear and shouting for Dovey at the top of her lungs. Even though she was frazzled from the return trip from Massachusetts and exhausted from the gamut of emotions her discovery about Junaluhska had triggered, she was still excited about the news she had to share.

"In here, dear, in the dining room."

Her heart sank at the somber tone of Dovey's voice. She took a long gasp of breath and ran the last few yards to the dining room. She burst into the room and halted in her tracks. The look on Dovey's face and the tears streaming down Angela's face confirmed her fear that something was very wrong.

"What is it? What's the matter?"

Angela turned her terrified eyes to Juanita. "Your sister, Isabella, is saying terrible, crazy things. She just ran out to find Senor Martin. She took a gun with her."

"Crazy things about what, Angela? What did she say to you?"

Angela shook her head slowly.

"Senorita, she tell me, 'I'll find that son of hers and kill him right before her very eyes.'"

Isabella had found out the truth! Dovey thought.

"We've got to stop her," Juanita said.

"Lord, forgive me," Dovey said as she unlocked the small drawer in the hall closet and took out an old Colt forty-five, which she handed to Juanita.

"I hope you don't need this," she said, "but take it just in case."

Juanita spun the cylinder, cautiously moved the safety catch backward and forward, and nodded her head. "I better go now." She hugged Dovey and quickly turned to leave.

It took a moment for her eyes to adjust to the darkness. The trail was treacherous, and she couldn't take any chances. She stepped quickly but carefully and quietly, hoping it wasn't already too late.

The sound of skittering pebbles nearby stopped Juanita dead in her tracks. She waited for a moment but heard nothing else. She moved onward, desperate to get to the ridge, where she'd have an open, moonlit view.

Her lungs were stinging when she finally reached the top. To her dismay, she could not see Jason or Isabella. But the bright light coming from the dining room was like a signal flare, and Dovey's image was plainly visible. She steadied herself and contemplated what to do next.

Suddenly, she felt a hand cover her mouth and an arm tighten around her waist. She struggled and thrashed out with the barrel of the pistol. She felt the gun slam into the side of her adversary's head, and the grip on her waist loosened. She fell roughly to the ground, and for a moment everything went black. The figure standing beside her slumped to its knees and fell across her.

With trembling hands she raised the gun and pressed it into the thick hair of the form holding her down. It was Junaluhska's hair!

She gasped and let go of the gun. He'd just been trying to keep her quiet. And she'd almost... Oh, God!

A rifle shot pierced the air like the crack of thunder. In the distance, glass splintered; then a second and a third shot, and Dovey's image was gone. Had she had time to place the full-length mirror as she had intended?

A chilling silence followed. Juanita waited for a moment. Then, raised her head.

Immediately, the rifle sent its whining message through the night air. She heard the thump of a bullet hitting a saguaro not three feet from her. She shouted, and the rifle fired again. A pistol shot answered. Two screams split the air.

With each muted shot she heard in the distance, icy fingers of fear and dread crept up Dovey's backbone. A bullet shattered the window and mirror, leaving the floor littered with shards of broken glass.

"Turn off the lights," she said to Angela. "Come with me."

She bent down below the windows and took refuge in the kitchen. She handed Angela a thick, cast-iron frying pan and grabbed a heavy skillet for herself. They stood, one on either side of the open kitchen window, and waited.

The minutes ticked away endlessly. The shooting had stopped. Please, God, let there be no deaths. There was nothing to do, but wait.

The odd thing was that it was her that Isabella hated, not Junaluhska. Ever since Henry had died, Dovey had to be on her guard on the rare moments when Isabella was around. She'd begged her to get help, but her pleading only fueled her stepdaughter's rage. So why on earth was she going after him?

"Senora, listen," Angela whispered. Dovey twisted her head toward the window and caught a slight sound of someone breathing deeply from somewhere up the hill.

"Who is it?" she mouthed. Angela shook her head.

The heavy, labored breathing was becoming more distinct. Now the clear sound of footsteps added drama to the other sound. Both were becoming louder, nearer. But whose steps were they? Dovey steeled herself and used every fiber of restraint not to peek out the window to see who it was. The risk was too great.

Suddenly a sharp, crashing noise reverberated through the still night. She could hear rocks tumbling down the hillside, almost masking the subdued cry of a woman's voice.

Dovey felt her heart tighten into a knot. Whose was it? She had to know.

She peered out the window and caught someone's shadow passing over the cars parked in the courtyard. The shuffle of footsteps on gravel became more pronounced as they landed on brick. Dovey gripped the skillet so hard it hurt her knuckles and prepared for the worst.

She saw the doorknob twist and heard the pounding of small fists on the glass door panel.

"Let me in, please. Hurry!"

Juanita!

Dovey let the skillet fall to her side and jerked the door open.

"Are you all right? Where's Jason? What happened?"

"There's no time to explain. Just call for an ambulance, quickly, and tell them we'll meet them at the intersection of the main highway."

Juanita turned to Angela. "Get a blanket and a few towels; dampen one of them and follow me."

Suddenly another figure came tumbling through the open door. It was Junaluhska, his trousers soaked in blood, which streamed from a matted mess of bloody hair.

Dovey screamed.

"Water, please," he said through his gasps for breath.

Juanita dashed for the water and a towel to clean his face.

Dovey spoke quickly into the telephone and hung up.

"My God, Jason. Are you hurt badly?"

The commotion in the room wasn't enough to distract her from the strange look he was giving her. There was intensity to his gaze, unlike any she had ever encountered. Yet, at the same time, it seemed to be a look full of confusion and anxiousness.

She let her eyes drop and for the first time realized how peculiarly he was dressed. A look of surprise crossed her face. Suddenly he smiled at her, then nodded almost imperceptibly before speaking.

"Isabella..." he said. "She's in the back of the car. We must get her to the hospital immediately."

The road to the highway intersection seemed much longer than the seven miles it really was. As her mind tumbled with strange thoughts, Dovey cuddled her stepdaughter's head in her lap, brushed the tangled blond tresses from around her face, and attempted to comfort her.

There was something taking shape in her subconscious, but she couldn't quite figure out what. Juanita's sudden, mysterious trip east, Isabella's attempt on Junaluhska's life and hers, his strange buckskin clothing, and that knife. Hadn't she seen it before?

Her heart was beating fast. She couldn't quite make sense of the thoughts and memories whirling around her mind, but something was starting to gel.

Isabella's eyes opened to slits for a moment. Dovey began humming a song she'd heard Henry singing to her years before, when she was still a child, although troubled even then.

A rare smile appeared on Isabella's face, full of beauty and innocence. What a beautiful creature she could be when the sadness and anger left her face. Her eyes opened completely and darted around to take in the surroundings. But when she saw Junaluhska in the front seat next to Juanita, her face clouded, and Dovey felt her muscles go tense.

"What are you doing, old woman? Where are you taking me? Why aren't you dead? I saw you die. I shot you. I know I did; I saw you fall. Damn you, die!"

She patted Isabella's head lightly, hoping to calm what she

sensed was an oncoming fit. An angry hand swiped away her caress.

"Leave me alone, damn you!" Isabella said, her voice surprisingly strong for her condition. "Leave me alone and let me die. Then that damn son of yours will get hanged for murder!"

Chapter Thirty-Six

Dawn was just beginning to paint the eastern Catalina Mountains when Junalhuska stepped from the police car and thanked the officer for returning him to the hospital. He paused for a moment before going inside, looked up at where he imagined Isabella to be and said a soft prayer for her.

He took the steps two at a time, crossed the hospital corridor quietly, wrinkling his nose at the antiseptic smell. He paused and peered through the glass door of the waiting room. A lump came to his throat, his eyes burned a little but he smiled at what he saw there.

Dovey was sitting upright on the couch with her head drooping toward her chest. Juanita was stretched out on the couch with her head on Dovey's lap. A few wisps of her beautiful long, brown hair had fallen across her face. Junaluhska watched for a moment as her upper body rose and fell with each breath. *How ironic that it had taken such a tragedy for him to experience this loving moment.*

The door responded to his soft push with a nearly inaudible squeak, but Dovey's eyes opened. She smiled broadly when she saw him, then put her finger to her lips. Juanita stirred but did not wake up.

Junaluhska walked up near the couch, leaned over for his lips to be near her ear and whispered, "How is Isabella doing?"

Dovey shook her head and then motioned for him to go into the corridor. She reached for a pillow, tenderly placed it under Juanita's head as she eased herself up from the couch.

"I was so worried, Jason. I expected you back ages ago. Were there problems with the police?"

Jason looked at his watch. 5:32 AM. He'd been gone nearly seven hours. "Well, I'm sure they'll have more questions for us, but I didn't get the impression we have anything to worry about."

"They're not going to prosecute?"

He shook his head. "Well, I don't think so. I believe they're perfectly willing to treat this as a private family matter, but they did suggest an interest in seeing to it that she gets some help."

"Thank heavens, Jason. Lord knows it's time."

He nodded.

"How is she?"

"The nurse says she's going to be okay, but the doctor's still with her. We'll know a lot more once he's finished."

Jason nodded, unsure what to say next. They hadn't yet spoken about what Isabella had said in the car. Yet there was no awkwardness in their silence on the matter. There was so much to be said, but they both seemed to sense that it would simply have to wait.

But, now they were alone together in the darkened hallway. It was almost impossible to believe he was really standing there, with her, not saying anything about what had happened.

He looked at her for a moment, wondering what she might be thinking. Her expression showed none of the confusion or anxiousness he felt at the prospect of confronting the truth. It was a look full of warmth and tenderness. Strange as it all was, what she'd learned tonight had obviously made her very happy.

She took his hand after a moment and locked her eyes on his. "Juanita was terribly worried about you."

Jason smiled. Just the mention of her name made him tingle.

"While we waited for you we had lots of time to compare notes. A good deal of the conversation was about the blessed good news we had learned. She told me about your pledge to confront your unknown adversary to attempt to put an end to your dilemma. Then just a few moments before she went to sleep you know what she said?"

Jason shook his head, perplexed by the tone of Dovey's voice.

"'Nothing sets you free like the truth'. Then she laughed and said she sure liked the sound of that."

She was smiling, but her words dripped with innuendo. He took a step towards her, paused momentarily, then put his arms around her in a slow, cautious embrace. They silently held each other as their tears mingled. He was reluctant to pull away when the elevator bell sounded.

Dr. Roberts stepped out, still attired in his bloodstained

surgical gown. "I'm sorry that took so long." He said, after nodding quickly to Juanita, who had awakened and was walking toward the group. "It was difficult to extract the bullet without risking serious damage and there were bone fragments to deal with. The good news is that she made it through just fine and will be good as new before you know it."

"Does that mean we can see her now?" Dovey asked, her voice full of relief.

The doctor was hesitant. "She'll be in the recovery room for a while. Maybe tomorrow afternoon would be better."

"Doctor, please. Even if it's just for a moment, I'd like to see my daughter, now."

Dr. Roberts looked over at Jason as though pleading with him to reason with her. Jason said nothing but never let his eyes leave those of the doctor. "Mrs. Stillwell, when you signed the admittance papers I believe you listed Dr. Levitz as Isabella's physician."

"Well, he's not really…"

He waved his hand dismissively. "Dr. Levitz and I have collaborated many times. I have great respect for his ability as a psychotherapist. But you should know that we did need to sedate your daughter before we could even examine her. I understand she was under extreme stress but the things she shouted out can't be taken lightly. And the truth is that I think it would be in everybody's best interest if he were here when she comes around. You all can do the most good by returning home to get some much-needed rest. Then you can direct your full energies to helping your daughter."

Jason put his arm around Dovey and squeezed gently. "I'm afraid he's got a point, Dov…"

The word caught in his throat. It suddenly seemed absurd to call her *Dovey*, but he couldn't quite manage *mother* either.

So he turned back to the doctor. "Can you please arrange to have Dr. Levitz here tomorrow when we return."

"I'd be delighted," he said. "And in the meantime, please don't worry. Isabella's going to be just fine."

Dawn was creeping across the Catalinas by the time the threesome left the hospital. The joy of being together was diminished by the tragedy of the previous evening but not obliterated.

At Juanita's insistence Dovey sat side by side with Junaluhska on the front seat. She was consumed by the joy of having her son next to her. After he steered the car out onto the long, straight highway and pointed its nose toward Tucson, he reached over and took her hand. She gently laid her other hand on top of his and smiled broadly. No words seemed necessary.

They road in silence, each knowing there was much to talk about but also realizing this was not the time. Junaluhska made the turn into the ranch road, sighed and said, "Well, we made it. I hope Isabella has done as well."

"Jason, I'm so pleased about the way you took charge of everything and about your concern for Isabella."

"Thank you, Mom." Jason took a short look at her smiling face and his heart seemed to beat a little faster. He looked away and saw one of the farm hands waving his big sombrero in salute. His bronze face caused Jason to transfer his thoughts to another bronze face, Wesa's.

"You know, I can't get Wesa out of my mind. It took a lot of fortitude for her to tell me her story. And, I thank God she did. It was strange; I hated her at first for telling me the truth. It hurt to know that my father was willing to sacrifice my happiness and yours for a stupid ideology."

"And now?"

"It's too early to say. The last two days have about drained my emotional tank. I need time… but, I also need to see Wesa again. Maybe then I can get closure."

"Perhaps we should visit her together," Dovey said.

"Yes, and Juanita too."

The morning rain cloud in the southeast gave comfort to Dovey as she stood at the foot of the simple cross on the hillside. The sun sparkled off the darkness of the cloud giving emphasis to its potential for bringing the succor that Henry was forever looking for during his lifetime.

Hatless, clad in her flowered dress and boots, Dovey stood for a long time looking at Henry's grave. The broad smile that had been on her face since she, Juanita and Jason had returned from their previous night's adventure had not diminished.

She leaned over to dust the cross and began talking in soft tones. She was alone with the memories of her husband and there were important things to tell him. Momentous things. This was not a time for silent reflection.

"Henry, I guess you never heard me laugh much during our years together but I think there will be lots of laughter from now on.

"I was thinking, Henry, I should offer a prayer for what happened last night but I'm as confused as Jason has been all these years. I can't decide whether the prayer should be to the Shaman, to God or to the Gray Wolf of whom he often talked to Juanita. I guess you don't know about the Gray Wolf but you will, I promise.

"First let me tell you that we have a son, yes, the boy you loved all along turned out to be Jason or Jerry or Junalhuska, take your pick. He wishes to be called Junalhuska. I will honor his request for I want him to be proud of his heritage.

"It's a long story that can only be told over time, but I wanted you to know that he intends to marry Juanita. You'll have a grandchild, soon, I'm sure."

Dovey laughed as she brushed a tear from the corner of her eye. "Before I go on let me tell you, old man, it looks like we'll have rain today. I know that'll make you happy. It's a day of blessings, Henry. Rain for you, a son for me, and a husband for our daughter. And the only sadness in my heart is that you can't be here in person to share it with us.

A sudden clasp of thunder split the air above her. Dust began whirling around Dovey's feet and the acrid smell of lightening assaulted her senses.

"Or maybe you are," she said, smiling and looking up at the sky.

"I'll have to go soon, Henry, but you should know that Isabella had one of her spells last night. In the darkness of the night Juanita and Junalhuska almost killed each other in an effort to prevent disaster, but everyone's fine now."

Another clasp of thunder rented the air, this time much closer to the hill.

"Mother, mother, are you there," A voice from behind her said.

Mother? He'd called her mother!

She turned slowly to Junaluhska's long, slender form, her heart bursting with pride. Whatever she'd endured from Blackjack was certainly worth it. She couldn't have asked for a finer son.

"Yes, yes, Junaluhska, I'm coming. We've got some living to do."

Junalhuska listened to the footfall of her boots and her happy words about the rain being evidence of Henry's blessing. They stood for a moment at Henry's favorite overlook.

After he and Juanita were married he would build a house over there, near the ranch house. He fixed the spot in his mind and could already see his mother frolicking with his children. The very thought began to soothe the agony of the past. He smiled broadly and stepped lively to her side.

He took her hand and together they began walking back toward the house, just as the first heavy drops of rain began to paint the ground.

He *was* now a man; a man loved by two wonderful women, who were eager for his love in return. His heart beat with pride. He would honor their love and trust.

He stretched his body, raised his arms to the heavens and silently made a vow of love, honor and respect, ending with a simple; thank you.

He now knew that the sheep's blood in his veins had been replaced by that of a lion.

Printed in the United States
918800004B